PROLOGUE

he first jagged splinters of light were glinting against the eastern sky, heralding the dawn of a day he would not see. He stood on a narrow plinth at the top of the Scott Monument, a thrusting shard of stone reaching up to pierce the firmament as though in defiance of gravity as much as mortality. The monument had been erected to ensure one man's legacy endured for centuries, a sight he had beheld every day. It looked like no other tower, no other object on earth, built to inspire as well as to honour. It had daily been his delight to behold; today it would be his deliverance.

He could feel the wind's bite as he looked about him, the city lying sprawled two hundred feet below. Two hundred feet between life and death, between this highest platform and the moment that would bring peace. To the south-east he could make out the roofs of the college buildings where he had once excelled, and the central tower of the Infirmary where he had engaged in true learning. To the south he could see the spire of St Giles, where he had married on a long-ago June morning. And to the north from this height, he could trace the clean lines of the elegant grid-like structure that was James Craig's New Town, neatly ordered in stark contrast to the ancient sprawling decrepitude of the Old Town. He could see his home, and the homes of so many he had ministered to. He had walked tall in that place.

They all knew his name. What would they think when they heard it hereafter? What would they think when they heard *her* name?

There was no hope of redemption for a person so comprehensively ruined. The people on the ground would not forget, would not forgive. Such was the nature of the city, and such was the nature of the sin. Even if they wished it other, once they had seen, they could not unsee. Perception would be irrevocably altered. Reputation irreparably destroyed.

The spiralling climb to the top of the tower had been a humbling one. There were statues representing Scott's work, celebrating his literary creations, and commemorating his peers. A towering monument to a man whose contribution the world would never forget as long as it stood.

But there would be no statues, no monument, no commemoration for a person so thoroughly shamed. The monument to his life would be a single image, defining his character in the basest way, and erasing all else. There was no undoing it, no retrieving it, and the proof was in the hands of someone unmerciful: someone who understood the control it conferred and who would never relinquish it. There was only one way to take that power from him.

The wind was stronger up here, cold upon exposed skin, cutting through cloth where it was covered.

It could not merely be a fall: it had to be a leap, to clear the platform beneath. That would take fortitude and resolve. Unquestionably there were other ways to do it, but with so much medical knowledge came the understanding of pain. No poison would be so swift, so instant.

Tormenting thoughts swarmed like winged demons, gargoyles taken to the air: thoughts of the delight with which the shaming would be seized upon. The alacrity. The perverse pleasure of unseen beholders. These were intolerable to contemplate.

Odd that there should be so little sound from below. Noises did not carry as they did on the ground, perhaps dispersed by the wind up here. Thousands of souls were obliviously asleep, or waking to commence their days a quarter of a mile away in the

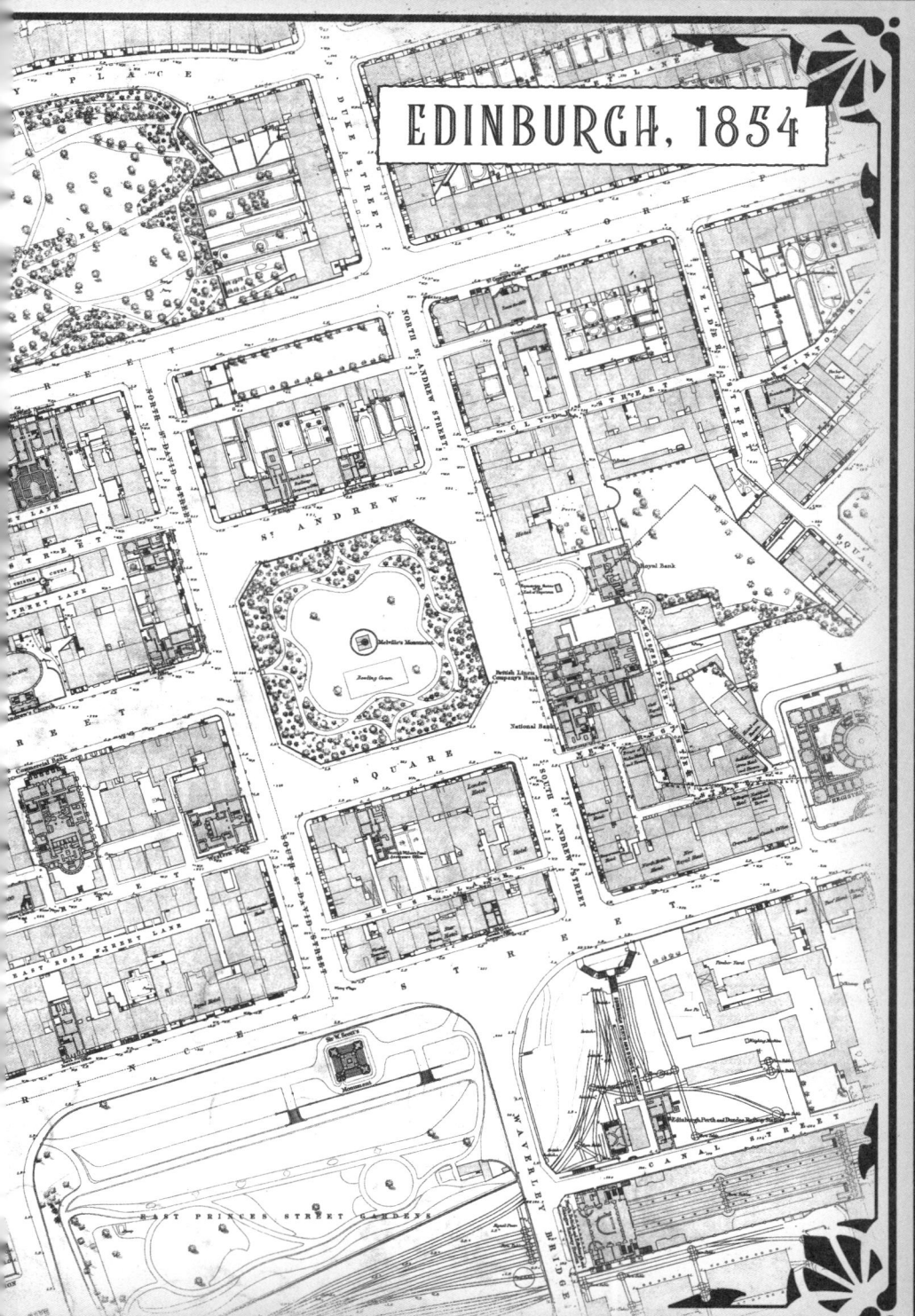

EDINBURGH, 1854

THE DEATH OF SHAME

Also by Ambrose Parry

The Way of All Flesh
The Art of Dying
A Corruption of Blood
Voices of the Dead

THE DEATH OF SHAME

AMBROSE PARRY

CANONGATE

First published in Great Britain, the USA and Canada in 2025
by Canongate Books Ltd, 14 High Street, Edinburgh EH1 1TE

Distributed in the USA by Publishers Group West
and in Canada by Publishers Group Canada

canongate.co.uk

1

British Library Cataloguing-in-Publication Data
A catalogue record for this book is available on
request from the British Library

ISBN 978 1 83726 343 1

Typeset in Van Dijck by Palimpsest Book Production Ltd,
Falkirk, Stirlingshire

Printed and bound by CPI Group (UK) Ltd, Croydon CR0 4YY

The manufacturer's authorised representative in the EU for product safety is
Authorised Rep Compliance Ltd, 71 Lower Baggot Street, Dublin D02 P593
Ireland (arccompliance.com)

In memory of Isabella Devitt and Annie Dougan,
two redoubtable women who won't be found
in any history books

Old Town, and less than a hundred yards distant in Princes Street hotels, but up here there was silence. There was stillness. There was peace.

The stone of the balustrade was cold to the touch. Surely no one had climbed upon it like this before. No one could have stood higher since the masons completed their work.

The higher he climbed, the further there was to fall. Wasn't that the truth.

The Bible said this would be a sin, but how could the Bible know people would ever be so tested? What the world would become, what it would make possible, what wonders and what temptations?

This was no sin. It could not be a sin, for ultimately this was an act of sacrifice. This was an act of love.

EDINBURGH

MAY 1854

ONE

t was the smell she noticed. Or perhaps the lack of it. Gone was the near-constant coal-fire fug of the winter months, replaced by the subtle perfume of cherry blossom. The crisp spring air had a freshness to it that held a promise of good things to come.

As Sarah approached Great Stuart Street, she noticed a new addition beside the door of No. 8 – a brass nameplate bearing the inscription 'Dr W. Raven MD'. Its shiny surface was marred by a number of fingerprints which Sarah removed by deft application of her handkerchief. Once a housemaid always a housemaid, she thought to herself as she put the handkerchief back into her pocket.

First impressions were important – that had been Raven's refrain for the past few months – and why his new home was situated in Edinburgh's New Town rather than a less salubrious but far more affordable part of the city.

It had taken them a long time to find the correct premises. It had to be home and medical practice combined: a consulting room and waiting room with family apartments upstairs, though Raven's wife, Eugenie, was already complaining that these were far too small and no improvement on the house on Castle Street that they had just moved from.

Eugenie was used to the better things, having grown up amidst wealth and comfort, and was finding the rigours of being a lowly doctor's wife demanding and unpleasant. Her father was a well-established, well-respected physician who had accumulated considerable riches as a result, but Eugenie always neglected to take into account that a significant proportion of his wealth pre-dated his medical career, having been inherited from several generations of landowning antecedents.

Setting up a successful medical practice relied on more than qualifications and talent. Fortunately, Raven had a sufficient quantity of both, but money and connections were also necessary. His origins were far less grandiose than those of his father-in-law, and as a result he was struggling to establish himself and make his mark, though being but twenty-six years old it was still early in his career. In his favour, Raven was the protégé of the famous Dr James Young Simpson and was both driven and ambitious, but the evolution of his plans – their plans – would take time. Sarah was willing to wait but Eugenie was impatient.

Sarah knew that Raven harboured his own doubts about the likely success of this venture, her involvement being only one of them. He often doubted himself, unable to shake the belief that there was some destructive element within him that would inevitably lead them all to disaster. He was haunted by the spectre of his father, a violent man but fortunately a long dead one.

The fact that Dr Simpson hailed from a humble background (the son of a Bathgate baker, educated in the local parish school, he had yet risen to the very top of his profession) gave Raven hope, but Sarah sometimes wondered if he had set his expectations rather too high. Simpson was world-renowned for his discovery of chloroform, something that Raven was unlikely to replicate. She worried that Raven had too much to prove – to himself as much as to others – and would perhaps not be content even if they managed to make a success of their current project.

Sarah pushed these thoughts aside and stepped through the front door.

All was quiet, in stark contrast to where she had just come from. Dr Simpson's house on Queen Street was a menagerie compared to this: full of children, pets, patients, doctors and visiting dignitaries wishing to speak to the great man, many waiting for prolonged periods of time to do so.

The fact that Sarah still resided amongst the chaos of Queen Street was something of a concern and a conundrum. She had first moved in when she became a housemaid there and had left a few years later as a doctor's wife when she married Archie Banks. Following her husband's death she had travelled around Europe for a while, but had moved back in again upon her return. It was supposed to have been a temporary arrangement – she had always intended to find a place of her own – but something always held her back. She worked there, helping out with the patients at Dr Simpson's clinic, but that was not the reason she stayed.

She was a woman of independent means, Archie having left her a considerable sum in his will, so there was no financial impediment to her leaving. Or at least not until now. She had sunk a considerable sum into Raven's new venture, but she had high hopes of a substantial return on her investment.

She was certainly attached to the Simpson clan, as they were to her, so perhaps her reluctance to leave was simply that – the desire to be part of a family. Or perhaps she was just afraid of being entirely on her own.

Part of the problem was that she wasn't sure where she belonged. Or perhaps she was, but *that* was clearly not an option open to her.

Sarah entered Raven's new consulting room and took off her coat. The room was almost ready to receive patients, with only a few crates left to unpack. Raven's degree certificate had been framed but was yet to be hung on the wall. Sarah picked it up and examined it. The Latin script, which would have been indecipherable to her only a few years ago, was straightforward to translate. Will Raven had satisfied the senate of the University of Edinburgh and the degree of Doctor of Medicine had been duly conferred.

Sarah would have liked to study as Raven had done, but the university did not admit women, its professors hostile to the very notion. The study of medicine by the fairer sex was considered particularly inappropriate, too taxing for their delicate constitutions or some other such nonsense.

Sarah placed the framed diploma against the wall and took a look around. A desk, an examination couch, a bookcase. Insufficient for such a large room. Sarah had questioned whether the space might be better divided up, providing a room where she might see and treat patients herself, or a small dispensary where she could make up Raven's prescriptions. Raven had demurred, suggesting that they take things slowly, especially given the unusual nature of their arrangement. He had been most resistant to seeing patients in what might be considered a confined space – back to first impressions again. 'I cannot expect to consult with and examine wealthy patients in some cramped little room,' he had said. 'I have to minister to them in an environment that gives the impression this is a burgeoning practice.'

Sarah hoped that the burgeoning part would commence soon, for all their sakes. Dr Simpson had said he would recommend Raven as an alternative to some of his patients when he himself was too much in demand, and Simpson was often too much in demand. But whether patients would take a chance on Raven rather than wait to be seen by the great man himself, that was the question.

A door slammed somewhere in the house, followed by raised voices and footsteps. Raven entered the room.

'Sarah, you're here,' he said. 'Thank God for that.'

He had baby Clara cradled in one arm, his other hand grasping the collar of his jam-smeared, squirming son, Jamie.

'Could you . . .?' he asked, indicating one or both of the children, Sarah wasn't sure.

'That's not what I'm here for,' she said, aiming for a firm tone but sounding a little tetchy. 'Where is their mother?'

Raven jerked his head to indicate the floor above. 'Resting.'

Eugenie seemed to spend a lot of her time resting.

Sarah looked at Raven's tired expression and felt her resolve crumble. She had known this man since he was a medical student apprentice at Queen Street, an unlikely-looking prospect, having turned up with fresh stitches in his face from a knife wound. She had watched him as he had evolved into doctor, husband and father. She loved him, and he knew it, but she was not about to let him take advantage of that.

'You need help,' she said.

Raven looked pleased and gave Jamie a gentle shove, sending him hurtling towards her.

'Not from me,' she added.

Raven sighed. 'Additional help is not within my current budget, as well you know.'

'And what of the help you already have?' she asked, aware that Raven had recently taken on a housekeeper.

'Mrs Balfour is even more insistent than you as to what her duties are – and are not.' Raven put on a weary voice, imitating Mrs Balfour: '"I can't get the cooking and cleaning done if I'm busy looking after your children."'

Sarah gestured for him to keep his voice down lest the house-keeper overhear.

'Oh, don't worry. She's not here. She's also very insistent about her hours, and we can barely afford those as it is.'

Sarah thought it time to mention the obvious solution. 'Eugenie could ask her father— '

Raven held up a hand to forestall any further discussion on the matter, but Sarah would not be put off. Raven had a blind spot where Eugenie's father was concerned. The reason Raven had agreed to go into partnership with her instead was so that he would not have to go cap in hand to Dr Cameron Todd for the finance necessary to set up his own practice, fearing the unwanted oversight and interference that would surely follow.

'He can easily spare the money . . . or one of the servants,' Sarah persisted. 'He's in that big house all by himself.' Raven's deepening frown suggested she was wasting her time.

She turned her attention to young James who, now freed from physical parental restraint, had wasted no time in picking up something he shouldn't have: a rosewood stethoscope that had been a present to Raven from Dr Simpson. Jamie was all set to start battering it off the leg of the examination couch when Sarah deftly removed it from his grasp and gave him some packing straw from one of the crates to play with instead.

'We can't go on like this,' Sarah continued. 'And with Eugenie—'

'What about Eugenie?'

'Well, it's been a year and she's not getting any better, is she?'

Raven's wife had been suffering from depressed spirits for some time, since the birth of her daughter the year before. To say it had been a traumatic birth would be a gross understatement. Eugenie had suffered from eclamptic seizures and was lucky to have lived, but the experience had left an indelible mark on her psyche. She had not bonded with the new baby, was frequently fatigued, took to her bed at a moment's notice, and was constantly short-tempered, arguing with Raven all the time.

'She remains in good health physically, at least,' he said. 'Apart from . . . no, that was nothing.'

'What was nothing?'

Raven looked flushed. Embarrassed more than concerned.

'She was ill a few weeks back. She left the children at her father's house and went out for lunch. She returned here around six, minus the children, barely able to stand, and took to her bed for about eighteen hours straight. I had the strong suspicion she was drunk, but she insisted she was not. Said she must have eaten bad oysters.'

'And you think that was nothing?'

Raven shrugged. 'I think it probably *was* bad oysters.'

He didn't sound convinced.

'Who was she dining with?'

'She said she was alone.'

'You don't sound like you believe her.'

'I am trying to give her space. Dr Simpson says— '

'I know, I know. It takes time to recover. Recuperation cannot be rushed. But in the meantime, what are we to do? You have a practice to set up and run, and an apprentice to teach.'

Raven sighed. 'Perhaps we *could* ask Dr Todd if he might spare one of his housemaids, just until Eugenie is back on her feet.'

Just then Eugenie walked into the consulting room looking tired and drawn, and not best pleased at being the topic of conversation between them.

'Eugenie *is* on her feet,' she said. 'Didn't you hear the door?' This was more accusation than question. 'You have a patient.'

She took the baby from Raven's arms and all but dragged young Jamie away with her free hand, a bunch of packing straw still stuck to the bottom of his trousers leaving a little yellow trail in his wake.

Raven and Sarah looked at each other.

'My first patient,' Raven said.

'*Our* first patient.'

Sarah quickly scooped up the straw from the floor as Raven tidied himself, tucking in his shirt and running his fingers through his tousled hair.

'Ready?' Sarah asked.

'Ready.'

They shared a smile, then Sarah went to the door.

'There was a crowd like an execution at Queen Street,' Miss Poole said as she took a seat. 'The butler mentioned that you had a surgery here. I wasn't too sure, but I'm pressed for time, and I didn't want to wait.'

Raven tried not to take offence. Given that this was currently his only patient, it was a luxury he could not afford.

Unfortunately Miss Poole was possibly the last person he wanted to see. She had plagued him at Queen Street and kept returning to see him even though she maintained that whatever he recommended or prescribed was completely useless. She had a long list of symptoms that seemed to grow rather than shrink, and always had new complaints that tended to reflect whatever she had most recently read about in the newspapers. Raven often thought it was as well she did not have easy access to medical journals or the meetings of the Medical-Chirurgical Society, as then who knew what exotic ailments she might decide she was suffering from. The cholera outbreak the previous year had seen her almost permanently stationed at Queen Street, her head swaddled in silk scarves in an attempt to keep the pestilence at bay. Raven had suggested that perhaps Dr Simpson's waiting room was not the best place to be if one was keen to avoid contagion, but that had only kept her away for a week or so before she returned with a cornucopia of vague and unusual symptoms.

He had tried everything – tonics, aperients, simple diet, fresh air (a walk in Princes Street Gardens was Dr Simpson's preferred treatment for hypochondriasis) – but all to no avail. She turned up regular as clockwork, ready to be disappointed in him all over again.

In his kinder moments Raven felt sorry for her, and now, given the lack of anything better to do, he sat back in his chair and decided to humour her. Simpson often said that a listening ear could be a potent treatment in itself.

'Terrible business on Princes Street this morning,' Miss Poole said.

'What's that?'

'Seems some poor soul threw himself off the Scott Monument.'

'I think I know how he feels,' Raven muttered. He risked a glance at Sarah, who was stocking up a cupboard at the far end of the room, and saw her stifle a laugh.

'You mustn't joke about these things, Dr Raven,' Mrs Poole chided. 'What would drive a man to do something like that?'

'Come back in another few weeks and I might have an answer for you.'

'At least she always settles her bill promptly,' Raven said, examining the fee that Miss Poole had deposited in his hand as she left. They were both back in the consulting room, Raven having seen Miss Poole to the door.

'That's something we need to talk about,' Sarah said.

Raven sighed. 'Money? Isn't that all we talk about? My lack of it. Your investment and what you expect in return.'

Sarah didn't like the way this was said. 'Are you having second thoughts about our arrangement?'

Raven frowned. 'I would be foolish not to have some concerns. If anyone finds out what we're up to here, my medical career will be over before it's even begun.'

'You talk as if it's some criminal enterprise we're entering into.'

'Might as well be, given what will happen if word gets out.'

Sarah knew he wasn't entirely wrong about that. 'We shall just have to make sure that it doesn't.'

She looked at his face for signs of a wavering resolve but fortunately saw none.

'So, what about fees?' she said.

'What about them?'

'Are you planning on charging everyone?'

'That is the general idea.'

'I thought you were modelling yourself on Dr Simpson and would be treating those with slender means for free.'

Raven shook his head. 'Dr Simpson has a surfeit of wealthy patients congregating in his upstairs waiting room, which allows him to do that. All I have here are three mouths to feed.'

'Forfeiting a few pennies here and there is not going to make much difference, is it?'

'Then who am I going to charge? What if word gets around and folk think that they can come here and get their treatment without paying?'

'And what if word gets around that your door is open to anyone in need? Not everyone who turns up will be poor.'

'I see your point,' he conceded.

Their conversation was interrupted by the doorbell.

'Could it be . . .?' Raven asked, taking his feet off the desk and sitting upright.

'Two patients in one morning,' Sarah said. 'Things are looking up.'

'Let it be a wealthy matron with a large family. Or a fellow professional, a man of business.'

Sarah made her way into the hallway and pulled open the door.

It was a man of business all right.

Police business.

TWO

aven cast an eye over the policeman standing at his front door. He did not appear to be in any way injured or conspicuously unwell, though he did seem a bit pallid for someone otherwise so physically hale.

'Officer Caldwell,' the man said nervously, as though trying to convince himself of his own name. He looked young to be in the job, but otherwise built for it, tall and strapping, suggesting he'd been reared on a farm rather than fighting for scraps in the Old Town. He reminded Raven of a few of the boys he had known at Heriot's: the type Raven could seldom resist getting into a tussle with. They had enjoyed throwing their weight about and he had enjoyed conveying that they would not do so with impunity.

'Are you Will Raven?' the lad asked.

'*Doctor* Raven,' he clarified, suppressing annoyance. Upon closer inspection the policeman really did look paler than was surely natural, as though profoundly anxious or recently shocked.

'Sorry, sir. I've been sent by Mr McLevy.'

'Is he ill?' Raven asked optimistically.

'No. He wishes your assistance. I've to escort you to Princes Street Gardens.'

Raven's instinct was to say he was indisposed and not about to be escorted anywhere. He did not like anyone assuming he was at their beck and call, least of all the snarling Irish detective.

'Someone has fallen from the Scott Monument,' the policeman added, perhaps sensing Raven's ambivalence.

'So I heard. Much as I am flattered by Mr McLevy's estimation of my abilities, I don't imagine there's much I can do for the victim.'

'No,' Caldwell agreed. The lad shuddered, becoming even paler, and put his hand on the railing to steady himself. Raven feared he might vomit, but the moment passed. No need to ask if he had seen the remains.

'How does Mr McLevy think I can assist, then?'

'He didn't say. He just told me to fetch you. I think he's maybe hoping you can help identify the man. There's nothing left of his face.'

'Bit difficult for me to identify him, then.'

Caldwell put a hand to his mouth, swallowed a couple of times, then shook his head as though trying to clear the image he had just conjured up.

'Mr McLevy believes the dead man to be a doctor, sir.'

'On what basis?'

'He did not say.'

Raven recalled Dr Simpson telling him it was wise to have a man such as McLevy owing you favours, but in practice such wisdom only applied if you were as esteemed as the professor. Over the years, Raven recalled doing McLevy a great many favours – often, one might even say, doing his job for him – but as far as McLevy was concerned, Raven's account was never in credit. Nonetheless, there was an enduring wisdom in not poking a bear, and Raven did not wish to give the Irishman any reason to add to his debit column.

'Let me get my coat.'

He stepped back inside the door. Sarah was waiting in the hall just outside his consulting room, while Eugenie had come to the head of the stairs to investigate what was happening. He could hear Clara fussing, an unquiet overture to a coming storm: one he had just been given the opportunity to escape.

'The police require my assistance,' he said. He tried not to meet his wife's gaze as he lifted his coat from the hook, knowing there would be accusation and rebuke in it.

Raven's thoughts were of Eugenie as he walked alongside Caldwell, of her perpetual melancholy and dissatisfaction.

Part of the problem was Raven's refusal to take any of her father's money, or indeed to simply take up the post of assistant in his practice. She could not understand why he would not accept the offer of help, but that was because, where she saw generosity, Raven saw something less altruistic. Raven had learned some harsh lessons about being in another man's debt, enough to understand that in certain men it established a hierarchy that neither time nor money could ever reverse. Cameron Todd was precisely such a man, the kind who would only ever see Raven as a subordinate, never an equal. Todd was one of the most financially successful physicians in the city, with a commensurate opinion of himself. Indeed, he was the type of man who might, under different circumstances, have refused to allow someone such as Raven to marry his daughter.

Unlike Dr Simpson, Cameron Todd did not minister to the needy, and treated nobody gratis. He was used to mixing in only the highest circles, tending to the wealthiest of patients. He was much in demand, providing the services such individuals required: treating their ailments when they suffered them, and listening sympathetically to imaginary complaints when they did not. He was also reliably discreet, to the extent that when occasion demanded, Raven knew he was a willing instrument in concealing their more squalid secrets.

Cameron Todd knew the value of such discretion because he had a squalid secret of his own, or at least that was how he regarded it. His only daughter, for whom he no doubt once harboured grand marriage plans, had some years ago become pregnant by a lover she would not name. Todd spirited her away to the country so that her condition would not be known, then spirited the child away too, a daughter whose fate to this day Eugenie did not know.

Eugenie thereafter became a problem to her father. She was not as gentle-mannered and deferential as suitors might desire in a bride, but far more importantly, she was not pure. It was not that some prospective husband from a great family would have the means to determine this in advance, but Todd no doubt feared for his standing were it to be discovered after the fact.

Raven vividly recalled the man's words when he had announced his intentions towards Todd's daughter. *She is not without . . . complications. But for that reason, I do believe you and she are a good fit.* There would have been a time when no man could have been good enough for Eugenie, but by then it was as though Raven had confirmed his lesser status by being someone suitable for Dr Todd to marry her off to.

Not that Raven cared back then. There was something wanton and untameable about Eugenie, and the very aspects that worried her father were what Raven had loved about her. She always had a lingering sadness in her though, and an anger. When they were first married, there were nights when Raven woke to find her weeping. She would not discuss the reason why, but Raven thought he could hazard a guess.

A woman unwillingly separated from her lover and their child.

When young James had come along, that seemed to soothe her for a time, although her sadness merely gave way to a restless dissatisfaction manifest in her impatience for Raven to spread his wings. To move on from Dr Simpson and set up on his own. To be more like her father, he realised.

And then had come the traumatic events surrounding Clara's birth. Even once she had recovered physically, something in her heart had changed. It was as though she did not love the girl. Raven could but speculate as to why. Was it because she was now more vividly reminded of the daughter she lost? Or more troubling, was it that she still had greater love for the *father* of the child she lost, and would rather have his daughter lying in the cot than Raven's? Would she rather it was her lost lover lying beside her too? Not that Raven had lain anywhere near her for some time. Before Clara was born, in fact.

He could endure all of this were it not that she seemed more distant from Jamie too. At times one might mistake her for his governess rather than his mother. She seemed at all times bitterly resentful of her duties.

Raven had hoped that finally leaving Queen Street and finding his own premises might provide the spark of change that would lift her mood, but it only seemed to open new fronts in their conflict. She was annoyed that their accommodations upstairs were too small, restrictions imposed by Raven's refusal of her father's largesse. But more problematic was from whom he *had* accepted money. Eugenie had always been suspicious of Sarah, aware that she had known Raven longer and jealous of what they had been through together. Part of Eugenie's design in getting Raven out of Queen Street had been to get him further away from Sarah. Instead, Sarah's investment had meant they were even more entangled.

Eugenie had been born into wealth, like her father before her, and did not understand that things did not come so easily to other people. But therein lay another unwelcome possibility: that it was not merely Dr Todd who had been forced to lower his standards and expectations in accepting Raven. Perhaps Eugenie had come to regard Raven not as her salvation but as a consequence of her fall. What increasingly worried him was not the thought that she did not love him any more, rather that she never had.

But perhaps he was suffering the greatest darkness ahead of the dawn. He had left Queen Street and founded his own practice, and today he had treated his first patient. One day they would look back and remember Miss Poole, and it would feel symbolic that Eugenie should have been the one who opened the door to her.

For all their cares, this was a new beginning.

★ ★ ★

As Raven approached the monument, he could see some of McLevy's men holding back a gathering of morbidly curious onlookers. Perhaps the detective should simply have posted young Caldwell at the gate, his pale, gaunt expression a more effective warning that no one would wish to set eyes upon what lay beyond.

The policemen parted, allowing Raven and Caldwell to pass. Raven recognised one of them and he him. Wilkie was his name. Their paths had crossed before, leaving neither of them enamoured of the other.

McLevy was leaning against one wall of the tower. He was a man who seemed to become physically smaller every time Raven saw him, but only because his physical incarnation could never measure up to the lumbering ogre that represented him in Raven's mind.

McLevy was renowned for his tenacity, or at least renowned for telling people about his tenacity; fond of declaring that no matter how long it took, he always got his man and the evidence to prove it. Raven would admit that this was true inasmuch as McLevy usually got *a* man and *some* evidence. However, the extent to which one related to the other was a matter many innocent individuals had a very long time to contemplate inside Calton Jail or on board their transportation vessels.

Raven chose to interpret McLevy's occasional request for favours as a tacit gesture of respect, though he knew that tacit was all it would ever be. Perhaps that was fair enough, because Raven's respect for McLevy went no further than wariness of the authority he wielded.

McLevy watched him approach, a nod dismissing Caldwell. The lad looked relieved to stand down, casting a glance beyond the tower where a shape lay upon the flagstones, covered by a dark cloth. Two more men were standing over it. There was a splash pattern of bloody matter emanating for several yards beyond the edge of the blanket, bits of bone and brain amongst it. What lay under the blanket was likely grim enough to turn most stomachs, even seasoned ones.

'Dr Raven,' McLevy said, 'thank you for taking the time.'

Did Raven detect something arch in McLevy's expression? An indication that he was aware Raven had fewer draws on his time than he would like? He could not discount it. McLevy had many sources: dozens of mouths whispering information in his ear, either in service of their own private agendas or merely to stay on the right side of him. In that respect, the only man through whom more gossip was trafficked in this city was William Sanderson, the former editor of the *Courant* who had recently graduated from distributing sensationalist pamphlets to setting up his own newspaper.

'I gather you have encountered an acute case of Newton's malady,' Raven said.

If McLevy got the reference, it did not raise a smile from him. 'The man must have fallen about two hundred feet,' he said.

'Aye, but I'm told it's the last inch that's the most dangerous.'

Once again McLevy did not smile. Raven thought it best to rein in any further attempts at levity. McLevy was not normally so reluctant to partake, morbid humour being a common defence against some of the grislier things both doctors and policemen were forced to endure. Such insistent decorum suggested that the victim must be a gentleman of some standing. But if McLevy knew that much, why was he seeking Raven's help?

'Some tragic misadventure, was it?' Raven asked.

McLevy shrugged. 'At this point it befits me to keep an open mind. The body was discovered at dawn, so he could have lain there for hours. Which would lead us to ask — what was he doing climbing the monument in the middle of the night?'

Raven assumed that this was a rhetorical query. He nodded towards the cloth and the shape beneath it. 'I'm told you believe him to be a medical man. Are you hoping I can assist with his identity? I can certainly make enquiries, but I would imagine his absence will become conspicuous soon enough.'

'I already have a notion as to his identity,' McLevy said. 'What I need from you is to confirm it.'

Raven felt a precipitous anxiety. McLevy's unusually respectful manner had suddenly taken on worrying implications.

McLevy nodded to one of his officers, who crouched down and delicately pulled back the cloth.

The body was lying in a supine position, smashed and twisted in ways that suggested only its clothing was causing it to retain a human form, and what lay at the top did not resemble a head any more than a crumpled mess of shell resembled an egg. The skull was extensively fractured, the head split into two parts, the skin of the face ruptured, its features completely obliterated.

Raven shook his head. 'Why would you think that I'd be in a position to confirm this person's identity? There's nothing left of him.'

McLevy reached into his pocket and presented Raven with a gold tie-pin smeared with blood. It depicted the Staff of Asclepius.

'The serpent and the rod,' McLevy said.

Raven recognised it, immediately and unmistakably. He looked again at the body, dumbstruck.

'Can you confirm who this is?' McLevy asked.

Raven simply nodded.

'I need you to say it, Dr Raven.'

Raven swallowed, found his voice.

'It's Cameron Todd.'

THREE

Sarah had spent the morning with Raven because she had been surplus to requirements at Queen Street. Dr Simpson was absent, hauled from his bed at an ungodly hour despite having been deprived of his sleep several times that week already, and his sciatica causing him significant pain when he did have the opportunity to lie down. Jarvis, Simpson's butler and general factotum, had suggested that the doctor's new assistant, Dr Ferry, be dispatched, but Dr Simpson had insisted on going himself. The patient, he said, had suffered much already, and would only fret if a substitute was sent in his stead.

That left Dr Ferry and the most recent addition to the household, Dr Emily Blackwell, to run proceedings.

Dr Ferry was a proficient but uninspiring man who was still wary of Sarah, unsure what to make of a former housemaid and now a nurse of sorts, who helped with the patients and administered chloroform when this was required. To Dr Ferry, Sarah was something of a conundrum: not sufficiently educated to be his intellectual equal, but knowledgeable enough to ask probing questions, the answers to which he didn't always have. He was by turns patronising and defensive, and that morning had decided that he would manage well enough without her.

Dr Blackwell had also been keen to manage on her own. Emily was sister to the famous Elizabeth Blackwell, the first woman to obtain a medical degree in the United States, and had followed in her sister's footsteps. She had managed to get a medical degree herself, albeit from a different institution, Elizabeth's alma mater reluctant to repeat their unusual experiment of accepting a woman into their ranks.

Sarah had hoped to find an ally in Emily, a confidante and a fellow combatant in the battle for women's rights, but she had been disappointed. Emily (or 'Dr Blackwell', as she insisted Sarah call her) was solely interested in furthering her own medical education. She tolerated Sarah's presence rather than welcomed it, possibly fuelled by Sarah having witnessed an early and embarrassingly incompetent attempt by Emily to apply leeches to a patient's cervix.

Sarah headed back to Queen Street following Raven's sudden departure to assist McLevy. The matter was obviously urgent and, given the pallor of the young policeman who came to the door, something rather nasty. She was shaking the rain from her umbrella – the spring sunshine having given way to a sudden downpour – when Jarvis appeared beside her and helped her off with her coat.

'I would avoid Dr Emily's company this afternoon if I was you,' he said, his voice low.

Sarah was immediately wary. 'Why?'

Jarvis held out a copy of the *Caledonian Mercury*, pointing to the headline A FEMALE MD, the article sandwiched between a piece about the last governors' meeting at George Heriot's Hospital and an intimation about the serious illness of a devoted missionary, the Reverend Dr Duff.

Sarah began to read aloud. '"Managers of the Royal Infirmary have received an application of a rather novel character. A lady graduate of Cleveland College, Ohio, named Miss Blackwell— "' Sarah looked up at Jarvis. 'They haven't used her proper title. No wonder she's angry.'

Jarvis raised an eyebrow. 'Read on.'

'"Miss Blackwell applied to the managers at the Infirmary for leave to visit the female wards of that institution. Permission to visit the Infirmary is, we believe, at all times most readily granted to gentlemen who have graduated at English and foreign universities, and who may, on visiting the city, desire it. The request of the lady however was an unprecedented one and they considered it their duty to respectfully decline acceding to it.'"

Sarah stopped and quickly scanned the rest of the article. Something about the medical gentlemen *vindicating their craft from the assumptions of the fairer sex*, whatever that might mean, and then the pièce de résistance: *Miss Doctor Blackwell* (Miss Doctor? They really couldn't deal with it, could they?) had apparently *quit the city in high dudgeon, appalled at the ungallant reception she had experienced from her brother practitioners.*

Ungallant. Brother practitioners. As though it was their lack of manners that Dr Blackwell might have objected to.

'Is she leaving?' Sarah asked, not sure if she was keen for this outcome or not.

Jarvis shook his head. 'Wishful thinking on their part. She wouldn't be so foolish as to do that. She's only been here a matter of weeks. Too much to lose in leaving early.'

'Doctor Simpson has her at the Maternity Hospital most days, so perhaps it's not such a loss to be barred from the Infirmary. Irritating certainly, but not that surprising.'

'You're missing the important part.'

Sarah was at a loss as to what that might be.

'The fact that it's in the newspaper is what has truly riled her,' Jarvis explained. 'She thinks someone gave them the story to make trouble for her . . .' He paused, offering Sarah a concerned look. 'And she thinks it was you.'

Sarah was barrelling through the downstairs waiting room, heading for the consulting rooms, determined to clear the air with Emily. Such an accusation would not stand. How could Emily think Sarah would do such a thing? She was so intent on her purpose that she didn't see the woman sitting there until she spoke.

'Mrs Banks?'

Sarah stopped short. No one had called her that in quite some time.

Mrs Banks. Her married name. A name she had relinquished when she became a widow, feeling that it was important to reclaim her own identity.

Sarah looked at the woman, who seemed vaguely familiar, but Sarah could not think from where. She was an unassuming soul, dressed in good clothes that had seen better days. She seemed apologetic for her presence, as though her very being there was an imposition.

'I'm sorry,' Sarah said. 'Have we met?'

The woman nodded. 'Once. Maybe six years ago. We are related.'

'Related?'

'By marriage. I, too, am Mrs Banks.' She stuck out a thin hand for Sarah to shake. 'Connie.'

Sarah took the hand and felt the bones beneath the skin. There was nothing to her.

'You're a relative of Archie's?' she asked.

'Married to his brother, Graham. Or was.'

It started to come back now. Sarah knew that Archie had a brother who lived in Perthshire somewhere, but the two had been estranged for years before Sarah even met him. Something to do with a disagreement over family money. Archie had seldom spoken of him, and Sarah had only been to one gathering of her in-laws, shortly after their wedding. She vaguely recalled meeting this woman then, and that it had been awkward as her husband, Archie's brother, had not attended. She looked frailer than she remembered, pale and gaunt. Then it struck Sarah that the woman's faded clothes were all black.

'Did your husband pass recently?' Sarah asked, as kindly as she could.

'Not long. A few months back.'

'I'm sorry,' Sarah said, and meant it. 'I know how hard it is.'

Connie Banks bit her lip. 'I won't lie to you. It has been very difficult. He didn't leave us with much.'

Sarah was immediately on her guard, anticipating a request for money.

'How did you find me?'

'The last letter Archie sent. It had this address on it.'

Archie had stayed at Queen Street while he was ill. Perhaps he had written to his brother in an attempt to smooth things over before he died. But Sarah still did not know or understand why he hadn't told her about it.

Connie seemed to sense Sarah's growing doubt. 'I know that you don't know me or owe me anything, Mrs Banks, but I have no one else to turn to.'

'It's Sarah. Sarah *Fisher*.'

Sarah wasn't sure why she had corrected Connie. Perhaps it was to weaken the familial connection this woman thought they shared. Connie didn't seem to notice.

'My husband wasn't like Archie,' she said. 'He wasn't good with money. Left us with nothing but debts.'

'Us?'

'My daughter, Annabel, and me. You met her that time you came to Perthshire.'

Sarah did remember. Annabel was the only child at the gathering but would have stood out anyway. She had been around nine or ten years old at the time, as pretty as she was precocious. Brightly intelligent in a way that had impressed Sarah and yet made her sad, for here was another girl whose potential would most likely be wasted.

'I remember her well,' Sarah said. 'She sang a Burns song for me. "Ae Fond Kiss".'

Connie glowed momentarily, then her pride faded into something darker.

'She's why I'm here. She left for Edinburgh. To work as a nursemaid. Good position in a good house. Much better paid than anything closer to home.'

Sarah was still bracing herself, waiting for the inevitable request for funds, funds that she did not have. She had sunk most of her savings into her investment with Raven. If that was what this woman was after, she was wasting her time.

'I haven't heard from her since she left home a month ago.'

'And you're concerned?'

'Wouldn't you be? She promised to write as soon as she was situated.'

'Perhaps she just hasn't had the opportunity.'

'What kind of place is she in where she doesn't have the time to write to her own mother?'

Sarah, having no knowledge of Connie Banks's relationship with her daughter, did not know what to make of this. Perhaps Annabel had been keen to get away, grateful to have escaped the suffocating sadness of this woman. Maybe she didn't want her mother to know where she was.

'Well, where is this house?' Sarah asked. 'Can't you go there and enquire directly?'

'That's the thing. I don't know. The position was organised through an agency. They match up employers with suitable candidates.'

'Do you know the name of the agency?'

Connie opened the embroidered reticule she had been clutching in her hands, fished about in it for a few seconds, then extracted a piece of paper. She handed it to Sarah. It was an advert cut from a newspaper: PIKE AND FEATHERSTONE. LADIES EMPLOYMENT AGENCY.

'Have you spoken to them?'

'I went to the office this morning, but it was closed. There was no one there.'

'I'm sorry, Mrs Banks— '

'Connie.'

'I'm sorry, Connie, but I'm not sure what you think I can do about any of this.'

Connie blinked a couple of times, looking to be on the verge of tears.

'You're the only person I know in the city,' she said, a plain-tiveness creeping into her voice. 'There's no one else, you see, and I was thinking that maybe you could go back there. To the agency. Try again.'

'I don't mean to be rude, Connie, but why can't you do that yourself?'

'I'm only in town for a few hours. I can't tarry. I must get back. I can't afford to lose my job.'

'Which is?'

'Housekeeper. The pay isn't great, but beggars can't be choosers. And I really can't be spared. I'm more nurse than housekeeper, if I'm honest. Had to beg for the time off to come here today as it is. And I'm no further forward.'

Connie Banks glanced anxiously at the clock on the mantelpiece. Sarah looked at the newspaper advert in her hand.

'I suppose I could— '

Sarah had no time to finish before Connie grasped her hand with a strength that belied her fragile appearance.

'Find her for me, Sarah. Please. She's all that I have.'

FOUR

s Raven stepped inside his front door, he realised he had no recollection of the walk home, as though his mind had become unmoored from his body. His face and clothes were damp from the rain, his shoes spattered with mud, but it was only as he stood in the hall that he became aware of it. Had anyone called his name he would not have heard.

He took off his shoes and ascended the stairs quietly, as he might if he was returning in the middle of the night and trying not to disturb anyone's sleep. He felt like a ghost passing through the house, or perhaps he merely wished he was, a being able to observe without being seen. For as soon as he was seen, he would have to speak, undertaking a grim aspect of manhood, a burden like none he had ever shouldered.

The door to his bedroom was open. He could see Eugenie lying on the bed, her back to the door. She was facing the tiny figure of Clara, who was asleep on top of the sheets. Jamie was sitting on the bedroom floor, quietly absorbed in pushing a toy cart around a course he had made. He would sometimes mark out a shape with wooden blocks and declare it his farm, his castle or his city. Jamie glanced up briefly at Raven, who worried that he might react with noisy excitement, but he was clearly busy.

It meant he could watch Eugenie just a little longer, lying next to their daughter. For now, his wife remained in a world where her father was still alive; where she would perhaps be taking the children to visit him later this afternoon, once Cameron Todd had seen all his patients. It was Raven's task to destroy that world.

He wondered how much Jamie would understand. Raven pictured him climbing upon his grandfather's knee as he sat in his armchair by the fire, a look of pride in Dr Todd's face. It was in such moments that Raven had come to see the man Eugenie must have known: a father transported by the simple pleasures of family life, unconcerned with career, status or reputation. It was in such moments also that Raven saw Todd regard him differently, as someone bonded to him through shared blood and shared love for the same precious people. A part of him had always believed he would eventually earn his father-in-law's respect in other matters.

Raven's dislike for the man now felt transmuted into regret. He would never get to change Todd's mind. He would never get to prove him wrong. But these were selfish thoughts, a distraction from what he didn't want to think about, what he now had to do.

In that moment Raven felt the depths of his love for Eugenie. He wanted to protect her and hated the thought of her suffering. That was why it troubled him so much when he could not please her. He wanted to make her happy. He loved the sound of her laugh, the mischief in her smile.

He missed that woman of mischief; she had been gone for some time. Now he feared she would never return.

Jamie was carefully turning the cart around a corner of his imaginary domain. His eye angled towards Raven briefly then he accelerated the little vehicle along the floor, sending it his way with a clatter.

Eugenie turned with a start.

'I didn't hear you come in,' she said. 'What did the policeman want? Was it McLevy?'

Raven did not, could not speak quite yet, and his hesitation was long enough for her to see what was written in his face.

'Will, what's wrong?'

'I don't believe it,' Eugenie said again. 'It cannot be so.'

These were the only words to have passed her lips in the hours since he told her. Upstairs in the bedroom she had kept saying them until the tears came and choked her voice. Then Raven had held her, knowing that loss was only the first blow. She was saying them again now that he had dealt the second, in telling her the nature of her father's death.

They sat in their small drawing room, the sounds of horses and passing conversations rising to meet them, dispatches from a faraway world beyond the glass. Eugenie looked numb, absent, an austere facsimile like the photograph that graced the mantelpiece. It had been taken by Dr Thomas Keith, Raven's predecessor as Dr Simpson's assistant. The detail was remarkable but to Raven's eye there was something stiff and formal about it that was unlike the Eugenie he knew. In her pose and her expression, she appeared to be approximating some notion of what a wife and mother should look like.

Ironically, Sarah had got her wish in that one of Cameron Todd's housemaids had been sent round to assist in taking care of the children, though the young girl had seemed as much in need of being taken care of herself. Not only was she shocked by the loss of her master but concerned for her own future now. She was upstairs, keeping a watchful eye on Jamie, but she had been unable to comfort Clara. The baby was asleep on Raven's shoulder, the smell of her in his nose and her warmth against him a reminder that life would go on. There would be another day tomorrow, when none of this horror would have gone away and more might arrive, but he would address it all as best he could.

Finally, Eugenie said something new.

'This cannot be as it appears.'

They both understood the implications of Todd having been the author of his own death. For a man of such standing, of such pride, for him not to be accorded a funeral and burial befitting his status would compound the tragedy. And the notion of Eugenie not having a grave to visit was not to be borne.

'I will speak to McLevy,' Raven assured her. 'There were no witnesses and therefore there is no definitive proof that it was other than an accident.'

Her face hardened. 'That is not what I am saying, Will. There is more to this. Why would he take his own life? He would not. He *could* not.'

Raven reached across to hold her hand. Clara stirred a little at the movement, then settled again.

'Then he did not. At least, not intentionally.'

Eugenie pulled her hand away as though in reproach. 'Do not talk of my father's intentions. He was not the agent of this. My father moved among powerful men, and you know that such men have secrets, have enemies.'

'I do,' he agreed, his voice tender.

Raven knew also that Eugenie loved her father deeply. In fact, she loved her father first and foremost: this was the root of much of their conflict. In times of anger she had sometimes spoken of taking the children and going to stay with him instead. Raven had thought it was because the house was bigger and grander and, more importantly, staffed with people who would assist. But he had sometimes wondered if part of Eugenie wished to return to a place and a time where life was simpler. Where she had been happiest. Now that such a place was gone for ever, she would have to build a monument to it in her mind instead.

Nonetheless, she was not the only one who could ill-conceive what might have driven Cameron Todd to kill himself. The very aspects of Todd's character that Raven least liked were also the reasons he was unlikely to have subjected himself to such an ignominious end. He was a man who had exhibited no remorse over what he had once done to Eugenie and to his own lost and unnamed granddaughter. Nor did he appear to feel any shame at his role in covering up his patients' wicked deeds as long as they paid handsomely enough. Eugenie was certainly speaking the truth when she cited the kinds of men he moved among.

'He was not himself of late,' she said. 'He was often short with me and with James, as though we were trivial, a distraction from something more important.'

'You had the impression he was burdened?'

'Very much so. I know he was deeply wounded by the death of a patient.'

Raven had not heard of any controversy, far less the suggestion that Todd had been at fault in a death. And in the back-biting realm of Edinburgh medicine, that was remarkable.

'Did he feel that a different course of treatment might have effected a different outcome?'

'No. It was a rich old man who died at home in his bed.'

'Why would your father be so troubled by that?'

'I do not know. Perhaps this was not the cause, but I had the impression he was hiding some worries from me.'

She grasped Raven's hand now, looking imploringly into his eyes. Raven squeezed her hand in response.

'Eugenie, you must understand that there is no explanation that will lessen the pain of what you have lost.'

She withdrew her hand once again, another reproach. 'Of course I understand,' she said. 'I am not a fool. But I also understand that having no explanation will be an endless torment.'

Raven leaned back in his chair and put a hand to Clara's head, stroking her hair.

'And what if the explanation itself brings endless torment?'

Eugenie looked at him awhile, considering this. There was no reproach this time, no flash of outrage in her expression. It was a moment of shared honesty. Of trust.

'I know who he was, Will. Better than anyone I know who he was. But that is why I am sure this cannot be what it appears. This disgrace is a fiction concocted to conceal a greater scandal.'

Or a harsh truth precipitated by a scandal Eugenie could never hope to escape, Raven thought, a door she would ever after blame him for opening.

'Your father did not share much with me,' he reminded her. 'Are you sure you want me prying through his private matters?'

'I want you to find out who or what killed him, for he cannot have been the true author of it. Promise me you will do that. For the sake of my name, and for that of your own children.'

FIVE

arah had to stand and wait a while on Great Stuart Street after ringing the bell, then finally heard the sound of footsteps from within. When Raven opened the door, his hair was unkempt, his shirt untucked and there was a yellow stain upon his chest that looked suspiciously like baby sick. He looked at Sarah with surprise bordering on confusion. He was clearly not expecting visitors.

'I thought I should see how you were all faring,' she explained.

'Thank you. Come in.'

She had been here with Dr Simpson the previous evening, as soon as they heard the terrible news. The visit had been meant as a gesture of solidarity, all of them sitting together in a vigil of mutual helplessness, though Mrs Lyndsay had insisted on Sarah taking a pot of stew she had made. The cook had always liked Raven, fussing over him all the more since he had got married and moved out.

He led Sarah towards his consulting room, but she continued past the door and into the kitchen. That was where they had retreated together so often at Queen Street. Raven's kitchen was far smaller, but warm and snug and without the threat of Mrs Lyndsay appearing at any moment to coo over Raven or glower at Sarah.

Sarah's ascension from the status of housemaid had been an

affront to Mrs Lyndsay's values; doubly so because if any house-maid was to make something of herself, to her mind it should not have been an insolent one who did not know her place. To Sarah's mind, it was only the insolent ones who did not know their place who would ever become something more.

Raven all but fell onto a chair. He looked like he had not slept, and probably had not eaten. Sarah filled the kettle and, as she placed it on the range, saw that Mrs Lyndsay's stew was untouched. She lifted the pot and placed that on the range too.

'Is Eugenie asleep?' she asked, aware of the quiet.

'No. She has taken the children to St Andrew Square.'

Sarah nodded, understanding. Her father's house. 'They will be a welcome distraction to the staff,' she suggested.

'Yes,' he replied. 'At such times it is better to have your hands full.'

A silence began to grow, all the more pronounced given the absence of the children.

'What about work?' she asked.

'Well, the patients haven't exactly been hammering on the door up until now, so it won't make any difference should I remain closed for business today.'

'Forgive me if it is too early to consider this, but perhaps some of Dr Todd's patients might be persuaded to come to you instead?'

Raven's expression was dubious. 'I very much doubt it. It's not as though I can slip behind the desk at his surgery and declare it under new management. His patients will likely seek the services of other, more established practitioners.'

The selfish side of her wondered, given Eugenie was to inherit, what might be the implications for her own plans with Raven. But now was not the time to discuss that.

She spooned some tea into the pot, noticing that the jar was almost empty. She wondered whether Mrs Balfour had simply neglected to refill it or whether she had not been given the funds to do so. Sarah looked at Raven, slumped in the chair, eyes blood-shot and unfocused. She stirred the stew as the first bubbles appeared on its surface. With her other hand, she gave his shoulder a squeeze.

'How is Jamie? What has he made of it?'

'He does not understand. He does not understand time, so how can he understand for ever?'

Raven's voice broke as he said this. Sarah stood closer and pulled his head against her chest. She wanted to comfort him, but she also felt her own need to be close to him in that moment. They stayed that way for a few seconds, then broke apart as the kettle boiled.

Sarah lifted it in two hands and poured water into the teapot. She let it brew in the next growing silence, pouring it out before she broached the most difficult subject.

'How is Eugenie?'

Raven took some time before answering.

'Broken. Angry and confused. She is refusing to accept the truth of it.'

Sarah looked at him in momentary confusion, concerned that Eugenie was so disturbed as to have lost her reason.

'She will not believe he is dead?'

'No: that he would take his own life.'

Sarah nodded, turning back to the pot on the stove.

There was a secret memory, one that Sarah kept prisoner in the darkest oubliette within her mind. This prisoner was one she never visited, but occasionally something would remind her of its existence. Remind her that it had never gone away.

Her mother had died in childbirth. The baby, a boy, had died with her and Sarah's father had followed soon after. The minister said he had died of a broken heart. For a time, Sarah had harboured the confused belief that such profound loss and sadness could precipitate the fatal failure of that organ. But she hadn't needed to study any medical textbooks to know that this was not a recognised condition. It was a comforting confusion, and a wilful one, because part of her always knew that something had been kept from her.

She remembered how the minister spoke softly to her, telling her that her father had been found dead. Through the window she had seen men from the village at the door to the barn. She had not been permitted to enter there.

She did not attend his funeral, as she had been sent away beforehand, but in truth she did not know if there ever was one.

'My father took his own life,' she said.

Raven looked up in shock.

'I have never said that aloud before. I suppose to do so, to acknowledge it to anyone else, is to accept the truth of it.'

He reached out a hand and took hers. 'Sarah.'

She felt a tear form and pulled her hand away to wipe it with her sleeve.

'I have been deceiving myself about it for a decade, and I tell you this now so that you will know to have patience with Eugenie.'

'Thank you.'

Sarah took a gulp of tea, her throat suddenly dry. 'What is McLevy's position on the matter?' she asked.

'With no firm evidence to say otherwise, he is content to rule it an accident and spare everyone the ignominy.'

'That is decent of him,' she acknowledged. She suspected he would not so readily afford such a mercy to a lesser citizen, but she left the thought unsaid.

'Of course, it means I will not be spared his funeral, and all of the eulogies declaring what a fine man he was.'

Sarah's expression betrayed her disapproval of Raven's sentiment.

'There are things you do not know about him,' he explained. 'I suspect there are things nobody knows about him. And perhaps it is best it stays that way.'

'Why wouldn't it?'

'Eugenie is convinced there must be more to this, but I think it is merely something she needs to believe until she can accept the loss.'

'There certainly must be more to it than we know.'

'You mean a reason why he did this?'

'Indeed. It makes no sense. He was one of the most respected doctors in the city.'

'Yes, but when one is so respected, one has much to lose. Further to fall,' he added ruefully. He sighed, gazing up at Sarah plaintively. A man lost, distraught. 'She made me promise I will look into it, but I doubt she will be comforted by anything I might discover.'

Sarah considered his dilemma. 'You can look,' she said. 'You *should* look, and knowing you, you will probably find. But that does not mean you need to tell. My father died of a broken heart. He died because he loved my mother so much that it killed him to consider life without her. That is the version I have clung to since I lost him. And despite what I've said to you today, I will cling to it still, for it is the version I prefer to remember. Eugenie needs a reason, but it does not have to be the truth.'

Raven smiled for the first time, albeit wistful and accompanied by a shake of the head.

'Why are you always so much wiser than me, Sarah?'

'It is easier to seem wise when talking of other people's cares.'

She spooned out a portion of the stew into a bowl and put it on the table.

'You must eat some of this.'

'I am not hungry.'

'That was not mere advice, Will, it was a command. You will eat this, and once it hits your stomach, while you have the peace to do so, you will lie down and sleep.'

'I would rather stay awake and talk to you.'

Sarah offered him an apologetic smile.

'I have business elsewhere,' she said.

SIX

he air was thick with plumes of steam and smoke wafting from the Caledonian Railway station as Sarah made her way along Lothian Road, which felt just as choked with people. A train must have recently disgorged its passengers, bodies spilling out to join the teeming numbers already crowding the pavements. She saw boys carrying trays of goods to and from the backs of carts, women clutching baskets tightly as they wove through the throng. Up ahead was a finely dressed woman in wide skirts, trailed by a maid bearing a teetering pile of parcels. Sarah shuddered to remember when that was her role, following faithfully behind Mina.

She recalled how intimidating she had found the bustle of this city when she first arrived here, wondering if young Annabel had been similarly overwhelmed. Like Sarah, she had been sent away because there was no future for her at home, and like Sarah, she had only known life in a village where everyone knew everyone else. The city was an easy place to get lost in.

Sarah had been fortunate in that her minister was acquainted with Dr Simpson, who was looking to expand his household staff. Following the deaths of her parents, a situation had been found for her, and though she did not appreciate it at the time, she could not have hoped for a better one.

Dr Simpson was already a man of some renown even before his discovery of chloroform, and when Sarah arrived at the four-storey townhouse on Queen Street, she had expected a household presided over by someone strict, rigid and authoritarian. That was not what she found. Dr Simpson was far from the stuffy patriarch she had anticipated. He was a warm, genial man, large of head and round of body, a physical softness to him that was in tune with his personality. His wife, Jessie, a woman of great patience, attempted to bring a good-humoured order to the chaos that constantly threatened to overwhelm things, providing nourishment to the needy who congregated in the doctor's overcrowded waiting room and caring for their ever-growing young family.

It was a nurturing environment, even for a housemaid.

Dr Simpson was an observant man. He had quickly noted that Sarah was an intelligent girl and had encouraged her to borrow books from his library, placing no restrictions on anything she might select. He was responsible for making her see that she was capable of so much more than she thought, giving her 'ideas above her station'.

Over time Sarah had become acquainted with other housemaids, many of whom were in far less favourable situations. Some she knew had worked for masters who mistreated them, sometimes in ways that could not be spoken of.

The threat held over maids who displeased their employers was that they might be cast out 'without character'. This meant that no other house would employ them, and they would thus be doomed to destitution, prostitution or both, a fall from which it was assumed there could be no redemption. But Dr Simpson had confounded expectation there too, taking in girls from the Lock Hospital and offering them an opportunity to better themselves. Sarah knew that there were good situations to be had as well as bad ones, but which kind had Annabel Banks been bound for?

Outside the station she passed newsboys selling the *Scotsman*, the *Caledonian Mercury* and Mr Sanderson's new venture, the *Capital*.

All of them made mention of Dr Todd's death, though none was going so far as to suggest he had been responsible for his own demise. Sarah had not heard the tragic news from Raven himself, but from Dr Simpson, who in turn had it from who else but Mina. The professor's sister-in-law still lived with the family at Queen Street, where she had all but given up her quest to find a husband, busying herself instead with other people's prospective relationships. Consequently she always seemed to be among the first to know the business of the city, to the extent she could offer her services to William Sanderson. Not that an Edinburgh newspaper would employ a woman as a journalist, any more than an Edinburgh hospital would employ one as a doctor.

On the wall of a timber-yard Sarah saw a playbill announcing, among other attractions, the Mysterious Lembik, who would be performing 'astounding feats of bladeless surgery and human levitation'. She allowed herself a smile. Edinburgh offered attractions, wonders and temptations aplenty. But it also offered dangerous illusions. Which of these might have befallen her niece?

She had come to recall the girl more vividly after Connie left. Sarah remembered spending time with Annabel in the garden of Archie's late father's house, a respite from the awkwardness of being around her new in-laws. Such a memory might not be much use in identifying the girl should she come across her, though. Sarah was picturing a tousle-haired and unselfconscious child, while Connie was missing someone six years older, years that changed everything.

The address she was looking for was on Bread Street, on the second floor, above a bakery and a dressmaker. She ascended the staircase and found a brass plaque identifying the premises she sought. The door was ajar so, after giving it a cursory knock, she stepped inside.

The office of Pike and Featherstone was spacious and well-appointed, presumably intended to reassure prosperous householders of the standards they set for themselves. There were two large desks by the windows, with one of the walls lined with wooden cabinets, the others with wood panelling. A sofa, upholstered in a tasteful floral material, was pressed against the panelling, a low table set before it.

Only one of the desks was occupied, by a neat and prim woman with her hair tied in a bun that might have seemed severe had it not been so large as to suggest quite the tonsorial volume. She rose as Sarah entered the room, though she did not rise very high. Her hair had to account for a good part of her height.

'Good morning, madam,' she said, offering a smile that was courteous but not familiar. 'How can I assist?'

Sarah noticed a nameplate on the desk stating 'Mrs Doris Pike'. To Sarah's mind, the name Pike suggested someone tall and angular, unlike the diminutive woman who stood before her.

'I am here regarding a young woman,' Sarah said.

'Then you have come to the right place. What manner of position would you be looking to fill?'

'I mean a specific young woman,' Sarah clarified. 'One for whom you arranged a situation. Annabel Banks?'

The name did not provoke any marked reaction, whether of surprise or other.

'Has she given you difficulties?'

'You misunderstand. She is my niece. She arrived in Edinburgh from Perthshire a month ago. She was told to report here.'

'I see. What was the name again?'

'Annabel Banks.'

'Let me check if there is record of her.'

Mrs Pike walked over to one of the cabinets.

'You arranged a situation for her,' Sarah repeated.

'Oh, I don't doubt it, but we arrange many situations. I don't remember the girl, but that doesn't mean anything. Much of our work is done by correspondence.'

Mrs Pike pulled a book from the cabinet.

'A month ago, you say?' she asked, leafing slowly through the volume and angling it away from Sarah's view. It was all Sarah could do not to snatch it from her and look for herself.

Mrs Pike appeared to alight upon a page and paused, nodding to herself.

'Yes. Here we are. From Luncarty, Perthshire. It appears she did not present herself here and we found her would-be employers a suitable replacement. I'm afraid the situation is now closed.'

Sarah endeavoured to keep irritation from her tone, knowing it would likely be counterproductive. There were people who struggled to comprehend anything that did not fit their expected frame of reference, and in such instances a combination of patience, persistence and explicitness was required.

'I am not here about her employment,' she said. 'She came to Edinburgh fully a month ago and her mother has not heard from her since. She is missing.'

Mrs Pike closed the book as though that in itself closed the enquiry. 'As I said, she did not present herself here.'

Sarah pointed to the room's other grand desk, taking in its nameplate. 'You have a partner in this business, do you not? What of this Miss Featherstone? Might she have seen Annabel?'

'If the girl had presented herself, it would be in the book.'

Sarah kept her tone even, concealing her frustration. 'Are you saying that if a girl is expected and she does not appear, you make no effort to ascertain her whereabouts? A girl who arrives in the city with only the address of your premises to orient her?'

'We get plenty of girls wasting our time,' Mrs Pike replied, putting the book back in the cabinet. 'We can't waste further time chasing after them.'

Once again Sarah bit back her exasperation. She reminded herself that this woman owed her nothing and Annabel even less.

'I appreciate that you must have your hands full. Running a business as two women cannot be easy.'

'No, it most certainly is not. Though some businesses are more suited to women, and ours is one of them.'

'How so?'

'An eye for the right type of girl. We have a talent for procuring them.'

'And what makes the right sort of girl?'

Mrs Pike considered this. 'That all depends. Different employers will be looking for different qualities. But we consider actually turning up to be a prerequisite.' She picked up a pen and dipped the nib. 'What is your name? In case we should hear anything.'

It sounded obliging but Sarah understood it as a prelude to her expected departure. She placed a calling card down on the desk. Mrs Pike glanced at it, then regarded her with an appraising eye, as though revising an opinion.

Sarah said, 'I would ask again that you enquire of your partner, please. The girl would surely have come here. She did not know anyone else in the city.'

'She knew you, surely, Miss Fisher. Did you not say she was your niece?'

'We are not well acquainted, with her mother living so far from the city. But I can assure you, the woman is distraught. Annabel is only a young girl. Fifteen years old.'

Sarah had been only a few years older when she started at Queen Street. She was twenty-four now and had learned a lot about the harsher realities of life in the intervening years.

Annabel's age seemed to strike the woman as significant. She responded with a smile, in equal parts sympathetic and condescending. 'Fifteen. And you say you did not know her. I wonder if her mother knew her well.'

'What do you mean by that?'

'Daughters are not always as innocent as their mothers like to believe. Or at least, it doesn't always take that much to persuade them out of their innocence.'

'I do not care for your insinuation,' Sarah warned.

Mrs Pike gave her that condescending look once more. 'Miss Fisher, perhaps you do not understand, as you are a maid, but—'

'I am a *widow*,' Sarah told her.

Mrs Pike nodded, as though an equation she was struggling with had resolved itself. 'Then perhaps you do understand. For how well did your mother know you when you were that age? The girl might have met a young man when she arrived in Edinburgh, or perhaps there was a young man she knew already. If this Annabel has not been in touch, then that is because she is her own woman now, and it is not for anyone else to interfere.'

Sarah bit back a refutation, for this possibility had occurred to her too. The city was an easy place to get lost in, especially if you did not want to be found.

SEVEN

ometimes you only appreciate the scale of a presence when it becomes an absence, Raven reflected. Cameron Todd had not been a boisterous or particularly demonstrative man, and certainly no one would have described him as flamboyant. But the lack of him felt stark in the stillness and silence of the house on St Andrew Square.

The staff were like automatons, going through the motions of their tasks with colourless expressions, doing their duties because they did not know what else they could do. Raven knew that their stunned condition was exacerbated by questions regarding their own futures, but he had little doubt that their concerns were not purely selfish. From the perspective of his own conflicts, he sometimes forgot how well-regarded Cameron Todd had been by other people. The staff were feeling the loss of a great man, but furthermore, they were feeling for Eugenie too. Many of them had known her a long time; Maxwell, the butler, since she was a child.

Raven could not help but think of his own father's house in the wake of his death. There had been an unusual sense of stillness and silence then too, but more like one that followed the passing of a violent storm. Nobody mourned the loss of Drew Cunningham, least of all his wife and his son. They had gone through the motions of their normal business, but that was because they had to pretend that they did not know where Raven's father was. Pretend he had not come home from a night of drinking and whoring. Pretend he had not attacked his wife yet again.

Pretend his son had not killed him to protect her.

Raven had no living relatives to remember his father by, something for which he was enduringly grateful. He knew he'd had an uncle who died when Raven was two or three, but he had never known his name and had only the faintest recollection of his father's tone of regret in alluding to his loss. More vivid was his memory of a discussion between his mother and her priggish lawyer of a brother, Malcolm, in which she had described someone as having 'gone the same way as Andrew's brother'. Raven had asked what she meant, and realising her child had overheard, she quickly got off the subject. How had he died? Raven wondered. Was it tragic, or was it shameful? His guess was the latter. Execution, perhaps.

Raven heard the doorbell echo from the hall. He hoped it was no one who might wish to speak to Eugenie. Every visitor who came offering consolation seemed to take something from her instead.

He was standing in the drawing room where he had first met Todd, and also the site of his first encounter with Eugenie. On that occasion, Raven had been staring at the largest of the paintings, the one above the piano. So entranced had he been by its scale, contemplating what deeper meaning there might be to the waterfall at its centre, that he had quite failed to realise she was there. She had commenced asking him questions that her father considered ill-mannered, before being dismissed lest she embarrass him further. Raven had sensed that she was trouble, and immediately wanted more of it.

They had courted in secret, with such discretion that it escaped even Mina's notice, but not so stealthily that it escaped Todd's. He was a man who felt he had paid a price for taking his eye off his daughter once before.

Eugenie was seated on that same couch now, the same place she always sat when she was in this room. Clara was lying alongside her, awake but peaceful, as though even she was reacting to the atmosphere of mournful reverence. In truth she was staring up in fascination at the play of light on the ceiling, refracted from the glass chandelier.

Their relative peace was shattered as Jamie burst through the door clutching a note, making directly for his mother. The butler followed on, making sure the recently delivered missive was transported to its intended recipient. Jamie ran to Eugenie and thrust the paper towards her. It seemed to take her a moment to pull herself up from the place she had retreated to in her mind, as though she did not at first recognise the object being extended towards her. When she belatedly took it from him, he jumped on the spot in expression of disproportionate satisfaction, then ran to the window as though hoping there might be another messenger any moment.

Eugenie looked at the note and her face lightened briefly.

'What is it?' Raven asked.

'A tender message of consolation from a friend,' she said.

She slipped it into her pocket, said nothing more. Raven wondered which friend had sent it, and why she hadn't come in person. The visitors thus far had only been acquaintances of her father, their cards sitting in piles on a silver platter in the hallway. He would have asked but Eugenie seemed to find even the simplest questions intrusive right now. Some more than others.

'Where is Grandpa?' Jamie asked, turning from the window.

Eugenie's eyes filled with hurt and exasperation. 'He won't stop asking that,' she said.

'Grandpa isn't with us any more, remember?' Raven told Jamie softly. 'Sometimes people die. That means they go away and don't come back.'

'Where has he gone?'

'I don't know.' Raven turned to Eugenie. 'He doesn't understand,' he told her.

'*I* don't understand,' she replied, tears spilling over again.

Raven went to her, and she leaned into him. He held her as he had done so many times since the tragedy, the greatest tenderness and intimacy they had shared in more than a year.

The consolation of Jamie's incomprehension was that when his question was not satisfactorily answered, he would forget he had asked it, then amuse himself with something else. Until he inevitably asked again. He may not have understood, but he was conscious that something was very wrong.

Raven heard the doorbell rattling from the hall again and Jamie scuttled away in excited anticipation, careening off the furniture as he went. He returned empty-handed, Maxwell at his back.

'Eugenie, Mr Golspie is here.' Maxwell's tone was apologetic, the familiarity of her first name testament to both how long he had known Eugenie and the affection with which he held her.

Eugenie looked pleadingly at Raven. 'Can you speak to him, Will? I have not the strength.'

'Of course.'

Raven walked out into the hall, where Cameron Todd's lawyer awaited. Frederick Golspie was a portly fellow, dressed in a finely tailored suit in an old-fashioned cut, grey whiskers framing his ruddy face.

'Mrs Raven is indisposed,' Raven explained.

'Of course, of course. Might we decant to Dr Todd's study?'

Raven showed him across the hall and through the door, feeling like some impostor as he did so, for Golspie had no doubt been in Dr Todd's private chamber more often than he had, and been given a far greater sense that he had the right to enter.

Golspie walked with a limp, his right leg never quite reset properly after an injury reputedly sustained falling from a moving carriage. How he had contrived to fall from said carriage was not something Golspie was ever forthcoming about, but Raven suspected that whisky had been a factor.

The study was a gloomy space despite its large windows, the wood panelling and rows of dark leather book-spines reflecting little light. There was an articulated skeleton in one corner, an object of constant fascination for Jamie. Todd had filled his grandson's head with nonsensical tales about its origin, variously saying it was the remains of a South Sea pirate captain, a cannibal savage, and a Turkish janissary. As it pre-dated the Anatomy Act of 1832, Raven suspected its provenance to be altogether more local.

Golspie took an accustomed position before Dr Todd's desk, where he must have stood many times in the past. Raven, by contrast, looked at the conspicuously empty chair and was not sure where to put himself. He settled for a spot by the window. He hoped Golspie didn't need any documents, as he would not know where to begin looking.

'I wished to speak to Mrs Raven concerning her father's estate,' Golspie said, his tone even but his manner stern. Raven did not know him well enough to discern whether this was his common register or a harbinger of troubling import.

'You're not about to tell me he failed to record a will, are you?'

Golspie regarded him as he might a simpleton, which Raven considered harsh but welcome, under the circumstances.

'Of course not. My business is not urgent but I thought that I should commence the preliminaries. Perhaps you can relay my query for Mrs Raven to address when she feels able.'

'You have a query? Is everything in order?'

Golspie's expression was equivocal. 'I have been gathering all the relevant documents, making sure that everything is as it should be, in order to smooth the process for Mrs Raven.'

'Everything is left to Eugenie?' Raven asked, seeking confirmation. It had been made clear to Raven when he married Eugenie that Todd's money would go to her and not him, but he had an irrational thought that Todd might have disinherited her while in the throes of the same madness that led to him taking his own life.

'Everything, yes. But I am still in the process of compiling and confirming what "everything" comprises. Thus far there is but one anomaly I hoped Mrs Raven might be able to shed some light upon.'

Raven doubted this, given how little her father divulged to Eugenie regarding his professional affairs.

'Morris Aitken at the bank said Dr Todd made a recent withdrawal intended for investments. Mr Aitken was only involved in the outgoing portions of these transactions, and I cannot find any documentation regarding the resultant holdings. The funds are therefore as yet unaccounted for. Dr Todd didn't happen to make mention of such matters to yourself or Mrs Raven?'

It was all Raven could do not to scoff. Dr Todd barely sought his counsel on matters of obstetrics, and that was his area of expertise.

'I don't know anything about any investments,' Raven replied.

Golspie frowned. 'Odd that he would not disclose the details to his banker.'

'Perhaps he considered the transactions too trivial to do so,' Raven suggested. 'He was a far from capricious man, but it's always possible he might have been persuaded to lay out a few guineas.' Raven thought about some of the ventures Dr Simpson had invested in of late – shale oil in West Lothian and guano from the New Hebrides – some more profitable than others.

'How much did Aitken say he was investing?'

Golspie's expression became stern once again.

'The withdrawal was for two thousand pounds.'

EIGHT

t was a cold morning for the time of year, the mist thick and stubbornly unmoving despite the chill breeze that found its way between every gap in Sarah's clothing. She could barely make out the outline of the castle even as they crowned the hill at Frederick Street, and there was only the most grudging light penetrating the cloud.

The weather was not her only source of gloom. Sarah had made the mistake of mentioning to Professor Simpson that she was bound for the High Street. 'Then you must accompany Emily,' he had said. 'She is leaving presently for the Maternity Hospital.'

'Presently' had in fact meant half an hour later, but the professor was always a difficult man to refuse, particularly when he made it sound as though he was doing both women a great favour. In truth, Sarah suspected that behind this morning's bonhomie was an awareness of the growing friction between the two women, but whether forcing them together was his idea of encouraging a rapprochement or merely typical mischief she could not rightly say.

Either way, neither of them was happy about it, and they had begun their journey wordlessly and at a stomping gait, as though each determined to reach their destination as soon as possible. Sarah had yet to confront Emily about the newspaper article and was wondering how to raise the issue, but Emily spoke first.

'I know what you did, and why you did it,' Emily said. 'Envy and spite.'

'If you are referring to the story in the newspaper, I had nothing to do with that.'

Emily scoffed. 'You feel threatened by me, and you bear a grudge towards my sister, Elizabeth, because she told you some unwelcome truths.'

'I am envious,' Sarah admitted, 'but also admiring.'

'You have a strange way of showing your admiration.'

Sarah stopped walking and turned to face Emily. 'I realise that you are angry and frustrated, but you are taking aim at entirely the wrong person. I wholeheartedly support your endeavours and one day hope to emulate your achievements. Where you lead others will surely follow. They can't hold out against us for ever.'

Emily tutted. 'Us? You clearly have a higher regard for the female of the species than I do. It is difficult to see how women will better themselves collectively when so few have the gumption to do so individually.'

Emily resumed walking, her pace as brisk as before.

'What do you mean?' Sarah asked, running to catch up.

'The problem is not the tyranny of men,' Emily stated, 'but the disappointing weakness of women.'

Sarah wondered if Emily was speaking generally or referring to Sarah in particular.

They were approaching Duncan and Flockhart's pharmacy at the end of the North Bridge. Sarah recalled when a position behind the counter there was the sum of her ambitions, and what unachievable ambitions they had seemed at the time.

'Women are not encouraged to make more of themselves and have almost no scope to do so,' Sarah said. 'It is not that they lack the capacity or the mental faculties. And as for those of us less fortunate, it is difficult to better yourself when your working day starts at five and ends close to midnight.'

'And yet many of them seem to find time for drinking and fornicating, otherwise I should not be so busy at Minto House,'

Emily replied. 'I find that I am very much in agreement with my sister. The root of much disease lies in moral degeneracy.'

Sarah was beginning to wish that she *had* been the one responsible for the story in the newspaper.

'And the root of much moral degeneracy lies in the disease that is poverty,' she retorted.

Emily seemed to be straining to outpace Sarah, so she could not fully see her expression, but she was sure Emily rolled her eyes at this.

'I have known poverty, Miss Fisher. When our father's investments failed, we all had to go out and work. We became teachers, opened our own school for a time.'

'Not everyone is blessed with the same opportunities. You were fortunate that kind of work was available to you.'

Emily snorted. 'I find that the harder one works, the more opportunity presents itself.'

'Fortune favours the brave.'

'My point exactly,' Emily said, finally slowing down a bit.

'Although friends in high places help a bit too.'

Emily drew her a look but said nothing further. Which was just as well. Sarah knew that Emily deserved to work alongside Dr Simpson as an assistant as much as, if not more than, any man, but she also knew that a crucial intermediary in this arrangement had been Lady Byron. Such opportunities did not necessarily present themselves to those without equally rarefied acquaintance.

'I do hope that you are right,' Sarah continued. 'That hard work will bring rewards.'

Sarah could see a frown forming on Emily's face.

'If you genuinely wish to follow in my footsteps, you will need a university education, Sarah. Occasionally administering a bit of chloroform does not make you anything more than a nurse, no matter how many books you read.'

Sarah knew that under other circumstances she would have found Emily's blunt appraisal of her prospects upsetting, but she had been busy making her own plans. If no university would admit her, she would gain an education by some other means. Apprenticeship had, until relatively recently, been the means by which surgeons had learned their trade and she and Raven had concocted a similar scheme. She would be his apprentice and he would teach her all he knew.

'As Miss Nightingale says,' Emily continued, seemingly impervious to the hurt her words might be causing, 'perhaps it is better that most women aspire to be first-rate nurses than third-rate doctors.'

'It will certainly be difficult for women to find positions as third-rate doctors when there are already so many men providing that level of service,' Sarah replied. They were almost at the High Street, about to go their separate ways. 'If the same instruction and education was offered to her, what makes you think a woman would make any less of a doctor than a man?'

Emily scoffed. 'The petty, trifling, gossiping, stupid, inane women of our day – you think we could make doctors of them?'

'I think that you have spent too much of your time in the wrong company,' Sarah said, surprised at her own equanimity in the face of this onslaught. 'In my experience pettiness and stupidity are not qualities exclusive to women. And as for gossip, how do you think your name ended up in the newspapers? I suspect it was one of those petty, trifling, inane and stupid *male* doctors. Because it's not me who's feeling threatened by you, Emily. It's them.'

NINE

moment later, Sarah was crossing Hunter Square when she heard someone speak her name. She turned and found Henry Littlejohn falling into step beside her. Having recently been appointed the city's police surgeon, Sarah assumed he was heading in the same direction as she was.

'I heard the dreadful news about Dr Todd,' Henry said. 'How is Eugenie?'

'As you would expect.'

Henry hung his head, shaking it gently. 'Will often mentioned how close she was to her father. He said she'd already been spending a lot of time with the children at St Andrew Square. They will all be moving there for good now, I should imagine.'

'I suppose so,' Sarah replied. She did not like to consider these implications. Without the need for Sarah's financial contribution, Eugenie might prevail upon Raven to break off their arrangement. And she would do so forthwith if she knew the true nature of it. Eugenie thought Sarah was merely lending the money, investing in the practice as a friendly favour and to secure her position as nurse, assistant, general maid of all medical works.

'How is Will holding up?' Henry asked. 'It is remiss of me not to have visited, but with the new position, I have been busy with various duties.'

'I think Will would be better if he was as busy. He is far from inundated at the moment.'

'Yes, at such times it helps to be occupied. All that will come, though. He is a good doctor.' They were almost at the door to the police office. Henry stopped outside, assuming Sarah was headed elsewhere. 'Anyway, I will try to drop in on him today,' he said. 'And I'm sure I will see you again soon.'

'Sooner than you think. My business is here.'

'You wish to see McLevy?'

'Oh, I do not wish to, but regretfully I must.'

Henry allowed himself a smile and held open the door.

Sarah found the detective sitting at his desk smoking his pipe as he pored over an edition of the *Capital*. His hat sat on the desk in front of him, indicating that he had either just arrived or was soon about to leave. There was another policeman standing at McLevy's side, his back to Sarah as he thumbed through a casebook.

McLevy looked up in curiosity and annoyance that a member of the public should have ventured beyond the constables at the front desk, then recognised who he was looking at.

'Miss Fisher,' he said, his tone guarded, holding back many complicated sentiments. 'Are you here on behalf of Dr Raven? Dreadful business.'

'A terrible, tragic accident,' she replied.

Their eyes met in acknowledgement of Sarah's understanding and McLevy's generosity in this matter. Branding Dr Todd's death a suicide would pile shame on top of grief.

'I'm actually here about another matter,' Sarah said. 'My niece, Annabel Banks, is missing. She travelled to the city a month ago to take up a position as a nursemaid, a situation arranged by an agency. She failed to present herself there and has not been heard from since. Her mother is gravely concerned about what might have happened to her.'

McLevy glanced again at the newspaper, as though reluctant to entirely disengage from his reading, then said, 'I know full well how sore it can go for mothers when their daughters fly the nest, but I'm not sure what it is you think I can do.'

'You can look for her. A young girl is missing. Isn't that your responsibility?'

McLevy snorted. 'What are my responsibilities, Officer Wilkie?'

Sarah recognised the name. Raven had spoken of him, and not fondly.

'Pavement repairs, the maintenance of street lights, the recovery of property and the protection of the Queen,' Wilkie replied.

McLevy nodded and looked to her again. 'To that I might add assembling and identifying murder victims from dismembered and charred remains, apprehending poisoners and baby-farmers, not to mention keeping order in this foetid labyrinth that is forever on the brink of chaos. So if a girl wants to take herself off, away from her mother's interference, then that's no business of mine. Not unless you can bring me evidence of a crime having been committed.'

Sarah looked at McLevy's expression, which was like a bolted door. Raven often complained that he and Sarah had repeatedly done McLevy's job for him, though they frequently arrived at answers different to those that McLevy had assumed. She was beginning to appreciate that there was a price to be paid for this.

'I suspect a crime *has* been committed. This girl did not run away. Her mother sent her to find work because, since her husband died, she could not afford to keep her. I have told you, a situation was arranged for her. She came to the city to assume a position, but never arrived there.'

'I'd wager she got a better offer en route and she's assuming a position right now,' Wilkie said, smirking.

Sarah glared at him. 'You are very rude, sir,' she scolded, and looked to McLevy to reprimand his officer, but the detective was regarding her with scorn.

'Oh, please, Miss Fisher. Don't try to play that card. Not given the horrors we both know you have insisted on witnessing. You will not move me with faux naivety. We both know the nature of this city.'

'The nature of this city is why I am here. She is a girl of fifteen, around five feet tall with dark hair and fair skin.'

McLevy continued to pay little attention.

'Perhaps if I said she was wearing a jewelled necklace and a tiara when she went missing you would show more interest. But you forget, Mr McLevy, that while possessions can be replaced, people cannot.'

McLevy met her indignation with a sneer. 'Ah, sure, that's where we differ, Miss Fisher. See, possessions can be very expensive to replace. But when it comes to daft wee lassies, there's a dozen more getting off the train every day.'

TEN

t took most of the walk back to Queen Street for Sarah to calm down. She imagined a dozen fiery ripostes in her mind, but they were merely barbs about McLevy's appearance and character. What she did not have, as he pointed out, was evidence of a crime, or a counter-argument any more convincing than the 'faux naivety' he had rightly dismissed. What most troubled her about their exchange was the harsh truth of it.

She decided she needed to distract herself, so she retreated to the upstairs drawing room with an apple and a book – *Villette* by Charlotte Brontë. Sarah remembered reading *Jane Eyre* as a housemaid, making her way through it in precious lulls and stolen moments, 'bits and pieces of time', as Dr Simpson would say.

She had just sat down to it when Lizzie opened the door clutching a duster.

'Oh, sorry. I'll come back,' she said.

Since marrying her late husband Archie and becoming, however briefly, a doctor's wife, Sarah's status in the house had been ambiguous. Mina and Mrs Lyndsay seemed the most resistant to the notion that Sarah was no longer under their command, and she had all but given up on trying to get Lizzie to call her 'Miss Fisher', but there was a note of deference in the girl not simply cleaning around her like she wasn't there.

It was an unnecessary deference on this occasion. Sarah well understood how many tasks Lizzie had to get through and did not wish to be an impediment. 'Not at all,' Sarah told her.

Lizzie bobbed her head in acknowledgement and entered the room.

When Lizzie first began working at the house, Sarah had had the strong impression that the girl thoroughly disliked her. She had worried why that might be until she realised that Lizzie gave the strong impression of thoroughly disliking everybody. She seemed to be permanently angry, but in time Sarah had learned not to be wary of her ill-temper but more sympathetically curious as to what she might be so angry about. Lizzie had exhibited a discernible mellowing towards Sarah of late, though Sarah was at a loss as to what she might have done to win her favour.

'Did you ladies enjoy your walk to the High Street?' Lizzie asked now, lifting a decanter from the sideboard as she dusted beneath it. There was an unusual hint of a smile in Lizzie's eyes, more unusual still that it bore more amusement than malice. Sarah realised she must have overheard Dr Simpson's unwelcome intervention.

'Dr Blackwell and I had a polite exchange of views,' she replied. 'She talked of her sister's correspondence with Florence Nightingale. I think she believes my ambitions would be best served volunteering as a nurse in the Crimea.'

Lizzie stopped to ponder this. 'I think we would all be best served if Dr Blackwell went to the Crimea,' she replied.

Sarah failed to stifle a laugh.

'I don't mean any disrespect,' Lizzie said.

'Of course not.'

'Because I want to give the woman her due: she's proved a lot of people wrong, including me. Working here, I used to think there was nothing more arrogant than a doctor. Now I know that there is: a doctor who is a woman.'

It now dawned on Sarah why Lizzie had become less chilly

towards her of late, and it was nothing she had done or said. In Lizzie's eyes, Sarah's stock had risen simply by not being Emily Blackwell.

Sarah watched her work, remembering how despairing Mrs Lyndsay had once been that she would ever make much of a housemaid.

'Lizzie, did you have a job before you came here?' she asked.

Lizzie put down the ornament she was holding and gave Sarah an admonishing look. 'I think you well know what I did before I came here.'

'I mean before that. Were you in service?'

Lizzie sighed. 'I was. For a year when I was fourteen.'

'What happened?'

'I was dismissed.'

'Why?'

'Master of the house took a special interest in me, and the lady of the house didn't like it. Why do you ask?'

'It doesn't matter,' Sarah replied.

'Yes, it does. You brought it up. Why?'

'It's my niece,' Sarah said. 'She's gone missing. She was offered work but failed to present herself as arranged. Someone implied that she may have found another occupation.'

Lizzie raised an eyebrow at this but said nothing.

'I find it difficult to believe she could find herself in such a predicament so swiftly,' Sarah continued. 'She did not even have time to commence work, let alone suffer the way you have.'

Lizzie sighed again, but the tone was of sympathy rather than the usual disdain.

'Did she come here from the country?'

Sarah felt something inside her stiffen. 'Yes. How did you know?'

'I met a few who had come to take up work but never got there. There are men at the railway stations on the lookout for young girls new to the city. They are easy to spot. These men will pick up their luggage and offer to escort them, maybe even tell them they've been sent to do so. The girls have no option but to follow.'

Lizzie resumed her dusting, as though there was nothing more to be said.

'And after that?' Sarah asked.

'They don't talk about what happens after that.'

ELEVEN

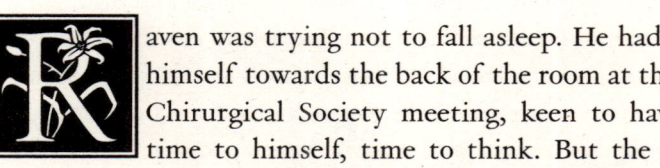aven was trying not to fall asleep. He had stationed himself towards the back of the room at the Medico-Chirurgical Society meeting, keen to have a little time to himself, time to think. But the room was pleasantly warm, the subject under discussion far from scintillating, his brain struggling to make sense of what was being said, his body exhausted.

He had attended several meetings of the society which were of great significance – Dr Simpson's first descriptions of the use of chloroform sprang to mind – but sometimes the presentations were of a more pedestrian variety. The subject currently under discussion was the management of cholera, the dull monotone of the presenter's voice lulling Raven towards sleep. Cholera was a frequently discussed topic, and obviously of great importance given the frequency of its visitations and the fact that the search for a useful treatment was proving elusive, but the presentation held little promise of anything new.

The speaker was in the process of listing the remedies in vogue: calomel and opium were his current preference, having also tried chloroform, ammonia, wine, brandy, the application of cayenne pepper, mustard, turpentine and other species of artificial heat without much effect. No mention was made of the recent enthusiasm in some quarters for castor oil, which to Raven's mind was as useless as everything else. Fortunately, the latest outbreak seemed to be receding, the quarantine ships now hosting a diminishing number of cases. Raven smiled to himself as he remembered Simpson finding a few escapees hiding amongst the laburnum bushes in his garden at Viewbank, the house he had recently purchased to provide himself with an occasional respite from the night bell at Queen Street.

The cholera man drew his presentation to a close, Raven having learned little of use. Cholera was a desperate thing to treat — copious effusions, cold extremities, sunken eyes, the skin taking on the curious blueish hue synonymous with the disease. Those who showed symptoms could sink with alarming rapidity, sometimes proceeding from perfectly good health to death in a matter of hours. When the state of collapse was extreme there seemed to be little any doctor could do to prevent a fatal outcome.

Back when he was still at Queen Street, Raven had experimented by treating the worst cases with infusions of saline solution through a hypodermic needle. This was inspired by a paper he had uncovered, written during the previous epidemic by a Dr Latta from Leith. But although his patient had rallied, getting everyone's hopes up, the improvement was only temporary, and she succumbed, as had the rest of her immediate family.

The next speaker was a Dr Lister, Syme's latest protégé: an unassuming gentleman, quietly spoken and a Quaker by all accounts. He stood at the podium, cleared his throat several times and then announced the title of the paper he was about to present: observations of the contractile tissue of the iris. Raven groaned, leaned back in his chair and felt his eyes close.

A smattering of applause roused him. He jolted awake and joined in, clapping his hands with a great deal more enthusiasm than he felt in a bid to hide the fact that he had been asleep. He watched as Lister took his seat again beside the usually taciturn Syme, who appeared to be smiling. Raven wondered if Lister was drugging the irascible old surgeon with something. Now *that* would have made for an interesting talk.

Raven looked around the room as everyone started getting to their feet, the educational part of the evening over. He often felt that the greatest benefit of these meetings was the informal discussions that took place after the presentations rather than the presentations themselves. As always, however, his eye was first drawn to identifying those he would prefer to avoid. Among them was Dr James Matthews Duncan – though avoiding him was seldom difficult as he seemed to make a point of ignoring Raven. Some might assume this was down to Raven's part in thwarting the man's plot to smear Dr Simpson several years back, were it not that he had behaved this way even before that.

Matthews Duncan had conspired to lay unfounded accusations against Simpson in the medical journals, in retaliation for – to his mind – being given insufficient credit for his role in the discovery of chloroform. Raven's recollection was that his role had been to dismiss the fateful bottle of viscous liquid and put it to the back of the cupboard, only for Simpson to retrieve it later. Matthews Duncan chose to remember it differently and had remained aggrieved ever since.

Raven spotted Dr Simpson on the other side of the room, surrounded as always by numerous friends and acquaintances. One man in particular caught his attention. He was dressed in a burgundy jacquard coat which made him stand out like a beacon from his more soberly dressed colleagues. Raven knew the man by sight (and reputation), but had never been introduced, for which he was grateful. His name was Stokes, a middling physician with delusions of grandeur; a teller of tall tales and notoriously difficult to get rid of. According to his victims, he clung on like a limpet, never responding to the usual polite verbal cues that he should go and bother someone else.

Raven instead fell into discussion with a surgeon he knew through Henry. As they chatted, he noticed the group surrounding Simpson one by one make their excuses and drift away, presumably lest they be the one who ended up with Stokes. This had the unfortunate result of leaving the professor alone with the man.

Dr Simpson generally enjoyed discussions of all sorts with all kinds, but in time even he began to look in distress. Raven decided an intervention was in order.

'Dr Simpson! I have an urgent matter to discuss with you,' he said, walking to the beleaguered man's side. Simpson looked up as Raven approached, gratitude writ large in his expression.

The limpet held his ground. 'I don't believe I've had the honour,' Stokes said, extending his hand. 'Dr Hedley Stokes.'

'Dr Will Raven.' He shook Stokes's hand briefly, then let go, trying to give the impression of being in a great hurry. To no avail.

'The professor and I were just discussing the Lock Hospital,' Stokes continued.

'Dr Stokes is on the board,' Simpson added wearily.

'As were you at one time,' Stokes observed brightly. 'Or so I'm led to believe.'

'I was. That's true,' Simpson replied. 'But I found I cared little for the emphasis on moral treatment when it was medical therapy that the women there were most in need of.'

'With such women, surely both are of equal import,' Stokes insisted.

'I remain unconvinced as to the therapeutic benefits of Bible study when dealing with the ravages of venereal disease,' Simpson told him.

'Come, come, Dr Simpson. We all know that the diseases these women suffer from are a small part of a greater ailment. And we do them no favours by treating their physical symptoms while ignoring the greater threat to their immortal souls.'

He flashed Simpson a slick smile.

Raven wasn't sure about Simpson's feelings on the matter, but his own tolerance for this man was rapidly depleting. Since subtle signs were being ignored, Raven decided to be more direct. He grasped Simpson's elbow and started to lead him away. 'As I said, it is something of great importance . . . apologies,' he added over his shoulder, but Stokes was already scanning the crowd for his next victim.

They kept walking until they had covered sufficient distance and were safely removed from the man's orbit.

'I'm indebted to you, Will,' Simpson said. 'I don't know how much more of him I could have taken. Half the time he talks complete nonsense. He was going on about his walking stick being a present from Garabaldi. Claims to have met the man in Italy last time he was there.'

'He had you cornered for quite some time.'

'Well, to be fair, it wasn't all nonsense. He was asking for my advice about something.'

'A medical case?'

Simpson shook his head. 'He claims he's the victim of blackmail.'

'Good heavens. What was he being blackmailed about?'

'He was disinclined to divulge any details. But he's under the impression that there's a lot of it about.'

Raven thought about Todd, and the recent withdrawals from his bank account.

'Do you believe him?'

Simpson gave Raven a grave look. 'I have reason to.'

Raven was still thinking about his father-in-law when he realised what Dr Simpson meant.

'You?'

Simpson nodded. 'A letter arrived in the night, so the messenger was not seen.'

'Can you tell me what it said?'

'I won't go into specifics, but it pertains to the fostering of children.'

Raven knew about this – Simpson placing the inconvenient, illegitimate offspring of Edinburgh society with adoptive parents. Obviously Simpson was the keeper of other people's secrets, but Raven could not understand why this made him a target himself.

'Does this concern a particular case, a particular child?'

'It does, but I can't reveal more without breaking a confidence, and that I will not do.'

Raven thought for a moment. 'Surely the information they have amounts to little more than gossip.'

'Gossip can tarnish a reputation whether there is any truth to it or not. They are threatening to take the information they have to the press.'

'Surely no one would publish unsubstantiated rumours—' Raven stopped mid-sentence, suddenly realising who would. William Sanderson: until recently the publisher of scandalous penny pamphlets but now editor of his own new venture, the *Capital*.

Raven looked at Simpson's face, his brow furrowed with concern. He would do anything for this man, loved him in a way he had never loved his own father.

'Can you think who might be behind this?' he asked gently.

Dr Simpson sighed. 'If we are looking for a rumour-monger in this city, I can narrow the list down to several hundred.'

'What about enemies, people who might wish you ill?'

'Also a long list.'

'What do they want from you? What are their demands?'

'Money. What else?'

'How much?'

'The sum is of no account. Whatever I pay, they can come back and ask for double tomorrow.'

Simpson sighed again, his shoulders slumped.

'The worst of it is,' he said, 'should these revelations be made, it is Jessie who would be hurt the most.'

Raven left the meeting room more burdened than when he arrived. Simpson had his fair share of detractors, had survived several attempts to besmirch his character and good name, but this was something new. What was the secret and how did it involve Simpson's wife? Raven knew that Jessie played an active role in the fostering process, keeping the natural parents appraised of their offspring's progress – should they want to know.

Raven wanted to help, but could not see how without the professor giving him more details. He thought with some discomfort about a

rumour circulating some time ago about Simpson's infidelity, a dalli-
ance with another woman and the existence of an illegitimate child.
Raven could not imagine Simpson betraying his wife like that but
recalled happening upon the professor making a discreet visit to a
New Town address many years ago. Through the window Raven
had spied the man being fondly greeted by a woman, then bouncing
an infant on his knee. Was that the secret? It would certainly hurt
Mrs Simpson if such a thing was revealed.

Raven shook his head. No, there was nothing that he could do
without more information and Simpson seemed reluctant to give
it. But was that not the very essence of blackmail's poison? Merely
to admit you were subject to it was to admit you had a secret
you would rather the world not know.

The question was how far a man might go in order to keep it.

TWELVE

here was a queue, of sorts, in Raven's waiting room when he emerged from what he had expected to be his sole morning consultation. There were two patients waiting to be seen, seated on the chairs nearest the door, as though claiming their spots ahead of an expected inundation. Raven would admit that two people was the bare minimum required to constitute a queue, and very much doubted that they had any need to worry about establishing their places in the hierarchy ahead of a sudden rush, but it appeared that Sarah was right. Word was starting to spread.

Sarah gave him a bright look, conveying her pleasure at this development combined with just a hint of vindication.

He enjoyed a brief moment of optimism, which was punctured by a sense of conflict as Eugenie entered the waiting room and deduced that he would be busy for a while yet. His mind went from gratitude towards his new patients to thinking: Where were you lot before, and why did you all have to turn up today? He wanted to be with his wife, concerned about leaving her alone with her pain.

'You are in demand,' she observed coolly. 'You must do your duty, and I mine.'

By that she meant looking to the children, and he knew what that implied.

'Will you take them to St Andrew Square?' he asked, trying not to make disappointment sound like disapproval.

'It will be our own home soon enough,' she replied, and once again Raven had to disguise his response. He hadn't told her about her father's finances, believing she had enough to deal with. The missing sum constituted a substantial portion of Todd's liquid assets, and without his income, Mr Golspie had warned that there was only money to pay the staff for another two months. Unless Raven rapidly expanded his practice, he would not be able to afford the upkeep of the premises. Eugenie seemed to think that Raven would inherit her father's patients as simply as she would inherit his house, but it appeared she was wrong about both of those things. To Raven's mind the solution would be to sell the house in St Andrew Square and buy somewhere smaller while he established his practice, but he could not envisage Eugenie agreeing to that, especially not in her current condition. And once they had moved into St Andrew Square, it would be all the harder to make her confront the harsh truth, that though they might own it, they could not afford to live there.

Sarah showed the first patient into Raven's consulting room, having already begun taking details to ascertain the nature of her complaint.

'This is Mrs Denholm,' Sarah said as the patient took a seat. The woman was thin, pale and held a white handkerchief to her left cheek.

Raven sat back in his chair as Sarah presented the case.

'Mrs Denholm is thirty-eight years old. She has been in delicate health for some time. For the last nine months she has been suffering from a neuralgic affection, a tic which principally affects her lower jaw on the left side. Paroxysms are frequent and can last for hours.'

'Any precipitating factors?' Raven asked.

'Currents of cold air, speaking or eating,' Sarah replied.

'Do you have difficulty nourishing yourself, Mrs Denholm?'

The patient nodded, disinclined to speak where she could avoid it.

'What remedies have been tried already?'

Sarah frowned. 'I didn't think to ask,' she said.

Raven gave her a reassuring smile. She had managed to garner most of the relevant clinical details and would become more proficient given time.

Mrs Denholm withdrew her handkerchief and spoke slowly and softly. 'Quinine, iron, various aperients, but nothing seems to help.'

'I've had some success with this in several cases,' Raven said. He picked up his pen, wrote down a prescription and handed it over. 'Veratria,' he said. 'Apply the ointment thrice daily and we will see you again in a week.'

He noticed Sarah smile at his use of 'we'.

After they had dealt with the second patient – a relatively young woman with a distressing case of uterine prolapse – Raven emerged from his consulting room to find that there was no inundation. There was not total silence either, though. He could hear the sound of weeping from the floor above and realised that Eugenie had not left.

Once upstairs he quickly ascertained why she had not gone out: both of the children were asleep, and she hadn't wished to disturb them. He found her sitting on the edge of the bed, her head in her hands, her eyes red and puffy. She had been sobbing for some time.

Raven sat down and put his arms about her. She stiffened at first, as she was wont to do of late, and he feared she would even shrug him off. It was as though she did not want to accept comfort if it was coming from him.

'I wake in the morning and there is a moment's grace before I remember,' she said, her voice brittle. 'Throughout my day, I am sometimes distracted enough to forget for a while, but then it comes upon me once more, crashing like a wave.'

'Those waves will keep coming,' he said softly, 'but they will lessen in time. You will never forget for long, but there will be less pain in the remembering.'

'It is what others will choose to remember that pains me,' she said. She glanced towards the dressing table, where a pile of newspapers lay in a scattered heap. 'I wanted to read the obituaries,' she explained.

Raven understood. She thought she would find comfort in other people's warm recollections, and in tributes to Cameron Todd's greatness. 'But they only served to stress how much you have lost,' he suggested.

Now she did shrug him off. 'No,' she said. She picked up one of the papers and thrust it at him. It was a copy of the *Capital*, open at a particular page, and not one that contained any obituaries. It took Raven little time to find what had upset her.

Edinburgh is mourning but puzzled over the mysterious circumstances of the esteemed Dr Cameron Todd's demise. It is not for us to suggest that his death was anything other than the accident that has been intimated by the authorities, but when a prominent citizen is so suddenly lost, people are naturally curious as to what precipitated the tragedy. Our curiosity extends to why Dr Todd should have been ascending the Scott Monument at the hour he did, in the dark of night. Such actions would, by any fair measure, constitute erratic behaviour. This unavoidably leads to questions regarding Dr Todd's state of mind at the time he undertook his ascent and thereby placed himself in the position from which he was to suffer such a tragic accident.

'They hide behind cowardly innuendo and weasel words, but their meaning is clear,' Eugenie said. Her anger was overcoming her grief, determination in her tone and a steadiness to her timbre. He was sure there was a note of accusation in there too. She had asked him to look into her father's death precisely so that such speculation might be averted, but with little consideration for Raven's likelihood of success.

'Sanderson has always traded in malicious gossip and sensationalised rumour,' Raven said, knowing it explained and excused nothing. He was merely trying to remind her who was the offending party.

'That is why I asked you to find out the truth,' she replied. 'Have you discovered anything?'

'I think you should try to put all this from your mind. It would only bring you more pain to immerse yourself in such speculation.'

'Then you have found nothing. Answers are the only thing that will provide a salve for my pain. Have you even asked any questions?'

Raven glanced at the newspaper, then closed it and placed it aside. He did not want to argue with her, but he knew he might need to hurt her a little right now so that he did not hurt her far more later.

'You say you want answers, Eugenie, but I am not sure you really want me asking the questions they might require.'

Her red eyes challenged his. 'You think there is something that can wound me more? Or that I am deluded into thinking my father some saint? Which questions do you mean? Tell me.'

Raven stood and walked to the window. He turned slowly and faced her.

'My first question, to you, is simply this: is it possible your father took his own life?'

'No,' she insisted immediately. She looked up at him and he held her gaze. 'Well. Yes, it *is* possible. But I consider it unlikely. Do *you* consider it likely?'

Raven took a moment. He had not told her about Dr Simpson's troubles. He had told no one, in fact, not even Sarah. She worried about the professor at the best of times, and she had enough to be concerned about. Her niece was missing in the city, quite possibly in a predicament nobody would wish upon anyone's daughter.

'I have learned that a respected citizen has been subject to a blackmail threat,' he said.

'Who?'

'I don't have any details,' he said, which was largely the truth.

'Are you suggesting that my father was blackmailed too?'

She sounded calm, as though determined to convince him that she could cope with anything Raven might tell her. He had no choice but to put that to the test.

'Eugenie, Mr Golspie brought to my attention that your father recently withdrew two thousand pounds of his funds, ostensibly to make investments. Golspie and I looked through all of the documentation we could find, but there is no record of what these investments might be, or any certificate of his holdings.'

'Two thousand . . .'

The scale of it struck her. This was a colossal sum, the implications only beginning to announce themselves. But now that Raven had broached it, he had to tell her the rest.

'Golspie said there is very little left.'

Eugenie looked stunned, the colour draining from her. She sat back down on the bed, picking up a cushion and hugging it to herself.

'I am so sorry,' Raven told her.

'It must simply be an administrative error,' she said. 'My father would not . . .' Then she stopped, briefly closing her eyes. Those last words hung in the air. *My father would not* . . .

From somewhere she found her voice again.

'I have no notion what my father would or would not do,' she admitted. She looked to the window, gazing east across the tops of the buildings opposite. Hidden beyond them, along her line of sight, was the Scott Monument. 'It is possible he took his own life,' she said. 'It is possible he was being blackmailed. I cannot think of any reason why, but of course the reason would be something so secret that none who knew him *could* think of it. But answer me this: if he had paid out so much money in exchange for a blackmailer's silence, why would he kill himself?'

Raven could think of a reason, and it was one that might offer her consolation.

'To protect you. So that they could not bleed him for more. If he realised that the blackmailer's demands would never cease, perhaps he chose a sacrifice that would preserve what was left for you and his grandchildren to inherit.'

Eugenie considered this, tears welling in her eyes again. Raven thought of what Sarah had said: *Eugenie needs a reason, but it does not have to be the truth.*

'No,' she said. She dropped the cushion. 'There must be more to this, Will. If my father habitually sinned, it was in protecting the secret shames of others. What if someone decided they could no longer trust him to do so?'

'That is also possible,' Raven conceded, though he kept to himself his reservations regarding how some malefactor could persuade him to the top of the monument, or even carry him there, whether against his will or already dead.

'My father seemed worried, more distant than I had ever known him,' Eugenie continued. 'I need to know why. I need to know whether or not he died by the hand of another before I can accept any other explanation.'

'Did your father have enemies?' Raven asked delicately, as though wishing to subtly dissuade her from this notion without dismissing it.

'Every doctor in Edinburgh has enemies, as well you know. They are at each other's throats when they're not stabbing each other's backs.'

'Yes, but the animus rarely spills over into physical acts. It usually involves smears and accusations, whispering campaigns and letters to the papers.'

'I told you my father was troubled by a patient's death. More troubled than I would have expected in the circumstances.'

'What do you mean?'

'The patient was not someone my father was close to, certainly not a friend, and he died peacefully in his own bed. Why should he be so distressed and moved over this old man's death?'

'Which old man?'

'Barrington Leitch.'

Raven nodded.

'You know of him?'

'I read of his death in the newspaper. He was a financier. One of those men who tells people he built a railway when he never so much as lifted a shovel, merely channelled money into a scheme.'

As he said this, Eugenie's eyes widened. 'Then perhaps my father gave Leitch this two-thousand-pound sum for an investment, and his death was catastrophic to the prospects of it paying out.'

'But why would there be no record of such a substantial speculation?'

Eugenie looked at him with weary eyes. 'I grew up on St Andrew Square, Will. I saw the statue of Henry Dundas every day.'

Raven understood. His mother had named him Wilberforce, after all.

'Not all investments are in noble enterprises,' he said, 'or even ones you'd want your name upon.'

THIRTEEN

arah stood outside the townhouse on Melbourne Place, having gone there direct from Great Stuart Street. She took in its noble exterior while bearing in mind the true purpose of the enterprise housed within. Parliament Square was only yards away, the Sheriff's Offices right across the street. She knew the nature of this place because she had been here before, but as she rang the doorbell she wondered just how many such premises there might be in Edinburgh: hidden in plain sight, known to their clientele and to the unfortunates who worked there, but unnoticed by the ordinary passer-by. Then she wondered whether she was in this instance being genuinely naive, for who was to say the ordinary passer-by did not know as much as she did about the House of Melbourne.

It was held over housemaids and governesses that if they were dismissed without character, they would surely end up working in prostitution. The late and – to Sarah, at least – unlamented Sir Ainsley Douglas had tried to raise an ordinance aimed at preventing the spread of infectious diseases in a city so full of prostitutes. But such a city must also be full of men eager for their services. Who was to say how many ordinary passers-by might be clients?

A young woman answered the door, initially confused at the sight of Sarah, then wary. She wore a red dress that looked cut

from expensively plush velvet, albeit with a neckline more revealing
than would be considered respectable around a New Town dining
table or even at a New Town ball. Upon first glance Sarah took
her to be around her own age, until she got a longer look and
recognised a much younger face, sixteen or seventeen at most.

'I wish to speak with Madame Bouvier,' Sarah said, stepping
inside without waiting to be invited.

'I will see if she is available,' the girl replied, her discomfort
sufficient that she hadn't the presence of mind to ask Sarah's
name before walking away. An unknown *woman* turning up was
evidently proof enough that the madam's attention was warranted.

Sarah waited in the hall, which was flamboyantly decorated
and hung with paintings. They were mostly classical landscapes,
wrought by a talented hand, but Sarah mused that in the realms
of pastoral mythology, surely some of the women would have had
the wherewithal to dress themselves. There was a strong smell
of perfumes. Not unpleasant, given what greeted the noses of
visitors to most dwellings, but strangely discordant, as though
multiple scents were clamouring for her attention. If this was
what it was like in the morning, she thought it must be over-
powering at night.

There were two young women sitting on a couch beneath one
of the paintings, wearing not much more than the women in it.
They were talking with a quiet furtiveness and amusement, the
ordinary and recognisable sight of friends engaged in gossip. They
seemed happy enough. Perhaps she was catching them during the
best part of their day, but they did not look broken or miserable,
she thought. Then she caught herself. Part of her was already
accepting Annabel's fate, she realised, and she wanted to believe
that the girl would not be irretrievably lost, irreparably damaged.

The doorbell rang again just as Madame Bouvier appeared,
descending the return staircase with a gloved hand sliding down
its dark wooden banister. She was dressed more modestly than
her charges, but still in a manner more suited to a later time of
day and a grander occasion. She wore a gold pendant upon her

decolletage, flanked either side by thick and flowing locks of a hue blacker and more uniform than a woman in her forties naturally enjoyed.

Another young woman emerged from off the hall and hurried to the front door, which she opened to a portly man with a bulbous, pockmarked nose and carrying a cane with a brass horse-head handle. Bouvier did not acknowledge Sarah for the time being, walking past her to greet her customer.

'Good afternoon, monsieur,' she said in her laboured French accent, as real and as convincing as her wig. 'A pleasant surprise to see you at this time of day.'

The man ambled in, lopsided in his gait, the cane sounding out against the polished floor. 'I was disappointed in another arrangement,' he said.

'But you know you won't be disappointed here,' Madame Bouvier replied.

The man regarded Sarah with an appraising and entitled gaze, like he was choosing steak from a butcher's slab. There was a flicker of perplexity in his expression, as though something about her was not in order, though the true implications of her garb and demeanour failed to fully register.

'Someone new, I see,' he remarked approvingly. 'And who would you be, my lovely?'

Sarah folded her arms. 'I am a widow despairing of divine providence that my husband should have died while the Almighty would spare the likes of you.'

The man barely blinked at her broadside. In fact, he looked mildly amused.

'Another moral campaigner. I didn't know you were opening the door to them now, Madame Bouvier.'

Madame Bouvier put a hand upon his shoulder and gestured to the young girl who had let Sarah in.

'I have not yet ascertained the lady's business, monsieur. But while I do so, why don't you allow petite Nicolette to serve you a drink through by.'

Sarah smiled to herself, Madame Bouvier's 'through by' betraying her affectation. She occasionally presented herself under her real name as a wealthy, 'upstairs' patient at Queen Street, which was how Sarah knew the woman was no more French than she. Sarah had recognised her on her last visit here some years back, and the fear that her two separate personae might become more widely discovered had been enough to make her divulge important information.

A shudder ran through Sarah as she watched poor Nicolette lead the horrible old man away. Madame Bouvier waited until the door to the sitting room closed, then turned to her with a smile as genial as it was conspicuously insincere.

'Miss Fisher,' she said, dropping the accent now. Sarah noted that the two girls remained in earshot, so the French business was largely for the clients. 'What brings you to my door? Is he right? Are you with the Butlers on this crusade against the evils of prostitution?'

Sarah had not heard of any such crusade and had still less of a notion why butlers might be leading it.

'I am looking for my niece. Her name is Annabel Banks.' She looked the woman sharply in the eye as she said this. Did she hope to see a flicker of recognition? If so, there was none. 'She came to the city for a job as a nursemaid, but she did not arrive. I have been led to believe that certain newly arrived and unsuspecting girls might be conveyed to establishments such as yours.'

Madame Bouvier put a hand to her pendant as though wounded by the accusation.

'There's nobody here against their will, Miss Fisher. My girls are well looked after. Living somewhere much finer than the tiny upstairs cupboards they'd be given were they in service in the New Town. And I'd wager there's not many housemaids enjoying fine dining and nights at the theatre.'

Sarah glanced at the two girls on the couch, who were clearly paying attention now. They still seemed giddy, but it was as though Sarah had become the source of their amusement.

'Have you had anyone new arrive in the past month?' she asked, loud enough to ensure they heard. Out of the corner of her eye she scrutinised them for their reactions but saw nothing of substance.

'That's none of your business,' Madame Bouvier replied. There was a hint of cruelty to her smile, born of the mutual under-standing that Sarah was supplicant in this exchange. Bouvier could toy with her, pretending she knew something, or with-holding what she genuinely did.

'My niece is fifteen,' Sarah told her.

'There you are, then,' she replied. 'If she's over twelve it's her own business where she goes and what she does.'

'You have girls here who are twelve?'

'Not here, no. My regulars' tastes don't run to that.'

The unspoken part of her statement made Sarah feel sick. 'Annabel is an innocent from a country village,' she said.

Madame Bouvier rolled her eyes. 'If you mean a maid, everyone here was once that, including you, *Mrs Banks*. Such humbug.'

Sarah felt a chill run through her at the woman knowing her married name. She had largely put Madame Bouvier from her mind after their previous encounter, but evidently the woman had not put Sarah from hers. She would not be intimidated, though.

'I know what it is to be a young girl fresh from the country, shy and afraid. These girls surely do not subject themselves voluntarily.'

Madame Bouvier leaned closer, her tone sincere but patronising. 'Let's be honest, none of us enjoys it the first time, do we? But we all learn to like it. A woman's virtue is something we are all commanded to protect and yet none of us miss it once lost.'

'They have lost much if they are ruined.'

Madame Bouvier gestured to the pair on the couch. 'Do my girls look ruined? Would you insult them thus? Why don't you tell them to their faces that you consider them beneath you?'

The girls went quiet, eyes averted, as if they did not want to meet Sarah's gaze any more than she theirs.

'Yes, I think you do belong with the Butlers,' Madame Bouvier continued dismissively. She began reaching for the door, by way of telling Sarah they were done.

'The butlers?'

'Campaigners against prostitution. Arrived from London. Probably chased out of there and come to plague us instead. Fools who think it something that can be stopped while men have the needs and appetites that they do. I would warn you to stay away from them, because there are people here who are not prepared to tolerate their nuisance.'

Sarah stopped on the threshold and turned around, glancing towards the couch.

'It is not I who would regard any such girls as beneath me, *Morag*,' she said. 'We both know that.'

Bouvier's expression hardened. 'Aye, I do,' she replied. 'It would be the upstanding, pious and respectable citizens of this town, many of whom can be seen walking through my door on any given night. I didn't make the world this way, and you're another fool if you believe you can change it. Would you rescue them all, Miss Fisher? All those lost little girls?'

Sarah felt the woman's scorn kindle a flame inside her.

'I would start with rescuing one.'

FOURTEEN

he day of Cameron Todd's funeral was hardly one that Raven anticipated being in any way auspicious, but he did not anticipate that it would get off to such a dreadful start. As he was fetching himself a slice of bread by way of breakfast, there had been a messenger at the door from Mr Golspie, asking him to make a discreet visit to his offices nearby on Charlotte Square. This told Raven that the lawyer had news he did not wish to impart directly to Eugenie – but she had seen the messenger from their bedroom window as she dressed. She then watched from the stairs as Raven read the note, and had read his expression just as clearly.

Eugenie stated that he was not to protect her from the truth and had sent for Golspie by return. The lawyer arrived at Great Stuart Street within the hour, though not long before they were due to leave for Greyfriars Kirkyard.

'The situation is worse than I had appreciated,' Golspie told them, standing in Raven's consulting room. 'Considerably worse. It has emerged that Dr Todd had secured a loan on his property. The two thousand pounds withdrawn from the bank was in fact borrowed against the house on St Andrew Square.'

Eugenie said nothing, merely stared numbly out of the window. Raven reached a hand out to hers but she folded her arms.

'Why would he need to borrow?' Raven asked.

Golspie sighed. 'It appears that some months ago he invested in the voyage of a trading vessel. An outbreak of cholera on-board meant that the ship was not permitted to land. It had to serve quarantine of forty nights, and much of its most valuable cargo was perishable. With his income, I am sure Dr Todd would have made up the loss in time, but I do wonder if this investment was an attempt to recover more rapidly.'

Golspie apologised profusely for being the bearer of such unwelcome news and promised to continue his search for the missing documentation. Once he had departed, the news remained in the room like an unwelcome visitor, one who was here to stay.

'You knew nothing of this?' Raven asked Eugenie. He tried not to make it sound like an accusation. This was nobody's fault. Nobody's but Todd's.

'Not about the borrowing. I am sure I told you about the ship.'

He doubted this but he could not say for certain that he always paid attention when she spoke about her father undertaking grand schemes far beyond Raven's ambit.

'You certainly didn't tell me about the loss.'

'No,' she admitted. 'I remember him saying he was investing in a voyage. I do not remember him discussing the outcome.'

This sounded about right. Todd was a proud man, and vain with it. He liked to talk about his successes and his prospects. Failures he kept to himself.

Some hours later, Raven watched as Cameron Todd's coffin was gently lowered into the gaping maw of the grave. He felt Eugenie grasp his arm for support, heard her whimper as the coffin reached its final resting place. He had tried to dissuade her from coming, suggesting that she might be better remaining at home with a friend for company, but she would not hear of it.

The days since Dr Todd's death had been consumed with making the requisite arrangements. McLevy had been content to release the body, convinced that there was nothing suspicious in the death that required his attention. This should have put Eugenie's mind at rest regarding the possibility of murder but hadn't. She was still adamant that things were not as they seemed and was growing impatient with Raven and his inability to get to the truth of the matter.

The words of the minister faded in Raven's ears as he stared down at the coffin, struck by how unthinkable this circumstance would have seemed only a week ago.

He glanced to the north-east end of the cemetery, towards the Covenanters' Memorial and the nearby tomb of Black Mackenzie. He thought of the evil deeds he had uncovered in the past, wondering whether Eugenie was right that similar evil deeds had led to this moment. But as he looked around at the people gathered to pay their respects, he realised that, to his knowledge, the only person present to have ever wished Cameron Todd ill was Raven himself.

FIFTEEN

That afternoon Raven found himself in the grand drawing room of Dalton's Hotel on Princes Street, to which they had invited the mourners for a light meal and refreshments. This had been Eugenie's idea, or rather, insistence.

There had been few callers to the house prior to the funeral, the sudden and violent nature of the death keeping them away. Eugenie said she wanted to provide an opportunity for friends and family to pay their respects; Raven suspected it had more to do with demonstrating an absence of shame, cementing the notion in the minds of the attendees that Dr Todd had not died by his own hand.

Looking at the assembled throng, Raven was torn between reassurance at the comfort Eugenie might derive from the large attendance and wincing at the prospect of what it was going to cost them. After Golspie conveyed the true state of Todd's affairs, Raven had suggested that they might cancel the hotel and ask people back to St Andrew Square instead, but Eugenie was having none of it.

'We must not, by action or omission, convey to people that we are financially embarrassed. It would only encourage more speculation.'

If it was Eugenie's intention that the gathering be a fitting testament to her father's status, then she was thoroughly vindicated, not merely by the numbers inside the hotel, but by the calibre too. The assembly was an impressive representation not only of Todd's patients but of his peers – half of Edinburgh medicine was here, though Raven wondered how many of the latter had turned up in the hope of poaching the former. In truth Raven was among them, under instruction from Eugenie, despite his qualms about it being both inappropriate and improbable. 'Such wealthy patients will be looking for a more renowned doctor,' he had said.

'Most of them will not be *looking* for a doctor until they urgently need one,' she countered. 'At which juncture, if you have made a sufficient impression, the son-in-law of the man they trusted should be the first option that comes to mind.'

The last time Raven had stood in this room had been after his wedding. The proprietor and his wife, Mr and Mrs Dalton, had been Todd's patients. Raven wondered if this meant he'd get any kind of discount.

He stood at Eugenie's side as the Daltons came over to offer their condolences and express their admiration for the deceased.

'We don't know what we will do without him,' Mr Dalton told her. 'So I cannot begin to imagine how it must be for you.'

'I have my husband,' Eugenie said, with a warmth that had not been in evidence privately. 'And so shall you, for he is taking over the practice.'

There was an awkward pause in response to this, precisely as Raven had feared.

'And is everything here to your satisfaction?' Mrs Dalton asked, bidding to move the conversation on. 'If there is anything our staff can do . . .'

'Your staff have been most accommodating,' Eugenie replied. 'It is a comfort to be here. My father always loved this place.'

'As have we,' Mr Dalton replied.

'Have?' Eugenie asked.

Mr Dalton gave her an uncomfortable smile, as though apologising for his own happiness in the light of her pain. 'We are planning to undertake a grand tour. I did so in my youth, and when we met, I promised Winnie that one day we would reprise it together. I made that promise forty years ago, and I am finally ready to keep it. The hotel will soon be sold.'

'Oh,' said Eugenie. 'Who will be buying it?'

'There are a number of bids, but nothing has been concluded.'

'A number of bids, yes,' said Mrs Dalton. 'Some higher than others.' There was an archness to her tone, evidently alluding to some private dispute. She leaned closer to Eugenie and gave her shoulder a squeeze. 'If your husband is stubborn now, do not delude yourself that time will alter him,' she said. 'Men do not change.'

Mrs Dalton gave Raven a smile intended to convey that the remark was largely in jest, but regardless, it was not a welcome sentiment.

The Daltons moved on, their withdrawal unfortunately revealing the sight of William Sanderson across the room, helping himself to whisky. Raven had spied him at Greyfriars and been relieved that Eugenie had apparently not, but there was no missing him now.

'What is that man doing here?' she asked. 'He should be thrown out.'

'I will deal with him,' Raven told her, keeping his voice low and thereby encouraging her to do the same.

Raven crossed the room, catching Sanderson's eye and gesturing him towards a quiet spot by the wall where they might speak privately.

'What are you doing here?' Raven asked.

'I am paying my respects to the late Dr Todd.'

Raven glanced at the drink in his hand. 'You are taking money out of my pocket is what you're doing. And you paid him no respect when you wrote that rubbish in your newspaper. My wife would like me to throw you out of here, but I better appreciate that such a conspicuous action might only serve your interests.'

'I did not print anything untrue. People *are* curious. I merely report what I see and hear. Speaking of which, I saw you talking to Reginald Dalton just now. Has he sold up yet, or is he still holding out, hoping someone will bid more than Cunningham?'

Raven stiffened, as he did any time he heard that surname. It had once been his own, but he had shed both it and his given name following his father's death. 'Thomas Cunningham' had made himself anew, taking his mother's maiden name and the middle name she had given him. He was always wary that anyone should connect him to the late Andrew Cunningham, particularly a prying soul such as Sanderson, but fortunately today his prying appeared to be focused elsewhere.

Raven was about to recount Mrs Dalton's remarks regarding her husband's stubbornness when he stopped himself. 'You know, just once I'd like to have a conversation with you where I don't walk away feeling like you've been rifling through my pockets,' he said.

'Every conversation is a transaction, Dr Raven. Don't pretend you have not on occasion come away the richer for the deal.'

'And yet I still felt dirty afterwards.'

'Where there's muck, there's brass.'

'I see you are editor of a new publication. Did you find yourself another master to serve as his attack dog?'

Sanderson had once been editor of the *Courant*, where he helped prosecute the interests of its proprietor, Sir Ainsley Douglas. The latter's death had led to Sanderson having to plough new furrows.

'I founded the *Capital* myself,' he said. 'That way I can report the truth without fear or favour. But it is an expensive business. If I am to stay afloat, I need to build a readership. To do that, I need to offer stories my competitors don't have.'

'I would sympathise, for I am trying to build something myself. But in the absence of a scandal, it appears you have made a story of mere speculation, heedless of the hurt it would cause.'

'Sometimes you must shake the tree and see what falls from the branches. Come on, Dr Raven. You knew the man. You're telling me Todd decided the dead of night was the ideal time to take in the view?'

'I only know the facts, and they do not support your insinuation.'

Sanderson's smirk told Raven he knew he was lying. He began to worry what else the man knew.

'An inquisitive man such as yourself must suspect there's more to the picture than meets the eye,' Sanderson said. He glanced down at the glass in his hand. 'There are rumours Todd was in financial difficulty. Is that why you're worried about the drinks bill?'

Raven leaned in closer, taking the man's arm and squeezing it just enough to hurt.

'Mind you do not shake the anvil tree, Mr Sanderson.'

SIXTEEN

arah climbed a narrow staircase taking her above a timber merchant's off St Mary's Wynd, near to the Cowgate. It had looked a thoroughly unpromising premises from the outside, and yet the meeting room within still managed to disappoint. It was small and low-ceilinged, with benches to seat a hundred at most. Only a quarter of these were occupied, mainly by women, a mix of middle and working classes by the look of their attire. Sarah was therefore heartened by the sight of several young men at the back, standing apart from the main body of the gathering, as though unsure they belonged. She wondered at their interest and what it suggested about public feeling towards this matter. Some of them gripped bottles in their hands. Perhaps they were early for whatever the room would be used to host next.

She wondered still more at her own interest, though. Was it a way of feeling useful, evidence of her lack of progress in the hunt for the elusive Annabel Banks? Or was it merely somewhere else to be on the day of Dr Todd's funeral, Raven having intimated that Eugenie would not welcome her attendance?

On a small raised dais, a well-scrubbed group of individuals sat on wooden chairs, talking amongst themselves. In contrast to the make-up of the rest of the room, only one was a woman, dressed in black, stiff of posture and serious of expression.

This was presumably Dorothy Butler, founder member of the recently established Edinburgh Society for the Suppression of Vice. Alongside her was a rather dapper gentleman with enough of a facial resemblance as to suggest he must be her younger brother. He carried himself with a certain confidence, and Sarah glanced again at the young men present, considering whether he was perhaps a charismatic figure who had been able to rally them to his cause.

Sarah took a seat and pondered her own willingness to get involved. She had only met Annabel once, for a few hours one afternoon, and yet she felt a compulsion to assist. It was the echo of her own past that was driving her, she knew: the fate that might have been her own had she been less fortunate in her destination. What form that assistance might take remained obscured, but what harm could it do to ask a few questions? And with a bit of luck the girl would turn up, unscathed, offering a banal explanation for her lack of contact with her mother.

The dapper gentleman reached into his jacket pocket, checked his watch and then, after conferring with the others on-stage, stood, cleared his throat loudly and asked for quiet. The hubbub of muted conversation died down.

He introduced himself as Nathaniel Butler. He seemed polished, self-possessed, confident in addressing a crowd. Sarah wondered if he was a member of the clergy, though his well-cut suit suggested otherwise. Even so, Sarah was expecting a prayer to be said. At these meetings the Almighty was frequently invoked to intercede in favour of whatever righteous crusade they had embarked upon. But Mr Butler merely thanked the audience for their attendance and applauded their willingness to discuss an age-old problem: the moral evil that was prostitution.

Sarah was soon reflecting that a prayer might have made for a better start. At the mere mention of the word prostitution, the young men at the back of the room began to barrack, whistle and stamp their feet. The question of their interest was rapidly answered: their purpose was simply to disrupt the meeting.

Mr Butler made repeated calls for calm and for the resumption of gentlemanly behaviour but to no avail. If anything, things deteriorated, with the young men making suggestions as to where the various committee members might go to avail themselves of what the local prostitutes had to offer, of which they seemed to have an extensive knowledge. Their profanity was profuse and esoteric, several terms being used that Sarah was unfamiliar with. She would have to ask Raven when she saw him next. It might cheer him up to thus enlighten her.

With no prospect of order being restored, the audience began to drift away; a trickle at first, but soon most of the rag-taggle congregation was heading for the door. The jeers of the disruptors were ringing in their ears as they left, quite possibly discouraging them from ever returning if this was what they risked exposing themselves to.

Those on the platform also got to their feet, looking more resigned than outraged, suggesting that this was not an unusual experience for them. Dorothy and Nathaniel gathered some books and papers together as their colleagues departed, also subject to catcalls as they left, though the enthusiasm diminished in proportion to the size of the target group. Nonetheless, the young men remained. Sarah watched as one of them approached Nathaniel, a fellow with curly brown locks beneath his stove-pipe hat.

'Here,' he hailed aggressively, 'who are you to tell us what we can and can't do? What we can and can't avail ourselves of should a lassie be offering?'

Nathaniel did not respond. Stove-pipe looked like he'd had a few drinks and seemed unlikely to be open to Socratic discourse.

'Maybe you'd like to show me what happens if I defy you, eh?' Stove-pipe added, his tone becoming more aggressive. 'Because if you're laying down the law, you need to be able to back it up.'

Nathaniel looked afraid but was trying to remain dignified in the face of his own fear. Sarah suspected he was not used to defending himself in a pugilistic manner, and utterly certain Stove-pipe had detected as much. His friends were amused by

Nathaniel's discomfort, smirking and guffawing as though the threat of a fight was only half-serious, although everyone in the room knew how quickly it could become real.

Dorothy led her brother away towards the stairs, his cheeks flushed with the humiliation of one who knew he could not face up to his would-be opponent. But why should he have to? Sarah could not abide violence being meted out, but an unworthy part of her wished to see the change in this drunk lout if he found himself facing Raven. She was sure his friends would also be rapidly dissuaded in the sight of that.

Sarah made her exit too, suddenly conscious that she was the last attendee. One of Stove-pipe's friends handed him a bottle and he took a triumphant swig at having emptied the room, several of the group looking her up and down as she hurried past. She could hear them break into a bawdy song as she descended the stairs.

Dorothy and Nathaniel were standing on St Mary's Wynd, both looking shaken. Dorothy's expression became apologetic as she noticed Sarah emerge from the building.

'Forgive me. I thought it prudent to get my brother out and I hadn't noticed there was someone still present,' she said.

'You did the right thing,' Sarah assured her. 'But why didn't one of your group send for the police?'

'The police are generally unsympathetic to our cause,' Dorothy replied. 'In fact, I wouldn't be surprised if some of them *were* police.'

'No,' said Nathaniel. 'I'm fairly sure they were medical students.'

'Also unsympathetic to your cause?'

'It would certainly appear so. You would think medical men might show greater concern and decorum.'

Sarah could have made a great many replies to this statement, but just then the individuals in question came spilling out of the building. A couple of them were laughing, but others had a look of hungry malice, fuelled further by drink. One of those was Stove-pipe, who was clearly not satisfied with merely driving them off. Henry had once talked of Raven's 'appetite for mayhem'. Was this what it had looked like? She could not picture Raven picking fights with frightened, weaker men. Indeed, as Henry had complained, 'Raven only picked a fight when the odds were against him. I was never sure whether he factored me into his calculations, but I found out the hard way how dangerous it was to be the one standing at his side.'

'We need to get away from here,' Sarah said. Her preference would have been to go north up the hill towards the High Street, but that would take them straight towards the gang. Instead she led them around the corner onto the Cowgate at as brisk a pace as she dared, aware that breaking into a run might be the thing that precipitated something worse.

'I don't really know the Old Town so well these days,' Nathaniel confessed anxiously. 'I've been living in London for some time.'

Sarah would wager he hadn't known the Old Town terribly well before moving away either. She hazarded a glance back. The gang was still following.

'What is their issue with this?' she asked.

Dorothy tutted. 'Someone might have put them up to it. Or if their protest was of their own volition, it might be that they object being lectured to, especially by a woman. The abuse is always greater when I elect to speak.'

Sarah nodded. That seemed about right.

Somewhere behind her she heard a bottle smash. It felt like a resolute act, a worrying moment of decision.

Sarah looked back in time to see a coach and four cross the Cowgate at the foot of High School Wynd, temporarily obscuring them from their pursuers.

'This way,' she said, hurrying into the dank and narrow vennel that was Dickson's Close.

'Are you sure about this?' Nathanel asked, following her into the gloom.

'Quiet,' she urged, shepherding them into a doorway out of sight. Sarah normally avoided such alleyways specifically because of the ne'er-do-wells she might run into, but reasoned that these particular ne'er-do-wells would not expect her to seek refuge in such a place.

Sure enough, as she peeked from the doorway she saw them barrel past the mouth of the close and continue along the Cowgate.

She did not wait for them to find out their mistake. Venturing further along Dickson's Close was a far from inviting prospect, but it would take them away from the Cowgate, and Sarah knew a place they might find sanctuary at the top of it.

Ten minutes later they were comfortably ensconced in a temperance tea-room on the High Street. Sarah felt certain that Stove-pipe and his crew would be unlikely to follow them into such an establishment, though truth be told she could have used a strong drink at that point.

Over the course of two pots of tea and several fruit scones, Sarah was given details about the Butlers and the aims of their committee. Both had been born and raised in Edinburgh, although Nathaniel had some years ago moved to London to pursue a career in the law. He had recently returned to see to their late father's affairs. Dorothy seemed keen to highlight her brother's many attributes, which Sarah took to mean that Nathaniel was unmarried.

Sarah had been worried that the pair of them might be self-righteous, religiously motivated and insensitive to the realities of life on the streets (moral crusaders often were), but they seemed warm, compassionate and knowledgeable, taking the refreshing approach of not blaming the prostitutes themselves for their miserable lot. Dororthy, it seemed, was well acquainted with the inmates of the Magdalene Asylum. She made frequent visits to the fallen women housed there, talking with them, knitting with them, praying with them, convinced that they could be re-educated and returned to respectable society. She had even had a few live with her for a time as they made the transition back to normal life.

'Unfortunately, not everyone shares Dorothy's enlightened views,' Nathaniel added. He had said little during the course of the conversation, allowing his sister to take the lead.

'Some condemn the women as irrevocably soiled, incapable of living a moral life,' Dorothy explained. 'And some are merely protecting their own business interests. Vice is a trade, after all, and a profitable one at that. Hence someone is likely paying those students to make a nuisance of themselves.'

'I worry how far certain of them might go to protect their interests,' added Nathaniel. 'Though I was the target today, it is Dorothy's safety I particularly worry about. Men really don't like being told what to do by a woman.'

'It's becoming increasingly difficult to find places where we can meet,' Dorothy told Sarah. 'We hired a room in Leith recently, but when we arrived for the meeting the place had been so liberally dosed in cayenne pepper it was difficult to breathe.'

'More imaginative than shouting abuse from the back of the room,' Sarah suggested.

Dorothy smiled. 'Perhaps, but just as effective in disrupting the whole thing.'

'You shouldn't make light of it,' Nathaniel warned. 'You cannot deny that there has been a palpable increase in hostility, and who knows where it might lead.'

He turned to Sarah and addressed his next remark to her.

'I have had to delay my return to London because of it.'

Dorothy scoffed, apparently sceptical of this. A look was traded between the two, but nothing more was said. An awkward silence started to grow, and Sarah felt compelled to intervene.

'I think I know someone who might be able to help.'

'Well, any assistance you could give would be most welcome,' Dorothy said. 'We must forge alliances where we can.'

Sarah wondered whether they would be so keen to forge an alliance with the man she had in mind were they made aware of his unexpurgated history.

'We are already grateful for your assistance today,' Nathaniel added.

'You are welcome,' Sarah said. 'But now I need something from you. Information, if you have it.'

Dorothy leaned forward in her chair. 'Of course.'

Sarah took a breath. 'It's my niece, Annabel. A girl of fifteen. She came to the city a month ago to take up a situation. It appears she never presented herself, and her mother has not heard from her.'

She looked for the same blithe dismissiveness she had seen in McLevy's face, hoping for reassurance that things weren't as bleak as they appeared, but Dorothy's expression was anything but reassuring.

'Her mother is worried,' Sarah added.

'She's right to be,' Dorothy replied.

SEVENTEEN

aven watched Sanderson wander off to rifle someone else's pockets, and turned to look for Eugenie. She was not where he had left her, and his heart surged as he scoured the room in case the occasion had proven too much for her and she had left. He felt an unexpected sense of loneliness and yearning: a need for solidarity, a need for companionship, and a need to know that Eugenie was all right.

His eyes found her. She was with her friend Agnes, who had made the effort to attend despite a recent bout of ill-health. They had withdrawn to a table where they could enjoy a seat together, and where Eugenie might be left alone from receiving condolences.

Raven felt a sense of relief that he need not be worried for his wife, though the other yearnings remained. He was there to support Eugenie, but he realised there was a part of him that needed support too. More than that, he needed it from someone specific, and that someone was not his wife.

He wondered where Sarah was right then. Perhaps looking after the Simpson children so that Jessie could attend. Raven could see Mrs Simpson and the professor deep in conversation with a white-haired gentleman he thought to be a judge at the High Court.

Raven decided he badly needed a drink, especially as he was paying for them all. He was about to signal to one of the staff when he saw Simpson's brother, Sandy, making his way purposefully towards him accompanied by an older woman dressed in the black of first mourning. Raven did not recognise her, but knew her not to be Sandy's wife.

'Dr Raven,' Sandy said, addressing him with unaccustomed formality, 'allow me to introduce Mrs Gertrude Leitch. She and her late husband were both patients of Dr Todd.'

Late husband, Raven thought. This could be none other than Barrington Leitch's widow.

'I wish to convey my deepest sympathies to you and to dear Eugenie,' Mrs Leitch said.

'That is very kind. Let me take you to her.'

'Not at all. I can see she is with a friend, and having been through it recently I know only too well how exhausting this must be. But I wished to pay my respects. Dr Todd was always courteous and obliging. He has been in my prayers. All of you have been in my prayers.'

Raven sometimes wondered at his status in the eyes of Todd's wealthiest and most prominent patients. Was he regarded as a disappointment, given the husband they perhaps expected such a man's only daughter to have found? He felt the contrast to how he had been regarded when introduced as Dr Simpson's assistant.

'Thank you, Mrs Leitch, and please may I express both of our condolences at the loss of your husband. I am told Dr Todd was deeply upset at the news.'

Mrs Leitch gave him a fleetingly odd look: not exactly surprise at what he had said, but certainly a moment's confusion. Perhaps he had overstated it, and she, like Eugenie, knew that Todd and her husband did not have the closest acquaintance.

'Yes, it was so terribly sudden,' she said, straightening herself as though drawing upon reserves of stoic fortitude. 'He was fifty-nine, but strong as an ox. His heart, I am told. But I will endeavour to ensure that his work – that his passions – survive.'

'His investment projects?' Raven enquired, trying to sound encouraging and not too inquisitive.

'Charity and the Lord's work. Spreading the Good News among those who most need to hear it, but practical assistance too, for each is diminished without the other.'

'Mr and Mrs Leitch supported missionary work among the poorer souls of the city,' Sandy said. 'He was a subscriber to the Lock Hospital,' he added with a knowing look to Raven.

Mrs Leitch caught it, tutting. 'You need not be so delicate on my account, Mr Simpson. We are cowardly when we shy away from the truth of these matters. Indeed, our reluctance to confront sin when it is in our midst is what allows it to fester. The tide is turning though, mark my words. There are campaigns afoot up and down the country. And the anger of our enemies is merely the sign that we are winning.'

Raven presented a sincere expression, as was his typical response when confronted by someone so effusive in their convictions, all the while hoping they would find someone else to talk to. On this occasion he was blessed by good fortune, in that Dr Hedley Stokes happened into view nearby. Also being on the board of the Lock Hospital, Stokes was no doubt as acquainted with Mrs Leitch's late husband as he was with her evangelical zeal, and the match happily spared two other people their tedious company.

This left Raven with Sandy, whom he had expected would depart having discharged his polite duty. Rather, it became clear that the man had an agenda. He looked agitated, gripping a glass of whisky in both hands as though unsure whether now was a good time to drink from it.

'Have you spoken to my brother of late? He seems unduly troubled.'

'He does?' Raven replied neutrally.

'You have not noticed it?'

'I am no longer at Queen Street, so I am less party to his thoughts than before.'

Sandy glanced inconspicuously towards the professor and his wife.

'I appreciate he seems fine today, but today of all days you must know how one can disguise these things in the service of decorum. I am concerned James might be on the verge of one of his episodes.'

Raven knew what was being referred to, having witnessed several of these episodes himself. The professor could occasionally descend into a state of depression that might last for days, withdrawing from all contact.

'Would you have any notion what might be troubling him?' Sandy asked.

'Who knows what goes on inside that great head of his,' Raven replied with a smile, but the words sounded both insincere and unconvincing in his mouth. Sandy's love for his brother deserved better. He looked Sandy in the eye and dropped his voice. 'He came to me with a concern but, were I to tell you the nature of it, I would be betraying his confidence. However, you can be sure I am assisting him in this matter.'

Sandy nodded, grateful if not entirely reassured. 'And how are you and Eugenie dealing with everything?' he asked. There was a gravity in his tone that sounded deeper than the standard platitudes. 'Frederick Golspie has been in touch concerning certain matters,' he added. 'Working at the bank, I am aware that a substantial loan was recently secured against Dr Todd's house.'

'We have some difficult decisions ahead of us,' Raven said. 'Todd and I were not close, but I am confounded by how little it seems I knew the man.'

Sandy took a sip of his whisky, nodding his understanding as he swallowed.

'Your father-in-law was a successful man, but if comparison can be a route to unhappiness, then constant exposure to the truly, vastly wealthy can poison a man's mind. One sees it enough in the world of banking to recognise it elsewhere: men who have plenty but believe that the right investments would allow them to have considerably more.'

'Surely he would not be taken for a fool, though.'

'Not a fool, but . . . such men can become credulous of advice from those far richer than themselves.'

'I had wondered whether Dr Todd might have speculated on the advice of Barrington Leitch. Eugenie said her father was upset by his death, and yet the men were not close. What do you know about him?'

Sandy glanced towards Leitch's widow, as though making sure she was not in earshot.

'I must be delicate. Barrington Leitch was a divisive individual, never shy of a fight. I recall him saying a man should be judged by the anger of his enemies.'

'Yes. His wife echoed that sentiment. But what of his business? Was he honourable? Might he have guided Dr Todd towards investing in something unsavoury that would give him reason to keep it secret?'

Sandy frowned, as though weighing a complex verdict. 'Leitch's father supported Dundas in his attempts to delay the Abolition Act. The family still has substantial holdings in American enterprises. Cotton, sugar.'

'You mean slavery. So his piety was a facade? Or a vanity?'

Sandy gave Raven a curious look, as though he was being naive.

'You will find few more devout believers than the extremely wealthy, Dr Raven. It is easier to have faith in the divine plan when that plan has such a privileged role in it for yourself, and if you believe your success to be divinely ordained, then all of your actions must therefore be divinely sanctioned. Thus displays of piety are not merely for show. Every donation made to a noble cause is not to salve a conscience; rather it justifies the action that generated the money and thus facilitated this beneficent contribution.'

'I see,' Raven said, though he was not sure he did, beyond that the rules of morality were particularly twisted in the world of finance. 'Sandy, Cameron Todd borrowed two thousand pounds, ostensibly for investments, and we have no record of where it went. So the fidelity of his beliefs notwithstanding, what I am asking is, was Leitch a rogue?'

Again the frown, an equivocating expression. 'He was a shrewd investor most of the time, and particularly shrewd about protecting himself. He made many people a great deal of money. He lost some people a great deal of money too, though he remained rich because he knew that the golden rule of speculation is to never risk your *own* money. But I never heard of him defrauding anyone.'

Sandy finished his drink, wincing at the burn of it as it went down. 'My brother is hopeless with money, and I'd wager you're not particularly familiar with the complexities of financial matters yourself, are you?'

'No,' Raven admitted.

'Nor is Mr Golspie as sharp of mind as he once was.'

'What is your point?'

'Just because you cannot find a record does not mean none exists, especially when you don't know what you're looking for.'

EIGHTEEN

arah left the tea-room feeling shaken and grubby after all she had heard. The Butlers confirmed what Madame Bouvier had suggested: that a trade in young girls was taking place in the city. It was well known in certain circles and the police were utterly indifferent, largely because the girls were over twelve and therefore 'responsible for themselves'.

Fresh girls were lured into the trade under false pretences, entrapped and enslaved. If this had been Annabel's fate, she could be in any number of establishments: there were dozens of them, and they didn't advertise in the Post Office Directory or the newspaper. Sarah needed to narrow her search, though she had no notion how. But as she approached her destination on George Square, she realised that in agreeing to help the Butlers find a safe venue, she had come to the right place to enquire about Annabel too.

Sarah pulled the bell and waited. As she did so she looked out across the private gardens at the centre of the square. The fact that Callum Somerville, or Callum Flint as he was previously known, now lived here should have been an inspiration to those born into poor circumstances, but in truth he was the exception to the rule. To Sarah's mind, individual successes should not be held out as a stick to beat others. They usually relied on a combination of inherent skills, the wit to use them, and a degree of luck, which could not be replicated by everyone. And in Somerville's case, success had also involved ruthlessness and criminality, the true extent of which she wasn't sure she wished to know.

The door was answered by a woman wearing a stained apron and a sour expression.

'I'm sorry, Margaret,' Sarah said. 'Have I interrupted something?'

'Just cooking the master's dinner. Is he expecting you?'

Sarah shook her head. 'I was just passing. Is he in?'

'He's in his study. Go on through.'

The housekeeper stood aside to let Sarah pass and she headed towards the study at the back of the house. She knocked gently on the door and entered.

Somerville was seated behind his desk writing in a ledger, and looked up.

'I apologise for the intrusion, Mr Somerville,' Sarah said.

Somerville was surprised but clearly delighted to see her. 'Sarah,' he said, getting to his feet. 'It's been too long.' He made his way towards her, leaning heavily on a walking stick. 'I'm so glad you're here.'

'Are you well?' she asked.

'As well as can be expected. Thanks to you.'

'Thanks to Will Raven.'

Somerville nodded an acknowledgement that was just the right side of grudging. 'But where would I be if you hadn't nursed me back to health?'

It was true that Sarah had helped to look after him for several weeks after his accident as there was no one but his housekeeper to do so. Somerville had no family, or so he said. In Raven's opinion, it was simply that Somerville did not trust anyone else enough to do the job properly.

Once he had recovered his strength, Somerville had made his intentions and his affections towards Sarah quite clear. Although he had not been born a gentleman, he was making every effort to live like one, and his multiple business interests and a large income meant he could offer Sarah the life of a lady, wanting for nothing. But Sarah was not interested in becoming a mere appendage to a man, ensnared by the vicissitudes of domestic life. Somerville had been adamant that he would never stand in the way of her ambitions, but she sensed he had no real concept of where her ambitions might lead, or what their pursuit would require. Whatever else he saw in her, she suspected he principally wanted a wife and a stepmother for his young daughter, not a woman with plans for an unconventional life and career. She did not wish to be distracted from her main aim, which was to educate herself about the theories and practice of medicine. The theories she could read about in books, but the practical application of such knowledge required access to patients, which was what her arrangement with Raven was giving her. When the rules about women practising medicine changed, which Sarah was increasingly convinced must be soon, she wanted to be ready: not starting from the beginning, but already there, the process of obtaining a qualification merely a formality.

But more than all of that, she knew that she did not love Callum Somerville. She was not so steeped in romantic notions as to believe that was always a prerequisite, and there was much to commend the idea of a companionate marriage to a man who undoubtedly respected and even admired her. But if she was being honest with herself, she wasn't convinced that she would ever be able to entirely trust him. When they first met, he had been evasive about his past and had still not revealed that much about it. If she was going to spend her life with someone, she needed to know everything about him. Honesty was important. Secrets were potentially disastrous.

Sarah had declined his offer of marriage as gently as she could, insisting that they should remain friends, and that had been her intention. However, she had allowed herself to drift away, busy with other things, and Raven's continuing hostility towards the man hadn't helped.

'How is life at Queen Street?' Somerville asked now.

'Busy. Crowded. I'm still in Will Raven's old room.'

Somerville flashed her a look, as though there was some significance to Sarah sleeping in a bed that Will Raven had once been in.

'The Simpsons have been so kind to me,' she continued. 'Letting me stay with them after my husband died. Making me feel like part of the family. But I think it may be time to move on.'

Sarah had been thinking about this for a while, but now her funds were limited, as was her time. Ideally, she would have moved in with Raven and his family, given that to all intents and purposes it was her money that allowed them to live where they did, but this had never been suggested. Eugenie would not have allowed it, and even had the thought been entertained, Sarah knew she would have been treated like a housemaid, housekeeper and nursery-maid all rolled into one. Eugenie was a remarkable woman in many ways, but she did not seem cut out to be a wife and mother, at least not without the help of a large domestic staff.

'If you're looking for a place to live, I could help you with that.'

For an uncomfortable moment Sarah thought he was about to suggest again that she marry him and move in here.

'I've just bought a nice little property near Dean Village,' he clarified, 'a cottage with a view of the river.'

'That's kind of you but that's not why I'm here.'

He indicated a chair. Sarah sat down and adjusted her skirts, watching with a surge of sympathy as Somerville gingerly lowered himself onto the chair opposite, grimacing as he did so.

'It still gives you pain? Your leg?'

'More stiffness than anything else,' he said, though the perspiration on his forehead suggested otherwise. 'Now, as this is evidently not a social call, what can I do for you?' The disappointment on his face was obvious and Sarah felt guilty for not calling on him before this, only turning up when she needed something.

'I have friends . . . well, acquaintances really, who are in need of somewhere to hold meetings.'

'What kind of meetings?'

Sarah realised that this might be more awkward than she had first thought.

'The Edinburgh Society for the Suppression of Vice.'

Somerville snorted. 'The suppression of vice? Well, good luck to them if they think their meetings will have any effect on that.' He seemed to find the idea highly amusing.

'And there's something else,' Sarah said. This was going to be a difficult conversation, she realised, because merely by asking she was going to acknowledge some of the less savoury aspects of Somerville's previous life. 'It's my niece. She's missing somewhere in Edinburgh, and I'm worried what might have happened to her. I think she might be . . .' She paused, trying to think how best to put it. 'I think she might have fallen in with the wrong people.'

'The wrong people?'

'I think that she might be in a house of ill-repute.'

Somerville sighed. If he had looked disappointed before, that was as nothing to the look of regret that haunted his features now. 'If we are going to talk about this, Sarah, let's not use coy terms. What makes you think your niece is in a brothel?'

Sarah told him what she knew and what the Butlers had said to her. Somerville listened attentively, sighed deeply, then spoke.

'There are many reasons why a young girl might go missing, but I won't lie to you. It's entirely possible that's where she is. Probable, even.'

'How do I find her?'

Somerville rubbed his face, got to his feet and hobbled back towards his desk. He scribbled something down on a piece of paper and handed it to her. A name and address in the Old Town. 'She might be able to help you,' he said. 'She's a reformed character now, but she was in the business once.'

'Will she speak to me?' Sarah asked.

'She will if I tell her to.'

NINETEEN

arah entered the consulting room at Great Stuart Street to find Raven at his desk, head in his hands, surrounded by paperwork. He looked like he had been there for some time. The fire had not been lit and the room was cold. It was the day after Dr Todd's funeral, and though the calendar indicated that it was early May, in Edinburgh winter was often reluctant to relinquish its grip and give way to spring.

Sarah approached and laid a hand gently on his shoulder.

Raven started and looked around. He seemed relieved to see her. 'Sarah. I didn't hear you come in.'

Sarah noticed that his eyes were bloodshot. He looked like he hadn't slept.

'Were you called out in the night?' she asked hopefully, giving his shoulder a squeeze. She was surprised by how natural this felt, to be this close to him. She was aware how informal they were with each other when alone, something that would be frowned upon if witnessed by anyone else.

'No,' Raven said. 'I've been trying to make sense of all of this.' He indicated the mess on his desk.

Sarah noticed that in amongst the letters and invoices was an old copy of the *Lancet*. The journal was open at an article, Raven's scrawl of notes running along the side of it. She felt a sudden panic as she read the title.

'"The Treatment of Cholera by Saline and Aqueous Injections" – you've not seen a case, have you?'

Raven shook his head. 'No. Just been thinking about it after the Med-Chir meeting the other night. I didn't have any success with it in treating cholera, but I wondered if it might be useful in haemorrhage.' He leaned back in his chair and sighed. 'I don't really have time to look into it at the moment. Too many other things to deal with.'

Sarah picked up one of the invoices. Spence and Son, Undertaker. The expenses incurred by Cameron Todd's funeral were itemised in cold, dispassionate detail: A hearse with four horses, two mourning coaches, an oak coffin with brass fittings, an embroidered cambric shroud, black velvet pall. The list went on and on.

Sarah put the invoice down and went to light the fire. She got down on her knees and started to add some coal to the small amount of kindling already in the hearth.

'Leave it,' Raven said. 'It's not cold enough for a fire. And anyway, we need to make economies where we can.'

Sarah leaned back on her heels and looked at him. 'I don't mean to be indelicate, but won't you and Eugenie be coming into money soon?'

'Not as much as we were anticipating.' Raven sighed again and rubbed his face. 'In fact, there might not be much at all. Todd was in debt, borrowed against the house.'

'Does Eugenie know?'

'Yes. But she seems to think all will be well, I think because she has never known otherwise. Financially, at least.'

'How bad is it?'

'Bad.'

Sarah got to her feet. 'What about all this?' she asked, indicating the consulting room. 'Are *we* in trouble?'

He looked at her and bit his lip. 'I think that we might be.'

Sarah walked over, pulled up a chair and sat down beside him. 'We always knew it would take time,' she said gently. 'And there were more patients yesterday than the day before.'

Raven looked at her, desperation in his face. 'Unless things change, and soon, I don't know if we'll be able to continue.'

Sarah paused for a moment. Raven seemed utterly convinced about the parlous state of their finances. She felt a sudden surge of annoyance that Eugenie's spendthrift ways had brought them so precipitously to the edge of disaster. But then she remembered herself. Eugenie had just lost her father. It was wrong to blame her for their present predicament.

'There are people who would help us,' Sarah said. 'People who would not wish to see you fail.'

Raven looked at her as though this was news to him. 'Who did you have in mind?'

'Dr Simpson. He would lend you money.'

Raven shook his head. 'Dr Simpson has enough on his plate at the moment.'

Sarah wondered what he meant. She knew that the professor had many investments, not all of them sure to succeed. Perhaps he had suffered a loss too. She thought for a moment, weighing whether she should risk mentioning the other person who leapt to mind.

'There is someone else who has offered to help, should you ever be in need,' she said, her tone cautious.

Raven made no attempt to disguise his annoyance. 'I hope you're not suggesting who I think you are.'

'You saved his life.'

'And I made it quite clear that I do not expect anything in return. I imagine, given the nature of the man, he's forgotten all about it anyway.'

'I don't think that he has.'

'You've seen him?'

Sarah nodded.

'When?'

'Today.'

Raven snorted. 'And did he propose again?'

'That is really none of your business.'

Raven looked entirely unchastised. 'I don't like you seeing him.'

'Why?'

'I don't trust him, that's why. I'm not convinced that he is the reformed character he pretends to be.' He looked more intently at her, his face serious. 'He's dangerous, Sarah.'

Sarah scoffed. 'Dangerous? You think I am in danger when I'm with him?'

'I don't like to think about you with him at all.'

'Are you jealous, Will Raven?'

Raven looked away.

'I'm a married man, Sarah,' he said. 'It's not my place to be jealous.'

TWENTY

Raven had left Sarah back at the house on Great Stuart Street, but she was with him every step of the way as he set off for St Andrew Square later that morning. She was in his head, taking up space where his wife should be. How could she make everything seem simpler and everything more complicated all at the same time? Simpler in that his path always looked clear when she was close. More complicated in that the path was always leading into a place that was forbidden.

His desire for her company was constant, even when she was exasperating him. But there were other desires, more dangerous ones. Desires for something that right now would be the worst kind of betrayal. Even entertaining these thoughts was a betrayal in itself.

He knew he should be thinking solely about his wife, but he simply could not, and it was pulling him apart.

Perhaps he would not be prey to these feelings were it not for the difficulties he and Eugenie were going through. They were spending too much time apart. He wanted to be close to her, to hear her voice, to smell the scent of her hair and feel something other than worry. He missed who they used to be together.

Eugenie had seemed adrift from him for the past year; in fact she had seemed adrift from everybody since the traumatic night of their daughter's birth. He sometimes worried that she blamed

Clara for how close she had been brought to death. But her manner towards Jamie had altered too. Sometimes he worried that it was because she saw too much of Raven in him, and not enough of herself, or her father. That when she looked at the boy, she saw all that dissatisfied her about her husband.

But these were temporary things that could surely be overcome. That was what marriage was. Beyond the early bloom of excitement there would be trials, and true closeness was forged in sharing the hard times, not the easy ones. But progress could only come through being together.

As he walked past 52 Queen Street, he saw a patient at the door being politely turned away by Jarvis. Given the hour, that meant the waiting room must already be full. 'But it's desperately urgent,' he heard the patient say.

The man noticed Raven and recognised him. Raven knew him too: a Mr Muir, whom he had treated on several occasions. The man hurried to intercept him. 'Look, it's Dr Raven,' Muir said, mostly addressing Jarvis. 'Another doctor means more of us can be seen, surely.'

'Alas, I no longer work for Dr Simpson,' Raven told him. 'But I can see you at my practice at Great Stuart Street tomorrow morning.'

Mr Muir tutted, shaking his head. 'I'll be better by tomorrow morning,' he said, walking away.

Jarvis sent Raven a wry smile of acknowledgement, closing the door as Raven strode on past.

Raven thought of the noisy chaos doubtless unfolding within, then thought of the professor and his troubles. He had promised Dr Simpson and indeed his brother that he would assist, and felt a degree of guilt and shame that thus far he had not, having been too occupied by other concerns. In truth he did not know where to begin, for the blackmail letter had come through the door in the night. There was no messenger boy to be questioned about the sender.

Simpson had been told there would be a further note concerning the arrangement of payment. To Raven's knowledge that had not arrived, so he told himself it was not yet truly urgent. It might even prove an empty threat, someone merely leaning upon rumour and hearsay to torment the professor. But Raven knew that if Todd had indeed been blackmailed, then the threat had proven real enough for him to take the worst of actions.

That brought to mind the other, more optimistic possibility regarding the missing funds, that the documentation regarding Dr Todd's investment had simply not yet been discovered. Raven had already spent hours in Dr Todd's office and found almost nothing that was not of a medical nature. The man's record-keeping was fastidious, his discretion in correspondence scrupulous, none of it indicating an interest in anything illicit. Despite the importance of his search, Raven was not sure he could face another hour looking through leatherbound encyclopaedias and other scientific volumes in the hope of finding a share certificate pressed between the pages.

As he neared the end of George Street, he recalled the caution with which he used to approach St Andrew Square when he and Eugenie were trying to keep their courtship secret. He felt an echo of that thrill of anticipation, the soaring inside him in those last few moments before she would emerge from behind a tree or turn around to face him from a bench where they had agreed to meet. If he remembered how that once felt, then surely she could too. He had to be patient. It had been a difficult year, and that had been compounded by Eugenie's great loss, but perhaps in that loss there was an opportunity. Now that her father was no longer here, perhaps she would come to appreciate Raven's full worth to her.

He opened the front door to the unexpected sound of Clara crying out in something other than distress. This was followed by the hurried gallop of Jamie's feet on the tiles as he raced up the stairs from the kitchen. The boy always sounded like he ought to be twice the size given the noise he made. Raven crouched, thinking Jamie on his way to greet him, but he charged blithely past in pursuit of some phantom: an invisible foe or runaway horse. More and more Raven envied his son his retreats into realms of the imagination.

Maxwell appeared, also climbing the stairs from the kitchen, albeit far slower. He bade Raven good day with the weary expression of one trying to go about his business while at the same time charged with keeping a careful eye on an object never at rest.

Again Raven heard a squeal of delight coming from nearby, and hurried into the drawing room, hoping for the sight of Eugenie tickling their daughter, the balm his soul needed. He did not find it, however. Rather it was Louisa, the housemaid, who was bouncing Clara on her knee.

Maxwell followed him into the room. 'Mrs Raven is not at home, sir,' he offered apologetically.

'I know she is not at home for I have just come from there,' Raven replied, irritated but directing his frustration at the wrong target.

'Apologies. I mean she has gone out.'

'Did she say where?'

Maxwell glanced out of the window as though he might see her. 'She needed to take the air. She has done so often, of late. I think she needs respite from the children sometimes.'

And respite from me too, Raven thought. He recalled the incident with the bad oysters. Pictured her walking through the city alone. Dining alone. He felt a hollow sense of loneliness, as though experiencing the sum of these absences at once. He was hurt by the idea that she found consolation in being alone rather than with him.

'Of late?' Raven asked. 'Since Dr Todd died?'

Maxwell shifted uncomfortably. 'No. Since before. A few weeks now. We don't mind. We love the children.'

Just then Jamie charged past the door towards the stairs with a look of eager determination that was worrying enough to send Raven into the hall. It was only as the child reached the return landing that Raven could see he was carrying a wooden hammer, a meat tenderiser he had swiped from the kitchen.

'Jamie,' he called after him. 'Stop!'

The boy let out a giggle as he gave his father a thorough and considered ignoring. If the vignette upon the staircase had been an etching, the word 'Mischief' would have been written beneath as a title.

When Raven reached the top of the stairs, he could neither hear nor see his son, which was always a portent of trouble. Jamie was only ever quiet when he did not wish to attract attention, and the only time that he did not wish to attract attention was when he was doing something he shouldn't. Raven's mind filled with images of smashed ornaments as he hurried after him.

He opened the nearest door into what had been Eugenie's bedroom. Indeed, it frequently still was, for in truth she had never entirely moved out. There were still many of her clothes here, and since they married there had barely been a week when she had not spent at least one night in its bed.

He did not see Jamie but nor did he see any debris. He stepped back into the hall, listening out for the sounds of syncopation wrought upon something not built to withstand hammering. There was only silence. Raven realised the game had changed. With his father in pursuit, Jamie had probably forgotten whatever he intended to do with the hammer. It was now hide and seek.

He called out 'Jamie' again, in a singsong voice. Even as he did so, he realised that the name itself had become another rift between him and his wife. As the child had become more autonomous, a boy rather than a baby, Raven had started calling him Jamie. Eugenie pointedly had not. He tried to tell himself that in her eyes he would always be the same little James she had nursed, but in his more worried moments he detected a formality to it, as though she would not accept the boy he was becoming.

Why was everything an occasion of conflict?

Proceeding slowly along the hall, Raven saw that the door to Dr Todd's bedroom was ajar. He pushed it open with some trepidation, as though afraid the man was about to catch him intruding. It seemed absurd, yet something did feel inappropriate about entering his private quarters without his permission. He was reluctant to venture beyond the threshold, for even standing there, Raven could smell the man still: pomade and pipe tobacco. It was unnerving.

He looked around this grandest of bedrooms, full of the finest furniture and dominated by a great four-poster. Seeing the bed, Raven suddenly had a sense of the man's loss and loneliness. Todd had slept there alone since his wife died giving birth to Eugenie. It was easy to understand why he would have become so protective of his daughter, how she would have become the only person that mattered to him, and he to her. He thought also of Eugenie being raised without a mother. Raised at the hands of kindly women, for certain, but not the one who would have loved her most. He wondered if that was a factor in her conduct now. Did she not fully know what a child needed from their mother because she had never known it herself?

He was about to turn around when he heard a giggle from somewhere in the bedroom. He found himself smiling in response. Raven hoped there was no anguish in this world that could not be alleviated by that sound. If he could put it in a bottle, there would be no more need for laudanum.

'Where on earth is Jamie?' he asked aloud, striding into the room.

His first thought was the mahogany tallboy. Its doors were closed, however, and he could not envisage Jamie pulling them firmly shut behind him. Equally, though the child could easily fit inside one of the dresser drawers, he would not be able to close that either.

Raven then noticed a bulge in the curtains. He finally stepped into the room, striding briskly towards the windows. He whipped the heavy cloth aside but there was no one behind it. The bulge had been merely an illusion of how the material was gathered.

He heard the giggle again and now more clearly detected where it had come from. Jamie was hiding under the bed.

'He is not in this room, alas,' he announced. 'I must seek him elsewhere.'

Raven began walking away then doubled back and dropped to his knees. He heard more laughter but could not see the boy, only a low trunk beneath the bed. Jamie was hidden behind it.

He ran around the bed and dropped again, scrambling underneath. Jamie, smaller and nimbler in the narrow space, crawled swiftly to the other side of the trunk, keeping it between them. Raven laughed in his exasperation but then realised how to effect a victory. He slid the trunk aside, out from the foot of the bed. No sooner was the obstacle removed than Jamie scurried out from underneath. He climbed up onto the bed, where he began rolling around, still giggling.

Raven sat on the edge of the bed, also laughing. He realised suddenly that he could smell Eugenie's scent, stronger than he had smelled Todd's. Maybe it was from Jamie, but he suspected she had come in here and lain on her father's sheets, surrounded by his things.

Raven placed his foot on the trunk, about to slide it back out of sight, when a possibility occurred to him. Her father's things. He had found no personal documents in the office.

He knelt on the carpet and flipped open the lid. The trunk was full of notes and letters. Raven enjoyed a moment of excitement that here might lie some clues to the answers Eugenie was seeking. Then it dawned on him how much he would have to sift through. This looked like several years' worth of correspondence.

Raven picked up a handful from the box. He reasoned that the most recent would be at the top, likely to be the letters most indicative of what had been troubling Todd towards the end. Jamie hopped down and did likewise, grabbing a handful before Raven could stop him.

'Take care with those,' he said. He was about to take them from him but anticipated that this would only cause Jamie to head off elsewhere, and he would be bound to follow.

Jamie stayed close and began arranging envelopes into a shape on the floor.

Raven opened a letter from a Mrs Butler. She was informing

Todd that her husband had died and her son was returned from London to assist her daughter in settling the estate.

He very quickly ascertained he would need hours to look through this, possibly days. He was about to put the handful back in the trunk when his eye was drawn to a torn edge of paper sticking out between two envelopes. Separating them, he found that there were actually four pieces, one on top of the other. It looked like a note had been torn up in anger. But if torn up, why kept?

Raven pieced them together on the floor and read:

Dr Todd,

Thank you for your discretion in such a delicate matter. I believe this marks the beginning of a mutually profitable relationship. I hope we both share an eye for a long-term investment, as well as a mutual understanding that any breach of trust would advantage neither of us.

Magnus Cunningham

Cunningham. That name again. Sanderson had mentioned it, though the surname only. More intriguing was the mention of an investment.

Raven turned to the box again, remembering a trunk with a false bottom he had once searched. He turned it on its side to empty its contents, much to Jamie's delight, and examined the base. It was a sturdy piece, made for a doctor, not an illusionist. There was no false bottom, no secret compartment, and he had now jumbled the contents as surely as a magician shuffled his cards. But as he was about to begin shovelling the letters back inside, he noticed the envelope now at the top of the pile was both larger than the rest and a crisp white rather than yellowed. It was comparatively new, but had been put to the bottom. To hide it.

He felt his pulse surge. Finally he might have found what he sought: kept safe and secret, away from all of Todd's everyday business matters.

Raven sat on the bed and slid out the contents. He somehow managed to stifle a gasp, his need not to draw Jamie's attention narrowly winning out over his reaction at what he saw.

It was not the stock certificate he was searching for, but rather a number of photographs. The images were sharper than either calotypes or daguerreotype plates, evidencing a new technology which might under other circumstances have piqued his curiosity. But by some distance the greatest part of his astonishment was that all of these photographs showed young women.

Naked young women.

TWENTY-ONE

ater that day, Raven walked the short distance from Great Stuart Street to the Clarendon Hotel, named for the crescent on which it stood. Raven had seldom given much thought to who owned such places, but clearly there was as much in the way of intrigue and politics in this field as in any other. He had learned that Magnus Cunningham owned two other properties, but that this was considered his flagship, being the largest and the best situated. Nonetheless, it was tucked some way down the hill from the castle, so Raven understood why Cunningham might covet the Daltons' property on Princes Street.

He was asked to wait in the lobby, where he took a seat with a view of the orchard on the other side of Queensferry Road. He had made an appointment, these days always assuming other men were busier than he. He had sat there only a few minutes before he was addressed by a young lad in a uniform somewhat too large for him.

'Dr Raven? Mr Cunningham is ready to receive you now.'

The lad escorted him through to the back of the building and down a flight of stairs, where he was shown into a spacious office. It was situated on a basement level, but the slope meant its large windows offered a view towards Canonmills and the Forth beyond.

Seated in front of the windows, behind a large desk, was a

man in perhaps his late fifties. He was sharp-featured, with a face that might have been handsome once but now looked strikingly weathered. His skin was leathery, in a way Raven associated with sailors: men who spent their days exposed to the harshness of the elements, and in this case particularly the sun. His dark-blue suit was finely tailored, understated in both colour and cut. Raven thought of Callum Flint's transformation into Callum Somerville. He had spent a lot of money on clothes, hoping to make himself look like a gentleman, but what he had chosen was too ostentatious, and served only to signal to those in the know that he was not of the right breeding. Cunningham did not look to be either, but he clearly knew how to imitate it better.

His fingers had calluses and other marks on them, the hands of a man who had worked with them, not of someone who had spent much of his life behind that desk. Raven wondered where he had made the money that allowed him to become a hotelier.

'Dr Raven for you, sir,' announced the young lad, before being dismissed.

'Good afternoon, Mr Cunningham. Thank you for agreeing to see me.'

Cunningham looked at Raven in a way that was both appraising and inquisitive.

'Have we met before?' the hotelier asked.

Raven thought about it. 'I do not believe so.'

'You seem familiar.'

'Have you ever consulted with Dr Simpson? I assisted him for several years.'

'The chloroform man? No. Though I'm always looking for the services of a reliable doctor. What can I do for you?'

Cunningham's accent was strange, one Raven had not heard before. He wondered where the man hailed from, and how long he had been in the city.

'I am Dr Cameron Todd's son-in-law,' he explained. 'I am endeavouring to put his affairs in order.'

'You are taking over his practice?'

'I wish it were that simple,' he admitted. 'I am trying to trace some of Dr Todd's investments, and in looking through his effects I found a letter from you.'

Raven placed the letter on the desk, laying it out carefully in its four pieces.

'Can you tell me what this was concerning?'

Cunningham pored over it, then looked up again with a thin smile. 'That I was grateful for Dr Todd's discretion should tell you I would not wish to discuss such matters with anyone else.'

Raven had anticipated this answer, but it had been more about how Cunningham responded to the sight of the letter. The four scraps posed an unasked question: why would Todd rip up a letter and then hold on to the pieces, as though thinking better of it, or thinking he might need it?

'Can you at least tell me what this long-term investment was, that you hoped he shared an eye for?'

Cunningham seemed more relaxed at this. 'I am looking to expand, seeking to purchase another property.'

'So Dr Todd gave you money?'

'I believed he was about to invest in my next hotel venture. But alas it was not to be.'

'It's Mr Dalton's hotel you're trying to buy, isn't it? I gather he won't sell to you. Why would that be?'

Cunningham eyed him sharply, much as he had done when he first entered the room. 'Raven,' he said, rolling the word around in his mouth, making it clear he was ignoring the question. 'There was once a woman of this parish by the name of Margaret Raven, who married a relative of mine.'

Raven looked to the floor, hoping to conceal his shock at hearing his own mother's name.

'She had a son by the name of Thomas, if that helps.'

'She is no relative of mine, no. My family is in St Andrews,' he added, anxiety making him embellish. At least he had remembered that, when lying, one should stay as close to the truth as possible for fear of tripping oneself up.

'That's a pity,' Cunningham replied. 'I have no idea what became of them after Drew died. He was a vintner, officially dealing in wines, but he was a good source of whisky. Highland whisky, if you know what I mean.'

Raven did. As opposed to Lowland, on which the distillers paid their duty, albeit for vastly inferior product. Highland whisky was far finer, but for a long time had been mostly distilled and distributed illegally: smuggled and sold by men like his father.

'What relation was he to you?' Raven asked, for he needed to know.

'He was my brother.'

TWENTY-TWO

he afternoon sun was shining through the window of the consulting room on Queen Street, warming the room, and making Sarah's hairline prickle with sweat. She was wrapping a swollen leg in a flannel bandage, only vaguely aware of the patient's occasional wincing, caught up as she was in her own thoughts.

Was her arrangement with Raven really under threat? Would their joint project have to be abandoned? It seemed so unfair that a sudden catastrophic event could upend everything they had been working towards.

Sarah knew there was no one to blame. No one was at fault. She hadn't been misled in any way and had always known it was going to be a risky undertaking. But still the injustice of it gnawed at her.

She couldn't just sit back and let it happen. There had to be some way of pulling this out of the fire. She thought again about Somerville, about his willingness to assist her where he could. She had no way of knowing what he might expect in return, and if his generosity would extend to funding Raven's new practice. Raven would never accept his help, but then perhaps Raven didn't need to know.

The thought of what else Somerville could offer her kept bobbing unhelpfully to the surface of her mind.

Her task nearly complete, she forced herself to stop ruminating on her own problems and focus on the poor woman seated in front of her.

'What have you been eating, Mrs Scott?' she asked as she tucked the end of the bandage in. Mrs Scott was a poor-looking soul, dishevelled and none too clean. She was in her forties – although she didn't seem to be sure of her exact age – but looked older, evidence of a hard life etched into the deep lines on her face. There was a sour, acrid smell emanating from her.

'Just my usual,' she replied. 'Bread, butter, tea. Bit of porridge on occasion.'

'Have you any family?'

The woman shook her head. 'No. I'm on my own since my husband passed.'

'Have you eaten today?'

The woman shook her head again. She became tearful, then looked away, as though ashamed that she had not the means to feed herself.

Sarah stood up. 'Wait here,' she said and gave Mrs Scott a reassuring smile. 'Dr Simpson insists that all of his patients eat before they leave.'

Sarah fed and dispatched Mrs Scott with as much as she could carry from Dr Simpson's larder. Mrs Lyndsay, the cook, made her usual complaints about being expected to feed 'everyone who comes o'er the door', but given that the Simpson household was always well-supplied with comestibles it was unlikely anyone would even notice, never mind have to do without.

She then carried a tea tray into Dr Blackwell's consulting room. As she placed it down on Emily's desk, she took in how tidy and organised it was compared to Raven's, which itself was a model of disciplined order compared to Dr Simpson's.

Emily looked up from the notes she was making. 'Thank you, Sarah.'

Sarah was beginning to detect a thawing in Emily's frostiness towards her. Perhaps she had realised her error in attributing the newspaper article to a loose tongue on Sarah's part. She suspected Emily now accepted that one of the male members of the Infirmary board or one of the consulting physicians was a more likely source. Idle gossip at a dinner party, perhaps, rather than a story given to a journalist with malicious intent, although when dealing with the medical profession in Edinburgh, malicious intent could never be ruled out.

Emily put her pen down and lifted the tea Sarah had poured for her.

'What did you make of our last patient?'

Sarah smiled. If Emily was seeking to catch her out, to illustrate Sarah's ignorance, she would be disappointed. The diagnosis was not a difficult one. Sarah recognised the signs.

'Painful swollen legs, firm to the touch with diffuse petechial haemorrhages. Gums swollen, tender and bleeding.'

'You examined her?'

Sarah nodded.

'And you are permitted to do that?'

'The patients don't seem to mind.'

'Depends very much on the patient, I should think.'

'The downstairs patients tend to be less fussy about such things,' Sarah said. 'They're just grateful for anything that they get. I generally don't have much to do with the upstairs ones.'

'No,' Emily agreed. 'I have found that Dr Simpson likes to keep those to himself.'

Sarah bristled at the implied criticism of the professor. Dr Simpson had welcomed Emily into his home as his assistant, giving her every opportunity to make the most of her time here. To Sarah's ears this seemed like ingratitude.

'So, what is your diagnosis?' Emily asked.

'Scurvy,' Sarah said.

'You've seen it before?'

'There was a spate of cases here not so long ago. Railway workers kept on short rations for months at a time.'

Emily nodded as if this explained why Sarah had managed to arrive at the correct answer. She took a sip of tea and peered at her over the rim of the cup.

'Have you given any thought to what I said? About your further education? You wish to study medicine, do you not?'

'I would like to, yes.'

'Then why don't you do it?'

Sarah was taken aback by the question. Emily knew better than anyone that such a thing was almost impossible here. The colleges she and her sister had attended in America were reluctant to repeat their experiments in the medical education of women, and Sarah had given up on the notion of travelling the globe in the hope some other foreign university would deign to let her study there.

'Do you really think you have what it takes?' Emily continued. 'Are you prepared to sacrifice everything for what you want?'

Sarah was wary of overstepping her bounds here, but she did feel the need to defend herself.

'Why should I have to sacrifice everything? I am prepared to study, to work as hard as any man would do. What else should be required of me?'

'But you're not a man.'

'I am aware of that.'

'My point is that in order to succeed in a profession completely dominated by men, we women have to work twice as hard, be twice as good. You are naive if you think otherwise.'

Sarah could feel tears pricking her eyes. She felt scolded, belittled.

'And *my* point,' she countered, 'is that medical education should be open to all women of sufficient ability. We shouldn't be made to beg for special favours.'

'If that is what you are waiting for, might I suggest that you satisfy yourself with your current duties here, or, as I said before, perhaps apply to join Miss Nightingale and her band of nurses in Scutari.'

Sarah didn't know what to say to this. Emily seemed to think that she and her sister were truly a breed apart without acknowledging the considerable advantages they had enjoyed compared to other women of equal intellect. They had been brought up in a middle-class household, had received a comprehensive education from an early age, and enjoyed the patronage of many notable people. Sarah felt that a little encouragement towards other women should not be too much to ask.

'You are obviously a woman of some intelligence,' Emily continued.

Sarah was grateful for this small compliment but braced herself for what was to come.

'But you have no husband, no family, no ties here. So perhaps you ought to ask yourself: what, or perhaps who, is holding you back?'

TWENTY-THREE

squall of rain blew through the window of the carriage, spraying Raven's face with cold water, the short interlude of sunshine having given way to thick cloud. It was about the only thing that could have brought him back to the here and now, as well as fully woken him up. He had not slept well, unable to put Magnus Cunningham from his mind since yesterday's revelation that he had an uncle living in the city. He wondered for how long. The man had clearly built up a successful business, so he must have been here for some time. But here from where? He had that weather-beaten face, that strange accent.

Raven had thought of writing to his mother to ask what she had not told him as a boy, but he did not wish to alarm her, and this news surely would. If she had remained ignorant of Magnus being in Edinburgh thus far, there was no reason to enlighten her. Raven had never encountered him here, so there was little chance of her doing so in St Andrews. Being in medicine gave the impression it was a small city, where everyone knew everyone else's business — or at least reputation — but this served to remind Raven of how his circle was only one small part of a much greater whole.

Another squall pelted him with raindrops, causing him to close the window. He considered Forbes, the poor driver at the reins, exposed entirely to the elements. Then he considered what he was paying him, though again his resentment was misdirected.

The carriage would reach Craiglockhart in a fraction of the time it would take for Raven to walk all the way out there, which struck him as ironic given that these days his problems lay in having time to spare. At least he would not arrive at his destination drenched, so taking the carriage did not seem like an entirely unnecessary extravagance. Or rather, at least he had reason to make *use* of an unnecessary extravagance. Dr Todd's coach and driver were near the top of the list of expenses Raven had identified to be cut, but though Golspie had made it clear how soon the money would run out, Eugenie refused to countenance his dismissal. She remained determined not to do anything that might spread news of their financial predicament, even if by her actions she was exacerbating it.

She kept asking if Raven had found the investment records, as though this was all an administrative oversight that would be made right as soon as the correct certificate was uncovered. Even if such a document turned out to exist, who was to say it would be worth anything? Or that the recovery of its value would be a quick and simple process?

Of course, he could not tell her about what he *had* uncovered. The photographs indicated a side to Todd of which Raven was hitherto unaware, but unless they cost two thousand pounds, they told him nothing useful about where the man's money had gone.

As he had said to Sarah, Eugenie tended to believe all would suddenly be well because, in her experience, it usually had been. The problem with Eugenie's blithe attitude was that she seemed to forget that the man who had ensured all would be well was no longer here, and nor was his money. She expected things to simply fall into place, which was why she had assumed such an air of vindication this morning when a message arrived from none other than Gertrude Leitch, urgently requesting Raven's medical attendance at her home.

'It is as I told you: people do not think to seek a doctor until they need one, at which point there is not the time to search far and wide. They will reach out to the first good name that comes to mind, and that good name is Will Raven. Mrs Leitch will only be the first. This is why it was worth the expense of the funeral.'

Raven did not think Mrs Leitch was about to pay what that occasion had cost him, but nor should he be churlish. If he made a happy patient of her, then it would be easier to attract more of Dr Todd's list. And if it made Eugenie happier, that would be a victory in itself.

The coach made its way down a grand avenue off the Colinton Road, drawing up outside a mansion house. The address on the message said simply 'Meggetland', which meant nothing to Raven but was well enough known to Forbes. A lad emerged from the stables to tend the horses as soon as they stopped. Raven saw two further carriages: a brougham and a phaeton.

A butler greeted Raven and showed him briskly inside, leading him upstairs.

'Mrs Yates is in the blue room,' the butler told him.

'Mrs Yates?'

'Mrs Leitch's youngest daughter. Recently married and now with child.'

So the patient was not Mrs Leitch herself, though a pregnant woman from a wealthy family was a prize too. There might be regular consultations, to say nothing of the delivery.

Raven was shown into a bright and airy bedroom, decorated in various shades of blue, where a woman was sitting up in bed. She looked plump and pink and far from unwell.

Her complaints were those associated with the early stages of pregnancy — loss of appetite, nausea, fatigue. Raven listened attentively, reassured her that her symptoms would soon improve and prescribed a tonic to be taken in the meantime.

'When did you last see Dr Todd?' he asked, hoping to effect a seamless continuation from his care to Raven's.

'Dr Todd?'

'Yes. My late father-in-law.'

'Oh. Never. My physician is Dr Agnew, in Corbridge. I am only visiting my mother. I wish I could stay longer. She needs company since Father died, but my husband wishes me back in Northumberland.'

Raven disguised his disappointment as he saw those regular consultations vanish.

The butler was waiting for him when he emerged from the bedroom. 'Mrs Leitch would like to speak with you,' he was told.

Raven was escorted downstairs to a room at the rear of the property, which appeared to be Mrs Leitch's private study. The walls were decorated with religious paintings depicting Christ's suffering and humiliation, all of which the Saviour apparently endured while wearing little more than a loincloth. Raven suspected the artist had been rather taken with his model, and wondered if Mrs Leitch was oblivious to the lasciviousness of the painter's gaze.

Mrs Leitch was sitting at a desk, once again dressed in black, though women these days seldom subjected themselves to the full restrictions of first mourning, which dictated they should withdraw entirely from society for at least three months.

She was not alone. Standing alongside her behind the desk was a tall gentleman in a smart grey suit. Raven estimated him to be in his sixties, but healthy with it. His expression was solemn. He regarded Raven with a sharp gaze, as though taking his measure.

'Dr Raven,' Mrs Leitch said. 'Thank you for attending Alice. Is all well?'

'Your daughter is quite well, madam, merely suffering from the symptoms of early pregnancy. They are not only to be expected but are usually taken to be a good sign.'

'Indeed.'

'If I might speak confidentially,' Raven said, glancing to the man at her side.

'Please do go on,' Mrs Leitch urged, evidently untroubled by issues of privacy.

'Very well. She seems concerned as much for your wellbeing as over her own condition.'

Mrs Leitch responded with a sage nod. 'She worries, yet she will have no idea what worry truly is until she is delivered.'

'How true,' Raven replied. He glanced again at the other man, which Mrs Leitch noticed.

'Dr Raven, allow me to introduce Mr Leonard McMurdo. He helped manage Barrington's business affairs and has been indispensable since his death.'

Raven shook his hand.

'You are Dr Todd's successor?' the man asked.

'I am Dr Todd's son-in-law. Whether I succeed him as anyone's doctor is entirely at the patients' discretion.'

Raven glanced towards Mrs Leitch, hoping for at least a glimmer of intent, but her expression remained inscrutable.

'You worked for James Simpson, I understand,' McMurdo said. 'The chloroform man.'

Raven normally welcomed the possibility of greatness by association with the professor, but on this occasion he wondered whether this was McMurdo's way of conveying that he had been vetted ahead of his visit.

'I did, yes.'

'Then Alice is truly fortunate,' McMurdo said. 'Perhaps she should come back to Edinburgh for her confinement.'

He added this as though he knew how unlikely it was. Raven wondered if he also knew how much Raven might wish for it. There was something detached and calculating about the man but also something protective: a man Mrs Leitch trusted, and whose husband must have too. If anybody knew whether Todd had lodged monies with Leitch, it would be him. Unfortunately, Raven had the strong impression he was about to be thanked and sent on his way.

'Mrs Leitch, we were interrupted the other day when you began to tell me about your campaign,' Raven said.

'We were,' she replied, suddenly animated. 'Is it something in which you are minded to assist?'

'I have a good friend to whom it is a personal matter. She fears her niece has been drawn into the clutches of such an enterprise. She recently attended a meeting of the Society of the Suppression of Vice, and nothing she learned there was of comfort.'

Mrs Leitch nodded solemnly. 'Yes, it is when someone close to us is affected that it brings home the cruel truth of it. Too many people remain blithely ignorant, or wilfully so: reluctant to confront what is going on behind doors that they walk past every day. What drives our campaign is that, by the time these girls are in the grip of sin, it is already too late. They become inured to the wickedness.'

'It is my understanding that they are often lured away when they have just arrived in the city,' Raven said, 'before they can take up their situations.'

'Sometimes they are lured even after they are in work,' she told him. 'Devils whispering in their ears, promising them earthly delights, trinkets and distractions. They succumb to temptation not knowing where it leads. Lied to about what seemingly kindly men truly want from them.'

'And then they are ruined,' McMurdo said.

'The Society for the Suppression of Vice seeks to raise the age of consent,' Mrs Leitch stated. 'For as it stands, these girls are regarded by the law as women, and all of their actions by their own volition.'

'What would a change in the law effect?'

'If a man keeps a girl in his house of assignation,' McMurdo replied, 'he needs only insist that she wants to be there. The police cannot intervene.'

'Not that they would,' said Mrs Leitch, 'for many of them are in league with the brothel-keepers. But if the law said these young girls were children, if people *realised* that these were mere children . . .' She sighed, glancing at a painting of Jesus dragging his cross upon muscular shoulders. 'It would be the most fitting monument to my husband should his funds help drive such a change.'

'A noble legacy,' affirmed McMurdo.

'But I forget myself, Dr Raven. You are here all this time and I have not asked how young Eugenie is faring. She was so brave at the funeral. To have to face everyone when you are laid so low is a dreadful burden.'

Young Eugenie. Eugenie was not much younger than he was himself, and the same age as Sarah, but this was a reminder to him of how long Todd must have had dealings with the Leitch family. People who knew someone as a child would often refer to them as such ever after.

'She will heal in time, as must we all,' he said. 'I think it was all the harder for her because she could not be permitted to see him. There was no opportunity to bid him goodbye. But equally, I cannot imagine how distressing it must have been for you, Mrs Leitch, being present alongside your husband when he so suddenly passed.'

She looked strangely at him, confused and uncomfortable. He immediately regretted mentioning it, bringing her back to such a painful memory.

'Or perhaps it comforts you that he knew you were with him at the end,' he suggested.

Mrs Leitch bowed her head. She seemed at a loss for a response.

'Mr and Mrs Leitch had separate bedrooms,' McMurdo said, his tone both deferential and matter-of-fact, as though indicating that no inference ought to be drawn from this that was anyone else's business.

Raven nodded his understanding as reverentially as he could. He wasn't about to infer anything. He was conscious that the only reason he and Eugenie were not in separate bedrooms was that they didn't have a room to spare.

The Leitches had been married a long time, with grown children: a successful but perhaps a companionate marriage. He was not sure he could tolerate that. He needed the feeling of closeness, the physicality of mutual desire. Not merely the lying together but the anticipation: the stolen glances, the sense of something secret shared only between the two people, an unspoken thing.

'This is why you must cherish every moment of your marriage,' Mrs Leitch told him. 'For you know not the day nor the hour. I last saw Barrington at breakfast the morning before he died, commencing a typical, normal day. No notion it would be the last time I saw him alive.'

'You did not see him that evening?'

'I dined at a friend's house, and when I returned, he had already gone to bed. I knew he'd had a busy day and I assumed he was unusually tired, but perhaps it was a sign of something more profound.'

'That was the only indication?' Raven asked.

McMurdo gave him a look: not quite a warning, but notice of a warning.

'Forgive me, professional curiosity, and quite inappropriate.'

'Don't mention it,' said Mrs Leitch. 'But no, there was no indication. I choose to look upon the suddenness as the Lord's mercy, for I have known those whose spouses wasted away before their eyes, over months or years. I went to bed knowing him as he was, then Leonard woke me with the news.'

'You were the one who discovered him?' Raven asked McMurdo.

'No. His butler woke me with it just after dawn. I summoned Dr Todd, who was good enough to come, though it was merely a formality. Then I informed Gertrude.'

Todd had been present. Raven had not known this. He now understood why Mrs Leitch had reacted strangely at Dalton's Hotel when he talked of Todd learning the news, as though he had found out like everyone else.

'You were staying here that night?'

'I stay here frequently. We had business matters to go over in the morning.'

'Were you Mr Leitch's amanuensis?' Raven asked. He tried not to make this sound like some kind of accusation, aware that this profession had been rendered forever suspect in Raven's mind. Many years ago, Dr Simpson had employed a Mr Quinton as his secretary, the fellow pilfering from the professor's coffers, all the while altering the books to point suspicion elsewhere.

Mrs Leitch let out a polite little laugh. 'His amanuensis? No, no. Leonard is a businessman in his own right. He and Barrington were always thick as thieves. But forgive me, I must go and see Alice. Thank you again, Dr Raven. Mr McMurdo will settle your bill.'

With Mrs Leitch gone, Raven watched McMurdo slowly count out his fee at the desk. He thought of what the widow had just told him.

'You had a hand in Mr Leitch's business affairs?' Raven asked.

McMurdo fixed him with a stern look again. 'What of it?'

Raven put the fee in his bag and closed the hasp.

'This is a delicate matter, but in attempting to put Dr Todd's affairs in order, I am struggling to trace an investment he might have made.'

'*Might* have made?'

'This is not a world I understand, Mr McMurdo, and I'm trying to piece something together from second-hand information. Dr Todd withdrew funds from the bank, who said it was for an investment. Is it possible Dr Todd lodged these monies with Mr Leitch?'

'I can look into it, but it would help if I knew the nature of the investment.'

'I recall him mentioning something involving a hotelier named Cunningham a few weeks ago,' Raven lied. 'Does that name mean anything? Is it someone Mr Leitch might have done business with?'

McMurdo straightened, as though giving this serious thought. 'I know Magnus Cunningham was raising funds to buy new premises, but I don't believe he would have approached Barrington. I'm not sure my late friend altogether approved of the man.'

'Why not?'

'I would not be so indiscreet as to trade in gossip. I will leave that to the likes of Mr Sanderson.'

Raven recognised the self-righteousness in McMurdo's tone and knew he would not be pressed. He tried another tack.

'Would these new premises be Dalton's Hotel? Mr Dalton told me he is selling, but his wife suggested – to her chagrin – that he was minded to accept an offer other than the highest.'

McMurdo smiled for the first time. 'I think Mr Dalton simply doesn't want Cunningham to have it. Barrington wasn't the only one to disapprove of him.'

Raven would have asked again why, but knew he would receive the same answer. He picked up his bag, a prelude to his leaving.

'Mr McMurdo, everyone has been passing on their condolences to Mrs Leitch, but it must have been a painful thing for you also to lose such a friend.'

Raven was watching him carefully for his response. There was a tremble to McMurdo's lip. He seemed taken aback by his emotion, as though he had only now thought to consider his own loss.

He cleared his throat. 'I had known him almost forty years. We did great things together.'

'And it is as Mrs Leitch says? Nothing to indicate he was ill?'

McMurdo gave him a severe look once more. This time Raven met it with no apology.

'It has been my duty and my misfortune to witness some startling things in my time as a doctor. I am naturally curious when a healthy man dies suddenly, and the explanation is not always medical. Was there anyone who might have wished him harm?'

McMurdo looked puzzled, as though this notion would never have occurred to him had Raven not raised it.

'Are you insinuating foul play, Dr Raven? Poison, perhaps? Dr Todd would surely have brought it to our attention had he found sign of that.'

'Nonetheless, Mr Leitch said he should be judged by the anger of his enemies.'

McMurdo gave him a cool smile, both wry and patronising. 'Sometimes we are injudicious in our choice of words. Barrington talked of enemies, but he meant adversaries, opponents, rivals. In the realm of finance, we do not fear each other as mortal threats.'

'But that was not the only realm he had ventured into.'

McMurdo scoffed. 'You mean politics? This campaign? I can't imagine some vengeful whore having the wherewithal to sneak in here and murder him in his own bed for threatening her livelihood.'

'I mean no disrespect,' Raven assured him. 'I am inquisitive by nature, exacerbated in this instance by professional curiosity.'

'I fear your profession drives a darker curiosity than mine,' McMurdo replied.

Raven nodded. 'Of that there can be no doubt.'

TWENTY-FOUR

When Raven returned to Great Stuart Street, he found himself alone, Eugenie and the children again at her father's house.

The stillness was oddly unwelcome. Where once he would have given anything for some respite from Clara's crying and Jamie's noisy bluster, this quietness felt merely empty. As though the house itself was incomplete.

Having made himself some tea, he went into his consulting room, where he had placed the trunk he had transported from Todd's bedroom. With no distractions, he would make use of the time to sift through more of the letters. He had found an old crate in which to store the messages he had already looked through, its paltry contents testament to the speed of his progress.

He really wished he hadn't upended the trunk looking for a secret compartment that didn't exist.

So far, he had found little of relevance, though his spirits brightened when he encountered something from the time he was first courting Eugenie. It was like glimpsing into the world she lived in before he knew it first-hand. He also found one missive from the time of her secret confinement: a letter from a friend of Todd's asking how Eugenie was, as the correspondent had heard she was spending some time in the country and was concerned she might be unwell.

Unfortunately he had found precisely nothing that made mention of an investment opportunity, or anything to do with Todd's newly discovered interest in photography.

Raven had just picked up a letter from 1847, around the time he first arrived at Queen Street, when he heard the unmistakable sound of Jamie's voice amid footsteps outside. He went to the door and helped Eugenie in with Clara's baby carriage, one Eugenie had been carried in herself before it spent two decades in Todd's attic until Jamie's birth. Clara was sleeping, as was often the case when she was being transported.

'I have just made some tea,' Raven said.

He was about to lead Eugenie to the kitchen, but Jamie charged into the consulting room, climbing onto the chair behind Raven's desk. Raven wasn't about to leave him in there unattended.

Eugenie followed Raven into the room, impatient to hear about his trip to Meggetland.

'Will Mrs Leitch be your patient now? This could be the beginning of— '

She stopped, taking in the trunk, which was close to the window where the light was best.

'What is this?'

'It is your father's correspondence.'

'I mean what is it doing here?'

'I am looking for something that might point us to the missing money. And you asked me to look into whether anyone might have wished him harm.'

Eugenie walked over to the trunk and lifted out a handful of letters.

'But this is his private correspondence.' Her tone was accusatory, even offended. 'You should have asked me.'

Raven was grateful he'd had the good sense to remove the envelope containing the photographs. He had placed it between the pages of the grindingly tedious physiology textbook sitting on his desk. He was reluctant enough to open that particular volume himself, so he reasoned there was little chance of anyone else doing so.

'What have you seen?' she asked, sounding both concerned and annoyed.

'I have barely scratched the surface,' he replied, indicating the crate. 'Clearly the most recent correspondence is the most likely to be helpful, but unfortunately the contents were spilled and jumbled. I will have to go through everything until— '

'*I* will go through it,' Eugenie insisted. 'And if I find anything that I feel you ought to know, I will inform you.'

'Lady ready for bath,' Jamie said, both of them ignoring him.

'Be my guest,' Raven told her. 'As you can see, the only ones I have read are those in the crate. Incidentally, did you ever hear your father mention someone by the name of Magnus Cunningham? A recent letter mentions a "mutually profitable arrangement".'

'I don't believe so.'

'It's just that this letter had been ripped into four pieces, as though in anger, and— '

'Other lady bath too,' Jamie said.

Raven realised only too late what he was talking about. Eugenie glanced towards the desk, where Jamie had found the envelope and emptied its contents. She got there before Raven could reach, picking up one of the photographs.

'In the name of God, what are these?'

'Ladies,' Jamie informed her.

'Don't touch those!' she shrieked at him, slapping his hand away from the pictures. 'Get out. Get out of this room at once.'

Jamie burst into tears, slid from the chair and ran off.

'Don't shout at him,' Raven said. 'The child has done nothing wrong.'

'The child saw these! What are they doing here?'

She began spreading them across the desk, gazing upon them in fascinated horror.

'Are these for your gratification?' she asked, her lip curling in disgust.

Raven could say nothing. If he told her where he had found them, then everything she was appalled by, everything she was accusing him of, she would know of her father. Or she would simply refuse to believe it and think even worse of Raven that he should try to blame a dead man for his own perversions.

'I cannot believe you would have these things under the same roof as me, as our children.'

Eugenie picked up the photographs and threw them at him.

'Perhaps these can keep you company from now on. I am taking the children to St Andrew Square. And I am not coming back.'

TWENTY-FIVE

arah finished ladling a quantity of ointment into a small jar and affixed a lid and a label. She handed it to the grateful patient, Mrs Heaton, a woman who had sustained a burn to her arm. The salve was a recipe handed down to Sarah from her grandmother, one she remembered making up for Raven on the first day she met him, applying it on top of the stitches that were holding his face together.

Perhaps she ought to have seen that as an omen and been wary that this was a man who brought trouble with him. When he turned up that day as Dr Simpson's new apprentice, bruised and bloody, she had assumed he would be gone even sooner than his predecessors. Yet here they were almost seven years later, still entangled in each other's lives.

There was a small part of her that was still angry about how he had distanced himself from her back then, forsaking what was blossoming between them, concerned about the consequences for his reputation as a doctor should he become involved with a mere housemaid. The irony of it was that he had remained involved with her, nonetheless. She wondered sometimes what would have happened if things had been different, and she had married Raven instead of Archie. Would she now be content as a doctor's wife? Or would there always be something unfulfilled at her heart, something she could not quite identify? Would her ambitions even have occurred to her? And, though it felt wrong to contemplate it, would she have known greater peace had they not?

She saw Mrs Heaton out, the final patient of the day. The waiting room was empty, but the traffic had been steady throughout the morning. Unquestionably, it was becoming busier every day here. She would have thought Raven might seem happier about this, but he had seemed quiet and weary throughout, not himself. She suspected one or both of the children had kept him awake through the night.

It struck Sarah then that there had been neither sight nor sound of the family. She went back into the consulting room where Raven was still seated at his desk.

'Has Eugenie taken the children to St Andrew Square?' she asked.

Raven said nothing for a moment. He nodded solemnly, his eyes glazed.

'Is something wrong?'

'She took them away last night, but when they will return is altogether less certain.'

Raven's weariness now seemed more explicable, and more troubling.

'What do you mean? What has happened?'

Raven sat back in his chair, cleared his throat, composed himself. 'She discovered some . . . photographs.'

'Photographs? Of whom?'

'I cannot say.'

Sarah was confused. 'Do you mean you cannot say, or you *will* not say?'

'Cannot.'

'Then why would they upset her?'

Raven looked exasperated, as though he did not know how to explain. 'I could show you, but my concern is that you might react as she did.'

'Oh, for heaven's sake, Raven. Given all that we have been through together, you know that I am not easily shocked.'

Raven sighed. He opened a drawer in his desk and produced an envelope. 'Just remember you insisted,' he said. From the envelope he removed several photographic images printed on stiff paper.

Despite her protestations, Sarah did feel taken aback at what she saw. 'Where on earth did you get these?' she asked. She thought of the paintings she had seen at the House of Melbourne. If paintings could be used for the express purpose of titillation, then it was inevitable that photographs would be too. But there was something starker and more immediate about these. In painting there was an element of interpretation, the images derived partly from the imagination of the artist. Women may well have posed for the paintings at the House of Melbourne, but they had displayed fantastical ideas, visible fictions. What was so arresting about these photographs was the sense of stark, unvarnished reality.

One of the first photographs Sarah had ever seen was an image of herself, taken at Rock House by David Octavius Hill and his collaborator Robert Adamson. Simpson's then assistant, George Keith, had been a friend of the pair and had brought her and Raven there on a visit, where she had been asked to pose. She recalled how strange it felt to see such a vivid likeness, as though looking in a mirror. What felt stranger still was to look at others without them looking back, without the need to lower your eyes and hide your own curiosity. But that was the purpose here, was it not? To permit the pleasure of looking, of staring.

'Why do you have them?' she asked. 'Where did they come from?'

Raven held her in his gaze, reluctant to answer but clearly aware an answer would have to come. His eyes strayed to the trunk he'd told her he brought back from St Andrew Square. Sarah understood.

'They belonged to Eugenie's father,' she deduced, many things becoming clear. 'And you didn't tell her.'

'How could I?' he asked, looking helpless.

'Oh, Will.' She stood next to him, pulling his head to her chest. 'You did a good thing, a noble thing.'

'It doesn't feel good.'

She held him a few moments. This did feel good. Too good. She stepped away.

'Why do you think he had them?'

'I suspect for precisely the reason Eugenie feared I did.'

'Anatomy illustrations?' she suggested.

Raven managed a glimmer of a smile. 'Todd was a man who lost his wife more than two decades ago. I would not judge him for a secret vice.'

'Others might, though. If Todd's possession of these was known to someone else, would that be grounds enough for blackmail?'

'It would certainly be enough for many of his patients to take their custom elsewhere. But would that be enough to make him take his own life? I cannot think so. Besides, these were carefully hidden, at the bottom of a trunk under his own bed.'

'Yes, but someone knew he had them: whoever he acquired them from.'

'Indeed. That is something I must endeavour to discover. You said I need to give Eugenie an explanation, and I think that is now true more than ever. But if I cannot exonerate myself without delivering painful knowledge about her father, there may be no way for me to placate her.'

Sarah wanted to hold him again. She offered him a reassuring smile instead. 'She will come around. Right now, her wounds are just too raw. But there will be a time when she is ready to know the truth, when she would rather hear a painful secret about her father than believe the worst of you.'

He glanced again at the images. Sarah looked too. The unseeing faces looking back seemed strangely serene in the face of this exposure. Only two people had ever seen Sarah unclothed. The love and trust required for that had been high. How could anyone strip naked before a photographer, everything on display?

'When I think of the perverse notions of modesty that endure,' Raven said, 'the absurdity that dictates I have to examine women beneath the bedclothes, working by touch because it is considered improper that I should see their intimate parts – yet this feels like a disturbing, opposite extreme.'

'The euphemism is to talk of someone "having knowledge of you",' Sarah said. 'This is another form of that knowledge. But who would participate in this? Never knowing who might see it, conscious always that anyone you meet might have done. Who would allow it?'

'Only those with little dignity left in that regard,' Raven said.

They shared a look, then shared a word.

'Prostitutes.'

TWENTY-SIX

he pavement was crowded, Raven and Sarah struggling to make headway down Clerk Street against a flow of pedestrians travelling in the opposite direction. The morning's rain having let up, it seemed to Raven that half the city was now making for the town.

Sarah took his arm, presumably in an attempt to avoid being mown down or separated from him. He could feel the gentle pressure of her hand, perhaps more aware of it than he should have been.

He knew that he was thinking about her more than usual. He had counselled himself that this was to be expected under the circumstances. Eugenie had withdrawn from him, and Sarah was the only one he could confide in about what was going on.

They were on their way to Beatrice Hinchcliff's house, a meeting brokered by Somerville. When Sarah told Raven about it earlier that day, he had insisted on accompanying her; to offer his support, he had said, but also because the Butlers were coming along too. Given the letter from their mother that he had found amongst Todd's things, Raven hoped that an introduction might prove informative in some way.

Raven stopped suddenly, having seen someone he recognised approaching from the other direction.

'You didn't tell me Flint was going to be here,' he said.

'Somerville,' Sarah corrected him. 'He's trying to be helpful.

He thought it likely that Mrs Hinchcliff would be more receptive to my questions if he was also in attendance.'

'What is he proposing to do? Glower at her from the corner? Or perhaps make more explicit threats.'

'I imagine he will do neither,' Sarah said. 'His presence is to reassure Mrs Hinchcliff that I can be trusted.'

Raven scoffed. 'And you believe that?'

'Why must you always be so suspicious of the man? He's trying to help me.'

'I've known him longer than you have, remember. I've seen what lurks beneath this new veneer.'

Sarah tutted and let go of his arm. 'Look.' She pointed at a man and woman further ahead, looking lost. 'There are the Butlers. I'll go and retrieve them and, in the meantime— ' She gave him an admonishing stare ' —you behave.'

Sarah took off to intercept the Butlers, and Raven made his way towards Somerville, the man's obvious limp miraculously less pronounced as soon as he saw Raven's approach. Same as ever, Raven thought. Unwilling to show any sign of weakness.

'It must hurt,' Raven said.

'What, the leg?'

Raven shook his head. 'No. I mean Sarah. She's about to get a glimpse of who you really are. Meeting the kind of people you are associated with.'

'Who I used to be, and who I used to associate with,' Somerville replied.

Raven had never really bought into Somerville's reinvention of himself. He had been a money-lender when Raven had first met him, with a crew of heavy-handed thugs more than happy to mete out violence at his behest. Raven had always been wary of the brutality he felt lurked inside his own breast, something he feared he had inherited from his father, but that was as nothing compared to what he knew Somerville capable of.

'And as far as Sarah is concerned,' Somerville continued, 'I'd wager you are the more pained.'

'What do you mean?'

'Well, I did as you asked. I confessed to her about my real name, and yet she did not despair of me. Not quite the outcome you were hoping for, I imagine.'

'If you had been entirely honest with her, I doubt she would have anything further to do with you,' Raven replied.

Somerville looked Raven square in the eye. 'You don't need to protect Sarah from me, Raven. I only want the best for her.'

Raven shook his head again. 'You have no idea of what she wants.'

'I know that she wants to break through and succeed where she is not currently permitted. It's a battle with which I can identify.'

'You want her for a wife,' Raven said dismissively. 'She can be so much more than that. You tell her you will support her, and maybe a part of you even believes that right now. But you have no idea how difficult that will be. And you have no idea how difficult Sarah can be.'

Somerville shrugged, unperturbed. 'What about when she decides the fight is done? What if one day the battle is lost, and she is content to settle for the life of a lady. I can give her that.'

Raven scoffed. 'That statement merely illustrates how little you know her. Sarah will never settle. It's not in her nature. You forget that she has been married already, and it brought her nothing but sadness.'

'It is my understanding that it was not the marriage brought her sadness. Only that it had to end.'

Raven hated that the man would not be cowed, that he seemed so sure of himself with regards to Sarah.

'What of your own wife?' Somerville asked. 'How is she?'

Raven frowned, wondering why Somerville saw the need to mention Eugenie.

'What business is it of yours?'

'I merely wish to convey my sympathy. To her and to you.'

Raven was immediately on his guard, wondering if there was concealed meaning in Somerville's condolences. His wariness must have shown on his face.

'I think you forget that you saved my life,' Somerville said. 'Or perhaps you merely regret it.'

'I don't regret it. I simply knew that I would regret it more were I to let you die. I had no wish to be burdened with that kind of guilt. Not about you. That's what sent me back into the flames to save you.'

'Whatever your motivation, it was still a heroic act. And so it puzzles me: why would you continue to believe I wish you ill? I'm indebted to you, and grateful.'

'I don't want you to be indebted to me,' Raven replied. 'It's only marginally preferable to my being indebted to you. And as I recall you were determined never to let me pay what I owed.'

'Maybe I liked having you around.'

'I seriously doubt it.'

Raven disliked this dissembling from Somerville, who seemed to be making light of their past history. Raven still had the scar on his face to prove what a ruthless and violent individual Somerville once was. Sarah might be taken in by this act, Flint reincarnated as the respectable Mr Somerville, but Raven never would be. He was, however, not averse to making use of the man.

'I imagine that, even in your new incarnation, you still have your ear to the ground. What's being said about Cameron Todd?'

Somerville's brow twitched. He seemed pleased that Raven wanted something from him. 'You mean other than that he probably killed himself? Not much.'

'Nothing about blackmail?'

'Blackmail? You think he was driven to it?'

'There's no evidence that I have been able to find. I'm merely exploring the possibility because I am aware of someone else who has fallen victim to it recently.'

Somerville shrugged. 'I'm not sure I can offer you any advice on that score. As you know, my methods were altogether less sleekit.'

He glanced at Raven's scarred face as he said this. Raven felt one hand reflexively bunch into a fist, but he knew better than to be provoked by this man.

'I was always more inclined to have people threatened with being thrown off a tall building if they didn't pay what they owed,' Somerville continued, 'rather than compelling them to do so by their own grubby secrets.'

Raven looked to where Sarah was standing, still at some distance, chatting to the Butlers. He wished that she had been within earshot of this discussion. Raven was convinced that, however much Somerville had told her about himself, the more disturbing details of his past life had been omitted.

'Sanderson's more your man for that sort of thing,' Somerville continued. 'Knows everything that goes on in this town.' He gave Raven a knowing look as though party to information that Raven did not have. 'Though now he's back in the newspaper business, I imagine he has more to gain from publishing people's secrets than keeping them.'

TWENTY-SEVEN

'I don't think I can do this,' Mrs Hinchcliff said, eyeing the small gathering. Raven could see her hands shaking, hear the tremor in her voice.

Raven, Sarah, Somerville and the Butlers had all just taken their seats in the small but well-appointed parlour of the lodging house on Bristo Street of which Mrs Hinchcliff was the proprietor. 'It's a gentleman's boarding house,' she had clarified while showing them in, as though keen to distance her establishment from the low-quality doss-houses of the West Port. Her rooms were for professional gentlemen, she elaborated, and the house rules were rigidly enforced. Said rules were pinned to the wall in the entrance hall: Meals to be taken at set times, no visitors without prior approval, no noise, no singing and no intoxicating liquors of any kind.

Mrs Hinchcliff wore a fitted black dress with a white lace collar, her hair neatly pinned up, the picture of middle-class respectability. Nonetheless her discomfort was palpable. She was gripping the arms of her chair, her knuckles white. She shook her head.

'No. I'm sorry, but I can't.'

She got up and left the room. Somerville sighed and followed her out.

Raven looked at his companions, all currently examining their hands, their feet or the rug on the floor as they sat in awkward silence. He decided to try and make use of the time.

'I understand you've recently returned to Edinburgh,' he said to Nathaniel. Sarah had told him this much, which was why he thought Todd's letter might have made reference to this particular family.

Nathaniel looked up and gave him a tight smile. 'A temporary sojourn,' he said. 'Assisting my mother with our late father's estate.'

Nathaniel's accent was testament to his time in London, the raw edges of Edinburgh smoothed away.

'My condolences,' Raven said, wondering how best to enquire further. 'I believe your mother was acquainted with the late Dr Todd?'

'Yes.' Nathaniel looked a little confused by this question. 'Why?'

'I am married to Eugenie, his daughter.'

Nathaniel and his sister shared a look. Raven found he was becoming used to this: people's discomfort, not merely at the bereavement but at the nature of the death. The unspoken implications.

'I also met Mrs Gertrude Leitch recently,' Raven continued. 'Another acquaintance we have in common, I believe.'

'Yes, she sponsors our work,' Dorothy replied. 'She and her late husband have been most generous. Indispensable to the cause.'

'In that case, I'm surprised that their involvement is not better known.'

'They were never ones for public meetings,' Dorothy explained. 'Their motivations are more religious than political.'

'They accompany their minister in visiting brothels and giving out bibles to the prostitutes,' Nathaniel said, his voice replete with disapproval.

'But not to the men who visit them,' Sarah added.

'Indeed,' Dorothy agreed.

'A shameful inequality in judgement,' her brother added. Raven could see why Sarah had warmed to these people; their views neatly aligned.

Before he could ask anything further, footsteps could be heard in the hall outside, then the door to the parlour opened and

Mrs Hinchcliff reappeared, Somerville following her in and taking a seat.

'Mrs Hinchcliff has been suitably fortified,' Somerville said quietly, holding up a small hip flask then sliding it into the inside pocket of his jacket.

Mrs Hinchcliff was flushed now rather than pale, but still looked as though she would rather slit her own wrists than sit down amongst polite company and recount the sins of a previous life.

'I have reassured Mrs Hinchcliff that what is said here before you will be treated with the utmost confidentiality,' Somerville stated. 'And that any information she gives you will not be used against her.'

Everyone murmured their agreement and Mrs Hinchcliff sat down again. She looked at Somerville, who gave her a brief nod. Raven wondered what he had actually said to her, what he might have threatened her with. He looked at Sarah and hoped she was thinking the same thing.

Mrs Hinchcliff coughed a couple of times, clearing her throat.

'I was once a midwife,' she began. 'A respectable trade, and I was good at it too. Well respected. But times were hard, and I was offered money to provide additional services.'

'Additional services?' Dorothy asked.

'There are different types of brothels,' Mrs Hinchcliff continued. 'Some are on the lookout for fresh girls. And they need to be fresh. Virginity attested by a doctor's certificate. Or a letter from a reputable midwife.'

Mrs Hinchcliff looked down, worrying at a bit of rough skin on the palm of her hand. Then she looked up again, emboldened. It was as though once started she could not stop what was coming out.

'A premium is paid for those who are attractive, with good manners and so on. Good girls, you see. That's what some men have an appetite for. And there are women paid to find them. For commission. Half paid on delivery, half when she's confirmed pure.

'A lot of the time it's young girls from the country, arriving for a respectable job in the city, caught coming off the coach or at the train station. Some are promised a position and installed in service in what appears to be a nice house, unaware of what it really is until it's too late. They're never allowed to go outside alone, and if they ask to leave, they're told they must serve out their term, or that they owe rent. Most are of tender age, too young to understand what's happening to them. But once they've been had, well, there's really no hope for them. Their character gone, no money, no friends, no means of escape.'

'But what about the charitable societies who seek to reclaim these girls?' Sarah asked.

Mrs Hinchcliff scoffed. 'I know of a young girl, twelve years old, sold for twenty pounds to a clergyman who used to come to the bawdy house to distribute his tracts and pamphlets.' She looked round at them all, defiant now. 'No disrespect to present company,' she said, 'but some of these do-gooders are not all they seem.'

'We must write to other campaigners,' Dorothy said as soon as they were outside. 'Write to Members of Parliament with the details of what we have learned here today.'

'We're talking about rape, aren't we?' Sarah said.

Raven met her eye and nodded. She had a look about her that he knew well, knew to be wary of. Sarah on a mission.

'People need to be made aware of what's going on,' she said. 'It can't be allowed to continue.'

'What we've heard today,' Raven said, 'it ought to be enough to raise all hell.'

'And yet it does not even rouse the neighbours,' Somerville replied.

Raven thought he saw Sarah's expression harden in response to this, and a small, craven part of himself rejoiced at it. Surely she would see now what kind of a man he was: plying that poor woman with booze, forcing her to talk to them, and now hinting that any efforts to change things would be met with apathy and doomed to fail. And that he had first-hand knowledge of the whole thing seemed obvious.

'Well, we can't just ignore it,' Sarah said, addressing Somerville directly. 'We have to do something. We should go to the newspapers.'

'The newspapers won't touch it,' said Dorothy grimly.

There was a moment's disconsolate silence before Raven intervened.

'There's one that might.'

Sarah looked at him with an appreciative smile. He hoped Somerville had spotted it.

'The *Capital*,' she said.

'Not because Sanderson is in any way honourable,' Raven clarified. 'Rather that he is less bound by the standards of respectability that would hold others back.'

'But would he help us?' Nathaniel asked.

'I think he might,' Raven replied, 'but only if we make him believe we are helping him.'

TWENTY-EIGHT

aven arrived at Queen Street in time for dinner, hoping for a quiet word with Dr Simpson as well as several glasses of decent wine and the best of Mrs Lyndsay's cooking. He was there at the doctor's request and was hoping that the summons was something to do with a medical case and not about the blackmail issue on which he had made no progress. It had caused him to wonder about the profession he was part of. He supposed that his association with Simpson led him to foster idealistic notions about the noble aims of the healing art. The reality was often rather different. When they weren't at each other's throats, it seemed doctors of all stripes were ripe for exploitation and extortion.

As Raven crossed the threshold, he realised that a quiet discussion would be out of the question. How quickly he had forgotten what Simpson's house was like. He had once heard it described as being like a hotel: 'full of doctors and their patients, visiting dignitaries and cranks of all kinds'. An accurate depiction from someone who had experienced it first-hand.

The sound of many voices emanated from the dining room, but the entrance hall itself was unusually calm. The children were less in evidence than they had once been. The eldest, David and Walter, were now at Edinburgh Academy, and of the others, Jessie was constitutionally fragile, and Jamie near blind. The fact that William and Alexander were not visible or causing an audible ruckus somewhere in the vicinity suggested they were currently being successfully wrangled by Ruth, the long-suffering and saintly nursery nurse, or had been removed from the premises entirely by their Aunt Mina, who seemed happy enough to help with the children on occasion. Mrs Simpson was less in evidence too, frequently retreating to her room with religious tracts, leaving Dr Simpson to entertain his many guests alone.

Raven entered the dining room to find an even more eclectic group than usual seated around the table. There were few he recognised, which suggested most were not medical. He found a spare seat and sat himself down, resigned to spending more time here than he had intended. Under other circumstances he might have enjoyed it. Dr Simpson had a great fondness for diverse groups of people, and had a seemingly unquenchable thirst for information and intelligence of all kinds. He was a good listener, and his ability to knowledgably discuss just about anything — medicine, archaeology, the railways, literature — often led to a crowded dining-room table at breakfast, lunch and dinner. Today's group included an archaeologist, a poet, an inventor, and a surgeon recently returned from the Crimea.

On Raven's right-hand side, the inventor was talking about a new patent and his hope that Dr Simpson would be willing to invest. Not an unreasonable aspiration. Simpson always had an ear for a new opportunity. Raven wondered if he should ask him about Todd's unidentified speculation.

To Raven's left, the army surgeon was talking about the scourge of cholera, which seemed to be causing more fatalities than any engagement with the enemy. This led to a discussion about the recent outbreak in Edinburgh, which had fortunately not reached the New Town, though the fear of it certainly had. Raven remembered the near hysteria which gripped the populace, fomented and encouraged by the coverage of the outbreak in all of the newspapers. Herbal infusions had been sipped in drawing rooms and silk scarves tied around faces, with whiffs of chloroform being suggested as a means of avoiding the pestilence while traversing the city by carriage. In the absence of sound scientific advice, people were wont to believe anything, and the fact that medical men could not make up their minds about the contagious nature of the disease or its source did not help. As for treatment, nothing in their therapeutic box of tricks seemed to make much difference.

The local ministers had not helped matters either, suggesting that the disease was a God-given, divinely ordained punishment for sin, prostitutes of course featuring specifically in the condemnation of vice in the city. One had gone so far as to write to the Home Secretary, Lord Palmerston, suggesting that the Queen declare a national day of prayer and fasting. The response was perhaps not what they had been hoping for. Palmerston reputedly demurred, saying that a few prayers were unlikely to make up for the lack of drains.

Around the table there was also talk of the latest publication by John Ruskin, something about Gothic architecture. Simpson knew Ruskin – of course he did – and had treated his wife, Effie, on several occasions.

Raven found he was having trouble concentrating on any of the conversations around him. He had too much on his mind to relax and indulge in idle chatter, and could hardly bring up the subjects of blackmail or Dr Todd's suicide. Nor could he leave, though. He would have to wait until everyone else had gone to find out what Simpson wished to discuss with him.

He was on his third cup of coffee when the last of the guests finally departed. Once they were alone, Dr Simpson wasted no time in getting down to business.

'I've received another letter,' he said. 'With a demand for payment this time.'

Raven sat back in his chair, thinking, then said, 'Should we ask Stokes about what happened to him? How he resolved the issue?'

Simpson snorted. 'I suppose we could,' he said. 'But I'm not sure we could give his answer much credence. If that man ever tells the truth, it is only by accident.'

Raven sighed. 'Can you tell me anything more specific about the threat? Are they planning to expose one of your patients? Or is this something about you?'

Simpson thought for a moment, as if calculating how much he should reveal.

'It's about the placement of a child, the offspring of a lady of high birth.'

Raven thought he could have guessed this much already. He understood Dr Simpson's reluctance to divulge confidential information, but he was struggling to know how he could help without it. He thought he should perhaps ask Sarah, and was annoyed that he hadn't considered this before now. Mrs Simpson had always played an active role in the fostering operation, keeping in touch with the fostering family, ensuring payments for the upkeep of the child were being made and received, and conveying information about the child to its mother. Sarah had helped out with this on occasion when Mrs Simpson was indisposed.

'They are threatening to reveal her name and my role in the affair,' Simpson continued.

Raven wondered about this. Simpson's role in fostering children was not exactly a secret. Why would such a revelation be a threat to him or cause upset to his wife?

Simpson shook his head. 'It's not true. But that's not the point, is it?'

What's not true? Raven thought. This was like wading through treacle. 'Perhaps you should pay,' he said, this bold suggestion the only thing he could come up with given the paucity of information he had received.

'Really?' Simpson asked, sounding surprised.

'Yes,' Raven replied. 'Why not? Tell them you'll meet their demands. Let's draw this reprobate out into the open, and find out who they are.'

TWENTY-NINE

aven emerged from 52 Queen Street into the gaslit night. He would be back at Great Stuart Street in a matter of minutes, but as he began his walk, he realised he did not want to go home. It had lifted his spirits to be among vibrant company around that dinner table, even if he had left with part of the burden of Dr Simpson's cares, but now he was left with the prospect of returning to an empty house.

He felt a need for the night not to be over. That was a need he had not felt in a very long time. Not since he became a father, not since he became a husband. He thought of his friend Henry, who was rightly wary of what he described as Raven's 'perverse appetite for mayhem'. Was that what he was feeling? He did not think so, or perhaps merely hoped not. The feeling of want was troublingly familiar, but *what* he wanted was altogether less clear.

He felt restless and alone. There was a frustration in him, a hunger. He felt anger at the faceless man who was tormenting Dr Simpson, and at the dead man whose secrets were tearing his life apart.

He knew he would not sleep. He would be happy for once to be kept awake by Jamie having a restless night, or Clara's crying, but neither of these things awaited him. He needed a sense of purpose. Or was he merely seeking a sense of danger? Either way, he found himself heading east instead of west, and was soon crossing the North Bridge into the foetid labyrinth of the Old Town, in search of the one person he could usefully deal with at this time of the night.

He walked down the High Street towards the Canongate, passing a wretched-looking female, stick-thin and gaunt, walking on the arm of a young man in a shooting jacket and cap. She had the slow and deliberate gait of one who has had more than her fill of whisky, but Raven knew that most such unfortunates could not ply their trade without it. In years she was not so old, but there was no expression of youth in her hard features, course paint where adolescent bloom should be.

The windows were dark in the address he sought, but he could hear activity within. The newspapers were printed at night to be sold in the morning.

He went down Tweeddale Close and around the back to where he could see stacks of copies of the *Capital* being loaded onto a cart by two men in overalls, their fingers black with ink. One of them noticed his arrival, regarding him long enough to decide he wasn't drunk enough to be a problem, then turning away again.

'I'm looking for Sanderson,' Raven said.

'Paper's printed,' the man replied. 'He's gone for the night.'

Raven cursed. He was about to turn and leave when the man spoke again.

'Though gone doesnae mean turned in.'

'Where would I find him?'

'Och, he could be in any one of a dozen spirit shops.' The man gave him a gap-toothed grin. 'But a shilling might narrow the list.'

Raven reached into his pocket. There wasn't much money there, though what little there was brought satisfaction for the manner of its earning. It would not begin to fill the massive hole left by Cameron Todd, but at least there was more of it every day.

He flipped the man a coin and was given a name. Raven knew the place. Indeed, Raven had known most such places from growing up here, both the taverns and the night-houses where drink was sold illegally after the licensed premises had closed up. He had known the faces of many who drank in them too, be they thieves, fellow students or working women. He had befriended one of these last, a girl called Evie. He liked to say 'befriended'; he had paid her like everyone else paid her, but not everyone else waited around afterwards. Not everyone was invited to spend the night talking, sharing his naive notions of helping her escape. She had indulged him in his talk. Made him believe he could help her.

They had spoken of imagined futures, seldom the past. It never occurred to him to ask how she came to be in her position, though he remembered her hinting that she had once plied her trade somewhere finer, a 'dress house', she had called it. 'Furnished like a palace. But even in there, you knew you were one wrong step from walking the Cowgate.'

Raven was heading back up the High Street, bound for Blackfriars Wynd. Ahead of him on the pavement he saw the same poor creature again, on her own now. Her dress was in pieces, barely holding together. She had perhaps pawned whatever else might have kept out the cold to pay for a different kind of warmth, her bosom almost bare and her feet stuffed into a pair of old bauchles. She became animated when she saw him, and Raven braced himself for the desperate offer of the only thing she had to sell. But that was not her question.

'Sir, might you help with my friend Mary?' she pleaded. 'She's collapsed nearby with a fever and I dinnae ken what to do. I need to get her back to her bed, but I havenae the strength.'

'I am a doctor,' he told her. 'Where is she?'

Her face lit up with surprise, though her eyes remained tired and drunk. 'Hyndford's Close,' she said. 'Just here. Please hurry.'

The close was only yards away. She led him down the narrow passage, which was almost in complete darkness. Most of the windows above him were black, none having any glass in them or even frames, long since ripped out for firewood. He could see more of a glow ahead where the close opened out into a courtyard.

'Please, Doctor, this way.'

Despite the darkness there was an urgency to her gait, in contrast to her drunken meandering before she had noticed him. That was the first indication something was wrong.

She glanced slightly to her left as she entered the courtyard, which told him precisely *what* was wrong just a moment too late. Even as his thoughts were in train, he felt a hand upon his throat and saw a cudgel raised in the gloom. He had been lured down here to be beaten and robbed by her fancy man, the one he had seen her with a few minutes ago.

But Raven was not their normal prey. For one thing he was fairly sober, and for another he had grown up around these alleys. Most significantly, their normal prey did not have a perverse appetite for mayhem. An appetite he had been given the opportunity to feed.

Raven deflected the cudgel with one arm and sent his other fist into his assailant's chest. He felt something crack. A rib. The man staggered back into what little light there was, his hat falling from his head. Raven could see him properly now. He was younger than Raven, barely twenty if he was that, and as starved-looking as his girl. He fell to the cold ground, writhing in pain. Raven felt an inundation of the anger and frustration that had risen in him before, in need of an outlet. He had been looking for some monster to slay, some foe to vanquish. This was not it.

Raven wrested the cudgel with little resistance and spun around, conscious that sometimes these girls had been trained in pugilism, and that there were some who carried blades. This specimen would not have had the strength to lift one. She crouched down to check on her man, already weeping.

Raven felt the anger turn into something else. Sadness. Pity. He crouched down alongside the girl, dropping the cudgel to the flagstones and reaching into his pocket. He pressed the remainder of his coins into the young man's hand.

'Spend some on bread before you buy more whisky,' he said. 'If you do need a doctor, I can be found at Great Stuart Street. And I don't always charge.'

Even in the poor light, Raven could see the young man's expression, looking up at him with pain, confusion, disbelief. Raven was feeling two of those things himself. Stepping out of the close he could not quite understand his own actions. Then he realised that what he had needed more than anything in his anger, in his hurt, was to be the opposite of those things.

He'd needed to help someone. To heal someone.

THIRTY

aven found Sanderson in an establishment on Blackfriars Wynd known as the Coffin, ostensibly for the shape of the premises, but as much perhaps for how it portended many of its patrons' imminent destination. The gaslighting was off, probably because it hadn't been paid for in some time. The surprise was that it had ever been installed in this chamber at all. Illumination was provided by candles melting into the necks of ginger-beer bottles, giving about as much light as Raven thought was wise; he wasn't sure how much detail he wanted to see of the fixtures or the clientele.

He could see Sanderson at a rough-hewn table, in conversation with another man, though Raven quickly ascertained he was not so much talking to as being talked at. The man looked drunk, but Sanderson's eyes were the more glazed from listening to him.

As Raven progressed into the room, he heard voices rise in growing anger. He turned to his right, where two men were squaring up, or more accurately swaying closer on mutually unsteady feet. The nearer of them grabbed one of the candle-holder bottles for a weapon. Raven saw the proprietor move from behind the bar at remarkable speed. He grappled the aggressor from the back, causing him to drop the bottle, which hit the floorboards with a heavy but hollow chime. The proprietor then ran the drunk out to the street, leaving him on the pavement in a daze. Raven was fairly sure he dipped the man's pockets while he lay there, though he doubted he would have found much. On his way back he told the other quarrelling party that he was on his last warning. 'We don't want the polis in here, sure,' he said, eliciting a woozy placatory gesture in response.

Raven reached Sanderson's table, where the journalist appeared as grateful as he did surprised to see him.

'We'll have to conclude this another time, Tommy. I have business with this gentleman.'

Tommy looked Raven up and down, a flicker of curiosity indicating that he didn't seem as though he belonged here. Raven took it as a compliment. The man went off in search of someone else to talk at.

'Dr Raven. A timely intervention. Twenty minutes of how the Jews are in control of everything. I should be putting it in my paper, apparently. Take a seat.' Sanderson made a subtle signal which was picked up by the proprietor even in the gloom. 'Fetch Dr Raven a whisky, please. A Highland whisky,' he added.

Raven was grateful for the distinction, a coded instruction to get the good stuff, but after his encounter with Magnus Cunningham he was wary of what might be implied. He shook it off. If Sanderson had any inkling about Raven's provenance, he would have played that card by now. Besides, he had a more immediate worry.

Raven made a gesture of patting his pockets. 'I am financially embarrassed,' he said.

'So I've heard. But fair's fair. You stood me a few whiskies at Dalton's. Whether you wanted to or not.'

The proprietor returned with a bottle and a fresh glass, or what passed for a fresh glass in here.

Raven recalled the altogether more salubrious circumstances in which they had first met, at a garden party hosted by Sir Ainsley Douglas at his Crossford House estate. Raven had subsequently sought Sanderson out in hostelries favoured by journalists, but even those seemed palatial compared to the Coffin. Sanderson still dressed as though attending a society event, his appearance fastidious to the point of dandified, making him all the more incongruous in these surroundings.

Raven took a sip, wincing at the burn. He didn't want to know what the other stuff tasted like. 'I'm guessing you're not flush either if this is where you're drinking,' he said.

'There are stories and sources to be found here. Reporters who would not condescend to patronise such an establishment will miss them. Besides, the Ship Tavern shut an hour ago. Now, to what do I owe the honour? For you to seek me out at this hour and this venue would indicate that you must want something, and want it badly.'

'Quite the opposite. Though I came with empty pockets I am not empty-handed. My friend Miss Fisher, with whom you are acquainted, has fallen in with the Society for the Suppression of Vice, and they have a story they would like to see told.'

'What kind of story?' Sanderson replied wearily. 'Another of their meetings disrupted with cayenne pepper? Speakers sworn at by rowdy medical students?'

'An account of this city's trade in virgins. A story your competitors refuse to print for reasons of decency, and yet it is their refusal that allows it to fester. Young girls are arriving in the city on the promise of a respectable situation, only to find themselves diverted or abducted. Then imprisoned. Then raped. Their virtue stolen and sold as a commodity.'

'I thought you had news,' Sanderson said. 'These are rumours.' As he spoke, his countenance remained blank, but Raven could tell he was putting effort into keeping it this way. Every conversation with Sanderson was not merely a transaction, but a negotiation.

'Not rumours,' Raven said. 'I can get you first-hand testimony. The most gruesome confessions of a penitent procuress in need of absolution.'

Sanderson said nothing for a moment, taking a sip of his whisky. 'What's her name?'

That was when Raven knew he had him. He was interested: he just didn't want Raven to appreciate quite how interested.

'We'll get to that,' Raven told him. 'But I'd hate you to think you were in my debt.'

'What do you want in return?'

'What do you know of blackmail in this city?'

Sanderson's normally inscrutable expression was sharply defensive. 'What are you suggesting?'

'There is no point in acting like you're being impugned. I know that when you were the editor of the *Courant*, your value to the late Ainsley Douglas was often in the stories you did *not* publish, for the threat of it bent people to your master's will. Some would call that blackmail.'

'And they would be wrong, for there was no money involved. The term derives from money, not letters, for your information.' He took another sip of whisky, eyeing Raven across the table. 'You're talking about Cameron Todd.'

Raven had forgotten that with this man, every question you asked told him something about yourself. He felt a degree of relief, for if Sanderson thought he meant Todd, there was no danger of him thinking about Simpson.

'Have you heard anything?'

Sanderson shook his head. 'Much as I would like to dangle a nugget before you, I have heard nothing, and there is a good reason why not. I don't doubt there is blackmail in the city, but by its very nature it remains hidden. For who would confide that they are being blackmailed? To do so is to confess that you have a secret shame. Are you asking if I know Cameron Todd's secret shame?'

Raven nodded reflexively, disguising his fear that Sanderson might detect that *he* knew it, or at least what it might be. He was not entirely sure he succeeded.

'Again, I cannot help you,' Sanderson said. 'But I can help your friend, so give me the name of this procuress and I will seek her out tomorrow.'

'Not in exchange for two don't knows. Let's try again. What can you tell me about Barrington Leitch?'

Sanderson shrugged. 'That's a very broad question, Dr Raven. Perhaps you would care to narrow it down.'

This suited Raven. It was not Leitch he was primarily interested in, but he did not want Sanderson to realise that.

'You asked me recently whether I knew anything about Reginald Dalton's refusal to sell his hotel to Magnus Cunningham. I have since heard a rumour that Leitch might have been an investor in Cunningham's proposed venture. I put this to an associate of Leitch who suggested it highly unlikely on the grounds that Leitch disapproved of the man. I was wondering whether you knew why that might be.'

Even in the gloom of guttering candlelight Raven could see the glint in Sanderson's eye. He was not so disciplined as to be able to disguise that he had something.

'For that, I'm going to need more than what you've brought me.'

'Don't push it,' Raven replied. 'This story will be the making of your newspaper and we both know it.'

'A sad old woman's testimony might raise a few eyebrows, but it will not draw many tears. For this story to really take off, I would need the voices of the girls.'

Instinctively, Raven knew he was right, just as Flint had been in his cynicism. But if a newspaper told the stories of the victims, in their own words, that really would rouse the neighbours.

'Then tell me what you know about Leitch and Cunningham, and I will deliver those too.'

Sanderson pretended to be weighing this up, but Raven knew they had a deal. The journalist finished his whisky and signalled for another. Then he glanced either side and lowered his voice.

'Cunningham owns some hotels which are just as they appear. But he owns other establishments catering to select patrons, if you catch my drift.'

'Brothels,' Raven replied. As he spoke, he realised that he felt little surprise that his uncle's business should not be quite as he presented it.

'I believe the more polite term is "house of assignation",' Sanderson said. 'Or in this case, a dress house, a very exclusive enterprise.'

'I've met Cunningham. He speaks with an odd accent and he looks like a sailor. I assume he has a colourful past.'

Sanderson seemed amused by this. 'A sailor? Aye, he's certainly spent some time aboard ships. But that's because he was transported to Australia. He made his way back though, somehow the richer for it. So I can only imagine someone else is correspondingly poorer.'

Now it made sense. Magnus had been transported. That was what his mother had meant when she referred to someone having 'gone the same way as Andrew's brother'.

'And what of Leitch. Are you saying he knew about the brothels, or about the transportation?'

Sanderson affected a pious air. 'As you know, Leitch was a demonstrably religious man. He and his wife engaged in missionary work among the ladies of the street.'

'He was also funding the Edinburgh Society for the Suppression of Vice, who are campaigning against the prostitution trade,' Raven said, beginning to wonder now whether Magnus had a reason to want Leitch dead.

'Yes, one way or another he spent a lot of money in that particular area,' Sanderson said. He had that glint in his eye again.

'What am I missing?'

The proprietor arrived at the table and refilled both their glasses. Sanderson waited until he was gone before he resumed speaking.

'Barrington Leitch was a man of, not so much hidden depths as hidden shallows. I believe you've met some of his children.'

Raven wondered how he knew this. 'Only his daughter, Alice. I treated her a few days ago.'

'No, I mean you encountered several of them at Bonnington Mills.'

Sanderson gave him a nasty smile and took another sip of his dram.

Raven needed another sip himself. What had been dredged up from the canal at Bonnington Mills remained a memory that forever haunted his sleep. Dozens of tiny corpses, starved or poisoned by a baby-farmer who had been paid ostensibly to look after them, but in truth to dispose of them. Many of them the children of prostitutes.

'Who knows this?'

'Not his wife, obviously. Many a hoor knows, but their golden rule is you never talk about who your clients are, or you'll soon find you don't have any. I'm sure he paid well. He certainly paid often.'

'His piety was a blind?'

'He found it advantageous to be perceived that way. All those walks among the fallen, handing out bibles. Leitch was praised for taking the time to talk to them when others would not sully themselves. But were you to observe you might notice he only spoke to the pretty ones. Like he was perusing a menu.'

'You're sure about this?'

'I can tell you this now because he's dead. But if you would indulge my alliteration, he was the most prolific patron of prostitutes from Polmont to Prestonpans. Or in the common tongue, the biggest hoormaister in all Edinburgh.'

THIRTY-ONE

Sarah was working in silence, trying to determine what she was feeling.

She was performing a bimanual examination of the uterus, the patient asleep – under the influence of chloroform – on Raven's consulting room examination table. Sarah closed her eyes, trying to visualise the structures between her palpating fingers.

'Assess the uterine size,' Raven said. 'Determine if anteverted or retroverted. Note mobility and shape. Does it feel normal to you?'

Sarah opened her eyes and looked at him. 'Hard to say given that I don't know what normal feels like.'

'Is it smooth?'

Sarah closed her eyes and concentrated again. 'No. I can feel a lump, I think.'

'Good. Yes. A fibroid.'

Sarah withdrew her hands while Raven jotted something down in his casebook. She looked at the patient, who remained blissfully unaware of what was going on. She wondered what the patient would have said had she known. She might well tolerate Sarah asking questions and even performing a rudimentary examination – taking the pulse or listening to the chest – but would likely draw the line at her doing anything more. Sarah disliked the secrecy but what other option did she have?

If anyone found out what they were doing – that Raven was teaching and training her as he would a medical apprentice – there would be repercussions. Nonetheless, Raven had not needed much persuading, agreeing to provide Sarah with a medical education (of sorts) in exchange for her funding the establishment of his practice. Emily Blackwell seemed to be under the impression that Sarah's reluctance to travel abroad in search of a medical education was down to something or someone holding her back, but she could not have been further from the truth. Raven was not holding her back; he was helping to propel her forward. If this was as close as she could get to being a medical practitioner in her own right, she was happy to accept it for the time being.

Sarah washed and dried her hands, picked up her pen and began to write in her own notebook.

'What is the treatment?' she asked.

'Larger tumours sometimes require excision, but this one is small. An iron tonic should suffice.'

Sarah noted down what had been said, one eye on the patient, who was beginning to rouse. The room was quiet, with only the sound of her pen nib scratching the paper and the patient's breathing. The house was quiet too, Raven's housekeeper having finished for the day.

Sarah became aware of Raven looking at her.

'What?' she asked.

'Just thinking.'

'About what?'

'Dr Simpson's fostering arrangements.'

Sarah put her pen down, immediately suspicious. 'What's got you thinking about that?'

Raven ignored the question, asked another. 'You used to help Mrs Simpson with the letters, didn't you?'

'I did. I wrote out what she dictated to me when she didn't feel up to writing herself. And there was a register kept of monies paid.'

'Did you ever notice anything that struck you as suspicious in any way?'

'Suspicious?' Now Sarah really was curious about Raven's interest. 'The whole thing was steeped in mystery. If you are looking for specifics, I can't give you any. I didn't even know who the letters were addressed to. Although I do know that Mrs Simpson has been paying for the upkeep of a boy. Twelve pounds a year since 1845.'

Raven, who had clearly been trying to affect an air of nonchalance, was unable to keep the surprise from his face at this revelation.

'What's this about?' she asked again.

Raven leaned back in his chair, put his hands behind his head and sighed. 'When I find out I'll let you know.'

Raven was staring out of his consulting-room window, thinking. Thin shafts of sunlight were penetrating the ever-present low cloud, the sudden brightness making his head ache. His conversation with Sanderson the night before had been informative but had come at a cost. Gone were the days when he could consume a skinful and then function normally the next day.

His conversation with Sarah was also troubling him. Why was Jessie Simpson paying for the upkeep of a child? That usually fell to the child's father or mother. And what was the secret about himself that Simpson would not share? That same memory came back to him once more: seeing Simpson with a woman and young child through a window, looking more like a doting father than a visiting physician. A meeting that Simpson's coachman, Angus, had tried to keep secret, that Raven was not supposed to know about. Did it mean anything? Raven wasn't sure then and it didn't seem any less suspicious now, but he knew better than to jump to any conclusions. He needed more than a memory to go on.

Angus evidently knew more about the professor than Raven did, but he could hardly ask him sensitive questions about his employer. Even if he knew the answers he would be unlikely to tell Raven. Simpson's employees were loyal to a fault, as Raven knew from having been one.

He wasn't getting anywhere with this, much as he wasn't making progress with his enquiries into Todd's death. Simpson had rejected the idea that he accede to his blackmailer's demands; for the time being at least. He had yet to receive details about how the payment should be made, he said, and was disinclined to pay anyway. His intention was to ignore the correspondence for a while yet. 'They won't reveal anything until all other options are exhausted,' Simpson had said. 'We'll make them wait. They'll become impatient and then desperate, and desperate people make mistakes. Either that or they'll give up on the whole enterprise.'

Raven thought that this was wishful thinking at best, naivety at worst, but knew better than to push when Simpson had already made up his mind.

The sound of Sarah coming back into the room roused him from his introspection. She bore a letter. He put out his hand for it.

'It's for me,' she said. 'Came this morning and I haven't had a chance to read it yet.'

She sat down heavily in the chair opposite, opened the letter and scanned the contents.

'It's from Connie Banks,' she said, 'asking for an update as to my progress and imploring me to keep looking.'

'I still don't know why the woman thinks she can task you with this,' Raven said. 'You don't owe these people anything. You barely know them.'

'They're family, I suppose.' Sarah didn't sound convinced of this herself.

'That's as may be, but for all we know this Annabel has run off with the love of her life, is now happily ensconced in her marital home and delighted to be away from her mother.'

'That's true,' Sarah conceded. 'Annabel could be perfectly happy, the lack of communication with her mother a conscious choice. Or she could have come to harm. She could be lying dead somewhere or being held against her will as Mrs Hinchcliff described. I can't do anything about the first two options but perhaps I can do something if it's the third. And anyway, this is about so much more than Annabel now.'

Raven knew this was true. Their investigations, such as they were, had uncovered some truly disturbing facts. This was not about one girl.

All right. For argument's sake, say she has fallen victim to entrapment. How would you even go about finding her?'

'Mrs Hinchcliff said that these girls are often picked up at the railway station.'

'You can hardly camp out there, hoping to catch them in the act, and then ask them politely where Annabel has been taken.'

Sarah scowled at him. 'I appreciate that it's not a practical option, but there is no need to be facetious.'

Raven held up his hands in apology. 'You're right. I'm sorry.' He smiled at her, hoping for a softening of her features, worried that he might have soured her mood for the rest of the day. He didn't think that he could bear it if she withdrew from him too. Fortunately, she returned his smile and adopted a more concilia- tory tone herself.

'What do you suggest?' she asked.

'The brothels themselves.'

'I doubt anyone would talk to me there. I've been to one, remember, on Melbourne Place. The girls are wary of strangers asking questions. And Melbourne Place aside, we don't even know where they all are, do we? They don't advertise and we're unlikely to find them listed in the Post Office Directory.'

Raven nodded in acknowledgement, then sighed and looked down at his hands. 'Which leads to our other problem.'

'And what is that?'

'Sanderson will only publish if we can get some of the girls to talk to us.'

'How are we going to do that?'

'I wish I knew.' He looked at Sarah for a moment. 'If Sanderson does publish, it could be cataclysmic.'

'That's the point, isn't it?'

'My point is that it's likely to cause trouble, and specifically for you if your involvement becomes known.' He was thinking about Dorothy Butler and the abuse Sarah said she'd had to put up with. 'You'll be exposing yourself to risk, and for what?'

'You sound like Somerville.'

Raven rankled at the very mention. 'I am nothing like Somerville.'

There was a moment's silence between them, the name hovering like an unwelcome guest.

'What we need are girls who feel they are free to talk,' Sarah said eventually. 'Like Mrs Hinchcliff: people who are finished with the business.'

Raven sat up a little straighter, realising a possibility. 'And who maybe have an axe to grind.'

'Do you have something in mind?'

'The Lock Hospital,' he said.

Sarah's smile returned, a balm for his aching head.

'I suppose they might be amenable,' she mused. 'Cast out for becoming diseased. Bearing the consequences of what's been done to them.'

'Though there is an obstacle to our admittance.'

'What?'

'Not what but who. The man in charge, Hedley Stokes.'

'Is he very strict? I suppose he would have to be, given the nature of the establishment.'

'It's more about the nature of the man. He's likely to be obstructive simply because he can.'

'Can't we appeal to his better nature?'

Raven snorted. 'He's a pompous, self-satisfied arse. So, no. There is no better nature to appeal to.'

'Well, then, there's your answer.'

Raven's confusion must have shown.

'If we can't appeal to his good nature,' Sarah explained, 'then we appeal to his vanity. Tell him Sanderson wants to run a big report on the great work he is doing.'

This was such an ingenious suggestion that he wanted to kiss her.

That and a thousand other reasons.

THIRTY-TWO

he world of Edinburgh medicine was replete with redoubtable characters and formidable individuals; strong personalities and towering intellects. Hedley Stokes, as far as Raven could surmise, was none of these things.

The fact that he was in charge of the Lock Hospital was an indication of the status with which the position was regarded, in that nobody else wanted it. But in compensating for this, Stokes acted as though it were the most coveted situation in the city, conferring great power and status. Raven was therefore not looking forward to having to feign interest in the man, but needs must.

Sarah had been absolutely correct in her assertion that his vanity was the key to their success. When it had been suggested to him that the *Capital* might like to publicise the good work he was doing, he had seized the opportunity. His cooperation had not come without stipulations, however. Raven as a medical professional and Sarah as a member of the Society for the Suppression of Vice would be admitted, but he had drawn the line at Sanderson, a decision which Raven had to grudgingly admit was to his credit. Sanderson had not been happy with the prospect of second-hand information, until Raven pointed out that the girls might be more forthcoming to Sarah than to a journalist. Either way, they both knew that the story was more important than who it was first told to.

As Raven and Sarah walked along High School Yards, Raven marvelled at her willingness to be drawn into other people's problems. Raven often felt he had worries enough of his own. He also felt like a bit of a fraud. His interest here today was not so much the plight of fallen women but what information he might be able to extract from Stokes about his recent experience of blackmail.

'Are you sure you want to do this?' he asked. 'You can trust me to ask the relevant questions if you'd rather not go in.'

'You should know me better than that, Will Raven,' Sarah said, a smile indicating she had taken no offence at the suggestion. 'In all my years at Queen Street, I'm sure I will have seen and dealt with worse.'

'I wouldn't count on it,' he replied.

Sarah's experiences had largely been confined to Dr Simpson's clinic and occasional visits to the Maternity Hospital with himself. The poor souls she had seen there were as nothing to the destitute wretches that swarmed the closes and wynds of the Old Town and who were likely to be the sort of women being treated here.

They crossed Surgeon's Square towards the Lock Hospital, a small building within the grounds of the Infirmary, but situated at the back of the Surgical Hospital, where the smaller Burns and Fever Hospitals were also placed. Tucked away in a far corner like an afterthought, Raven supposed it ranked below even these.

Raven had half expected Stokes to greet them at the door, but they were met by a functionary who escorted them to the great man's office. Stokes was seated behind a desk from which he did not get up as they entered. It was a small room but it had been decorated with care, little expense having been spared on the desk, the upholstered chairs and the wallpaper, not to mention the bookcases and their contents. Given the on-going difficulty in raising subscriptions for this lowly hospital, Raven wondered at the decision to spend money here rather than on more staff, or even some new linen for the beds.

Stokes smiled with quiet satisfaction as he noticed them taking it all in.

'You like my office?' he asked.

'It's . . . remarkable,' said Sarah, a diplomatic answer if ever there was one.

'I believe that it is an important part of my role here to elevate the place, to improve the impression most people have of it. I'm under no illusions that these lock wards are viewed with disdain by some of my medical brethren, but the work we do here is important, perhaps more important than any other branch of the healing art.'

Raven refrained from pointing out that the disdain was as much reserved for the doctor in charge as for the institution itself. He nonetheless failed to suppress a scornful expression, and Stokes noticed.

'Impressions are important, Dr Raven. People need to see that everything here is of a high standard. We must make our donors feel that this hospital is a suitable repository for their charity. I said this much to James Paget when I visited London last month.'

'You visited St Bartholomew's?'

'Yes, I was given a private tour.'

Raven found this hard to believe. He very much doubted that someone of Sir James Paget's standing would have any interest in Hedley Stokes or the fortunes of the lock wards in Edinburgh.

'Have a seat,' Stokes said.

Sarah sat down on a plushly upholstered chair and Raven reluctantly followed suit, concerned for how long he might have to sit and listen to the man.

'Can I smell ether?' Raven asked. There was a distinct scent of it coming from somewhere in the room; possibly Stokes himself. Raven knew that the pungent – and highly flammable – chemical tenaciously adhered to clothing, one of many reasons Simpson had been determined to find a better means of rendering patients unconscious. Sarah nodded, wrinkling her nose, confirming that she could smell it too.

'Ah, yes,' Stokes said, displaying unexpected coyness. 'Well observed. I have been working on a new tonic, one likely to outsell Gregory's Powders once perfected.'

'In here?' Raven asked sceptically, unable to imagine this office a suitable location.

'At home. I have my own laboratory. But enough about me,' he announced. Raven hoped that this was a prelude to his showing them to one of the wards, but he was to be disappointed. 'Let me tell you more about the institution itself. The number of cases treated here in the last year,' Stokes began. 'Can you hazard a guess?'

Raven hated this sort of question, but fortunately Stokes didn't wait for a reply.

'Six hundred and twenty-six. Three hundred and thirty-one of these were cases of gonorrhoea, and the rest syphilis.'

Raven had to admit the numbers were considerable, more than he would have thought.

'What age are the women who come here?' Sarah asked. Stokes looked at her as though he had only just realised she was still there, his attention having been firmly focused on Raven.

'Most are between the ages of fifteen and twenty-five,' he replied. 'Some are the victims of misplaced affection; others are born into a world of vice. But here we work on the principle that among those who have sinned there will be many who, by kind treatment, strict discipline and religious instruction, may be reclaimed from a vicious mode of life and restored to society.'

Raven recalled Dr Simpson's objection to the Lock Hospital's emphasis on religious instruction, his feeling being that the focus should be placed firmly on the treatment of the diseases the women presented with.

'Are you still using mercury?' Sarah asked. Stokes again gave her a quizzical look, as though unused to women asking him questions; and even less used to them being medically informed questions. His expression softened, replaced with an oleaginous smile, as though suddenly deciding to humour her.

'We are currently moving away from the old system of administering mercury in every case,' he replied. 'Although it still has its place.' He got to his feet, presumably to forestall any further questions from Sarah. 'Time for the tour,' he announced.

Raven silently thanked Sarah for her insatiable curiosity. It had probably saved them at least another half-hour of Stokes's pontificating.

THIRTY-THREE

arah had hoped that she and Raven would be left alone to interview the patients on the hospital's wards, but the insufferable Stokes had not finished with them. The man wished to inject himself into every story, every conversation. Whenever Sarah ventured to ask a question, even of the most innocuous sort, the girl's tentative answer would be immediately interrupted by Stokes answering for her and thus directing attention back to himself. But even if they were permitted to answer for themselves, it was clear that the girls would not be candid while he stood at their shoulders.

Fortunately, Raven decided to intervene. 'Dr Stokes, I wondered if I might have a word in private. There are matters I would like to discuss that are not for delicate ears.'

Stokes looked at Sarah, then touched the side of his nose in a conspiratorial gesture that she found deeply annoying. 'Indeed,' he said to Raven. 'I quite understand.'

Stokes began making his way to a corner of the ward, intent on finding a place out of earshot, but Raven strode out into the corridor. The sense of relief when Stokes followed him was palpable, from the girls as much as from Sarah herself. It wasn't just that he was the authority in this place, it was also the fact that it was utterly draining to be in the company of someone so relentless in pulling the focus of attention onto himself.

But though the two young women had said next to nothing while Stokes was present, once he was gone it appeared they still had little to say.

'What's it like here?' Sarah asked. 'Are you treated well?'

The two looked at each other as though deciding how forthcoming they should be. One shrugged a scrawny shoulder.

'It's all right,' she said.

Her friend scoffed and looked round, taking in the row of mainly empty beds. 'Not exactly Tait's Hotel, is it?'

'Better than we're used to, though.'

The two of them looked as though they weren't used to much. Both had the emaciated appearance of the chronically underfed. One had an old bruise around her left eye.

The bruised one looked Sarah up and down, trying to gauge what her agenda might be. 'You another one come to save our souls? If that's the case, I'll save you the trouble. Mine's not worth saving.'

'I'm not here about that,' Sarah said.

'What are you here about?'

'I'm trying to find someone.'

'Oh, aye.'

'A young girl who came to Edinburgh about a month ago and hasn't been heard from since.'

'You think she's fallen on hard times?'

'Possibly.'

'Well, it's not like we all know each other.' The bruised woman lifted her hand to scratch her head, revealing rough reddish-brown spots on the palm of her hand, the characteristic rash associated with syphilis. She noticed Sarah looking and dropped her hand back down into her lap. 'I don't think we can help you,' she said. 'Now if you don't mind, we're supposed to be resting.' She scowled at Sarah and then gave her groin a vigorous scratch for good measure, presumably hoping that if the scowl didn't send Sarah on her way, the fear of fleas would be the clincher.

Sarah took the hint.

THIRTY-FOUR

'erhaps I might see more of the place while we talk,' Raven suggested. Having got Stokes out of the ward, he wanted to keep him away from Sarah as long as he could, or at least as long as he could tolerate. 'It would be best if the majority of the account came from someone qualified to understand the work you do here,' he added.

'Quite,' Stokes replied. 'Let me show you some of the non-clinical aspects of our rehabilitation.'

Stokes's accent was English, though Raven did not have the experience to identify it more specifically. Wherever it was he had worked before, they probably had a celebration when he left.

'Allow me to say that I was most sorry to hear about the death of your father-in-law,' Stokes continued. 'Dr Todd and I were good friends.'

Raven had only ever heard Todd mention Stokes disparagingly. He could not imagine Eugenie's father having time for the man, as Cameron Todd was nothing if not a snob. He could, however, vividly imagine Stokes also claiming that Professor Simpson and he were good friends, as well as Professor Syme, Professor Miller, Professor Gregory and Professor Christison.

'Thank you,' Raven said. 'He is greatly missed.'

'We had much in common: the joys and the trials of successful practices.'

It was widely assumed that Stokes was from a wealthy background, but it was clearly important to him that people knew he had made money from medicine. Raven could not imagine how. He had been asking himself of late what properties rich patients might look for in a prospective doctor, and found it difficult to picture anyone encountering Stokes and thinking: Yes, this is the man to take care of me. For one thing, it would be difficult to tell him about your ailments while he couldn't stop talking about himself.

But to give Stokes his due, being in charge of the Lock Hospital was not an easy thing. Subscribers and board members were an opinionated lot at any hospital, expecting to exert influence in exchange for their contributions, and at an establishment like this, it would be even more pronounced. Maybe it took a personality likes Stokes's to run such a place: someone whose own self-importance made him impervious to the self-importance of the donors.

They had reached a doorway through which Raven could see several young women working in pairs to fold bedsheets.

'These are patients, not nurses,' Raven observed.

'Yes. Once they have made good their physical recovery, that is only the first part of their rehabilitation. We need to know they are disciplined and ready to be of use, so that they do not quickly find themselves back where they were when they fell.'

Stokes led him down another corridor, which Raven estimated would take them back to his office. Raven noticed that staff and patients alike would stop and clasp their hands as he passed. Stokes acknowledged them with a nod, sometimes saying their names.

'What was the medical matter you wished to discuss?' he asked.

'It was not actually medical, but sensitive,' Raven explained, waiting until a nurse had passed out of earshot. 'As you know, I am well acquainted with Dr Simpson. He confided in me that you had been subject to threats from a blackmailer.'

Stokes looked at Raven as though he had no idea what he was talking about. Then his countenance darkened into a look of regret.

'I did ask his advice regarding that, yes.'

'I gather he had little to offer. Are you still under threat or has the situation . . .?' Raven did not know how to put it.

'The situation is resolved,' Stokes told him, his voice low. 'I gave him what he asked for.'

'You paid? But how can you know he will not come back with the same threat and ask for more?'

Stokes looked confused for a moment, as though at a loss how to answer this. Surely he was not foolish enough never to have considered it.

'Because money was not the price,' he eventually said.

'What was, then? Payment in kind? Services rendered?'

'I was asked to desist from something. It was a personal matter, regarding a lady I was courting. She was the daughter of a duke, who evidently considered me unsuitable.'

'So you know who your blackmailer was?'

Stokes took a moment, glancing along the corridor as though assuring himself they were still alone.

'You must understand that my on-going regard for his daughter dictates that I do not identify him. I will not importune her family name the way he threatened to shame mine. I would have made her happy; but alas I must make do with simply not making her sad.'

As Raven listened to Stokes's wistful tone, conveying a sentiment ostensibly humble but in fact entirely self-regarding, he had an epiphany. Stokes was not merely pompous and insecure: he was a fantasist. Raven thought of his claim that he had been touring St Bartholomew's as a guest of Paget, and now this story about courting the daughter of a duke. He was a man looked down upon by others in Edinburgh and had consequently constructed a fiction of himself.

Raven recalled what Sanderson said, that to tell someone you were being blackmailed was to tell them you had a secret shame.

He had wondered, therefore, why Stokes would tell Simpson. The answer was that Simpson was esteemed and important. Quite tragically, Stokes had told him he was being blackmailed because he thought that might make himself seem more interesting. That look of apparent confusion moments ago had been something else: Stokes had forgotten telling Simpson this lie and consequently needed to come up with a second part to it.

Also, as Stokes had vividly demonstrated, he could not hear any conversation without making it about himself. Which made Raven think he must have overheard someone else talk of blackmail at the Medico-Chirurgical Society meeting. He recalled Simpson's words: *He's under the impression that there's a lot of it about.*

'I am pleased the matter has been put to rest,' Raven said. 'But tell me, have you heard of any other doctors falling prey to such threats?'

'Fortunately not,' Stokes replied curtly. 'Now, please, here is something else for the newspaper report.'

He led Raven towards a small room where a minister stood before a group of girls at a long table, each with a bible open in front of them.

'That is the Reverend Lochlan McLean. He is a trustee and gives generously of his time. The Bible has a vital role in preparing the girls for a better future.'

The minister noticed them, and introductions were made. 'There is nothing so inspiring to a penitent sinner than a story of redemption,' McLean told Raven. 'That is why eighty per cent of girls who receive this instruction do not return to vice.'

Raven was fairly sure the man had misread that statistic, or indeed inverted it, and he was inclined to ask some awkward questions when instead he became distracted by the sight of one of the girls looking up from her bible. Her head had been down while she thought McLean's eyes were on her, glancing up curiously once the men were focused on one another. When Raven saw her face, he felt an unsettling jolt of recognition. He did not know from where but the sight of her prompted troubling feelings;

an association with something deeply uncomfortable that he could not pin down. Had she been a patient? One he had failed, somehow?

It was as Stokes led him away again that it came to him: she was in one of the photographs.

His face must have betrayed him. 'Dr Raven, is all well?' Stokes enquired.

'I need to speak to one of the girls.'

'I think I have already been most accommodating in that regard. Your friend Miss Fisher is speaking to some of them still.'

'No, I mean one specifically. One of those we just saw with Reverend McLean.'

'Specifically? Can you tell me what it is regarding?'

'I don't want the girl to get into any trouble, but there is a matter about which I would like to ask her some questions.'

'As I would hope you have ascertained, we are not in the business of allowing our girls' past misdemeanours to be hung around their necks like an albatross. So please do elaborate.'

Raven took a breath. 'I believe I saw her in a photograph. I would like to know more about her involvement.'

'Why would a photograph get her into trouble?'

'It was not the kind that might be placed on one's sideboard,' Raven replied.

Stokes paused, then said, 'Part of our purpose here is to encourage these young women to put certain things behind them, and thus we do not encourage them to revisit undesirable recollections.'

'But you know of such photographs?' Raven asked. 'You understand what I am talking about?'

'Sadly it is my business to know. It is my job to help repair the damage done by men's basest appetites, Dr Raven. Though I am curious as to how *you* know about them.'

Raven wondered how he might answer this without giving anything away.

'I recently encountered such an item and have been unable to discover its provenance. It may yet shed light on a matter concerning a patient.'

Stokes considered this. Or rather, savoured it. This was what such a man lived for: exercising the power to withhold something.

'I understand,' he said. 'But I cannot have it getting out that there exists such an image of someone under my care, or the hospital having any kind of association with such practices.'

Raven had expected the refusal, but in making it about himself, Stokes had just reminded him of where his vulnerability lay.

'No, you absolutely cannot have it getting out. Which is why it would be far better were I to talk to the girl about such matters than talk to Mr Sanderson.'

Stokes's eyes flashed in annoyance, but it was an acknowledgement that Raven had him over a barrel. Raven knew he had made an enemy, though he was hardly bringing down the wrath of God, or even the wrath of Syme.

Stokes escorted him back to the Bible class, where he offered apologies to the Reverend McLean and summoned the girl from her seat. Stokes closed the door and led them down the corridor.

'We will have privacy in my office,' he said.

Raven knew he could insist that he speak to the girl alone, but in that circumstance, Stokes would most likely go back to bothering Sarah. He would have to keep him here, though it might have a dampening effect on the girl's candour.

Her name was Nell, and she looked younger than she had in the photograph, timid and shy. Raven put her at around eighteen, though she had seen a lot of life in her short time, little of it kind. When Stokes gestured for her to take a seat she looked around the office, then at the chair, as though unsure it was not some kind of test.

'Nell, Dr Raven has something he'd like to ask you about.'

Raven thought of what Sarah had said after he showed her the photographs, of how vulnerable and afraid the girls would feel to know that any man they thereafter met could have seen them.

Raven said gently, 'Nell, I believe I saw you in a photograph. A candid photograph.'

The girl looked confused. She glanced at Stokes as though for permission to answer.

'It's all right, Nell,' Stokes said. 'We appreciate that these are memories it might not be good for you to revisit.'

'What memories?' Nell whispered.

Raven wondered how to make this explicit without inflicting humiliation upon the poor girl. 'Do you recall posing for a picture?' he asked.

'Posing?'

'Remaining still for a long time, as if for an artist. With no clothes on,' he added.

She coloured now, shrinking into herself. 'Yes,' she admitted.

'Were you coerced?' Raven asked. 'Were you compelled by threats or force?'

'I was paid,' she replied. ''No' as much as they said I would get, but more than I would have got otherwise.'

'When was this?'

'Must have been nine months ago or so. Before I got sick. It was high summer, though. Had to be.'

'Why?'

'It was outdoors, in a garden, but made to look like inside. They had big sheets for background, like at the theatre.'

Raven recalled the same arrangement when he and Sarah visited Rock House, where she posed for David Hill and the late Robert Adamson.

'Where?' he asked.

'I don't know. I was taken in a carriage. A big house somewhere.'

'Who operated the camera?'

She looked confused. 'What camera?'

'To take the picture of you?'

'There was no camera. There was an artist. He sketched me.'

That was when the true vileness of it dawned on Raven. The camera must have been concealed. The girl did not even know she had been photographed.

THIRTY-FIVE

arah made for the door, wondering whether she might find someone more amenable in one of the other wards. She was beginning to doubt anyone would be willing to talk to her, with or without Stokes's smothering presence. These women had suffered and been shamed by society. Who wanted to confide in a stranger about that?

Then she heard a voice from the other side of the room.

'Whatever you're selling, I'm willing to listen.'

Sarah turned to see an older woman sitting up in a bed, her sheets folded neatly around her.

'That pair haven't been in long enough to appreciate fresh company,' the woman added.

'I'm not selling anything,' Sarah said.

'Sure you are. Repentance and salvation, is it?'

Sarah shook her head. 'No. Nothing like that. My purpose here is to learn, not to preach. I have come on behalf of the Edinburgh Society for the Suppression of Vice.'

The woman patted the low stool beside her bed. 'You've got me curious now. Sit yourself down.'

Sarah did as she was asked. The woman was older than Sarah, but probably not by much. She had some grey in her hair and a tinge of jaundice about the eyes. She was in the process of knitting something, yarn and needles moving with practised precision.

'She has us that are confined to bed knitting socks.'

'Who has?'

'Matron. Have you met her yet?'

'No.'

'Best keep it that way. She's the worst of them.'

'The worst of who?'

'The reformers. They think that a dose of mercury and a few prayers will sort us all out. They don't know the half of it.'

'That's precisely what I'm here about,' Sarah said. 'To find out the truth of what goes on. The *Capital* newspaper is going to publish it. That way it can't go on being ignored.'

The woman gave Sarah a shrewd look. 'You really think that would make a difference? That anyone would care?'

'I do,' Sarah said.

The woman put her knitting down. 'Then tell me what you want to know.'

Flo confirmed most of what Sarah had already learned. Young girls were lured into the life, violated, and ruined so that they felt they had no option but to stay where they were.

'"Against their will and without their consent",' Sarah repeated as she scribbled down Flo's testimony in her notebook.

'Sometimes without their knowledge,' Flo added.

'Without their knowledge?'

'Some of them are given a drowse. The black draught they call it. Dosed so well with laudanum or chloroform they don't know what's happened to them until they wake up the next morning, bleeding and sore. Some of them are in such a state they need to be taken to a midwife or doctor to patch them up. And they're the lucky ones.'

'The lucky ones?' Sarah felt a sudden nausea grip her stomach, unsure if she wanted to hear what was next.

'Some men wish them to be awake. They prefer to take them by force. Like them to make a bit of noise.'

Sarah felt her gorge rise, a salty rush of fluid at the back of her throat. She swallowed it down.

'But that's rape,' she said feebly.

'That's as maybe, but nobody cares about that.'

Sarah couldn't believe that such blatant criminality – a capital offence no less – would go unpunished.

'Can't the girl report it?'

Flo gave Sarah a pitying look. 'Who would she tell? The folk in charge that organise the whole thing, earning a pretty penny in the process? The police who know what goes on but turn a blind eye? And even if she did, who would believe her?'

Sarah could see the truth of this. A woman who had lost her virtue would never be believed, was destined to be viewed as a discredited witness.

'So, you're stuck there,' Flo went on, 'and you make the best of it, hoping maybe that one day you'll snare a nice rich old man who'll die on the job and leave you all his money.'

She laughed at this, but Sarah was struggling to find any humour in it.

'That or a handsome young man,' Flo continued, 'who'll keep you in fine style for his exclusive use.'

'Does that happen much?' Sarah asked.

'Don't know anyone it's happened to, to be honest, but we all live in hope. You have to, don't you? You need something to hold on to. It's either that or the drink gets you. Or the pox. And no one wants you once you're diseased.'

Sarah found she was gripping her pencil so hard she thought it might break. She had known some of this before coming here, but the raw details and the matter-of-fact way they were being discussed were making her stomach contents curdle. She understood that it was this brutal reality Raven had wished to spare her from.

Flo sighed and picked up her knitting again. 'They send us here for treatment, claiming they can save our souls if only we'd repent. I ask you, after what's been done to us, what have we to repent for?'

Sarah sat back against the wall, not knowing what else to say. She spotted a door on the far side of the ward. It looked stark, heavy and imposing.

'Where does that lead?' she asked.

Flo shook her head. 'The end of the line. No one is allowed in there – or out. It's where they keep the ones that've gone mad with it. Brains are mush. Dosed with calomel till their mouths rot and the teeth fall out of their heads.'

Sarah felt a sudden need to be away from this place. It all felt too much, too overwhelming. And what if she did provide all of these details to Sanderson, and he did publish them, would anyone care? Would anything change?

Amidst this overwhelming awfulness she realised there was something she hadn't asked, perhaps because she was reluctant to hear the answer. She closed her notebook, laid it down in her lap.

'I'm looking for someone,' she said.

'Aren't we all, dearie.'

'A girl. My niece. She was supposed to be taking up a situation as a nursemaid, but— '

'Young?'

Sarah nodded.

'A maid?'

Sarah was about to repeat her previous statement about Annabel being a nursemaid when she realised what Flo meant. She blushed at her own misapprehension, while feeling revulsion at what might have been taken – forcibly – from the girl.

'A maid. Yes.'

'Pretty?'

Sarah nodded again. 'Bright too. Clever,' she added, feeling a need to value the girl for more than her appearance.

'If she's bright, she might have found ways to delay the inevitable. Girls can make themselves useful in a house by other means, as well as having the guile to stay out of sight where possible.'

Sarah dared allow herself to hope. 'And the madams, they permit this?'

'Only for so long, while the fee ticks up. An attractive young girl, and a maid? She would fetch a price from the first man to have her. Fresh girls are always in demand.'

'But they have no choice in the matter,' Sarah said.

Flo gave her a sorrowful look, then her expression became more resolute. 'You say you'll put this in a newspaper? And people will hear the truth?'

'That's right.'

'Well, the truth is that sometimes it's worse. Sometimes the gentlemen get rough. And sometimes there are lassies you just don't see again.'

'You mean . . .?'

She clutched her knitting and nodded. 'They don't make it through the night. Bodies flung out like they're rubbish. Heard tell it happened recently. At the Castle.'

'The castle?'

'A dress house. They call it the Castle. The lassies do, anyway.'

'You worked there?'

Flo gave her a scornful, mirthless chuckle. 'The likes of me? No. Only the young and very pretty there. But I know a girl who does, Liza. A kind lassie. Comes to see me every week. She said one night, just after Easter, they were all told to stay in their rooms because of a commotion, but she peeped out the door and spied them carrying a dead body wrapped in bedclothes.' Flo shook her head solemnly. 'There had been a new girl. Pretty and bright. Kept her head down, but Liza never saw her again after that night. Poor wee thing.'

Sarah felt something inside her turn to stone.

'Did she say what the girl's name was?'

'Aye. Annabel.'

THIRTY-SIX

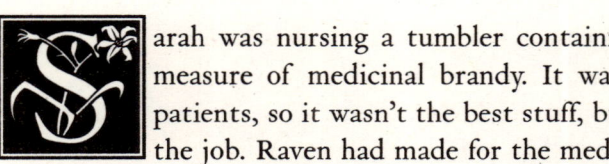arah was nursing a tumbler containing a generous measure of medicinal brandy. It was intended for patients, so it wasn't the best stuff, but it was doing the job. Raven had made for the medicine cupboard as soon as they returned to the house on Great Stuart Street, poured them both a drink, and handed Sarah hers without a word. It was quite clear what they both needed; a cup of tea was never going to be enough. Sarah knew that she should really have returned to Queen Street, but she didn't want to be with others who would not have understood her mood, and she was not capable of disguising how she felt.

She could still see Annabel standing in that Perthshire garden, still hear her singing, *Ae fareweel, and then forever! Deep in heart-wrung tears I'll pledge thee . . .* She wasn't ready to contemplate the finality of it quite yet, though she knew she could not outrun it for long.

She shivered, a chill running through her. Although the weather was unseasonably cold, she didn't think the outside temperature was responsible for how she was feeling. She wondered if she would ever be warm again. As well as cold, she felt unclean, as though by hearing about the depraved behaviour of others she had somehow become contaminated herself. She pulled her shawl tighter round her shoulders.

Raven noticed and added more coal to the fire. 'Come sit by me if you're cold,' he said.

Sarah looked over at him. After the day she'd had there was nothing she would have liked more than to sit beside him, feel the warmth of his body, rest her head on his shoulder. She wanted to feel his arms around her, feel the comfort of another's embrace. *His* embrace. But it was not possible, and she would not torture herself further by thinking about it.

'I'm all right where I am, thank you.'

Raven turned back to the fire, jabbed at it with a poker in a desultory way. The house was eerily quiet, just the spit and crackle of the fire and the ticking of the clock on the mantelpiece.

'When is Eugenie coming back?' Sarah asked.

Raven shrugged. 'She hasn't said.'

'I'm sure she just needs some time.'

He looked up at her, pain in his eyes. 'What am I going to do if she doesn't?'

Sarah wasn't sure how to answer that question. 'It won't come to that,' she said firmly. 'You're her husband, the father of her children. She'll return when she's ready. When she's had time to grieve.'

Raven said nothing, went back to staring at the fire.

'How are you managing without her?'

Raven sighed. 'I would feel better if I had made some headway in my investigations regarding her father.'

Sarah wasn't sure that Raven solving the mystery of what had happened to Cameron Todd would be the answer to his problems with Eugenie – they had been present long before her father's sudden death – but she also knew that Raven's failure to do so would probably make things worse.

'What have you found?'

'Money missing. A letter, torn up but not discarded. And the photographs.'

'What is the significance of the torn-up letter?'

'I don't know. But it was from Magnus Cunningham.'

'Cunningham? Who's he?'

Raven seemed uneasy at her question, as though not sure how to answer. 'A hotelier,' he eventually said, 'among other things. Sanderson said he has links to prostitution.'

Sarah thought about this for a moment. 'What was he writing to Todd about? Was he a patient? Or has this something to do with the missing money?'

'I don't think Todd was Cunningham's doctor, no. As to the money, I can't be sure.' Raven leaned back in his chair, swirled the brandy around in his glass. 'Dr Todd had also been upset about the death of a patient, but as the patient died at home, in his bed, of natural causes, that makes little sense. So you see I'm no further forward.'

He seemed so disconsolate that Sarah reached out, put her hand on his arm and gave it a gentle squeeze. He looked up at her, the intensity of his gaze disconcerting. Sarah felt the heat rise to her face, removed her hand and looked away. She took another sip of her brandy.

'Was Dr Todd a friend as well as a doctor to the patient who died?'

'That doesn't seem to be the case.' He drained his glass, wincing a little at the burn of the brandy as it went down. 'I had thought that they might have entered into some business together, a risky investment, as an explanation for the missing money. But the more I look the murkier things seem to get.'

'How so?'

'The patient in question is, or was, Barrington Leitch.'

'He funds the Butlers' campaign, doesn't he? Or his wife does now.'

Raven nodded. 'Yes, he was quite the moral crusader, in public. But according to Sanderson, in private he was a customer at a variety of brothels, regularly partaking of the very vice he purported to campaign against. And he was on the board of the Lock Hospital.'

Sarah reeled. That someone who purported to be campaigning against this vile trade was actually revelling in it made her feel like its tentacles were everywhere. She thought of Somerville's scorn that her quest was futile.

'Are all these things connected somehow?'

Raven shook his head. 'I don't know if I'm looking for connections that don't exist, that in an attempt to placate my wife I'm looking for answers that just aren't there. I mean, it's possible that her father did simply kill himself, for no reason other than he despaired of his present life and wished it to be over. It's a more common occurrence than people would care to admit.'

Sarah thought of her own father, the solemn gathering of men at the barn behind their house, shortly after the death of her mother.

She felt sorry for Raven. There was no way he could win. Self-murder as an explanation for Todd's death was unacceptable to Eugenie, but alternatives, if there were any, might not be any more palatable. What was she hoping for? A grand conspiracy?

'So, you have missing money, the death of a patient and the photographs.'

Raven nodded his head. 'That's about it. And I still don't know if any of it means anything.'

'Given the reaction of your wife to the photographs I would contend that they are not nothing.'

'Pales in comparison to what we heard today though, doesn't it?'

Sarah couldn't argue with this. That the naked human form should be considered shameful was anathema to her, but these photographs spoke of other, less healthy desires. Women put on display to satisfy the appetites of men. And did such an unhealthy attitude to female nudity lead to other, more unsavoury obsessions?

'I still can't believe that she is dead,' Sarah said. It was the first time she had stated it out loud, yet when Flo had said it, it had felt oddly inevitable. *Fare thee weel, thou first and fairest! Fare thee weel, thou best and dearest!*

'The shock of it has taken me by surprise,' she admitted. 'I thought I had prepared myself for the worst. I always knew that it was one of the possibilities, but it feels different, so much more devastating, when the theory of a thing and the reality collide.'

She put her glass down, didn't want to drink any more. 'What am I going to tell her mother? She won't even have a body to bury.'

'No,' Raven agreed. 'They'll have disposed of her remains as they have probably done to others' before.'

'We're no longer talking about just rape,' Sarah said. 'We're now talking about murder too. And yet we still can't go to the police. No corpse. No evidence. Just the testimony of a prostitute.'

Raven put his head in his hands, ran his fingers through his hair, then sat up and gave Sarah a steady look, his face serious.

'We should think again about giving this to Sanderson.'

'What do you mean?'

'I mean that these are dangerous people we're dealing with here.'

'Obviously. But after what we heard today it is even more important to publish. It's imperative. I was unable to save Annabel but there are others just like her. We cannot leave them to their fate. We can't know this and do nothing.'

She held Raven's gaze, not looking away this time.

'We need to find out who is responsible for this and bring them to justice. And if you won't help me, then I'll do it myself.'

THIRTY-SEVEN

ugenie's perfume was in Raven's nose as he walked into the hallway at St Andrew Square. The smell and his surroundings instantly took him back to happier times, in a way that made him believe they were possible again.

He had received a message from her that morning, asking him to come here once his clinic was done. It had greatly lifted his mood, particularly after seeing that morning's edition of the *Capital*. Sarah had evidently ignored his misgivings and given Sanderson his story. Raven often admired her fortitude, but he feared she was playing with fire on this. He suspected the tragic news about her niece had been a factor: feeling she needed to do *something* because she had been unable to save Annabel.

Raven was reluctant to hope that Eugenie's message signalled a reconciliation was on offer, but the scent told him she must be feeling better, for she hadn't worn any fragrance in some time. In truth it was only in believing their rift might be over that he allowed himself to admit how much he had missed her. Almost as much as he had missed the children. He listened out for Jamie coming to investigate the sound of the front door, but the place seemed unusually quiet.

Maxwell appeared from the kitchen, offering an explanation. 'Louisa has taken young James and Clara to Princes Street Gardens, as it is fine out,' he said. 'They should be back soon. How are you, Dr Raven?'

'I did not sleep a great deal last night, but I should be used to that.'

Maxwell responded with an oddly conspiratorial smile. 'So, it was a happy reunion,' he said.

Raven looked at him quizzically. 'I beg your pardon?'

Maxwell coloured a little. 'My apologies,' he said. 'Suffice to say we were happy to care for the children while you and Eugenie spent some time together.'

'Last night?' Raven asked. He hadn't seen Eugenie in two days.

Maxwell's eyes widened in realisation that he might have said the wrong thing.

Just then, Eugenie appeared from the drawing room. She looked at the two men in the hall and read it instantly: the awkwardness. Maxwell absented himself, looking mortified.

'I gather you were not with the children last night,' Raven said, once he was gone. 'Maxwell was under the impression you were at Great Stuart Street.'

'I needed an evening away from them,' she replied, turning on her heel and retreating to the drawing room. Raven followed her in. 'And a good night's sleep,' she added, yawning as she said so.

'Where were you?'

Eugenie glanced out of the window as she sat in her preferred spot. 'With Agnes,' she answered. 'I needed the company of a friend.'

'So did I,' Raven replied, though he knew it sounded pitiful.

'You have your photographs for company.'

Raven wanted to hold back but found that he could not. 'They are not my photographs.'

'Then to whom do they belong?' she asked.

Raven felt an urge to defend himself, to tell her the truth, but found that he could not. Nor could he let her believe they were his, if he wished to effect a reconciliation.

'They were in a textbook I borrowed from someone, a fellow doctor. Under the circumstances you will understand if I don't wish to identify him.'

Eugenie looked at him, an expression of disdain on her face. 'And you will understand if I don't believe you.'

Raven hadn't the heart to press on with a lie, and decided to change the subject instead.

'You sent a note requesting my attendance,' he said, his heart already low at having grasped that this was not for the reason he had hoped.

Eugenie reached into her pocket and produced a letter. 'I found this,' she told him flatly, holding it out.

Raven stepped closer and took it, his finger barely brushing hers. He wanted to grasp her hand, hold her to him. He wanted her to love him again. But merely liking him would be an auspicious beginning.

He unfolded the note.

Dr Todd,

This city will see something you would rather it did not unless you stay in my good graces.

'It was with my father's things,' Eugenie said. 'I do not know what it is referring to, but I know that its being anonymous is not good.'

Raven examined it carefully. It did not appear to be in the same hand as the letter from Cunningham. Its intent was starker than his, though.

'I believe your father was being blackmailed.'

'I grasped that much myself,' she said icily. 'Do you know anything more?'

'I have heard of other doctors being blackmailed recently. Over what, I don't know. But the implication we cannot avoid is that this might account for the missing money.'

Eugenie glanced around the room. Raven could read her thoughts. She was looking at what she knew she might lose.

Her expression became stony, her jaw firm. 'No, this cannot be. My father was a good man, a respected man. He had his faults, but he would not . . . He would not . . .' Her eyes filled as she failed to find the words.

'Eugenie, it may transpire that there are things about your father you would rather not know; and perhaps you will never know them because he paid dearly to ensure that. Whatever he did, I'm sure it was to protect your future. Why don't you and the children come back to Great Stuart Street? My practice is growing. We are building a home there.'

'I hate that place,' she retorted, loathing in her eyes. 'It will never be my home. This cannot be so. You need to look harder. Find those investments. Or perhaps *not* finding them suits you.'

Raven was losing patience, wounded by her last remarks. 'How in God's name could this ghastly mess suit me?'

'With me entirely reliant upon you, nothing more than an adjunct looking after *your* children. In the little doll's house you've made for me.'

With that, she got up and left the room, slamming the door on her way out. Raven thought it safe to conclude that she wasn't feeling better.

He sat down and looked around the room, taking in the grandeur, the furniture and paintings, the view of the square. The little rooms above his practice were no comparison, but surely what they could build *together* was worth more, a monument to their partnership. Like their children.

With that, he heard her words echo. *Your* children, she had said. Not *ours*.

Moments later he heard the front door slam and saw Eugenie stride out purposefully in the direction of the square.

There was a quiet knock at the door, followed by Maxwell carrying in a tray bearing a bowl of broth and a glass of wine. An act of apology, though an unnecessary one.

'I'm sorry, Dr Raven.'

'It's all right, Maxwell. It is difficult when your place of work becomes the site of someone else's battles. This is most welcome. As I said, I got little sleep last night.'

'What kept you awake, sir?'

Raven took a mouthful of wine before answering. 'I was required to deliver a woman in Fountainbridge. When the patient's need is pressing, you must come running, no matter the hour. That's what Dr Simpson told me.'

'Or if the patient is rich enough,' Maxwell replied. 'That is what Dr Todd told me.'

Raven managed a smile. 'And if they're as rich as Barrington Leitch,' he said, 'you must come running even when the patient is already dead.'

Maxwell looked stern all of a sudden and Raven feared he had overstepped the mark.

'Dr Todd did not know that when he was summoned,' Maxwell told him. 'As was his duty, he answered the call swiftly, though it was the middle of the night.'

Raven straightened in his chair. 'The middle of the night?'

Maxwell nodded. 'About two o'clock.'

'Two o'clock? You are sure about that?'

'Perhaps a little earlier, but it had struck two by the time Forbes had the horses ready.'

Raven considered this. 'Can you summon Forbes now?'

'Certainly, Dr Raven. Have you a patient to attend to?'

'Indeed I have. A gentleman with a suspected case of forked tongue.'

THIRTY-EIGHT

aven had returned to Meggetland merely to ask where he might find Leonard McMurdo, but upon arrival discovered the man precisely where he had left him. He was shown to the same study towards the rear of the property, the one with several paintings of a scarcely clad saviour. McMurdo was alone this time, seated behind the desk and looking very much at home, though it was Mrs Leitch's private study. Gertrude herself was not at home, perhaps out saving prostitutes from their sins before they had to service the likes of her late husband.

McMurdo looked surprised to see him, but not alarmed. He seemed relaxed, gesturing to Raven to take a seat. There was a smell of tobacco in the air, a pipe recently smoked.

'Dr Raven. What brings you back this way?'

'I was wondering whether you had found time to look into my query,' he said, thinking he should address that before he burned this bridge.

'Indeed. I'm afraid I have not been able to find any indication that Dr Todd lodged an investment with Mr Leitch.'

This came as little surprise, but the confirmation felt like a blow nonetheless, the slamming closed of a door.

'I see.'

'I could have conveyed this by messenger had you sent a note,' McMurdo added. 'Or do you have other business here?'

Raven glanced at one of the paintings, as though distracted. 'If you would indulge me, I would just like to clarify some matters regarding the morning of Mr Leitch's discovery.'

McMurdo stiffened a little, but his expression remained amenable.

'You said you found him and then you summoned Dr Todd, is that right?'

'No, the butler woke me with the news,' McMurdo corrected him. 'He went to bring Barrington his breakfast and found that he had passed in the night.'

'Sorry, I misremembered. But perhaps you might clarify something else. It's just that Dr Todd's butler recalls the summons coming before two o'clock in the morning. What was Dr Todd doing here all that time, Mr McMurdo, and why did you lie to me?'

McMurdo retained his composure, though his eyes did flash. It was a deliberate use of language on Raven's part. A man who had acted in good faith would be rightly outraged by the word 'lie' and surprised by the accusation. McMurdo's shock was merely at being discovered in his deceit.

His brow narrowed. 'What is the name of Dr Todd's butler?' he asked. A question of little relevance. He was stalling for time while he calculated.

'Maxwell.'

'Then Mr Maxwell is confused. These were the small hours, after all. Perhaps Dr Todd was first called out to another case that same night.'

Raven raised his palms in a gesture of concession. 'It's possible I misinterpreted what Maxwell told me. Much as I misinterpreted it when you told me Mr Leitch spent a lot of time among prostitutes.'

Raven let this hang, meeting McMurdo's eye across the desk. McMurdo tried to appear sanguine, but the effort required was telling its own story.

'I know the truth about your late friend,' Raven said quietly. 'This information was not easy for me to procure, but I could certainly make it easier for others to do so.'

There was ire in McMurdo's expression now, a warning of claws about to be bared.

'I only want the truth,' Raven said. 'What happened that night? When did you really summon Dr Todd?'

McMurdo sighed. He went to a cabinet and produced a decanter, pouring himself a glass of whisky. He did not offer Raven one.

'I did not summon Dr Todd at all,' he admitted, sitting back down. 'That is the truth of it. Barrington's carriage arrived in the night with him already dead inside and Dr Todd in accompaniment. Todd had been summoned when Barrington fell ill, but there was nothing he could do. He acted to protect Mr Leitch's reputation by having him apparently discovered dead in his own bed. A deceit I willingly went along with.'

'In his own bed,' Raven said, working it out. 'As opposed to some prostitute's boudoir.'

McMurdo did not answer.

'Where was this?'

'I did not share his appetites,' McMurdo replied. 'Though he knew I was aware of them. We trusted each other.'

'That's not what I asked. Where did he die?'

'He referred to it as the Elysian Fields.'

'A house of assignation? Where is it?'

'I don't know. I never went.'

'Does it belong to Magnus Cunningham? You seemed very keen to put distance between the two of them when last we spoke.'

'I believe so. Though as I say, I did not share Barrington's appetites.'

'No. You merely helped conceal them.'

McMurdo slammed a hand on the desk. 'I was trying to protect Gertrude,' he retorted.

So that was why the claws were bared. McMurdo's being ever-present here began to take on a different hue. Raven wondered what might have been going on right underneath Barrington Leitch's nose, the man too caught up in his own predilections to see that his wife might be involved with someone else. He found it difficult to envisage there being anything unchaste about it, but love was not always manifest that way.

'I don't know how much Dr Todd knew before,' McMurdo said, 'but he certainly grasped the nettle on the night. One could say Gertrude was the patient he was truly caring for.'

'And the death was definitely as it appeared?'

'I'm not qualified to judge. But Dr Todd certainly was, and he said it was Barrington's heart.'

Raven could only think of Eugenie's insistence – and confusion – that her father had been upset by this death. Todd had been complicit in this deceit in order to protect Barrington Leitch's reputation, but he had covered up worse things to protect the reputations of worse people. Why would this upset him?

Raven could think of only one answer: because it wasn't a heart attack.

He thought of the letter from Magnus, the one torn up in anger but retained. *Thank you for your discretion in such a delicate matter. I believe this marks the beginning of a mutually profitable relationship.*

Raven had no notion what Todd was getting out of it, but he suspected he knew what Magnus had. Leitch had died in his brothel. Todd certified the death as being by natural causes, and the man had been buried without any further examination.

THIRTY-NINE

arah entered Princes Street Gardens through the gate beside the Royal Institution, the glowering spire of the Scott Monument at her back. It had been erected in tribute to a giant of literature but now it would always be associated in her mind with something more sinister. She kept thinking about how Cameron Todd must have seen it from his window every day, coming to loom over him in his despair until it appeared to offer the only way out.

She was glad she had insisted that this meeting take place outside, the trees, cherry blossom and spring flowers a temporary balm for the ache in her head. Since the revelations at the Lock Hospital, she had an almost permanent tension at her temples, and an intermittent stabbing pain around her left eye.

Sarah saw him before he spotted her, taking his ease on a bench beneath a willow tree, reading a newspaper. Callum Somerville looked like the epitome of a modern gentleman, suited and booted, the spring sunshine reflecting off the shiny black silk of his hat. He was indisputably a handsome man, though 'rugged' might be a better descriptor. She knew that she was attracted to him in the physical sense, and he had been nothing but kind and solicitous towards her, but something had changed. His past had begun to intrude on the present.

Intellectually she understood that forgiveness for past crimes and misdemeanours was important if remorse was genuine, but the things he had been involved in – particularly his knowledge of the vice trade – were now making her deeply uncomfortable. If they were to remain friends, she felt that she needed to know everything, and yet should she know everything she doubted that friendship, or anything more, would be possible.

Did that make her a hypocrite? Probably. And yet here she was, taking advantage of their relationship for her own ends.

He got to his feet upon seeing her, his expression one of concern.

'Shall we walk?' she asked. Sometimes difficult conversations were best had on the move. There was something she wanted to discuss with him, but Somerville got in ahead of her. He held out his newspaper, that day's edition of the *Capital*.

'What were you thinking?' he said without preamble.

Sarah was unapologetic. 'It had to be done.'

Sanderson's story had run after she gave him the information Raven was keen to withhold. 'Virgins for Sale' was the headline. The copy itself contained all of the relevant facts but was padded out with salacious detail, some of it purely speculative. Sanderson was clearly happy to outrage his readers if it meant sales.

'But you are mentioned by name,' Somerville persisted.

'Only as a member of the Society for the Suppression of Vice.'

'That might be enough.'

'Enough for what?'

'To cause you trouble.'

She was already in trouble. Raven had barely spoken to her after seeing it, communicating that morning only in grunts and terse instructions.

'Am I not allowed to be a member of a society concerned with the wellbeing of fallen women?' she asked.

'Don't treat this lightly, Sarah. You have placed yourself firmly in the sights of ruthless people. You should step back from this. Do not become any further involved.'

'But I am involved,' she said, her voice rising. 'Annabel is dead.'

Somerville stopped walking. If Sarah was expecting an apology in response to this, or even an expression of sympathy, she was to be disappointed.

'This is exactly what I'm talking about. You've blithely put yourself in harm's way.'

'I haven't "blithely" done anything. My actions have been quite deliberate.'

'Which makes things worse.'

Sarah turned to face him. 'I know what I am doing.'

'I don't think that you do.'

They walked on in silence for a while, both too angry to say anything.

'It's just that I care for you, Sarah,' Somerville said eventually. 'A great deal. You know that. I can't just stand by and watch you walk towards danger.'

'Someone has to.'

Somerville sighed. 'But this is not your fight,' he told her.

'This *is* my fight, just as it is your daughter's fight. It should be everybody's fight.'

Somerville scoffed at this. 'My daughter won't want for money; she'd never find herself in that position.'

Sarah stopped again. 'But don't you see? All women are vulnerable in a society where such evil goes unacknowledged, never mind unchecked. And ignoring it is tantamount to condoning it. Violence against women – any women – should be taken seriously and punished for what it is. A crime. The law is there to protect all of us. Not just the wealthy. And not just men.'

Somerville had the decency to look slightly shamefaced. 'I don't disagree,' he said. 'But this is the real world, Sarah. And I would not see you put yourself at risk for the sake of some crusade.'

'I think you might be overstating the danger.'

'I don't believe that I am.'

They walked on a bit further, Sarah needing a few moments to calm her righteous anger. She still had questions she needed answers to.

'Does it mean nothing to you that my niece is dead?' she asked, her tone a little softer now.

'I'm sorry for your loss, Sarah. But I never knew the girl.'

'She was last seen at a place called the Castle. Are you familiar with it?'

'Should I be?'

'It's a brothel.'

Somerville gave her a sad smile. 'I see that you've ceased using genteel terms to describe such places.'

'Do you know it?' Sarah persisted.

'I don't know of any establishment by that name.'

'Do you know the name Magnus Cunningham?'

Somerville responded with a guarded expression, from which she inferred that he did, and that his reasons for knowing it were not something he was comfortable discussing with her.

'You have had dealings with him?' she pressed. Somerville seemed reluctant to answer. 'I'll take that as a yes. I understand he runs brothels in the city.'

Now Somerville did reply. 'That was not the nature of my business with him,' he said, sounding indignant. 'And it was a very long time ago. Before he was . . .' He tailed off. 'Never mind. The point is I've had nothing to do with him in twenty years.'

'Before he was what?' Sarah insisted.

Somerville sighed again. 'Before he was transported.'

'Transported? For what crime?'

'Most of them, if memory serves. But he made his way back here several years ago. He presents himself as a legitimate businessman these days, a hotelier. But it's well known he made his money in the flesh trade. And still does.'

'What are the names of Cunningham's establishments?'

'I have heard of a house named the Elysian Fields. And I think he used to have one called the Garden of Eden.'

Sarah snorted. 'Appropriate, I suppose, signifying as it does man's fall from grace.'

'As a result of temptation by woman,' Somerville added.

'I'm going to pretend I didn't hear that.'

'Cunningham's not the only one who owns such places,' he said. 'There are a number of individuals in this town posing as respectable gentlemen, whose incomes derive in large part from enterprises most people don't know about. Or don't care to know about.'

Sarah looked at him, his face in profile. What he had just said could have applied to him not so long ago.

He turned to face her, held her gaze. 'It's amazing what some people are willing to overlook if the circumstances are right,' he continued. 'The same good folk who have made it so difficult for me to operate as a respectable citizen are altogether more accommodating of Cunningham.'

'Why should that be?'

'Why do you think? It is because he caters to their basest needs and desires, and he does so with the utmost discretion.'

FORTY

he rain became dramatically heavier just as Forbes stopped the horses in front of the police office on the High Street. Though Raven would only have to walk a few yards, he decided he would wait a while to see if it eased off, reasoning that he might as well keep his suit dry while its pockets were being emptied by Eugenie's insistence on maintaining the carriage.

On the journey he had been thinking of how his uncle had been living – and thriving – in the city for years, without him knowing of his existence. He might have walked past him in the street, stood next to him in a public house. But what did it matter? What was blood but happenstance? He used to worry that it meant more than that, but he now knew better. He and Magnus shared no connection. If he had known the man in his childhood, it must have been in his infancy, the years he had no memory of.

Nonetheless, it still troubled him because of whose brother Magnus was, and clearly he and Raven's father had much in common. Their attitudes to women for one thing, as well as their tendencies towards criminality, operating businesses that skirted either side of the law. But how deep did Magnus's crimes run? That he had operated brothels was not in dispute, nor that he continued to do so. But what had been his relationship with Cameron Todd? Had it truly been Barrington Leitch whom Todd was protecting in his deceit, or had his actions been at the behest of Magnus?

The police office's door swung inwards, and from the carriage Raven saw the object of his visit intent upon heading elsewhere. Henry screwed up his face at the sight of the downpour, but he was not to be deterred. He was about to bolt.

Raven leaned out of the window. 'Henry! Over here. I need to talk to you.'

Henry looked for the source of the shout then hurried across the pavement, his shoes splashing mud from the puddles beneath him.

Raven felt an unexpected surge of warmth at the sight of his friend, and a profound sense of closeness. The times they had shared flashed through his mind, from raucous nights in taverns to quiet confidences, from Raven fending off attackers to Henry stitching his face. He suspected that recent events had left him feeling vulnerable, so his instinct was to cleave to what was dear for fear of losing anything else.

'You have use of a carriage?' Henry asked with delighted surprise.

'For now, at least. It was Dr Todd's.'

'Excellent. Then you can save me the bother of trying to summon one on such a day.'

'Where are you headed?'

'Bellevue Terrace,' Henry called to Forbes.

'On what business?' Raven asked.

'To examine a body.'

The horses trotted back towards the New Town through the rain, the wheels throwing spray in arcs before the open window of the cabin.

'Why isn't the body being brought to you? Isn't that how it normally works?'

'I was told I would have to make a determination, presumably regarding the cause of death. I find that there is much can be inferred from context that would be lost once the body is removed.'

'Who is the subject? Someone important, as you are going to such trouble?'

'Professor Duncan Conville. I'm not familiar with the name. Yourself?'

Raven frowned and shook his head.

There was a lull in the conversation as they crossed the North Bridge, but Raven decided not to lead with his request. It was something he would be wiser to build up to.

'How is Eugenie?' Henry asked, making Raven wish he had led with his request after all.

'I'm told she's fine.'

'You're told?'

'She insists on staying at her father's house.'

'I suppose she's still adjusting to his loss.'

'It's more than that,' Raven said.

He told Henry about the photographs.

'I have heard of such things,' Henry said. 'There is a great trade in them, apparently. Holywell Street in London, Bookseller's Row, has become so inundated with them that the moralisers are seeking an Act of Parliament to ban such obscene materials.'

'I don't believe these came from London. One of the girls depicted currently resides in the Lock Hospital. Which is neither here nor there. The point is Eugenie was sufficiently horrified that she now wants little to do with me.'

'You did not inform her as to the photographs' true provenance?' Henry asked.

'How could I?'

'You're a good man, Will.'

'People keep saying that. But the person who most needs to hear it is the one person I can't tell.'

'Do you think these photographs are in any way related to Todd's death?'

'Possibly. Eugenie found what looks like a blackmail letter. An anonymous note. It mentioned the city seeing something he would rather it did not. And there's money missing. Two thousand pounds. No sign of where it has gone. We stand to lose the house on St Andrew Square.'

'Dear Lord.'

'There's more. The death of Barrington Leitch.'

'What about it?'

'He didn't die in his own bed. He died in a brothel called the Elysian Fields and his body was brought home by Cameron Todd.'

Henry looked briefly surprised but then frowned. 'What did Todd say was the cause of death?'

'His heart.'

'Seems a reasonable supposition. What is your concern?'

'Eugenie said Todd was upset by the death.'

'So?'

'The Todd I knew would have had no compunctions over protecting a patient's dirty secrets, so why would he have been upset? And why did he take his own life shortly afterwards?'

'What are you suggesting, Will?'

'I'm suggesting that there is more to this and Leitch's body was never properly examined.'

Henry sighed as the carriage drew to a halt. 'He's already buried. An exhumation is no small thing.'

They had arrived at the address, a dwelling at the centre of a semi-circular terrace to the north-east of the New Town. Raven followed Henry across a platform that ran above the basement-level apartments like a drawbridge over a moat.

'What manner of professor was this Conville?' Raven asked.

'A professor of classics. At the university.'

Raven felt a twinge of embarrassment that it had not occurred to him Conville would be anything other than medical.

They were greeted by Conville's son, George, a smartly dressed man probably of around Raven and Henry's age, though he looked older today.

'My mother is with her doctor in what used to be my bedroom,' he said. 'She is in a state of grief bordering on delirium. She has barely spoken a word since she found him.'

'Why *your* bedroom?' Henry asked.

George bowed his head and led them upstairs to a closed door on the first landing. Mr and Mrs Conville's bedroom.

'If you don't mind, I will be in my father's study. I do not wish to look at him again.'

Henry waited until George had descended before pushing the door open.

Conville was naked, recumbent in a bathtub on the floor between the windows and the four-poster bed. He was a bearded man in his forties, portly and grey-haired. His head hung backwards over the rim of the tub, as though he had fallen asleep. His hands were in his lap, one of them resting on a knife, which he had used to slice open the major vessels in each groin. The bloody bathwater was several inches deep all around him, but mercifully contained.

'Classics,' Henry said with a sigh.

'What?' asked Raven.

'This is how the Romans killed themselves.'

'Little for you to determine, then.'

'No. I don't think we will be able to spare the family by saying this was an unfortunate accident.'

'Slipped while trimming his beard in the bath?' Raven suggested. 'It's about as plausible as Todd's nighttime sightseeing misadventure.'

They descended the stairs and found George Conville waiting in his father's study. His expression was grave, burdened. Raven recognised it. He was not dealing merely with loss, but contemplating shame and the dreadful hurt to his mother. Raven also knew the question he would be asking himself: What could make his father do this? Unless that burdened look was because he knew. Or suspected.

'I have seen all that I need to,' Henry said.

George stared at the floor, seemingly unable to meet Henry's eye.

'No, you haven't,' he eventually replied.

'What do you mean?'

'I found this.'

George picked up a folded piece of paper from his father's desk. He handed it to Henry, who opened it, then showed it to Raven.

Professor Conville,

This city will know your true nature unless you stay in my good graces.

'He asked me for money,' George said. 'A few days ago. Me. His son. I am a lawyer's clerk. I asked him why he needed it, and he would not answer. He was not himself.'

Henry folded the note and put it in his pocket. 'I shall have to inform the procurator fiscal,' he said.

'About the nature of my father's death?'

'Yes,' he replied, then he turned to Raven and spoke more quietly. 'That and an imminent exhumation.'

FORTY-ONE

wo days later, Raven was walking past the Royal Infirmary towards the Surgical Hospital when he was assailed by a memory, one he had thought long buried. The sight of the old High School building had long since ceased to intimidate him, but for some reason his mind had chosen to dredge up a recollection of his experiences in the theatre there as a student, when he had been humiliated by Professor Syme for vomiting during a procedure on a hot and stuffy afternoon. It was Syme's acolytes who had been particularly merciless, and there had been a time when Raven vowed revenge upon them all, but in truth they had seldom crossed his mind once he had changed paths and followed Simpson instead. He didn't think he could name them now, or even recognise them.

He still preferred to avoid the Surgical Hospital, not least because of the enmity Syme continued to foster towards man-midwives in general and his nemesis Simpson in particular, but on this occasion Raven had been asked here by Henry, who was about to conduct his post-mortem examination of Barrington Leitch.

Raven was passing the resident officers' houses at the eastern end of the Infirmary when his eye was drawn to a man striding towards him on the path through the gardens. It was Dr James Matthews Duncan. Raven reached a hand to his hat by way of acknowledging him, but Matthews Duncan did not reciprocate, which was not a surprise. Indeed, Raven's hat tip had been partly out of mischief. Though they had once worked together and even lived beneath the same roof for several months at 52 Queen Street, he continually affected not to know Raven.

Raven glanced back and watched Matthews Duncan climb into a private brougham: the mark of a successful individual. He was a clever man. An accomplished man. But he was someone who would never be content with those things as long as there were more accomplished men in his midst. And unlike Raven, he evidently *could* still name and recognise those he felt had wronged him.

Raven proceeded beneath the marble colonnade and into the entrance hall. He saw a group of surgeons gathered at the foot of the staircase, and wondered what a fitting collective noun for them might be. A 'scar', perhaps, or a 'bleeding'.

He felt a tap on his shoulder and started just a little. It was Henry.

'I didn't mean to startle you. Is everything all right?' he asked as he led Raven down a corridor towards the mortuary.

'My reflexes have been primed by too many bloody encounters in dark alleyways,' Raven replied.

Henry looked sceptically at him. 'I was there when you precipitated certain of those encounters, remember.'

'That was a long time ago. And I did not precipitate all of them. I was attacked recently, in fact, just off the Canongate.'

Henry looked concerned. 'What happened?'

'I was lured into a close by a prostitute, then ambushed by her fancy man. He had a cosh.'

'You? Lured by a prostitute? How bad *are* things with Eugenie?'

Raven gave him a glare. 'She said someone needed help. A friend with a fever.'

'Oh dear. I remember reading about a case like that in Glasgow a few years ago. A gentleman was badly beaten and robbed. I'm assuming he hadn't your reflexes. What did you do to him, the fancy man?'

'I gave him what money I had,' Raven replied.

Henry looked astonished. Raven was not sure this was a good thing.

'So, he beat you down?'

Raven snorted. 'I'm not so changed that I couldn't defend myself. No. I took the cosh from him but did no more than that. I didn't feel the need to hurt him. The rage that I'm usually prone to, the anger you are so wary of, did not arrive. I felt only pity. And disgust at what he and the woman had been reduced to.'

Henry nodded sagely. 'Poverty is at the root of most crime, like filth is at the root of most disease. The moralisers would have us think that if people could only accept the word of God and behave themselves, then all would be well. But it's hard for God to reach the heart when the belly knows only hunger. We cannot expect people to be gentle and polite when they are living like animals, mired in filth and ordure. An unsanitary city is an unhealthy city, and the corollary holds true.'

Henry led Raven down some stairs, trading nods with two gentlemen on their way up. Raven recognised one of them as Lister, having heard him speak at the Medico-Chirurgical Society meeting.

'Syme's new anointed,' Raven said quietly once they had passed.

'And possibly more than that in future, if the rumours are to be believed,' Henry replied. 'I've heard he has taken an interest in Agnes, Syme's daughter.'

'Good heavens. I wouldn't have thought someone might find a worse father-in-law than Cameron Todd, but there you go.'

His jocularity concealed the regret he felt in knowing that this morsel of gossip was the sort of thing Eugenie might previously have shared with him, she being Agnes's friend. He missed her confidences.

Henry led him into a high-ceilinged room with windows to the south, an altogether brighter and more salubrious space than the grimy quarters at the back of the police office where he had conducted so many other such examinations.

'Even after death it appears the wealthy enjoy better accommodations,' Raven observed.

'Everything is more delicate when the rich are involved. The procurator fiscal sanctioned the exhumation, but it was requested that everything be as discreet as possible. Leitch's widow has not been told, and Mr McMurdo was adamant that no one should be able to say his body was laid out in the police office like some criminal.'

'Did you explain that it's usually the victims of crime who find themselves lying there?'

Henry ignored this.

Leitch's coffin was lying on the floor against one wall. It looked finely made, and probably cost more than most men in this city would earn in a year, but Raven's nose was telling him some things were universal. There was a reek coming from the corpse lying underneath a sheet on Henry's table, but in Leitch's case he suspected the rot had started a long time before he died.

Henry placed his instruments on the table then pulled the sheet away. Raven had never seen Leitch alive, but now understood why his wife had described him as being strong as an ox. He was at least six feet tall and broadly built, with powerful arms. Raven might have said he had shovel-like hands, but doubted those hands ever touched such an implement.

Henry began his examination, making notes in his book with a pencil.

'So, the thesis is that he died of a heart attack,' he said, 'perhaps brought on by over-exertion.'

'There are worse ways to go.'

Even as Raven said this, he thought of another death in another brothel, one that shamed his levity.

'Have you heard of a brothel known as the Castle?' he asked.

'I've heard a few names, but not that one,' Henry replied. 'Though I believe there is one on Ramsay Lane, just shy of the Esplanade. Close enough to the castle for it to be a nickname. Why?'

Raven took mental note of this. He would investigate Ramsay Lane later.

'Sarah's niece is missing. We believe she was abducted and forced into service in this place, then murdered there.'

'Murdered?' Henry shook his head. 'Sadly, I don't doubt it. She won't have been the first and she won't be the last. I saw in the *Capital* that Sarah is campaigning against the vice trade. Good for her, but you ought to warn her she might make herself the target of reprisals.'

'I've tried warning her. But I would remind you who we're talking about.'

Henry picked up a probe and a pair of forceps. 'Speaking of Sarah,' he said, 'I saw her acquaintance Mr Somerville the other day. I hadn't thought of him in some time.'

Raven's hand went to his scar. 'I think of him every time I look in the mirror.'

Henry glanced up, contemplating Raven a moment. 'One of the men responsible subsequently became your friend, did he not?'

Raven thought of Gregor, the giant who had held him in that dark alley while an accomplice cut him with a knife. He had proven himself an altogether more noble man than Raven could have imagined that night.

'After a fashion,' he replied.

'But you forgave him, clearly.'

'He was but an instrument of someone else.'

'And will you never forgive the man who commissioned the deed?'

'I pulled him out of a burning building. I saved his life.'

'That's not the same thing.'

Raven knew this well enough. He had gone back into that theatre because the burden of hatred was something he needed to extinguish. But that did not mean he had absolved Flint.

'Even were I to forgive him, that does not mean I can forget what he's capable of.'

'You just told me you've lost all appetite for brutality. If you truly believe you have changed, then you must be prepared to believe the same of him.'

Raven said nothing, just watched Henry work. Henry was as wise as he was compassionate. Sometimes annoyingly so.

'I think of you every time I look in the mirror too,' Raven told him. 'It's your handiwork I see.'

Henry glanced at the scar on Raven's face. 'I would be neater now, I'd like to think.' Looking back to his work, Henry's brow creased, the expression he wore when confronted by something unexpected. Raven thought it was some past memory, then realised it was Leitch.

'Help me here,' Henry said. 'I need to put him on his front.'

Raven braced himself against the cold, clammy feel of Leitch's flesh, then put his shoulder to the task of rolling him over on the table.

Henry was feeling around at the base of the dead man's skull.

'Look at this. A couple of stitches in a ragged laceration, the hair arranged over the wound.'

Henry took a knife and cut into the scalp, folding back a flap of hair and skin. He prodded at the underlying skull with his finger, nodding to himself.

'Depressed skull fracture. Indicative of a severe blow to the back of the head with a blunt instrument. I'll know more when I open up the skull and remove the brain.'

'He was assaulted,' Raven said.

'It looks like he was on the job at the time, his attention firmly elsewhere as someone snuck up behind and delivered a fatal blow.'

Raven looked at the damage. 'Leitch was murdered,' he said. 'And Cameron Todd covered it up. Quite literally.'

He thought again of the torn-up letter from Cunningham, its reference to *a mutual understanding that any breach of trust would advantage neither of us.*

'I must visit the Elysian Fields,' he said.

'You're waxing poetical, Raven. What do you mean?'

'The house of assignation Leitch was transported home from, remember?'

'Oh yes. Of course. Where is it?'

Raven considered this.

'That's the problem. I have no idea.'

FORTY-TWO

arah was restocking one of the cupboards in Dr Simpson's consulting room. In contrast to Raven's practice, the bustle of Queen Street had left her little time to brood, but as she reordered the medicine bottles in the cupboard – haphazardly replaced by Dr Simpson – her thoughts drifted back to Annabel and the scale of the operation that had ensnared her and got her killed. Prominent among them was whether and what to write to Connie Banks.

Annabel's case was not an isolated one. It wasn't merely bad luck that saw her entrapped. She was a young woman of some intelligence, not likely to be completely unsuspecting, naive, or easily lured. The procurement and certification of these girls suggested a degree of organisation, a business, but one naturally shrouded in secrecy. Sarah dearly wished to expose it, but how did one investigate something so carefully hidden?

'Is this place always so busy?' Emily asked as she entered the room, notebook in hand. She looked tired, the night work at the Maternity Hospital evidently taking its toll.

'It's worse in August and September,' Sarah replied. 'The Glorious Twelfth and all that.'

Emily looked confused.

'Grouse season. Gentlemen come north to shoot, and they leave their wives to spend their time and money in pursuit of better health. They consult whatever doctor is popular depending on the current vogue. Mostly menstrual complaints.'

Emily scoffed, the minor issues of wealthy women of little interest to her.

'When is your cousin due to arrive?' Sarah asked. Emily's cousin Kenyon had brought his wife Marie to Edinburgh to consult with Dr Simpson. They were struggling to conceive a child, the blame for this falling squarely on Marie.

Emily looked at the clock on the mantelpiece. 'They'll be here soon.'

'I assume she is coming on your recommendation.'

'Kenyon made the decision himself without consulting me,' Emily replied a little testily. 'And probably without asking Marie either.'

'Women should be able to make decisions about what happens to their own bodies,' Sarah suggested.

Emily snorted. 'When are women ever in charge of anything?'

Sarah wondered what had happened to provoke Emily's ire today. Perhaps it was that, despite her qualifications and Dr Simpson's prodigious use of her title, the patients remained wary of her. A female MD was a novelty they preferred to do without.

Sarah began laying out the equipment Dr Simpson would need for Marie's procedure. The diagnosis was cervical stenosis, a constriction at the neck of the womb, and the remedy was to make several incisions in it with the intention of opening things up. The metrotome was the implement used to achieve this. When inserted into the cervix, it made an incision along the length of it.

Emily picked up the metrotome to examine it, depressing the handle and watching the blade project out.

'Wouldn't it be better to use something softer to dilate the cervix?' Emily mused. 'A cylinder of waxed cotton or a piece of sponge, perhaps. Surgical scarring is likely to make things worse rather than better. And there is always the risk of bleeding.'

Sarah's immediate impulse was to defend Dr Simpson. He was Professor of Midwifery at Edinburgh University, and consulting physician in the diseases of women and children at the Infirmary.

There was a reason patients came from all over the world to see him. She felt that Emily was in no position to judge or to criticise; she was only at the start of her career and had no real experience to speak of. But Sarah held her tongue. Emily was already in a bad mood and she did not wish to provoke her further. In addition to that, as Sarah looked at the bladed implement Emily held in her hand, she had to admit that the woman had a point.

'Maybe that's what we are needed for,' Emily continued, testing the sharpness of the metrotome's blade against the skin of her thumb.

We? thought Sarah. She wondered if this was a deployment of the royal 'we' or if she was being included in this. She wondered too what might have provoked such a change in Emily's attitude towards her. Perhaps she felt in need of a confederate. Sarah could certainly relate to that.

'A woman's role in medicine should not merely be to fight for the scraps men are willing to throw our way,' she said, 'such as the treatment of women and children, for example: things they are willing to give up. Perhaps a woman's role is not simply to try and emulate the men.' She put the metrotome down and looked at Sarah. 'Perhaps our role is to see things differently and to change how they are done.'

FORTY-THREE

On the afternoon following Leitch's post-mortem, Raven accompanied Sarah to the next meeting of the very society the old hypocrite had funded. He climbed out of the carriage behind her, feeling a chilly wind whip along the High Street, carrying the first spit of rain. He had all but given up on finding any missing investment documents and knew that the money he was continuing to pay the coachman would be sorely needed elsewhere, but he was disinclined to cross Eugenie any further at the moment. It was therefore some consolation to be able to convey Sarah to their destination in comfort and safety, particularly as it was in the Old Town.

The Butlers had convened another meeting and Raven had offered to escort Sarah, ostensibly as a show of solidarity, but as much because he was worried about the target she was painting on herself. The Edinburgh Society for the Suppression of Vice had already attracted hostility, and with the articles in the *Capital* being the talk of the city, he feared that there might be worse than cayenne pepper and harsh words aimed at its members.

The venue was halfway along Toddrick's Wynd, surrounded on all sides by the towering tenements or 'lands' that had been continuously subdivided over the years, housing more and more people, with little to no money spent on maintenance and repairs.

The air was filled with the stench of waste and the cobbled street ran with filth. Raven thought of what Henry had said as they trudged along the alley.

Up ahead he saw a figure step from a doorway onto the cobbles and felt himself tense as he recognised Somerville. 'What is he doing here?' he asked Sarah, trying not to sound accusatory.

'We have struggled to find anyone who will accommodate our meetings. Mr Somerville was good enough to call in a few favours on our behalf.'

'Best not ask who the favours came from.'

Sarah turned to him with a look he knew not to defy. 'I appreciate you coming, but I expect you to behave.'

'I will be the essence of civility.'

Somerville greeted Sarah warmly and gave Raven a curt nod.

'Thank you again for facilitating this,' Sarah told him.

'I will admit it's not exactly the Assembly Rooms,' Somerville said. 'It was a dance hall for a time. The owner charged a penny for entry, sold whisky and ale without a licence, and ran a profitable sideline flogging stolen goods from the premises.'

'So why has he made it available to us?' Sarah asked.

'He's currently being detained at Her Majesty's pleasure in Calton Jail.'

Sarah stepped through the entrance, then noticed that Raven was not following. He remained in the alley.

'I'll stay by the door for now, in case you get any more medical students,' he explained, though he thought them likely to be the least of the threats he might face.

She gave him that look again, by way of warning not to butt heads with Somerville, then continued inside.

'Up the stairs,' Somerville advised her.

Raven glanced inside. On the ground level there was a large space populated only by broken crates and several hay bales, as well as a doorway further in leading to the staircase.

'I thought you owned an assembly hall yourself,' he said to Somerville.

'Not any more. If you remember, dabbling in theatrical matters proved more hazardous than I had anticipated. I rented this room myself to conceal who it's really for. This society poses a threat to a very lucrative trade and so certain people are reluctant to accommodate it. That's why I won't be hanging around for the show. And be assured, I would not put myself on the wrong side of this for anyone else.'

'Are you saying you are afraid? Have you shed your old reputation so thoroughly that no one is scared of you any more?'

Somerville ignored this. 'It strikes me that Sarah's campaign will not merely pitch her against certain dangerous men,' he said, 'but against the *nature* of men. There will always be someone making money by catering to their needs.'

'So you believe her battle to be futile?'

'Not as futile as any attempt to change Sarah Fisher's mind,' Somerville said by way of a parting shot.

'Spoken like a man who has tried and felt the lash of her tongue,' Raven replied as he watched him walk away.

Somerville glanced back, offering a smile, which Raven shared. It was a rare moment of commonality, a glimpse of what forgiveness might feel like.

FORTY-FOUR

arah headed up the stairs, grateful to be away from the smells outside. This was not an area of the city the members of the Society were likely to have visited before, but she thought it would do them good to be reminded of how some of their fellow citizens were forced to live. She wondered if that had been part of Callum Somerville's plan when he suggested it.

Given their limited numbers, the Society had elected to use the smaller upstairs room rather than congregate in the larger space below, and she could hear a few low voices as she reached the landing. The room looked like it had once been a large office or storeroom, but a number of chairs had been laid out in rows, so it did appear a fit venue for their purpose. Sarah placed herself towards the front this time, determined to make a contribution. The Butlers, the minister from the previous meeting and several other men were already seated, facing their audience. There were only a few others in attendance, many perhaps scared off by reports of the harassment the Butlers had endured on previous occasions.

Sarah had invited Emily to come along, keen to foster their growing camaraderie, but she had declined. She wanted to keep an eye on Marie following her procedure, convinced that the threat of haemorrhage had yet to pass.

As before, it was Nathaniel Butler who stood up to make the introductory remarks, reciting a lengthy agenda. This was a meeting about women's wellbeing, founded by a woman and yet led by men. *When are women ever in charge of anything?* Emily had asked. The truth of this was obvious here.

She saw Raven slip in quietly at the back just as Nathaniel sat down. The minister then stood.

'Let's begin with a prayer,' he said.

Let's not, thought Sarah. She felt an aggravating restlessness. Given what she now knew to be going on, she felt that there was no time to waste. Girls were being murdered and these men were wallowing in self-serving piety.

As soon as the minister finished his prayer, Sarah stood up.

'There is something missing from the agenda,' she said.

Nathaniel looked as though he was about to interject but Dorothy placed a restraining hand on his arm.

'The Society should be shifting the focus of its attention to the slave trade.'

The minister promptly cut in, giving her a patronising smile. 'Slavery has been abolished, my dear.'

'I'm referring to the white slave trade. The trafficking of young girls. It's happening here in Edinburgh, and we need to do something about it.'

Nathaniel did intervene now. 'I'm not disputing what you say,' he stated. 'But it's difficult to do anything without evidence of criminality. Those involved are reluctant to speak out, will not bear witness to what is going on. Without credible witnesses there is no prosecutable crime.'

There it was again. The question of credibility. The testimony of prostitutes would count for nothing. A woman who had lost her chastity would always be viewed as a discredited witness by the authorities, by the courts.

'That is why we are focusing our efforts on rescuing these women,' one of the other men continued, 'giving them the means to financially support themselves, reintroducing them to society.'

'Absolving them of their many sins,' the minister added, nodding sagely.

Sarah thought of Flo at the Lock Hospital. Given what had been done to them, why was it necessary for them to repent and seek forgiveness? What sin had Annabel committed, that she should deserve such a fate?

Sarah sat down, not sure what else she could say, or how civil her tone might be in saying it. Nathaniel was right. There was little they could usefully do without evidence.

There followed more discussion about restoring fallen women to society, encouraging all of the middle-class ladies present to consider giving them employment as well as guidance and support.

'And where better than in the bosom of a good Christian household,' the minister intoned. 'Saving their souls from the eternal fire.'

Sarah thought she could detect the faint aroma of smoke as he said this, though there was no fire lit in the room and it couldn't be coming from outside as they had kept the windows closed against the putrescence emanating from there. She put it down to her imagination.

She thought about the women she had met. It seemed short-sighted to assume that all they needed was domestic work. It didn't seem to occur to anyone that they were being asked to trade one form of servitude for another.

Sarah found she was unable to concentrate on what was being said. She looked out of the window, watching the clouds as they drifted past, tried to empty her head. The tension in her temples and around her eyes was building again.

Sarah started as the scraping of chairs alerted her to the fact that the meeting was breaking up. As she got to her feet she heard the woman beside her question her companion.

'Would you consider it?' she asked. 'Taking in a fallen woman?'

'One ought to, I suppose,' her friend replied. 'But really, how can one be sure they are truly reformed? There must be certain risks associated with it.'

'A husband's wandering eye?' the first woman suggested.

'The sanctity of the home is our responsibility too. Though I'll consider a fallen woman if I don't find someone soon, as long as she knows how to scrub a floor.'

The two women started to make their way to the end of the row, Sarah following on behind.

'Are you still looking?' the first lady asked.

Her friend sighed. 'Reliable help is hard to come by. You don't have any recommendations, do you?'

'There's an agency. Fish and Feathers, or something like that.'

'Fish and Feathers?'

'I think you mean Pike and Featherstone,' Sarah said.

'That's the one,' the first lady said. 'Norma swears by them. Country girls mainly. Hard workers but not much to look at. I think it's by design: so that a woman need not worry about her husband.'

The exchange gave Sarah pause. Annabel had been a beautiful child, nothing plain about her. Sarah thought about Mrs Hinchcliff, herself once a procuress, and heard Emily's words again in her head. *When are women ever in charge of anything?*

Sarah had been thinking about men luring young women, but what if it wasn't men who did the luring?

Somerville had spoken of businessmen with a respectable front, an impenetrable barrier protecting them from public scrutiny. Hiding in plain sight. What if the recruitment agency was just that: a respectable front? A filtering process: diverting those deemed suitable – young, attractive, pure – to the brothels, while sending the others to legitimate places of work?

She knew then that she would have to go back to Pike and Featherstone. And do what, though? Confront them about it? She would have to come up with a better plan than that.

Sarah sniffed, realising that the smell of burning was becoming stronger. It hadn't been her imagination. Others were noticing it too. And it was no longer just a smell. Thick swirls of smoke were drifting up from the stairwell.

The place was on fire.

FORTY-FIVE

aven had felt anxious on Sarah's behalf as she stood up to speak, concerned she might be shouted down or talked over and simply ignored. It chilled him to think how that might make her feel. In the event, she had not prevailed, but nor had she shrunk away in the face of opposition. He and Somerville had joked about her determination, but there was something inspiring about seeing her embody it before an audience. He could barely conceive of what she might achieve, given the chance.

As the meeting began to break up, he found himself next to Nathaniel and Dorothy Butler, who thanked him for coming along.

'How is your wife?' Dorothy asked.

Damned if I know, Raven thought, though it was reassuring that very few people were party to the awkward details. He thought he could smell smoke and wondered briefly where it was coming from.

'You both knew my wife when you were children,' Raven said. 'Was she so . . . sensitive back then?'

Nathaniel smiled knowingly. 'You're not the first to wish you had the secret to staying in Eugenie's good graces,' he replied.

'The loss of her father is proving very difficult for her to recover from,' Raven explained. 'Are you married yourself?'

There was an awkward pause, Nathaniel appearing as though he did not know how to answer.

'Nathaniel lost his wife and daughter three years ago,' Dorothy said. 'An infectious fever claimed them both.'

'I am so dreadfully sorry.'

Nathaniel nodded and gave him a sad smile. 'It has been difficult. For the longest time I struggled to find a purpose, a reason to keep going. Happily, I have discovered one of late.'

'Nathaniel has been a driving force in our campaign,' his sister added, with a strange urgency.

Raven was about to ask Nathaniel what had first motivated him to get involved, when he noticed a plume of smoke curl around him. He turned and looked back, which was when he saw that it was coming from the stairwell.

There was a sudden sense of alarm as awareness of the threat passed through the room like a wave.

Raven was closest to the exit. He looked down the stairs and saw a dancing flicker of brightness in the doorway below. When he turned again, he could see that the smoke was beginning to rise through gaps in the floorboards.

'We must get out of here,' he said, heading for the stairwell. 'I'll make sure a path is clear.'

The smoke began to sting his eyes as he descended, the heat palpable too. As he neared the bottom, he could see that the hay bales were alight, and as he passed through the doorway he could also see why. There were two men standing by the main door, cloths wrapped around their faces and flaming torches gripped in their hands.

Raven charged towards them, and they both fled, but not before hurling their torches at him. One bounced off a pillar; the other Raven had to deflect with his arm. Both sent showers of sparks and ash into his face. Raven spluttered and forced himself to keep his eyes open. His sleeve was alight. He felt someone tug at him and saw that it was Nathaniel, helping him haul off his jacket and throw it to the floor.

One of the burning bales was directly in front of the exit. Raven got behind it, Nathaniel in front, and between them they were able to haul it through the door and toss it into the lane. It sent more sparks scattering as it landed, and it was only now it was outside that Raven could see the volume of smoke towering from it.

People were issuing past them now, covering their mouths as they made their way out into the lane. Most of them moved urgently, but pulling up the rear he saw Dorothy helping a gentleman who was overcome with a coughing fit.

Then it struck him.

'Where is Sarah?'

Dorothy spluttered, clearing her throat to speak. 'I don't know. I think she's still up there.'

There was another bale still ablaze further in. It wasn't an obstacle, but it was belching smoke, burning too hot and fierce to try and drag it out.

Raven ran back up the stairs. It was harder to see now, but he could make out a pair of legs on the floor, jutting from between two rows of chairs.

He ran towards the figure and saw that Sarah was crouched at the other end, trying to drag a semi-conscious woman from between the seats. He hurried to assist, getting hold of the lady under her arms while Sarah took her feet.

Nathaniel appeared as they reached the head of the stairs. He relieved Sarah and sent her ahead as they carried the casualty between them.

Reaching the bottom, he was dismayed to see Sarah tarrying a moment, staring fixedly at something.

'What are you waiting for? Get out!'

'Look,' she said, pointing as she withdrew.

Glancing down, Raven saw three wooden planks lying on the floor. Alongside these was a box of nails.

FORTY-SIX

arah brushed some soot from Raven's face as they sat together on the couch in his consulting room. She revealed a rash of tiny scorch marks where the black was wiped away.

There was an energy running through her, one she did not entirely trust. When she saw the flames, the shock had fast given way to fear, then the fear to action and resolve, but once outside in safety, the sense of relief was not enough. It was as though she had fuel unspent, feelings she did not know what to do with. She only knew she needed to be with someone who might share them.

She checked his arms next. There were only a few superficial abrasions – nothing serious – but she found she was reluctant to let go of his hands.

'One of them threw a torch at me,' he explained.

'They meant to barricade us inside,' Sarah said, finally speaking it aloud. They had not discussed it in the carriage. They had said almost nothing, in fact, sparing their voices while their throats recovered from the smoke.

'I thought that too,' Raven replied, 'but I have had time to reconsider it. They left the wood and nails at the door to the stairs. You don't start a fire around yourself and then set to work hammering battens as it burns around you. We were supposed to see them. This was merely a message.'

'Either way, it also tells us something else, something unintended.'

'What?'

'That they're worried.'

Raven looked exasperated. 'Do you not see the danger you are courting? The more worried they are, the more ruthless they will become. You must stop now. For your own sake as well as mine.'

'What do you mean: as well as yours?'

He touched her face with his thumb, gently wiping soot from her cheek. 'Don't you see, Sarah?' he said, his voice gentle, his head leaning close to hers until their foreheads touched. 'I can't risk losing you. You mean too much to me.'

Raven leaned back again, just enough to look into her eyes, their faces inches apart. Sarah thought he might kiss her, and then when she feared he might not, she leaned in and kissed him.

It was gentle at first, a tender brushing of lips, but it soon became fiercer and more urgent.

Then they broke apart, Sarah feeling breathless, Raven holding her at arm's length. He looked torn, but there was also an intensity in his eyes, an undeniable tension in the air between them.

Sarah was about to apologise, feeling at fault for putting him in such an invidious position, but before she could speak, he pulled her towards him and kissed her again. There was nothing tentative about it. It was as though a decision had been made, a bridge crossed, final boundaries breached, their need for each other transcending all other concerns.

All she could see was him.

All she could feel was him.

All other thoughts left her head.

As Sarah lay in Raven's arms, in his bed, sweat cooling on her skin, their clothes tangled and scattered about the floor, she felt a melancholy descend. She tried to make light of it.

'The minister will have to absolve me of my sins,' she said. 'Save me from the eternal fire.'

Raven sighed. 'I'm the one who has committed adultery. You are not married.'

'I think you'll find that the woman is always to blame. Those are the rules.'

Raven did not dispute it.

'This would be a most inconvenient time for your wife to decide to come home,' Sarah observed.

'I very much doubt it will happen so soon.'

Sarah sat up, wrapping the sheets around her. 'But it will happen,' she said. 'We both know that.'

They did not speak for a while, both lost in their own thoughts. The deed had been passionate, exquisite, necessary. But now it was done, and they were left to contemplate the consequences, or the lack of them. The fact that nothing had changed.

'What will we do now?' he asked.

'We have to decide what we want,' Sarah replied. 'Because we both know it cannot be this.'

FORTY-SEVEN

nly a couple of hours later, Raven was presenting himself at 52 Queen Street, aware that Sarah would be somewhere in the house. He felt that, should they see each other, it would be hard to act as though nothing had happened. Harder still to act as though he didn't want it to happen again. But he knew that it must not.

Jarvis opened the door to him with a warmth in his smile that was at odds with how he had regarded Raven during much of his time there. Perhaps being a professional associate and guest of the professor had conferred greater status upon him, or perhaps it was simply that, no longer being a fellow employee, Jarvis did not feel the need to keep Raven in his place. Either way, the joviality in his expression indicated that he had no idea why Raven had been summoned that evening. The note said Simpson needed him urgently, and if the professor was telling no one else why, then Raven could guess the purpose.

This was confirmed when he entered the study and found Simpson at his desk, a large pile of money in front of him.

'I did as you suggested and agreed I would pay. Today I received instructions for doing so.'

Raven took in Simpson's dark, burdened expression. He thought of George Conville saying of his father that he was not himself, and of Eugenie talking about her own father the same way. In this city a man's reputation was everything, which made shame a powerful weapon.

Raven's mind went back once again to what he had seen through the window of that house on Doune Terrace years ago, Simpson being greeted lovingly by another woman, and then equally lovingly playing with an infant. He had learned that this might not be as it appeared. Raven knew Simpson and his wife were instrumental in finding good homes for the unwanted offspring of the quality, often to women who were failing to conceive for themselves. That, he had often told himself, was all he had seen. But why had Simpson been so secretive?

'Did you hear about Professor Conville?' Raven asked.

'I did,' Simpson replied gravely. 'Do you believe it is connected?'

'His son found a note. Eugenie discovered one very similar among her father's things. Do you still have the original threat you received?'

Simpson's expression was uncharacteristically sheepish. 'I burned the letter in case Jessie should see it.'

'Do you have the one you received today?'

'Yes. When I saw what it was, I had Jarvis chase after the messenger and call him back. He caught him just in time. The lad said it was pressed into his hand by a man, with payment for delivery. He said he saw the man only briefly.'

Simpson handed the note to Raven, who read the instructions. The money was to be taken at nine o'clock to the summer house in Princes Street Gardens, close to the bowling green at the western end.

'I do not have the other notes to compare, but I am fairly sure the handwriting is the same,' Raven said.

'It is familiar to me too,' Simpson replied. 'Though for the life of me I cannot think from where.'

There was a leather satchel lying empty on the desk, waiting to be filled. Raven lifted it.

'How much is here?'

'One hundred pounds.'

The blackmailer had bled Cameron Todd until he had taken his own life so that he could be bled no more. It might have been the same with Conville, or perhaps he had taken his life because he could not pay. Simpson had a lot of money, more than either of those men. But that would not save him. The blackmailer would not stop until his coffers were emptied.

'I will need to borrow some journals,' Raven said. He lifted a handful from a shelf and began stuffing them into the satchel.

'What are you doing?' Simpson asked.

'I said to tell him you would pay. I never intended for you to *actually* pay.'

'What if this ruse angers him into releasing the information?'

'He has one card to play, and he won't play it until he has given up hope of getting your money. Even if you did pay him this, he would soon be back for more.'

'What do you intend to do?'

'I will persuade him that his best interests lie in not pursuing this course.'

'How?'

'A blackmailer's power derives from threatening people with exposure. I will simply do the same to him.'

FORTY-EIGHT

he lamplighters were commencing their rounds as Raven made his way to Princes Street. The cloud cover was heavy, making it seem as though the hour was later. He got to the summer house ahead of the appointed time then retreated to a covered spot among some trees, from where he could watch all routes of approach.

The Scott Monument loomed in the gathering dusk. Raven gazed up at it and thought, not for the first time, of Cameron's Todd's lonely ascent. It was surely more than money that had driven him up there. He had been prevailed upon to cover up the truth about his patient's murder. Having exhausted his funds, had his debt to the blackmailer caused him to borrow from Magnus Cunningham, who had extracted payment in kind, by services rendered? What was the long-term investment Magnus's letter alluded to? And what *breach of trust would advantage neither of us*? According to Somerville, Cunningham had risen in the city by meeting the needs of the rich and influential. Raven could not envisage Todd visiting brothels, however. If anything, there was always something bloodless about the man. And yet there were the photographs. It felt plausible to Raven that those might be the sum of his appetites, but had they led him somewhere more dangerous?

He had hoped that being able to offer Eugenie an explanation for her father's conduct might help her make peace with his death, but so far he was uncovering a picture that would be harder and harder for her to accept. Nonetheless, he knew that only the whole truth, however harsh, could dispel the phantom version of her father that was standing between them.

He had thought that lying with Sarah again would confuse his feelings, but surprisingly it had seemed to clarify them. He loved Sarah – of that he was in no doubt – and although part of him desperately wanted to be with her to the exclusion of all else, another part of him knew that it couldn't be so. He had taken the forbidden path but it had only led him back to the same place.

Henry had said that he was a good man and he hoped that was true. A good man would not turn his back on his wife, abandon her with all of the shame that such a thing would entail. Certainly not when she was grieving, still coming to terms with a profound loss and seemingly unendurable pain. To add to that would be unforgivable.

When confronted with the impossibility of one future, it made it simpler to see where his path must lie. He had to get Eugenie back, to reunite his family so that his children could have what he had not: both a mother and a father who loved them. If Eugenie could accept that her future lay with Raven, and that it would be a good future, she would surely remember how much she loved young James, and how much she loved Clara too.

Raven heard voices to the south. Crouching close to the wide trunk of a massive oak, he saw two men approaching from the direction of the castle. He hadn't anticipated this, only thinking of an individual. His plan might need to adapt. As they drew closer, he observed from their clothing that they looked like tradesmen on their way home. And from their swaying gait and garrulous demeanour, they had clearly visited a tavern after finishing their day's work. They carried on through the gardens, never noticing him.

A few minutes later, he saw someone else, this time a man on his own. He stopped by the summer house, looking back and forth. He was dressed smartly, in what Raven recognised as the uniform of a hotel concierge. The fellow looked anxious but sharp-eyed, alert: someone who would have observed and over-heard many things while doing his job, and perhaps made use of some of them. There were several hotels nearby on Princes Street, all of them looking towards the castle. It struck him that the Elysian Fields could be accommodated within one of them but known only to certain people. That way clients might come and go with the nature of their business remaining unknown.

The daylight was all but gone, the moon and the gas lamps of Princes Street now the only illumination. Raven waited a few minutes just in case he had it wrong and the man was meeting a sweetheart. The concierge continued to look back and forth impa-tiently. Raven decided it was time to make his move. He emerged from his hiding place and strode towards the summer house.

'Waiting for someone?' Raven asked.

The concierge regarded him uncertainly. He had been expecting Simpson.

'Do you have a package for me?' he asked.

Raven held out the satchel. The concierge reached for it eagerly, but Raven pulled it back. 'You ought to check the contents. I don't want you claiming they were not as agreed.'

Raven placed it on the ground. The concierge crouched down to open it, working the clasp with both hands. As he did so, Raven slipped his Liston knife from his pocket and held it to the man's throat.

'Your sport is at an end,' he said.

The man whimpered.

Raven put a hand over his mouth. 'If you call out, I will open your throat before a sound can issue. Do you understand?'

The man nodded minutely, wary of moving his neck while the blade was pressed so hard against it.

'What is your name?'

'Robert, sir. Robert Graham.'

'You told Cameron Todd the city would see something he would rather it did not unless he stayed in your good graces. What did you mean? What did you have on him?'

The man whimpered again. 'I don't know what you're talking about,' he said, his voice tremulous. 'I was sent here on an errand. A gentleman came into the hotel where I work. Told me someone would deliver a package to me here at nine.'

Damn it, Raven thought. 'Did you do this before? Did you meet another man here and take delivery?'

'No, sir.'

Clever. He had used different couriers.

'What was his name?'

'He did not say.'

'Where are you to take this package?'

'I was . . . I was told I would not be paid if I divulged that to anyone.'

'Nor will you get paid if you're lying here bleeding to death.'

Raven felt his own voice tremble. He hoped the concierge did not call his bluff. He was willing to trade blows with any man in a fight, but he could not harm a fellow who was defenceless.

'I was to meet him at Gayfield Square, no later than nine-thirty.'

'What did he look like?'

'I only saw him for a few seconds, and he had his hat pulled down, covering part of his face.'

'How was he dressed? Height? Weight?'

'Average. I'm not sure. He didn't sound local, though.'

'An accent? Where from?'

'Hard to say. Just not Edinburgh, or Glasgow.'

Raven pulled the knife away and produced some coins from his pocket. He placed them into the man's palm.

'Buy yourself some whisky or whatever else is your choice, and sit yourself down an hour. I don't want you warning him in the hope of reward. If I see you again tonight, it will not end well. Do you understand?'

The man said nothing, just took the money and ran.

★ ★ ★

Raven approached Gayfield Square from the west, passing the United Presbyterian Church on Broughton Place. The streets were quiet, most good people in their homes by this time of night. On the far side he saw a coach and pair before one of the townhouses, a driver at the reins.

He tarried at the edge of the lane leading into the square, looking at the pools of light beneath the gas lamps and where illumination radiated from shutters that had not been pulled. He observed no one at a window watching for the concierge's approach, but he was sure he glimpsed a figure retreat inside a close.

He strode casually, staying beneath the lights lest he appear suspicious. Only when he got to the close would he rapidly turn and charge. But before he could do so, he glimpsed movement from the carriage. A hat-covered head emerged briefly from the brougham's window and ordered the driver with a single word: 'Go!'

Raven broke into a sprint, but the driver's rein was fast and his horses faster. The carriage turned hard on to Leith Walk and away, with no hope of him catching it.

What had given him away? he wondered. He was clearly not the concierge, but he could be anybody, just a gentleman making his way home. Then he deduced it. His mistake had been walking beneath the lamps. The blackmailer had sent a courier because he feared he would be recognised. He had identified Raven, and thus assumed Raven could identify him.

This caused something else to resolve itself. He had been puzzled by the blackmailer's delay in asking Simpson for money. Why send the threat and then wait so long to make your demand? The answer was cruelty, deliberately ensuring the threat was hanging over Simpson for a while before seeking his bounty. Had that been the case with Todd and Conville too? He could not say, but it felt like there was an edge of the personal to it this time, further borne out by the steps the blackmailer was taking to protect his anonymity.

Raven suddenly recalled the sight of James Matthews Duncan getting into a brougham at the hospital: a man who held a deep grudge against Simpson, and who had been in the household long enough to know there were whispers about him fathering another child. His accent did not sound local: he was originally from Aberdeen and had lived in France. He was an individual who might well prefer to release the information than be paid; and who might release the information anyway.

Raven wondered if there might be a way to get Matthews Duncan's driver to reveal where he had taken him. If anyone knew a man's secrets, it was the person who conveyed him hither and thither. However, he also knew that being so trusted, they tended to be loyal to their employers. Simpson's coachman, Angus, certainly was.

But with that, Raven realised something else. Barrington Leitch's coachman had driven Cameron Todd and his master's body back to Meggetland the night Leitch died. He would have been compensated for his discretion, as well as no doubt accepting the importance of keeping the truth from Mrs Leitch. But he had only driven part of the journey.

Dr Todd had been summoned from his home.

Forbes might not have known the true nature of his destination, but he had taken Todd to the Elysian Fields. And Raven was now his employer.

FORTY-NINE

he briefest glimpse of morning sun was extinguished by gathering clouds as Sarah walked up the High Street, paying closer attention to her surroundings than usual. She found herself scrutinising passers-by, wondering if they posed a threat to her or whether they might be involved in the darker deeds she was investigating.

She knew that, given recent events, vigilance was important, but she also knew that it was unhelpful if taken too far. She didn't want to live in a world where one had to assume the worst in everyone, but she was conflicted. The publication of the 'virgins for sale' story had caused a furore, but mostly it was other newspapers complaining that the subject was not a fitting one to be discussed in the press. What would it take to make the good people of Edinburgh sit up and pay attention? What would it take to get the authorities to register an interest?

They would have to produce irrefutable evidence that led to prosecutions. Nothing else would suffice.

Sarah hadn't told Raven she was coming here today. She knew he would not have approved. But it was clear to her that this was something she needed to pursue, even if it had to be done alone. They were not married, never would be, and he had no jurisdiction over her.

She was worried that their moment of passion might affect

their working relationship and she fervently hoped that they could continue as they had before. It was a risk they shouldn't have taken, but she couldn't bring herself to regret it. It had provoked an opportunity for truth and evaluation.

She had long ago accepted that they were not destined to be together, had convinced herself that friendship was all that she required. Whether this was true or not didn't matter, it was all that there was.

She thought again about Emily's comments regarding whether there was something or someone keeping her in Edinburgh when she should be pursuing her fortunes elsewhere. She worried about her own needs sometimes, whether she would be satisfied to live out her life as a solitary traveller, a widow, or whether she should consider other offers. Somerville's offer in particular.

Somerville was a man of some fortune now, and his wealth seemed likely to accrue. Although he was making all the correct overtures in offering his support for her ambitions, she could not convince herself that he would be so amenable when confronted with the realities of what she wanted to achieve.

But she was now starting to reconsider the wisdom of throwing her lot in with Raven. He had made it clear that his priority was his wife and his marriage. If his ongoing association with Sarah was an impediment to his reconciliation with Eugenie, their working arrangement may well have to be sacrificed.

And where would she be then?

Her exposure to the Butlers and their crusade for social reform was also causing her to re-evaluate what her future might hold. Would her energies be better spent trying to improve the lot of women and the poor? Might she do more good that way rather than pursuing an unlikely career in medicine?

She realised that Somerville represented security and stability, a useful platform for promoting social change. He was a man with connections, with power, and was unafraid to wield it. He was keen to leave his dark past behind and make amends. Together they could become a formidable force for good.

She did not love him. Not in the way she loved Raven, but mutual respect was a good starting point, and affection would surely grow. She knew she couldn't have children of her own, but she could be mother to Somerville's daughter and experience family life: her own family rather than forever being part of someone else's.

In short, she did not want to sacrifice everything for a career that might always remain out of her reach. But men were permitted to have everything: wife, family, and purpose. Why should she settle for anything less?

The premises she was looking for were not hard to find. A newly painted sign hung above the door on the Canongate, next to Tweeddale Close. The offices of Edinburgh's most recently instituted newspaper were impressive, though Dr Simpson insisted that the *Capital* should not be described as such, should not be mentioned in the same breath as the *Scotsman* or the *Courant*. Not so much a newspaper as a scandal sheet, he said.

Sarah did not disagree with this assessment, but it was the only publication willing to soil its pages with the sordid accounts of abuse that they had uncovered. And Sanderson, much as she disliked him personally, was a useful ally in the matter. She was grateful that he now had an office to conduct his business from. It made it easy to track him down and meant Sarah did not have to seek him out in the howffs and drinking dens he was known to frequent outside normal working hours.

The *Capital*'s headquarters consisted of several rooms, and it was clear that some money had been spent on the place, with freshly painted walls and good, solid furniture. It made Sarah think of Dr Stokes and the Lock Hospital, and his insistence that first impressions were of the utmost importance.

Sanderson was seated behind a desk in the largest room, reading a newspaper (not his own), when Sarah knocked on the open door to his inner sanctum.

'This must have cost a pretty penny,' she said.

Sanderson looked at her over the top of his paper. 'I am nothing if not resourceful when it comes to procuring investment,' he said.

Sarah knew that to be true. He had a history of using information to his advantage to get what he wanted.

He was as expensively attired as his office was decorated: dapper
as ever, dressed in a tailored suit, his gold-topped cane resting
against his desk. It was as though his immaculate appearance,
the clean-cut image he presented to the world, was a sartorial
shield, deliberately wielded to disguise the fact that he peddled
in scandal and filth. But when he lowered the newspaper, she saw
that his carefully curated image was marred by a recent, incongruous addition. Sanderson was nursing a black eye and a burst
mouth, his upper lip purple and swollen.

'What happened to you?' she asked.

Sanderson dismissed her concern with a wave of his hand.
'A minor altercation. Nothing for you to worry about.' He
folded his newspaper, put it down on the desk. 'I assume your
presence here indicates that you have something for me,' he
said, a leery grin on his battered face. 'Paper's been selling like
hot cakes since the virgins story. Struggling to keep up with
demand.'

Sarah often had the impression that Sanderson revelled a little
too much in other people's misery, and his current gleeful expression was doing nothing to disabuse her of that notion. He was
not a good man. Not the sort of man she would choose to do
business with, but in this matter, there was no alternative.

'I think I know who the procurers are,' she said.

Sanderson sat up ramrod straight in his chair. 'Who?'

'Pike and Featherstone.'

'The recruitment agency? What makes you think that?'

Sarah explained her reasoning. Annabel was supposed to go
there but apparently never arrived; the fact that only plain girls
seemed to find their way into genuine domestic roles.

Sanderson sucked air in between his teeth. 'It's a bit thin,
isn't it?'

'I know we will need evidence,' Sarah admitted. 'Problem is, I
don't know how to go about getting it.'

Sanderson thought for a minute, scratched his chin. 'Seems to me we would need to catch them in the act.'

'How might we do that?'

'Set a trap for them. Tell them we have a young woman that they might be interested in.'

The way he was looking at her was making Sarah uncomfortable. 'I hope you're not suggesting using me as bait.'

Sanderson snorted. 'No offence, Miss Fisher, but you're a little old and have been married. Not really the type they're looking for.'

'Well, we can't use anyone else either.'

''Course we can. I know a few likely candidates. We pose as sellers, looking for a slice of the commission. Insist on payment after chastity has been certified. That way we get the introducers *and* the doctor who is certifying the girls as virgo intacta.'

Sarah did not like the way this was going, thinking it best to draw a halt to his line of thinking immediately. 'We can't subject some innocent to an intimate examination.'

'It won't get as far as that,' Sanderson said, confidently. 'Anyway, the girls I have in mind are not so innocent, and certainly wouldn't pass any virginity test.'

She shook her head. Desperate as she was to see justice done, Sarah knew that she could not condone putting others at risk.

'I just can't see how it would work,' she said.

'I don't see that we have much alternative. You would need to pose as a mother or maybe an older sister. I can't be directly involved. Too well known in these parts.'

'You're forgetting that I've met one of them before.'

Sanderson was not to be dissuaded. 'Only once, you said. And only briefly. They must see a dozen women a day. Different dress, different hat, different name, they'd be none the wiser.'

'No,' she told him. 'It's too risky.'

'Think on it,' Sanderson insisted. 'The last story I printed certainly shook things up a bit. But this, this would be explosive. If we get the procurers and the doctor certifying, we can put pressure on them to give us the next one up. The man at the top.'

He leaned forward over his desk.

'Do this right,' he said. 'And we get everything.'

FIFTY

Raven was entering St Andrew Square from George Street when he saw Eugenie step out of the carriage, Forbes offering a hand to help her onto the pavement. He hastened to catch up to her as she approached the house. Maxwell noticed him and held the door open after she had entered, which caused her to turn. She seemed almost alarmed to see him, which was not the most encouraging response.

Jamie came thundering along the hall at the sound of their arrival. He charged past his mother and wrapped himself around Raven's legs. It felt so bittersweet that it was all he could do not to weep.

Eugenie observed this coolly, Raven unsure whether it was his very presence or Jamie's affection of which she was disapproving. Either way, the moment did not last, for Jamie soon went charging off again, into another world of his own.

Maxwell having departed for the kitchen, Eugenie finally met his eye.

'Are you all right?' she asked. 'I heard you got yourself caught in a fire.'

She made it sound as though it was a misadventure of his own making, or perhaps it merely sounded that way to his guilty conscience, his thoughts having already gone to the aftermath of the blaze.

'Heard from who?'

Eugenie did not answer, asking another question of her own instead. 'How is Sarah?'

Raven's guilt and anxiety made him wonder why she would ask, for she didn't normally enquire after Sarah's wellbeing.

'She sustained no injuries, but she is shaken.'

'It appears this Society has upset some dangerous people. These events should give Sarah pause.'

'I agree,' Raven said.

Sarah's anger at Annabel's death had motivated her to seek justice. He felt something had changed when he told Sarah he couldn't risk losing her. It was as though she had not thought what she might mean to anyone else, nor of her own safety. But she surely would now. For all she could be stubborn, she was not a fool.

Nor was Eugenie. She had a pragmatic side too, and he had to appeal to it.

'Eugenie, difficult as this feels right now, you know we must face the future, and soon. Your father's money is gone. We both must accept that. You won't be able to stay here much longer. You might as well come home now. With the children.'

Eugenie gave him that cool look again. At least it was not the angry one she'd worn last time, when she said the situation suited him, though in a way the neutrality of it unsettled him more.

'So he was blackmailed, you are certain,' she said.

'All but certain, yes. Though he was not the only one. Another man took his own life, a professor at the university, I believe for similar reasons.'

'Do you know what my father was being blackmailed over? Was it to do with those photographs?'

Raven felt some light get in through the crack of her tacit acknowledgement, but he didn't have an answer for her. 'No,' he said.

'What, then?'

He hesitated too long, and she misinterpreted that. 'Tell me,' she insisted, growing frustrated. 'You know *something*, clearly.'

'There are possibilities that I might be wrong about. I do not wish to say anything until I'm sure I can tell you the whole truth.'

'So instead you would rather leave me with the worst my imagination can summon?'

Raven felt his own frustration grow, not least because he was wondering what Eugenie might be keeping to herself.

'Then why don't you tell me the worst you can imagine,' he asked, 'and I'll tell you if you're right?'

That ended the conversation. He saw her eyes mist, whether with anger or sadness he could not say, then she walked away. He had been stupid to say it, but it hurt that he was trying so hard to protect her, and to find her answers, while in response she acted like she resented him for it.

He watched her climb the stairs, thinking about pursuing her but knowing he would only make it worse. Through the window he could see Forbes tending to the horses, causing him to remember the true purpose of his visit.

Raven stepped back out onto the street. It was early afternoon but it looked more like dusk, the sky so low and dark.

'Rain,' said Forbes, by way of acknowledging him.

'Forbes, I need to ask you about a recent journey,' Raven said.

Forbes stiffened, immediately uncomfortable.

'I want to know where you took Dr Todd on the last night he was summoned away in the small hours.'

'I took him to Meggetland,' Forbes replied. 'As I have taken you twice since.'

'No, you did not. You took him to a destination from where you were sent home again without him.'

Forbes winced. 'With all respect, Dr Raven, I worked for Dr Todd almost twenty years, and he always stressed to me that discretion was paramount, for the good of his patients.'

'I fully agree, but I have reason to believe the events of that night were what led him to the top of the Scott Monument. If you would honour him, I need you to take me where you took him, and now.'

FIFTY-ONE

he threat of rain loomed for much of the journey, the sky getting darker than Raven thought it possible without ever fully breaking. Forbes drove him further out of the city, bearing north. It made sense that the dress house should be away from the town, making clients less susceptible to being seen.

As they approached Trinity Grove, the first drumming on the roof of the cab commenced, very rapidly becoming a downpour as the carriage drove between the gates of a large property. With the rain so heavy and the sky so black, Raven could only see the building as a hazy outline. There was little light emanating from it, the curtains drawn and the gas lamps not lit at the door as it was still hours from twilight.

Raven alighted and sprinted the few yards from the carriage to the front entrance, the rain bouncing off his hat.

The door opened as he approached it, his arrival evidently having been noted. He stepped into an entrance hall where he was greeted by an attractive older woman attired as though she was about to attend a ball, allowing Raven to understand why they were called dress houses. She looked at him with a welcoming smile that failed to disguise wary suspicion, someone trained to be warmly hospitable but used to knowing to which gentlemen such hospitality should be extended.

'The Elysian Fields,' Raven said, taking in the opulent decor, the walls lined with wood panelling and draped with plush cloth.

'You are most welcome, Mr . . .?'

'Dr Will Raven,' he announced himself.

Given the secrecy surrounding the location, he suspected that simply presenting oneself here was probably an endorsement in and of itself, though as always he was unsure whether he passed muster sartorially. It must have helped that he had turned up in a carriage.

'Have we had the pleasure?' she asked, still smiling but also still looking as though she was on unsure footing.

'Pleasure is not my purpose here. I have come regarding another client, Mr Barrington Leitch. He was a patient of my late father-in-law, Dr Cameron Todd.'

Raven watched her expression, hoping to see recognition at the mention of each name. Her face gave away nothing, though her smile seemed a degree colder.

'We do not discuss any matters pertaining to our clients, and that includes confirming or denying who our clients are.'

'I don't need you to confirm that Mr Leitch was a client, because I know he died here.'

That snuffed the smile.

'Please bear with me,' she said, retreating down the hall. He watched her enter a room on the right and then re-emerge a few moments later, beckoning him forth. Perhaps it was the poor light, but she seemed paler.

'Right this way,' she said, indicating the door. She held it open for him, hurrying away before he had entered.

Raven stepped into a smoke-filled lounge where he found Magnus Cunningham upon a settee, drinking brandy, a cigar between his rough-skinned fingers. He was in the company of someone else Raven recognised: Wilkie, the policeman he had crossed paths with in the past. Wilkie got to his feet as Raven entered, more on guard than to greet him. He fixed Raven with a wary look, trying to seem intimidating but managing only to look anxious.

'Dr Raven,' Magnus said. 'What an extraordinary coincidence.'

Raven took in his surroundings. The room was luxuriantly decorated, almost to excess, with wall coverings and several large paintings, each of a pastoral landscape with a classical or allegorical theme. Sarah had told him about the nudes adorning the House of Melbourne, but this was altogether less vulgar, catering to men of refinement.

'Quite the place you have here,' he said.

'It's a folly,' Cunningham replied in that strange accent, forged in the Antipodes. 'Twice a folly, in fact, for I was foolish enough to purchase it, thinking its grandeur would make for a fine hotel. It is too far out of the way, though it has proven a worthwhile purchase in its own way.'

'I can imagine.'

'Please take a seat.'

Raven obliged, sitting on a most comfortable banquette.

'Wilkie, pour Dr Raven a whisky.'

The policeman went to a decanter and served Raven a large measure. Raven met his eyes as Wilkie handed him the glass. Pictured them above a scarf wrapped around his mouth and nose. He glanced at the policeman's hand, saw tiny specks such as dotted his own since the fire: the kind left by sparks.

Raven took a sip. 'Tastes smoky,' he observed, eyeing Wilkie.

'The good stuff,' Magnus replied. 'From the Highlands.'

Raven did not miss the significance.

'What brings you out this way?' Magnus asked. 'Did you discover any more about Dr Todd's investments? Where did he choose to put his money in the end?'

'I'm here regarding one of his patients. Barrington Leitch.'

Magnus took a sip from his glass. Taking time to think, Raven noted.

'A sad loss, but I don't know what it has to do with me.'

'He died here, that is what it has to do with you.'

Magnus said nothing, and in doing so said much. He wasn't going to deny it. Then he said, 'Discretion is an inestimable component of the service offered here. When a client dies in such circumstances, his dignity and that of his family must be preserved.'

'Such circumstances? Someone smashed the back of his skull. Then he was transported home and certified dead of his heart by a man you later thanked for his discretion.'

Magnus and Wilkie shared a look. Magnus appeared genuinely surprised, albeit just for a moment, though Raven could not say whether that was because Raven knew this or because it had come as a revelation to himself. He wouldn't have heard it from Wilkie, as Henry had only just submitted his report to the procurator fiscal, who had demanded complete discretion until he ruled on a course of action.

'Where did you hear this rumour?' Magnus asked, trying to lace his reaction with a scoff.

'I saw it with my own two eyes. The procurator fiscal exhumed the body.'

Magnus and Wilkie traded another glance, an unspoken question from the former, an embarrassed admission of ignorance from the latter.

Magnus put down his drink. His face was a mask now, a man who had suspicions of his own but was not about to share them.

'I know nothing about this,' he said. 'I was not present on the evening in question. It is my understanding that Mr Leitch died of his exertions, but it is possible he fell and struck his head. He did like a drink when he visited.'

Raven very much doubted this was the explanation, and very much doubted that Magnus believed it to be either. But nor was he certain Magnus had known about any of it until now.

'Who else was here that night?' he asked. 'Was there anyone present who might have wished Mr Leitch harm?'

'We do not reveal who our clients are here. As a doctor you should understand the importance of confidentiality.'

'Yes. It strikes me that you must know some highly delicate things about many people. The threat of their being revealed might make them most obliging towards you. Is that how you compelled Dr Todd to be so . . . discreet?'

Magnus sat up straighter on his settee. 'You fundamentally misunderstand what makes this business work, Dr Raven. Trust is my most valuable commodity. My clients here are among the most powerful individuals in this city: judges, generals, politicians, men of industry and commerce. I can take these people to paradise, and they pay handsomely for that, but if they thought for a moment that I could not be trusted, my business would be gone overnight.'

Raven could see the truth in this, but he also knew Magnus was needing money to expand. *If they thought for a moment . . .* Steps could always be taken to ensure that they did not. Such as couriers and concierges.

Raven knew he would get nothing more, so decided to change tack.

'Where was your man Wilkie yesterday evening? His hand looks like he's been playing with fire.'

Wilkie met Raven's gaze. There was no question that it had been him, and he knew it. His face remained impassive though, while Magnus's twisted into a snarl.

'He was sending out a warning,' Magnus said. 'I told you: I cater to the pleasures of the most powerful men in this city, and that will not be stopped by misguided fools making a nuisance of themselves. So tell Miss Fisher that she and her friends ought to find themselves some other pointless crusade.'

Raven tried not to flinch at the mention of Sarah's name, but he knew that was the reason Magnus mentioned it.

'Oh, does it trouble you that I know she is your friend?' Magnus took a puff of his cigar and blew the smoke towards Raven. 'When someone asks questions about me, I ask questions about them.'

There was a calm, a relish about Magnus's manner that sent a chill through Raven.

'You said your family were in St Andrews. I made enquiries and discovered there is indeed a lawyer there by the name of Raven.

Malcolm Raven. He has a daughter and two sons, neither of them named Will. But here's the thing, he's got a sister. Named Margaret. And by all accounts she is very proud that her son went to work for the great Professor James Simpson.'

Raven coughed at the smoke. He felt the room close around him.

Magnus fixed him with a penetrating stare. 'Why did you lie to me, Thomas?' he asked.

Raven got to his feet. 'Because I refuse to carry his name. When I hear it, I think only of him punching and kicking my mother and me in his rage.'

Magnus nodded regretfully. 'Aye. That's the danger when your livelihood is the bottle.'

'He didn't need to be drunk to beat her, or even angry. He enjoyed it. He relished her fear. But then, abusing helpless women would appear to run in your family.'

Magnus's sun-weathered face reddened in rage. 'Women are seldom as helpless as they like to pretend. They are schemers and thieves and tauntresses, and they need to be taught their place lest they run rings around you. They will be in your pocket when they're not in your ear, to say nothing of what they'll do behind your back. The only way they're worth something is with their legs apart.'

Magnus reached for his drink, his outburst spent. He made a contemptuous gesture with his free hand as though to dismiss Raven.

Raven gladly made his way to the door, then stopped to look at his uncle as he pulled it open.

'In case you didn't know,' Raven said, 'your brother was found dead in an alley. Beaten to death. I can only assume he made the mistake of picking a quarrel with someone who could fight back.'

Magnus regarded Raven with a quiet loathing. 'You should learn from his mistake, then,' he said, 'and mind who you pick a quarrel with.'

★ ★ ★

Raven stepped out into the courtyard. It was markedly brighter, the rain had stopped and there was some blue appearing between the dispersing clouds. Forbes was sitting inside the cab, having been sheltering from the downpour. He acknowledged Raven with a nod and climbed up to his seat, leaving the door open.

Raven strode across to the carriage and was about to climb inside, but turned to take in the building fully now that he could actually see it. A folly, Magnus had called it. It was an over-ornate construction, ostentatious in its grandeur, with crenelations atop towers either side of the structure intended to make it look like a palace.

Or a castle.

The implication struck him like it had been hurled from one of the parapets. Flo at the Lock Hospital had told Sarah that the girls had been ordered to remain in their rooms, but one of them had spied a body being carried out, wrapped in a sheet. If Elysian Fields was the Castle, then that body had been Leitch's.

Which meant Annabel might still be alive.

FIFTY-TWO

've found it,' Raven announced excitedly.

He was standing in front of the fireplace in the drawing room at Queen Street, Sarah having been summoned from her clinic duties by Jarvis. A matter of some importance, he had said. She had hoped — stupidly, she now realised — that he wanted to talk to her about what had happened between them, how he had reconsidered and decided he wanted her above all else. She hated herself for it. Saw it as a weakness in not accepting the reality of the situation.

'Found what?' she asked.

'The Castle.'

This *was* a matter of some importance.

'Where?'

'It's a place called the Elysian Fields, a folly that has turrets and crenelations, hence the nickname the girls had for it.'

'How did you find it?'

'Doesn't matter. It's what else I found that's important.'

'What?'

'I think Annabel might still be alive.'

Sarah sat down on one of the armchairs by the fireplace. She felt a bewildering array of emotions: hope, fear, anxiety.

'What makes you think so?' she asked. She wanted to believe

what Raven was saying, but after everything they had been through, she was finding optimism difficult to come by.

'The business of the body being removed, wrapped in a sheet,' he said. 'It was Leitch being taken away. It was Leitch who died there.'

Sarah took a moment, trying to assimilate this new information into what they already knew.

'But according to Flo at the Lock hospital,' she reminded him, 'after that night, Annabel was never seen again.'

'Magnus must have moved her on. To a different house.'

'Why would he do that?'

'I assume she saw something. Perhaps she witnessed what happened to Leitch.'

'Do you think it was Magnus who killed him?'

'I'm not sure that I do. But if Annabel was a witness, it would make her valuable to him.'

'That's a lot of assumptions,' Sarah said. At times it seemed assumptions were all they had. She felt the dull ache in her head again. Nothing was clear, everything becoming more complicated.

'Wilkie was there too,' Raven told her. 'The policeman. He's in Magnus's pay, which would explain a lot. He had scorch marks on his hands.'

'He set the fire.'

'You made yourselves a threat. Magnus boasted about his clients being military men, judges, generals and politicians. I think he enjoys the power he has over the women too.'

This made depressing sense. Power and the men who wielded it were at the heart of most of Edinburgh's problems. Sarah decided the time had come to share what she had uncovered and what she suspected.

'I believe Pike and Featherstone might be involved.'

'The recruitment agency? What makes you think so?'

'I've spoken to several people and some of the upstairs ladies have confirmed it. The girls they supply for domestic work are all plain, ordinary, nothing to look at; though some of the ladies used less polite terms in their descriptions.'

Raven looked confused. 'I don't understand.'

'Plain, ordinary, nothing to look at. Annabel was none of those things. What if Pike and Featherstone are part of the procurement process? What if girls like Annabel are sent elsewhere?'

'Somewhere like the Elysian Fields.'

'Exactly.'

'Well, if that's true, then perhaps Pike and Featherstone are connected to Magnus, part of his operation.' He frowned again. 'Still, it's not much to go on.'

'That's what Sanderson said.'

'Sanderson?'

'I took my theory to him first.'

Sarah hurried on before Raven could voice his redundant disapproval. She outlined the plan that Sanderson had proposed, Raven's expression becoming ever more dismayed. Sarah held up her hands to forestall the reprimand she knew was coming her way.

'It's all right. I said no. Told him it would be too risky.'

Raven's hunched shoulders dropped an inch or so. 'Good. Glad to hear it.'

'But everything has changed now. If Annabel is still alive then she can still be saved.'

Raven opened his mouth then closed it again. He knew what she said to be true.

'If I can prove that Pike and Featherstone are part of the procurement process, that gives me something I can work with. And if I can establish a link with Magnus, then that is something I can use as a trade.'

'As a trade?'

'If the information about his involvement in the procurement and rape of young women were to be made public, no decent person would patronise any of his hotels again, and perhaps those who frequent his brothels would think twice about their association with him too. It would ruin him.'

Raven frowned. 'So, you would see the story buried in exchange for Annabel?'

Raven had cut to the nub as usual. She remembered what Madame Bouvier had said to her. *Would you rescue them all, Miss Fisher? All those lost little girls?* It was what she had been trying to do, but now the stakes had changed.

'I don't see that I have much choice,' she said, though she knew this wasn't true. There *was* a choice to be made: Annabel or a newspaper story that could bring down the whole sordid edifice. But she knew that she could not sacrifice Annabel for a mere possibility.

Raven was still frowning. 'There's something else,' he said. 'Magnus knows who I am.'

'What do you mean?'

'He knows my real name.'

This was another significant development. Even Dr Simpson wasn't privy to that information.

'How did he find out?'

Raven blanched. 'Because Magnus Cunningham is my father's brother.'

Sarah suppressed her own surprise and dismay, as she could see how this must have burdened him. 'You never said you had an uncle.'

'I didn't know. As a child I heard him spoken of as though he was dead, but it transpires he was transported. This must have been when I was very young, as I didn't even know his name.'

'How long have you known he was your uncle?'

'Only since I spoke to him at his hotel. I deduced it from things he said. He mentioned how his brother had married a Margaret Raven, asked if she was a relative. It appears that, despite my denials, he made some deductions too, and he went to some lengths to confirm them.'

Sarah thought for a moment. 'It doesn't change anything though, does it?'

Raven looked directly at her, concern in his face. 'Only that I understand the nature of the man, as he is my father's brother in every respect. This ruse that you and Sanderson have cooked up together, it is high risk. Essentially, you'll be threatening him, and this dog bites.'

'It is a risk I have to take, though. For Annabel's sake.'

'But you've been to Pike and Featherstone's before, asking about Annabel. What if you are recognised? Is there no one who could go in your place?'

'I can't ask someone else to shoulder a risk I am not prepared to take myself,' she told him.

Committed to the idea, she thought again about Madame Bouvier's scornful taunt, *Would you rescue them all, Miss Fisher?* and remembered her reply.

I would start with rescuing one.

FIFTY-THREE

arah stood outside the bakery on Bread Street, wondering which came first, the street name or the business. It occupied the ground floor of the building, the office of Pike and Featherstone situated two floors above it. The yeasty smell coming through the open door of the shop was almost overpowering and made Sarah's stomach rumble. She had not eaten any breakfast this morning, too anxious about the task ahead of her.

She looked at the trays of tarts and pastries displayed in the window, thinking how far removed such colourful and sweet confections felt from the matters she was trying to expose.

'Should we buy something?' said a female voice.

Sarah turned to see Mary Anne, the girl Sanderson had assigned to the task of playing the untouched innocent, ripe for plucking. Sarah had been introduced to her the day before and had nearly called the whole thing off. Mary Anne was certainly young and beautiful, but she had hardly been the picture of purity and virtue.

'You're late,' Sarah told her.

Mary Anne was unperturbed. 'Took a while to find the right frock to wear,' she said.

Sarah had to admit it had been time well spent. The girl before her was transformed. Gone was the abundance of rouge and trussed-up decolletage. In its place a face scrubbed clean and a modest dress with a high, lace-trimmed neck.

'Where did you get the outfit?' Sarah asked.

'Pawnshop on the Grassmarket,' the girl replied. She sniffed one of her armpits. 'Think someone might have died in it.'

Sarah took the girl's arm. 'Come on. Let's get this over with.'

'Can we get a cake afterwards, then?' the girl persisted as Sarah dragged her away from the shop window.

'If this goes well, I'll buy you whatever you like.'

Sarah was still concerned about involving this young woman in their scheme, but Sanderson had assured her that Mary Anne knew exactly what she was doing, had agreed to all of it, and would come to no harm. Easy money, she had said when Sanderson outlined the job to her. In contrast Sarah was feeling nervousness bordering on nausea.

The painted sign for the Pike and Featherstone recruitment agency sat amidst those of other businesses beside the door to the close: dressmaker, staymaker, milliner. Sarah felt the doubt that had been plaguing her since her decision to go through with this. What if she had it all wrong? What if there was nothing to her suspicions? What if there was, and she was recognised?

She had worn her hair differently and donned some old clothes, pieces that had been mended one too many times. Respectable but well worn, Sanderson had advised. Present herself as too prosperous and the ruse was unlikely to work.

Mary Anne shuffled her feet. 'Will we be long, do you think? I've other things I need to be doing today.'

Spurred on by her restless companion, Sarah entered the building and climbed the stairs to the second floor. This time, the door was closed. She pulled the bell and took a deep breath as she heard the sound of footsteps. This could prove a very short visit if Doris Pike saw through her disguise, but the door was answered by a woman Sarah had not seen before. She heaved a sigh of relief.

'We've come about a position,' Sarah said.

'Then you've come to the right place,' the woman replied. 'Come away in. Take a seat.'

She had a friendly, professional manner. She looked to be in her mid-thirties, with fashionably styled hair, and clothes that were well made but sober and unostentatious. There was no hint of the disreputable about her. She lacked Mrs Hinchcliff's care-worn expression and world-weary attitude. Sarah wondered again whether this might be a colossal mistake, but then counselled herself that, if she was wrong, the worst that would happen was that she would give offence and be hastily shown the door.

The woman settled herself behind her desk and gave them both a smile. 'My name is Miss Lilian Featherstone,' she said. 'How can I be of assistance?'

Sarah felt her mouth dry. She was grateful that Sanderson had coached her, told her what to say. For her part Mary Anne was playing the innocent ingenue with aplomb, sitting demurely, gloved hands resting on her lap.

Miss Featherstone was studying the girl with an appraising eye. 'What is your name, my dear?' she asked.

'Matilda,' Mary Anne lied. 'Happy to make your acquaintance.' The falsehood tripped off her tongue easily, something she was used to. Telling people what they wanted to hear. Being who they wanted her to be.

'She's a good-looking young woman,' Sarah stated with a confidence she didn't feel. 'Don't you think?'

Miss Featherstone nodded her head. 'She is indeed.'

Sarah studied the woman's face for any sign she had been understood, but Featherstone's expression had not changed.

'A good girl,' Sarah continued, 'pure in every sense.'

She thought she saw the slight rise of an eyebrow.

'And how old are you?' Miss Featherstone asked Mary Anne.

'Sixteen next birthday.'

Miss Featherstone nodded again.

'Might I speak with you in private?' Sarah asked, looking across to the other side of the room.

'Of course,' Miss Featherstone said. She got to her feet, glancing at Mary Anne, who was making an impressive job of appearing guileless.

Sarah walked to the windows and lowered her voice as Miss Featherstone joined her.

'Matilda is too good for domestic work. If you know what I mean.'

Featherstone did not reply, fixing Sarah with a firm but neutral stare.

Sarah pressed on, endeavouring to keep her voice steady. 'A valuable commodity. In the right place she would surely attract a hefty price.'

Featherstone frowned now. If Sarah was wrong about this she was about to find out. She said nothing for a moment, the tension in the air thickening. Featherstone looked at Mary Anne, then back at Sarah.

'What is your relationship with the girl?' she asked.

'She's my sister. But I've been mother to her these last few years since our own mother died. She told me what to do when the time came. Who to go to and what to ask for.'

The woman gave Sarah a shrewd look. 'And what exactly are you asking for?'

Sarah held her nerve and the woman's gaze. 'Half your commission as a finder's fee.'

The woman snorted, shook her head. Again, Sarah was grateful for Sanderson's coaching. They had been prepared for this. A first refusal.

'If we can't come to an arrangement,' Sarah said stiffly, 'I'm sure I can find someone else.'

Featherstone looked unruffled. 'I'm not saying we can't do business,' she said.

Sarah felt her heart thumping in her chest, her elevated pulse audible in her own ears.

'I assume you know the rules about these things,' Featherstone went on. 'How this is done.'

Sarah nodded. She realised she had been right in her deduction but did not feel good about it.

'Before terms are agreed, there must be an inspection,' Miss Featherstone continued.

'I understand.'

The woman wrote something down on a piece of paper and handed it to her.

'Take your sister to this address at the time specified. She will be seen by a gentleman who will ascertain whether or not she is pure. If all is found to be as you claim, then we can discuss payment.'

'What gentleman?' Sarah asked. 'A doctor?'

Miss Featherstone narrowed her eyes and Sarah worried that she had given herself away by being too inquisitive.

'He is qualified to make the assessment,' Featherstone replied a little curtly, her air of friendly professionalism all but gone. 'That is all you need to know.'

Sarah decided not to ask anything further. She had what she came for. She looked at the piece of paper. It was the name of a hotel; one she knew belonged to Magnus Cunningham. Suddenly everything seemed to be falling into place.

Sarah took Mary Anne by the arm, hoisted her up from her chair.

'Thank you for your time,' she said to Miss Featherstone, concealing the growing urgency with which she wished to get out of there. She felt a vast sense of relief as she closed the door behind the pair of them and they began descending the stairs.

'That couldn't have gone better,' Mary Anne opined.

'Thank you. You put on a remarkably convincing performance.'

'Maybe I'm fit for the stage.'

They reached the front door and were stepping out onto the street when Sarah almost collided with a woman on her way in.

Doris Pike.

'Excuse me,' Sarah said, dipping her head and hoping her hat was hiding her face. She took Mary Anne's arm again and started walking down the street.

'What about my cake?' Mary Anne whined.

'Keep walking,' Sarah insisted, her pace brisk.

She waited a few moments then risked looking back.

Doris Pike was gone.

FIFTY-FOUR

Raven was heading for Charlotte Square, but his mind kept returning to Sarah, where she would be and what she would be doing.

He had offered to accompany her on her trip back to Pike and Featherstone, but she insisted that it would appear less suspicious if she went without him. Sanderson had heard tell of mothers selling their daughters, and his scheme required Sarah to pose as someone offering up a younger sister. Raven had to concede that he didn't really fit in with this plan, but he had at least got Sarah to agree that they would confront Magnus together once they had enough proof to bargain with.

He headed across the square to the home of James Matthews Duncan. It was a grand address for a man only a few years older than Raven: the kind of residence a man could more easily afford were he to supplement his income with thousands of pounds in blackmail money.

The true identity of the blackmailer still remained a mystery, Raven constantly changing his mind as possibilities presented and then dismissed themselves. He understood why Magnus had insisted he could not afford to be blackmailing his own clients, but perhaps it was more accurate to say he could not afford to be *caught* blackmailing his own clients.

That said, Dr Simpson was most definitely not a client of

Magnus Cunningham, and it was not his activities in a brothel that were being held over him. Raven also remained convinced there was a personal aspect to it. He suspected that the blackmailer was someone who bore a grudge against the professor, which was not true of Magnus. And yet the individual blackmailing Todd, Simpson and Professor Conville was surely one and the same. He used the same hand and the same phrase: *stay in my good graces*.

Raven was sure he had heard similar words spoken aloud recently but could not remember where or by whom. Raven hadn't spoken to Matthews Duncan in a very long time, but it was possible he had overheard him at the Medico-Chirurgical meeting.

He had thought of asking Simpson whether he possessed any correspondence sent by Matthews Duncan, to compare the hand-writing. It would have been some time ago as he and Simpson were no longer on speaking terms, but Simpson was a bit of a hoarder and likely to have kept the letters had there been any. Then it occurred to Raven that someone who sent couriers to protect their anonymity might also get someone else to write the notes, though it would have to be someone they were in league with.

Matthews Duncan and Magnus? Could it be? But how? Was he also certifying virgins for Raven's uncle? He had to confess he couldn't envisage *that* of the man. This whole thing was apt to drive him mad.

There were two carriages outside the address he was looking for. Raven called out to both drivers: 'Which one of you drives for Dr Matthews Duncan?'

'That would be me,' said a surly, grizzled man with an unruly beard. He was hunched in his seat, as though bent that way by too many hours exposed to inclement weather, a book open in his lap. Raven was reminded of Simpson's insistence about making use of bits and pieces of time. He thought also of Sarah when they first met, stealing moments in the chaos of Simpson's clinic to read *Jane Eyre*, the story of a resourceful young woman who chose to be with a damaged individual, despite knowing of his troubled past and the fact he already had a wife.

'Did you happen to be passing Gayfield Square last night?' Raven asked, trying to make the enquiry sound casual.

'I am not at liberty to discuss the doctor's movements with just anyone,' the man replied.

Raven wondered if he was holding out for an emolument in exchange for information, or whether he was being as discreet as Simpson's coachman, Angus, had always been. Given his aloof and frosty manner, he couldn't imagine Matthews Duncan engendering the same degree of loyalty from his staff. But whether money was expected or not was moot, as Raven was currently without the means of paying the man anything.

The coachman looked at Raven for a moment, then put his book down. 'I won't tell you where I took him,' the man said, 'but I can tell you it wasn't Gayfield Square. He was to the south of the city all day yesterday and into the evening, delivering a young lady of her firstborn. That's as much as I can say.'

Raven expressed his thanks as the man returned to his book.

A short while later Raven was making his way back along George Street, thinking about what the coachman had said. If he was telling the truth – and Raven could not think of any reason why the man should lie – it was not Matthews Duncan who had been in the carriage on Gayfield Square the previous night. In which case, who was it?

He was so engrossed in his thoughts that he almost bumped into someone coming out of one of the shops that lined the street. 'My apologies,' he said, tipping his hat before realising it was Agnes Syme, Eugenie's friend and confidante.

At the sight of her, Raven thought immediately of someone else who bore Dr Simpson a persistent grudge: Agnes's father, Professor James Syme. Raven dismissed the notion, however. For all their professional rivalries, Syme had very probably saved Simpson's life a few years back. Nor could Raven imagine the surgeon being sleekit and underhand in his dealing with Simpson, or anyone else for that matter. Syme was rather more direct with his professional rivals. Only recently Simpson had infuriated him by publishing a pamphlet about what he referred to as 'acupressure', suggesting the use of metal pins to ligate blood vessels, rather than catgut sutures. Syme had been incensed at the idea of an obstetrician invading what he considered to be surgical territory. He had apparently held up the despised pamphlet in the operating theatre, denounced it in front of his surgical class, torn it in half and then discarded the pieces into the surgical remains box under the operating table.

No, blackmail was definitely not in keeping with Syme's modus operandi, inclined to stab you in the front rather than the back, and watching your face as he twisted the knife. How he had managed to raise such a pleasant daughter had always struck Raven as something of a mystery.

Agnes gave him a warm smile. 'How is Eugenie?' she asked.

The way she was looking at him suggested that this was something more than a polite enquiry. He suspected she knew more than most about what had been happening of late. Eugenie had, after all, been spending a fair bit of time with this particular friend.

'Things have been difficult,' Raven admitted. 'But time is a great healer, or so they say. I'll just have to bide my time and be patient.'

Agnes put out a gloved hand and gave Raven's forearm a gentle squeeze. 'Perhaps not for too much longer,' she suggested. 'I saw Eugenie yesterday. She seemed that bit brighter.'

'And are you feeling better?' he asked. 'I heard that you were off taking the sea air.'

'I'm just back, actually. North Berwick. Have you been?'

Raven shook his head.

'It's a lovely place. A week there proved to be most restorative.'

'A week?' Raven asked, reeling.

'Yes. Did me a power of good.' She looked at him with concern. 'If you don't mind me saying, you look as if you could do with a dose of sea air yourself. Take care, Dr Raven.' She gave his arm another squeeze then walked away.

Raven stood watching her on unsteady feet as he processed

what he had just heard. No amount of sea air was going to blow away what was assailing him right then.

Agnes had been away in North Berwick on the night Eugenie claimed to have stayed with her at the Syme residence, here in Edinburgh.

FIFTY-FIVE

arah entered the lobby of the Clarendon Hotel, Mary Anne trailing behind her. There were bountiful amounts of chintz, velvet drapes, sofas and chairs upholstered in expensive fabrics, a tiled marble floor, potted ferns, and glass chandeliers.

Sarah spun round, taking it all in. 'Beautiful,' she said, impressed in spite of herself.

Mary Anne did not share Sarah's view. 'Been here before,' she said, clearly familiar with the opulence of the place. She was dressed in the same modest gown as before but kept pulling at the neck of it. 'This thing is near strangling me,' she complained.

Sarah looked around, worried that Doris Pike might be here, but was relieved to see Lilian Featherstone, unaccompanied, making her way towards them from across the lobby. She gave them both a smile, warm and friendly. No hint that she knew who Sarah really was, or that Doris Pike had recognised the woman who had passed her as she came in a few hours ago.

'The doctor has been delayed,' she said apologetically. 'Let's take a seat. I've ordered tea.'

Miss Featherstone seemed unconcerned that she had let slip a doctor was involved, something she had seemed guarded about previously. Perhaps she failed to realise she had done so, or perhaps this was a further indication that Sarah was being trusted.

She led them into one of the lounges situated off the lobby, sitting herself down amongst the frills and florals. Sarah's initial impression of the place was starting to tarnish. It all suddenly felt too much, oppressive and imposing rather than merely opulent. Suffocating. She worried her anxiety was getting the better of her.

As she and Mary Anne took their seats opposite Miss Featherstone, a young serving girl approached with a silver tray. Black uniform. Pristine starched apron. She placed the tray down on the table between them. Miss Featherstone gave the girl a smile. Sarah couldn't help but notice that the girl was plain to the point of frumpy. She wondered if Pike and Featherstone were responsible for her employment here.

'Shall I pour?' Miss Featherstone said. 'It's from Ceylon. Quite delicious.'

Sarah watched as Miss Featherstone went through the motions with teapot, strainer, milk and sugar. She offered the plate of biscuits that had come with the tea to Mary Anne, who politely shook her head. 'Thank you, no,' she said, eyes cast down, her voice just above a whisper.

She really should be on the stage, Sarah thought.

Sarah lifted her teacup and took a sip. It was warm, fragrant, and she drank some more. The heat it brought to her chest was comforting. It was only then she noticed a slight aftertaste, rather bitter. She wasn't sure she cared for it and wouldn't be ordering it again, no matter where it came from.

Mary Anne seemed to be enjoying hers. She still hadn't taken a biscuit and Sarah was impressed at this display of self-discipline. She had a liking for sweet things, something Sarah had learned to her cost having being dragged back to the bakery on Bread Street after Doris Pike had disappeared. Whatever Sanderson was paying her, he could probably have negotiated its equivalent in confectionary.

They drank in silence for a few minutes, then Miss Featherstone placed her cup down and looked directly at Mary Anne.

'Do you really want to be in service, Matilda?' she asked, her voice soft and silky. 'You strike me as a girl of taste and refinement.'

So this is how it's done, Sarah thought. Like a seduction. Clearly the girls who got this far had no idea what was going on.

'Do you like the theatre?' Miss Featherstone continued. 'Fine hotels and handsome gentlemen?'

Mary Anne looked up, paused for a moment before answering. 'Who wouldn't?' she said.

Miss Featherstone smiled again. 'Then perhaps we can find better employment for you. Would you like that?'

Mary Anne put her cup down, looked at Sarah then back at Miss Featherstone. 'I would, as it happens,' she said. 'Better that than scrubbing floors and cleaning out chamber pots.'

Miss Featherstone laughed. 'You have spirit. I like that.'

You don't know the half of it, Sarah thought. She wondered again how Annabel had been duped. Not like this, surely. This was too obvious for a girl of Annabel's intelligence. She thought about what Mrs Hinchcliff had said. How young girls started off as servants in some houses, unaware initially of the business that was really conducted there. These people had many ways to ensnare their prey.

Miss Featherstone reached for the teapot again and was about to pour some more when the serving girl approached bearing a note. Miss Featherstone read it, then folded it up and slipped it into her reticule.

'A change of plan,' she announced. 'Unanticipated complications. It seems we must go to him.'

She stood up, took Mary Anne's hand, and led her back towards the lobby. 'Our carriage awaits,' she announced brightly, as though they were going on some jaunt to the country rather than headed to some dubious medical practitioner to ascertain whether Mary Anne's maidenhead was intact.

Sarah followed, feeling suddenly lightheaded. The heavily patterned wallpaper seemed to be moving, heavy flower heads swaying in an impossible breeze. She paused for a moment, shook her head, waited for her vision to clear.

The fresher air outside the hotel helped. She hadn't been eating much of late, her appetite suppressed by a near-constant state of worry. She should have had one of those fancy biscuits with her tea.

They climbed into the carriage that was waiting just outside the door of the hotel. Sarah noticed the livery on the side: a lion's head, two unicorns and the initials M and C. She sat down beside Mary Anne. Miss Featherstone seemed to be looking at her strangely, examining her for some reason. Sarah wondered why she should be the focus of her attention.

The carriage moved off, the rocking motion making Sarah feel sleepy. She felt the dizziness descend again, her vision becoming blurry at the edges. She thought she might be about to faint. Not an unpleasant feeling. Like floating through water. Dream-like.

'Are you all right?'

She heard the voice vaguely, as though from a distance, before drifting off into oblivion.

She came to lying across the carriage seat, finding herself alone. Her mouth felt dry, her throat parched, her tongue sticking unpleasantly to the roof of her mouth.

She made to sit up, but the movement caused her head to ache, as though her brain was bouncing around her skull, entirely unrestrained. She thought she might be sick.

She lay still for a moment, trying to work out what had happened to her. She remembered the meeting at the hotel, the change of venue, the carriage. But then what?

A few disparate images drifted through her mind. Fleur-de-lis wallpaper. The smell of lavender.

She waited for the nausea to settle, trying to remember more. But there was nothing. A blank.

What had happened to Mary Anne? She thought of Sanderson's reassurances. Empty promises from a disreputable man. She had been wrong to trust him. He said nothing bad would happen. But something had: she just couldn't remember what.

She risked sitting up again, pulled the carriage window down and took a deep breath of cooler air. She saw that she was outside 52 Queen Street. But that made no sense. What was she doing there?

She opened the carriage door, stepped tentatively down to the street. Her legs buckled and she felt strong arms about her.

'Let's get you inside,' she heard someone say. A familiar voice but in her present state she couldn't quite place it. She felt herself drifting again.

The next time she woke, she was in her own bed, in her own room. There was a glass of water stationed on her bedside table, which she downed in one, slaking an appalling thirst.

She lay back on her pillows, trying to marshal her thoughts.

The hotel. Miss Featherstone. The tea. The carriage. Then what?

Everything after that was vague and blurry.

She felt a sudden chill as she recalled Mrs Hinchcliff talking about the black draught that was given to the girls to make them compliant. Thought again about the tea. The Clarendon Hotel. *Magnus Cunningham*'s hotel.

She had been dosed with something.

She closed her eyes. Tried to concentrate. Tried to remember. It was all broken fragments. Disordered. Disconnected from one another. Blue wallpaper, the smell of jasmine and lavender. Faceless people. Muted voices. Cool air. Someone's hands upon her.

So many images now. The colour blue, the fragrance of a summer garden. None of them coherent.

But one image kept coming back, becoming clearer each time it resurfaced.

And in it she was naked.

FIFTY-SIX

arah turned her head away, revealing the upper part of her chest. Raven placed his stethoscope on the exposed flesh, bent his head and listened, though it was his own heart that had been thumping since he learned of what happened.

They were in his consulting room at Great Stuart Street. He had insisted on taking her there and examining her for signs of any lingering issues after her poisoning. That was how he chose to refer to it. A poisoning. An intoxication. He was concerned about long-term damage given that they had no idea what agent had been used.

Sarah had tried to reassure him. She said she felt fully recovered, her only lingering fear the fact that she still had no memory of what happened to her; or no coherent memory anyway. She had expressed a desire to see Sanderson, to find out whether he knew what had happened to Mary Anne, but Raven would not hear of it. After what had just happened, he didn't want her going anywhere.

'Your heart sounds are pure, and your chest is clear,' he said. He stood back and looked at her as she buttoned up her dress. 'But I'm still worried.'

'As am I.'

'I agree Magnus must have had a hand in this. It was his hotel.'

'And a connection with Pike and Featherstone seems to have been established. So that's something, I suppose.'

'I think you've paid too heavy a price for that piece of information,' Raven said.

Sarah looked away from him, out of the window. 'I'm not sure I know exactly what the price was as yet.'

Raven thought of Magnus saying the fire at the meeting hall was only a warning. He felt anger growing in him, but alongside it was a deepening fear. This was not like butting heads with Flint and his rabble of cut-throats and ne'er-do-wells. This was a powerful man, connected to even more powerful people, whom he could call upon for favours.

The sound of the doorbell ringing out caused them both to jump.

Raven smiled, trying to make light of their exaggerated response. 'I'll go,' he said.

He strode into the hallway and opened the door to find Wilkie standing on the other side of it.

'Mr Cunningham wishes to see you and Miss Fisher at the Clarendon,' he said without preamble.

Raven wondered how Magnus was aware that Sarah would be there, decided he probably didn't want to know.

'Miss Fisher is indisposed,' Raven said. 'Something she imbibed disagreed with her.'

Wilkie gave him a vicious-looking smile. 'It's not an invitation. It's an order.'

They were shown into Magnus's office, with the view towards the Forth.

Raven's uncle sat behind his desk, master of all he surveyed. He had a self-satisfied look on his face, the expression of a man used to getting what he wanted.

'Take a seat,' he said, indicating two chairs positioned on the other side of the desk.

'I think we'll stand,' Raven replied.

'As you wish,' Magnus said, drawing a large cigar from a humidor on the desk. 'You might come to regret that decision, given what I have to show you. Especially you, Miss Fisher. We all know how delicate you ladies can be.'

Raven looked at Sarah, saw the worry in her face. They both took a seat.

Magnus rolled the cigar between his fingers, lifted it to his nose and inhaled its scent. Taking his time, he struck a match and inhaled deeply, blowing rings of pungent smoke towards them. Raven could see Sarah stifle a cough.

He opened a drawer in his desk, from which he pulled out two envelopes. He slid one over the desk towards Sarah. 'Open it,' he said, leaning back in his chair, a malicious leer on his pockmarked face.

Her hands trembling, Sarah reached for the envelope and fumbled with the folded edge. Something slipped out onto the desk.

A photograph.

Raven watched as what little colour was left drained from her.

The photograph was of Sarah, stripped bare, her body draped across a chaise longue, eyes glazed as though in a delirium of ecstasy.

Sarah flipped the photograph over, put a hand to her mouth.

Magnus took another puff on his cigar, leant back in his chair and blew smoke rings towards the ceiling.

'I have an associate,' he said. 'Clever fellow. He photographs certain ladies on occasion, and the pictures sell for a pretty penny. Uses some new process. He explained it to me. I couldn't follow the chemistry, but I did understand the part about being able to make as many prints as I want.'

He paused for a moment, letting that piece of information sink in.

'I can send prints of these to everyone who knows you,' he continued. 'I can hand them out to my clients. And of course I could sell them in any number of places up and down the country so that gentlemen collectors might gratify themselves.'

Raven saw that Sarah was gripping the arms of her chair, her knuckles white.

'What do you want?' she asked, her voice trembling in anger and despair.

'She gets straight to the point,' Magnus said, looking at Raven. 'I like that in a woman. Refreshingly rare. I prefer it when they don't make you dance around and play games before giving you what you want.'

Magnus stubbed his cigar out in an ashtray, grinding the end of it slowly, in no hurry to put them out of their misery.

'I've heard she fancies herself a doctor,' he said, still addressing Raven as though Sarah wasn't there. 'A woman doctor, eh? Makes me think of Dr Johnson and what he had to say about a woman preaching. Like a dog walking on its hind legs. It is not done well; but you are surprised to find it done at all.'

Magnus must have noticed the look on Raven's face.

'What? Surprised that I've heard of Johnson, is that it? Think I'm stupid? You'd do well not to underestimate me, Thomas.'

'My name,' Raven said through gritted teeth, 'is Will Raven.'

'Well, here's something for you, Will Raven.' Magnus slid the other envelope across the desk.

Raven looked reluctantly at it, feeling a growing dread as he opened it. It contained precisely what he feared most: another photograph, this one of Eugenie.

Raven closed his eyes for a moment. He thought of the time Eugenie had taken to her bed a few weeks ago, saying she had eaten bad oysters. She told him she had woken up outside their door, and assumed she had fallen asleep in the carriage. She must have been given the black draught too. Magnus had sought her out, sent this associate to target her, so that he could blackmail her father. The thought of someone following her, handling her, made him shudder, made him murderous, but he knew he had to stay in control of himself. Magnus had absolute power here, which was why the same feelings had ultimately driven Cameron Todd to his end.

'How did you get this?'

'I have my ways. You should know that by now. You ought to be keeping a closer eye on that wife of yours. Teach her what her place is.' He looked at both of them in turn, enjoying his moment of power. 'Personally, I think a bitch's place is on all fours.' He turned to Sarah. 'That's why you're going to come and work for me, Miss Fisher.'

'Work for you?' Sarah's expression was aghast.

Magnus laughed. 'No, nothing like that. You're a bit too old. But you have a face young girls would trust. You'll be invaluable in helping us find new recruits.'

Sarah's head dropped, unable to meet his gaze. She was trembling, though with rage, fear or despair Raven could not say.

'Speaking of which, I believe you're looking for a girl who worked for me.'

Sarah's head shot up again. 'Annabel?' she asked.

'That's the one. Looked like butter wouldn't melt in her mouth, and yet she robbed me, slick as any cut-throat. Absconded the night old Leitch died and took something that belonged to me. A ledger. I want you to find her and return my property. Return the girl as well. She belongs to me also.'

He turned to Raven. 'You're both going to work for me, in fact. I want Dalton's Hotel, and you, Thomas, are going to become Mr Dalton's doctor.'

'I take it Mr Dalton doesn't have a choice in the matter,' Raven said. 'Do you have a photograph of his wife too?'

Magnus laughed again, enjoying this too much. 'I have other means of influence. Dalton doesn't like me, but I know people he *does* like, and even now they are recommending you, so you ought to be grateful. But even if they are insufficiently persuasive, I will expect you to be resourceful in getting access to old Reginald, and you will find a way to make it discreet.'

'Make what discreet?'

'He doesn't want to sell to me, but his wife does. And a widow's will is not to be denied.'

It took Raven a moment to understand what was being asked of him. Not asked — demanded. The enormity of it hit him hard, like a blow to the temple. The implications were far-reaching, other things falling into place.

'This is what you asked Cameron Todd to do,' he said. He picked up the photograph of Eugenie. 'And this is what you held over him, how you thought you could persuade him to do it.'

Magnus smiled. 'On the night Leitch died — still not my doing, by the way — my associate dealt with it, and he compelled Todd to help him using that photograph you're holding. When I subsequently discovered that Dr Todd was Reginald Dalton's doctor, well, I saw a serendipitous opportunity. You learn to seize those when you've been banished to the other side of the world for a while.'

He gave an exaggerated sigh.

'I thought I had left Todd with no choice than to cooperate, but the awkward bugger found a way out, a way *not* to give me what I wanted.'

'Maybe you shouldn't have bled him of all his money, then,' Raven said. 'He knew a man like you would never stop. How much did you take from Conville before *he* killed himself?'

Magnus wore the same expression as he had back at Elysian Fields. Raven had just told him something he did not know. And just as at Elysian Fields, he quickly hid his surprise, composed himself.

'It's a shame that Todd frustrated my plans in such an extreme manner,' he said. 'But as it turns out, his son-in-law is now in a position to be just as useful. Family's a blessing, isn't it?'

'You can't choose your relatives,' Raven said bitterly.

He looked over at Sarah, who seemed to have closed in on herself. Magnus had them right where he wanted them. He held all the cards, leaving them with no option but to do as he directed. Play by his twisted rules.

'If we do this,' Raven said, 'you give us the original photographic plates. To both images.'

Cunningham gave an ugly laugh. 'Christ, no,' he said. 'We are not bargaining here, Thomas. Whatever gave you that impression?'

He leaned forward, elbows resting on his desk, then looked at them each in turn.

'I own you,' he said. 'Both of you. And if you don't like it, Dr Todd demonstrated the only way out.'

FIFTY-SEVEN

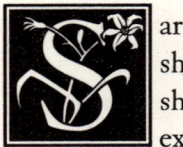arah took another mouthful of brandy, more than she knew she should try to swallow in one go, but she wanted to feel it burn just so that she could experience something beyond the emotions that had enveloped her since she saw the photograph. There were flashes of anger and hatred, but mostly she felt helplessness and fear.

They were in the kitchen at Great Stuart Street again, having retreated there after returning from the Clarendon Hotel. She hadn't spoken for the longest time; neither of them had, both sitting in dazed silence, contemplating the enormity of their situation. She felt almost as if she had been drugged again, detached from reality.

She could see the image every time she closed her eyes, and it turned her stomach to think of how easily Magnus could make good on his threat: how many people might see it then, and what that would do to her.

She would be ruined. Shamed. Shunned. An outcast.

How could she ever face anyone who had seen it? How would she know who had?

Magnus Cunningham knew what he was about. He knew that she would go to any length to prevent that photograph being distributed, knew that she would do exactly as he wanted. Then she remembered what that was. To be part of his abhorrent organisation.

To assist Pike and Featherstone. The very thing she had been fighting against, she would now become. And he wanted her to find Annabel, then give her up to him.

Two different versions of hell. And only one way out.

She had never felt such fear. She had never felt such powerlessness, such a sense of someone having control of her.

For his part Raven had looked equally adrift, eventually bestirring himself to pour two hefty measures of brandy. At this rate there would be none left for the patients, but then there were unlikely to be many patients after this. All of their plans, their arrangement, would come to nothing. All of Sarah's ambitions, crushed.

'Trouble always seems to find us, doesn't it?' she said, finding her voice.

Raven looked up from contemplating the brandy in his glass and gave her a rueful smile. 'My life has certainly been full of incident since I met you,' he said.

'Would you have had it any other way?'

Raven looked at her for a moment. 'It's hard to imagine my life without you in it,' he said.

Sarah felt a warmth in her chest that wasn't from the drink. She was closer to Raven than anyone, their relationship forged by shared experience, good and bad. She found it hard to contemplate any sort of life without him either.

'If there is any consolation,' he said, 'it is that we now know Annabel is alive. And Magnus doesn't have her.'

'Not yet, but he will soon enough. What choice do we have in any of this now?'

'This is exactly the situation Eugenie's father faced,' Raven said, glancing out of the window. 'I know that now too. He was asked to cover up Leitch's death, and then Magnus asked him to do away with a patient. He couldn't go through with it, and saw only one way to protect his daughter.'

'A man of honour in the end.'

'I suppose that might be of some comfort to Eugenie.'

'You can't tell her about the photograph,' Sarah said.

'I don't intend to.'

'What *are* we going to do?'

Raven had no answer for her.

'Part of me wants to pack a bag,' she said. 'Run away from all of it.'

'Understandable. Perhaps you should leave. Go where the photographs can't find you.'

'Banish myself?'

Raven shrugged. 'We don't have many options, do we?'

'What about you?'

'What about me? I can't go anywhere. My family and my responsibilities are here.'

Raven drained his glass, got up to pour himself some more but seemed to change his mind.

'When I mentioned the blackmail, Magnus taking money from Cameron Todd, he seemed surprised, didn't he?'

'I wasn't paying much attention at that point,' Sarah admitted. 'Couldn't bring myself to look at him.'

'He reacted in much the same way when I told him Leitch had his skull bashed in. He disguised it, but it was news to him.'

Raven put his empty glass down.

'This associate he mentioned: Magnus was able to compel Todd using the photograph he supplied, but it's my guess Magnus didn't know he was already extorting the man.'

'Apparently not,' Sarah agreed.

'So the photographer *is* our blackmailer,' Raven said. 'He was already blackmailing Todd when Leitch was killed; that's how he knew he could prevail upon Todd to cover it up. Though that doesn't explain what's happening to Dr Simpson.'

'Dr Simpson?'

Raven looked at Sarah. 'He has also been the victim of blackmail.'

Sarah's shock must have shown on her face.

'It has nothing to do with brothels,' Raven reassured her. Under other circumstances they might have been amused at her misunderstanding. 'It has to do with the adoptions he and

Mrs Simpson organise.' He put his hands up to ward off any further questions. 'I don't know the details, so don't ask. He wouldn't tell me.'

Sarah went to take another sip of her brandy then put it down. She was feeling muddled enough without adding any more alcohol.

'It's hard to see how Simpson's and Todd's blackmail might be connected,' she said.

'Then let's focus on the immediate threat. This photographer has been taking pictures for Magnus to sell using this new process, and blackmailing people on the side. If we find him, we can find the photographic plates.'

Sarah nodded firmly, seeing his logic. 'Destroy them, and the copies Magnus has already, and he loses his hold over us,' she said.

'Problem is, how do we find someone when all we know of him is that he takes photographs? I don't even know where to begin.'

'I do,' Sarah said.

FIFTY-EIGHT

eopold Place was not far from the studio where Raven and Sarah had first met Janet Mann. She had been working at Rock House as assistant to the photography pioneers David Octavius Hill and Robert Adamson, one of the first women to be involved in photography. She was a skilful assistant and on occasion took photographs on her own, most notably a portrait of the King of Saxony, who had arrived at Rock House with his entourage when neither Hill nor Adamson were present. The photograph had been credited to the men who owned the studio rather than the woman who took it, her contribution never acknowledged.

Would this always be a woman's fate? Sarah thought as they approached the front door: their influence and involvement forever overlooked, no more than a footnote, overshadowed by men? It made her recall a character in one of Jane Austen's novels discussing the shortcomings of history books: "'The quarrels of popes and kings, with wars or pestilences, in every page; the men all so good for nothing, and hardly any women at all.'"

Sarah thought of her own ambitions and how they were now grasped in the hand of a cruel and callous man, her entire fate suspended in chemicals on a glass plate, like some magic spell. It was absurd that it could be so simple and yet that was the truth of it. The photograph had an unanswerable power over her.

Miss Mann answered the door herself. She was a neat, compact woman, unprepossessing, her diminutive frame concealing her considerable talent.

'Miss Mann,' Sarah said. 'Please excuse this intrusion. My name is Sarah Fisher. We met a number of years ago.'

Miss Mann scrutinised her face for a moment, her brow drawn into a frown. Then her expression softened in recognition. 'I remember,' she said. 'I took your photograph. You were interested in the chemistry of it, as I recall.'

'Yes, that's right. This is my associate, Dr Will Raven.'

'I remember you too,' Miss Mann said. 'Bit of a poor subject compared to Miss Fisher.'

Raven tipped his hat. 'There can be no arguing with that,' he said.

Miss Mann opened the door. 'Do come in,' she said.

She led them to a modest parlour at the front of the house with a view of the gardens on the opposite side of London Road.

'Sit, sit,' she urged. 'My sisters and I don't get much in the way of company these days. To what do I owe the honour?'

'Our enquiry is photography related,' Sarah said.

'Oh?'

'I hoped that you might be the person to help us.'

'Well, I don't do as much of it as I used to,' she said, looking suddenly mournful. 'Lost interest after Mr Adamson died.'

'Yes,' Sarah said. 'He was so young. And so prodigiously talented.'

'Tuberculosis, wasn't it?' Raven asked.

Sarah drew him a look. The pathology that resulted in Robert Adamson's premature demise was surely irrelevant at this point, but doctors could not help themselves.

'We have a photograph we'd like to show you,' Sarah told her. 'The subject matter is rather— ' She searched for the appropriate word. ' —indelicate.'

Miss Mann looked at her and nodded. 'I'm not as fragile as I look, Miss Fisher.'

'We're trying to track down the photographer responsible for it.

Any information you might give us could prove invaluable in finding him.'

Miss Mann fished out a pair of spectacles from a pocket in her dress and held out her hand. Raven passed her the photograph featuring the girl he had recognised from the Lock Hospital. All of those found in Todd's trunk showed young women draped seductively over a chaise longue in various degrees of undress. The furniture and the wallpaper were the same in each image, including the ones featuring Eugenie and Sarah. Same place. Same photographer.

Sarah had speculated that Dr Todd had been sent the others merely to underline how his daughter's image might be easily distributed. Raven had countered that perhaps it was his interest in such images that had brought Todd to the photographer's attention. They would never know.

Miss Mann's eyes widened briefly. 'How did you come by this?' she asked.

'Probably best that you don't know,' Raven replied.

'We need to know who took it,' Sarah said. 'Have you any idea how we might identify the photographer?'

Miss Mann glanced at the back of the print. 'No signature, no notation of any sort,' she observed. She looked at the image again. 'These are quality furnishings. Throws, upholstery: all can provide clues. Portraits include them deliberately to give some sense of the sitter. Any indicators in this one would presumably be unintentional. I assume none of it strikes either of you as familiar?'

Sarah strained to remember, but her recall of her ordeal remained fragmented and occluded.

'Could the photographer be identified from some aspect of his technique?' Raven suggested, beginning to sound a little desperate.

'When last we met, I could have given you no more than half a dozen names for all of Scotland,' Miss Mann said. 'But things have changed. There are more practitioners all the time. New processes, new techniques.' She indicated the photograph. 'And with it, inevitable perversions of the art.'

'Can you tell us anything about the print itself?' Raven asked.

'The quality of it suggests Archer's wet collodion process. It produces multiple prints of extraordinary clarity and detail, over and over again.' She said this with an enthusiasm Sarah did not, could not share. 'Sharp like a daguerreotype, reproducible like a calotype.'

'Is there any way of finding out who is using this process in Edinburgh?' Sarah asked.

'Many people, I should think. It's become quite popular.'

Sarah and Raven exchanged a look. They didn't seem to be getting anywhere.

'What is collodion?' asked Sarah.

'Pungent stuff,' Miss Mann replied, wrinkling her nose. 'Gun cotton in ether.'

'Ether?'

Miss Mann nodded. 'The smell hangs around for days. Been dabbling with it myself of late. My sisters complain about it. They've started suggesting that if I want to pursue this hobby I might need to move out, find somewhere else to live.'

Sarah recalled smelling ether recently, off the clothes of someone who had told them he was working with it at home.

She looked at Raven, who had clearly remembered it too. They both said it at the same time.

'Stokes.'

They stood outside Miss Mann's front door, Raven's carriage waiting a few yards away.

'Could it really be him?' Sarah asked. 'That ridiculous man?' She felt a mixture of fury and mortification at the thought of him having touched her, undressed her, posed her and then captured the image.

'He is someone who might know that Cameron Todd was Leitch's doctor, something the blackmailer would need to have been aware of,' Raven replied.

'But why would he let you speak to that girl at the Lock Hospital if he was the one who photographed her?'

'Two reasons. One, because I threatened to tell Sanderson about her otherwise, which would have brought down far more trouble. But also because the girl didn't know he was the photographer. The camera – and presumably Stokes – were concealed.' His expression turned bitter. 'That was before he found other ways to ensure his subjects were oblivious of his actions.'

'But wasn't he claiming to have been blackmailed too?' Sarah reminded him.

Raven remained unperturbed. 'Stokes told me that his blackmailer was some duke warning him off wooing his daughter. Pure nonsense, a fantasy. The story he told Simpson was confected to allay suspicion, by telling the very person he was blackmailing that he was also a victim.' Raven gave a rueful laugh. 'Why didn't I see it before? I always thought him preposterous, couldn't understand how he made his money, how a man like that would ever attract the right sort of patient. But I can see now that this was also a blind, to conceal that he has been making most of his money working for Magnus. *He* is the doctor certifying virgins. He also makes money selling photographs of Magnus's prostitutes. And he is making money from blackmail.'

'But what grudge does he have against Dr Simpson?'

'I imagine he will be only too willing to tell you,' Raven said, hailing Forbes.

'Why would he do that?'

'Because I'll be holding a knife to his throat.'

FIFTY-NINE

quick look at Miss Mann's copy of the Post Office Directory had provided Stokes's address, not far to the east of where they were now. Raven instructed Forbes to go there directly, while it was not yet dark. Once again he had reason to thank Eugenie for her stubborn insistence on retaining the driver.

The more he thought about it, the more he realised he should have seen it before. Stokes was disdained by his peers, which would have made him secretly despise them even while he courted their approval. He would have felt no remorse about bleeding those who spurned him.

Sarah was gazing out of the window as the carriage clattered down London Road, deep in thought. She turned to face him.

'Why would Stokes have been present at the Castle on the night Leitch died?' she asked.

'It sounds like he was Magnus's pet physician. In such a place it might be valuable to have one on hand for all manner of eventualities. Though Magnus would have been a fool to trust him. He's as sleekit as they come, working many angles at all times.'

'Could he have been the killer, then?' she asked.

Raven considered it. 'Difficult to imagine how that would have come about. Leitch was a big man, physically powerful. Stokes is not.'

'It was a blow to the back of the skull. An unexpected attack from behind. Sleekit.'

Raven still couldn't see it. 'Why would Stokes want Leitch dead?' he asked.

'Perhaps Leitch had become a threat to him in some way.'

'Possibly,' he conceded. 'Or perhaps the answer lies in the ledger Magnus is looking for.'

'Yes. Why is this ledger so important to him?' Sarah asked. 'And why would Annabel steal it?'

'You said it yourself. She's a clever girl. Perhaps she thought it would give her leverage, something to trade.'

'She's not been seen since the night Leitch died. The place would have been in a ferment while Stokes was arranging for the body to be removed. She must have taken advantage of the commotion to escape.'

This made sense, but it left a big question.

'If she got away, where is she?' Raven asked. 'Why would she not return to her mother, where she would be safe?'

Sarah did not have an answer for him.

The carriage was approaching the turning onto Abbeyhill.

'We'll have to ca' canny,' Raven said. 'We're hanging everything on the smell of ether. We must bear in mind we may have this wrong.'

'So you won't be putting a knife to his throat as an opening gambit?' Sarah asked witheringly.

'I'll need a bit more information before we reach that stage,' he admitted.

'My memories of what happened to me are still jumbled but they're coming back,' Sarah said. 'I think I'll recognise the place if it's where I was taken.'

'I'm not sure you're going to get the chance,' Raven told her, pointing out of the carriage window.

The building they were heading to was on fire.

★ ★ ★

Raven and Sarah got out of the carriage and approached Stokes's house, where flames were erupting from the upper floors, smoke belching into the darkening sky. There were a number of bystanders milling around, as though unsure what to do. Raven had run into a burning building once, saving the lives of both Sarah and Somerville, but he wasn't running into this. It had been blazing for some time.

'Have the brigade been summoned?' he asked one of the spectators.

'On their way,' he was told.

He watched the flames lick up the side of the building towards the roof.

'I'm finding it hard to believe that this is a coincidence,' he said to Sarah. 'This has Magnus Cunningham's name all over it. Partial to a bit of fire-raising, isn't he? Him and his willing instrument, Wilkie.'

'Do you think Stokes was in there?' Sarah asked.

'I don't fancy his chances if he was.'

Sarah suddenly put a hand on Raven's arm. 'Did you hear that?' she asked.

Raven strained to hear anything above the roar of the flames.

'I heard something,' she insisted. 'Or someone.'

Sarah hared off towards the back of the building. Raven followed, trying to locate where the noise was coming from, both covering their faces against the smoke.

The damage was even greater at the rear. A whole section of the back wall had collapsed, the fire having exhausted all it could burn. There were smouldering timbers, sections of floor fallen from above.

'The fire must have started here,' Raven said.

There was a definite sound of banging and muffled shouts coming from somewhere inside. Raven thought he could make out a door behind a pile of smouldering debris.

'It's the cellar,' Sarah said, her voice muffled by the collar of her coat pulled tight over her mouth and nose. 'There's someone in there.'

Sarah made a move towards the building, but Raven hauled her back.

'Stay where you are,' he said.

He headed for a small outbuilding that sat on the edge of the grounds. Once inside, he began searching for something, anything he could use. There was a baling hook hanging on the wall next to a shovel and a rake. He grabbed it and headed back towards what remained of the rear of the building.

Raven stepped over what looked and smelled like the charred remains of a body, but there was no time to worry about whose it might be. Using the hook, he levered up a section of carbonised timber, the heat around him scorching the skin of his face.

It was just enough. The cellar door opened a fraction, and a figure squeezed through the tight gap, almost knocking Raven down as they both stumbled over the debris to reach safety.

Raven could not immediately see who it was he had rescued, but from the man's build it obviously wasn't Stokes. They both collapsed onto the grass, coughing and heaving.

Sarah approached, crouching down. She and Raven both looked at the man sprawled out beside them. His face was covered in soot, but they quickly recognised him nonetheless.

James Quinton.

His relief at his escape appeared to be short-lived when he realised who his saviours were, and understood that they knew him too.

Quinton was Simpson's disgraced amanuensis. Several years ago, he had been a trusted member of the Simpson household, until it became apparent that he was siphoning off money into his own coffers. Accused of fraud and threatened with prosecution, he and his wife had quit the city, heading south to England. Evidently he had returned, and presumably thrown his lot in with Stokes.

Quinton was a man in possession of confidential information about the professor, including details about adoptions. He and his wife had even taken one of the infants themselves, as they could not have children of their own. He was a man with a grudge, believing Simpson had treated him harshly when his larceny was uncovered. Raven had been correct about his blackmail having a personal element to it.

Looking at him now, Raven realised that it must have been Quinton in the carriage at Gayfield Square. When Raven had walked beneath the gaslight, Quinton had recognised him and ordered the driver to leave. He was more than assistant to Stokes in all this, then. He was his confederate.

'Where is Stokes?' Raven demanded.

'Dead,' Quinton said, his voice reduced to a rasping whisper.

'And what of your wife?'

'Works as his housekeeper. Mercifully she was not at home.'

'What happened?' Sarah asked.

Quinton got to his feet, starting to stagger away. Raven grabbed him, hauled him back.

'Where do you think you're going? You have some explaining to do.' Raven held him by the lapels of his smouldering jacket. 'You were a part of this, weren't you?'

'Part of what?'

'You know what. Blackmail.'

'Among other things,' said Sarah bitterly, her face a picture of utter loathing for the soot-stained specimen in front of her.

'Dr Simpson said the handwriting on the blackmail notes was familiar. That was because it was yours.'

Quinton squirmed from Raven's grasp. He let him, knowing he could grab him again if necessary.

'I don't know what you're talking about,' he insisted, but he would not meet Raven's eye.

'What happened here tonight?' Sarah asked.

Quinton coughed again. 'All I know is that Hedley and I took our dinner at the Sheephead Tavern,' he said, 'and when we returned we found that someone had been in the house. The place had been ransacked. Hedley kept his money in a strongbox in the cellar and I was sent down to check whether or not it had been taken.'

'And had it?'

Quinton nodded.

'How much was there?'

'I don't know.'

'I don't believe you,' Sarah replied. 'It was your job to know. Stokes would have had Todd's money, Conville's money, and who knows what else.'

Raven grabbed Quinton again, staring into his reddened eyes. The sound of the fire brigade could be heard in the distance, although given the time it had taken them to get here, there wasn't going to be much left to save.

'You're going to tell us everything you know or you're going back into the fire,' Raven snarled into his face. 'It's no more than you deserve, and no one will be any the wiser.'

Quinton's body sagged; his defiance gone. 'There was thousands,' he admitted. 'Close to three thousand in total. It was all gone. They took the lot.'

'Who did?'

'Magnus Cunningham and his policeman, Wilkie. When I came back up the stairs from the cellar I heard voices. They were still in the house, so I stayed hidden. They were asking about a ledger. Hedley said he didn't have it, and Cunningham didn't like that. I think Wilkie hit him. Sounded like it anyway.' Quinton shuddered. 'It was horrible.'

'And then?'

'I couldn't see very much but I know that Hedley hit the ground hard. Didn't get back up again. Cunningham was angry with Wilkie, complaining Hedley was no use to them dead.'

'They killed him?'

Quinton nodded. 'Maybe didn't mean to, but they killed him either way. Then Cunningham told Wilkie to burn the place. He said that if the ledger was destroyed, then that would have to be good enough.'

'And this ledger wasn't in the strongbox?'

'No.'

Raven loosened his grip on Quinton's jacket once more. Quinton wiped his face with his sleeve.

'The place went up like a roman candle, on account of all the photography chemicals Hedley kept about the place. I waited too long to make my escape. By the time I tried to get out, the door was jammed shut.' He paused for a moment, heaved in a great breath. 'I thought I was going to die in there.'

Raven surveyed the damage. That ledger was now ashes. But perhaps it was not the only thing.

'Stokes took photographs for Cunningham,' Raven said. 'You know the ones I mean.'

Quinton glanced at Sarah, then nodded.

'He took them of my wife too,' Raven added, injecting a deliberate note of menace. He could see Quinton shrink in the face of it. 'How did he manage that?'

'He used a concoction, of his own devising.'

'The black draught,' Raven said. 'I know. But how did he get to her?'

'He happened upon her. She was in a tea-room, on her own.'

This last sounded as though it had a note of judgement in it: though whether upon Eugenie for this apparent wantonness or Raven for permitting it, he could not say. Either way, he struggled to rein in his fury.

'He recognised her,' Quinton added hurriedly. 'And therein recognised an opportunity.'

'He *happened* upon her? And happened to have this draught upon him at the time?'

Quinton squirmed, as though considering whether it would be worse to answer or to abstain. Sarah got there ahead of him, though.

'She was not the first,' she deduced.

Quinton nodded, swallowing. 'He photographed Magnus's whores, who were happy to strip, albeit he hid the camera. But he wanted higher women. That thrilled him more. And so many of them can be seen out and about alone these days, exercising their . . . independence.'

Now it was Sarah who looked like she was endeavouring to contain her rage.

'Where are the plates?' Raven asked, indicating the wreckage. 'Were they in there too?'

Quinton looked at Sarah again, having the decency to appear shamefaced.

'Cunningham has the plates,' he said. 'I delivered them to him myself.'

SIXTY

arah watched the fire brigade do their best to douse the flames but there was not much left to salvage. Quinton allowed himself to be carted off to the Infirmary, desperate to get away from the two people who knew what he had done.

'Don't go far,' Raven had warned him. 'This is not over.'

Sarah stood watching as the roof collapsed, sparks shooting up into the darkening sky.

Part of the mystery had been solved. They had confirmed their suspicions, identified the blackmailer, but their situation had not changed. Magnus had merely demonstrated his ruthlessness. He had come to reclaim his property and had helped himself to Stokes's extortion money into the bargain. And he still had the photographic plates.

'Stokes had the ledger all along,' Raven said. 'He took it, not Annabel.'

'How did Magnus find out he had it?' she asked.

'I told him,' Raven said. 'When I accused Magnus of taking money from Todd and Conville. He knew what Stokes had on Todd, but not what he had on Conville. He must have deduced that Stokes blackmailed Conville using information from the ledger.'

'I don't understand,' Sarah said. 'Why would Magnus think that Annabel took it?' But even as she asked this, she worked it out.

'Because Stokes told him she did,' she realised. 'He needed someone to take the blame, divert suspicion away from himself.'

Raven had asked why, if Annabel had escaped, she would not return to safety. Now they had the answer.

'The night Leitch died,' she went on, trying to order events into a logical sequence, 'as well as summoning Todd, Stokes must have helped Annabel abscond, because if someone went missing along with the ledger, they would get the blame. And as long as Magnus was looking for Annabel, he would be looking in the wrong place and blaming the wrong person.'

'So, where is she?' Raven asked. 'What did Stokes do with her?'

'I don't know,' she admitted. 'But if I'm right about this, then Stokes could not afford for Annabel to be found.' She felt a tightness in her chest. 'I fear he killed her.'

Raven scoffed. 'Stokes? I very much doubt it. He was a buffoon, not a brute. Besides, there was no need for him to do so.'

Sarah looked urgently at him, daring to hope. 'Why not?'

'Because he had a place where he could keep her locked away. Quite literally.'

SIXTY-ONE

arkness had fallen as they approached Infirmary Street, the various hospital buildings made visible by the grid of lights from so many windows.

Sarah felt engulfed by the smell of burning, couldn't get rid of it despite having the cab window fully open. She thought of the body they had seen, convinced the smell of it was on her too.

Her anxiety seemed to be increasing the closer they got to their destination. She could feel her heart thumping in her chest, sweat forming on the palms of her hands. She could hear Annabel singing in that garden: *Who shall say that Fortune grieves him, While the star of hope she leaves him?*

It made sense that Stokes should use Annabel's disappearance to disguise his theft of the ledger, but what if Raven was wrong? What if he had decided to make her disappearance permanent? She already knew that Stokes had been capable of terrible things – she was proof of it. But was he capable of murder?

She and Raven knew for certain that Magnus was. But what he had inflicted on her was a fate worse than death. Sarah suspected he knew that, and relished the torment he was inflicting. But if she were to rescue Annabel, then that at least would be something. That was the star of hope.

Raven had Forbes take the carriage to the far side of High School Yards, beyond the Surgical Hospital. It was impossible to miss the significance of the Lock Hospital's situation, far removed from the rest: women with sexual diseases, prostitutes, regarded as the lowest of the low, even in the world of medicine.

The hospital was closed for the night, the door locked. Raven rang the bell and began thumping on the door.

After a while they heard a rhythmic jingle of someone approaching with a set of keys on their hip. The door was opened by the matron, a sourly disapproving look on her face.

'What do you want?' she asked, glaring at Raven. She noticed Sarah standing beside him and looked her up and down. 'This is no time for a new admission.'

Sarah returned the matron's hostile look, in no mood to be disparaged by anyone.

'We need access to the locked ward,' Sarah said.

'What is she talking about?' the matron asked.

'My name is Will Raven. *Doctor* Will Raven. I've come to see a patient and it is imperative that I see her now.'

'I will admit no one without the express permission of Dr Stokes,' the matron stated, standing tall and filling the doorway. Clearly a woman used to giving orders and having them followed.

'That might be difficult,' Sarah told her, 'given that he's dead.'

'Dead?' the woman repeated, taken aback.

'This very evening,' Raven confirmed.

She recovered her composure, stood her ground. 'Nevertheless, the rules are there for a reason. I can't let just anyone in.'

'Give us the bloody keys!' Sarah said, ripping them from the woman's grasp and marching away.

'Give those back!' she protested, following indignantly behind. 'I will be reporting this.'

'See that you do,' Raven told her. 'Dr Stokes was involved in a criminal enterprise that involved selling young girls into prostitution. If anyone working with him was complicit in that, we would like to know.'

The woman looked altogether less indignant now, though she kept following them along the corridor towards the locked ward.

When Sarah reached it, she looked at the vast ring of keys then back at the matron, who sighed and took the ring from Sarah. She selected a key and placed it in the lock.

'I should warn you,' she said, her expression grave, 'there is only one patient in the ward right now, and poor Peggy is quite delirious from syphilis.'

Sarah felt her heart sink in her chest. One patient, named Peggy.

The door opened onto a short corridor, doors either side of it.

'She rants and raves and claims Dr Stokes is keeping her a prisoner. They often say that sort of thing, though. She's taken to calling herself— '

'Annabel!' Sarah shouted. 'It is Sarah Fisher. Archie's wife.'

'Sarah!' a voice called in astonished reply from behind one of the doors.

'Release her,' Raven commanded.

The matron fumbled with the keys but complied.

The door was opened, revealing a young woman clad in a crumpled grey flannel dress. Standard hospital issue.

It was Annabel. Taller, older, but definitely the girl that Sarah had known. And she was still a girl, no matter what might have happened to her.

'Come with us,' Sarah said, reaching for her hand.

Annabel remained in place, arms folded. 'I can't,' she said. 'It's not safe.'

'Who told you that?' Raven asked.

'Dr Stokes. Kept me here for my own protection, he said.'

'He kept you here for *his* protection,' Sarah told her gently. 'Come on. Let's get you out of here.'

'Where will you take me?' she asked, fear in her eyes.

Sarah thought about Magnus's threat but reasoned that he wouldn't know they had found her, and was unlikely to keep looking now that the ledger had been destroyed.

'Home,' Sarah said.

At that, Annabel burst into tears.

SIXTY-TWO

hey were sitting in Stokes's office. Matron, full of apologies, had made them all tea, at pains to distance herself from Stokes and his activities. Raven thought her shock seemed genuine, was inclined to believe her.

He took a sip of his tea, wishing for something stronger.

'We need to know what happened,' he said to Annabel, putting his cup down. 'How you came to be here.'

Annabel had been wrapped in a warm blanket but was still shivering, though the room was not cold.

'Dr Stokes brought me here,' she said. 'He said I had to be kept hidden, my whereabouts secret, because Cunningham's men would be looking for me. But every time I asked if it was safe to go, he always said no. Then when I tried to leave, he had me locked up. He told the nurses I was mad, and that my name was Peggy. I must have been here a month. Any longer and I genuinely would have run mad, and started to believe Peggy really was my name.'

'The night you escaped from the Castle,' Sarah said. 'What happened? You saw something, didn't you?'

Annabel became pale, her cup rattling on its saucer. Sarah took the cup from her, held her hands.

'It's all right. You're safe now.'

'A man named Barrington Leitch died at the Castle that night,' Raven said. 'Were you there? Did you witness it?'

Annabel's eyes filled. She nodded.

'Did Dr Stokes kill him?' Sarah asked.

There was a long pause, then Annabel shook her head.

'Can you tell us who did?'

Annabel shook her head again.

'Maybe you saw them,' Raven suggested, 'but did not know their name?'

'Take your time,' Sarah told her, giving the girl's hand an encouraging squeeze. 'Tell us what you can. Start at the beginning.'

Annabel sniffed. 'I was taken to the house, the Castle, by Doris Pike,' she said. 'She told me I was lucky, that I was to be a maid there. I soon learned what the place really was. When I did, I tried to run away but I was caught and Mr Cunningham warned what would happen to me if I did it again. He said the policeman would catch me. Wilkie.

'I saw what went on there. I didn't want it to happen to me, so I stayed out of the way as much as I could. Made myself useful to the woman who ran the place, Mrs Gilroy. I have a head for numbers, so I helped her keep the ledger. The record of who had come, who they had been with, how much they owed.'

She glanced up furtively, gazing past Raven, scanning her surroundings as though still wary of what might happen to her.

'The girls warned me that my time would come, that it would happen eventually. Too valuable to be left unmolested, they said. The men pay a lot, you know, for virgins. They told me that the gentlemen could be generous. But that's not what I saw.'

She shuddered and Sarah put an arm around her shoulder.

'What did you see?' she asked.

'The girls were wary of Mr Leitch. Wouldn't tell me why. That night, the night I escaped, I was told to take a bottle of wine to one of the rooms. I heard a scream. Muffled, but definitely a scream. When I opened the door, I saw him. On top of a girl. His hands around her throat. Squeezing. And the look on his face . . .'

Annabel wiped her nose on the edge of the blanket.

'Then he saw me, and he shouted at me to get out. I obeyed.

I was scared. But I couldn't just leave her, could I? I thought he was going to kill her.'

'So what did you do?' Sarah asked.

'I sneaked back in. It wasn't hard: he was so intent upon what he was doing to her. I hit him on the back of the head with the bottle. Hard as I could.'

There was complete silence in the room as the truth of what had happened that night sank in.

'And did Dr Stokes deal with the . . . the situation?' Raven asked.

'Yes. Dr Stokes was often around in the evenings. The girl Leitch had been choking went to get him and he said he would deal with it. He also said he would get me out of the house and away, but I had to do something for him. It wasn't what I thought.'

'The ledger,' Sarah said.

Annabel nodded. She glanced anxiously past Raven once more. 'Where is Dr Stokes?' she asked. 'Does he know you've come here?'

Raven and Sarah exchanged a look.

'He's dead,' Raven said. 'Cunningham burned his house down tonight, with him in it.'

Annabel looked scared, pulled the blanket tighter.

'He was looking for the ledger,' Raven explained. 'That's why Stokes was keeping you here. So that Cunningham would think you had disappeared with it.'

'What if he finds me?' she asked, eyes wide.

'He won't,' Raven reassured her. 'We'll get you out of the city. And Cunningham was more interested in the ledger. He'll be content knowing it's been destroyed.'

Annabel frowned, gazing past Raven again. He realised she was looking at the bookcase on the far wall.

'But the ledger's here,' she said. 'Where Stokes left it.'

Annabel got up from her chair and selected a volume from the shelf, the spine a similar green to the books on either side of it. She placed it on the desk in front of Raven. Sarah got up and stood beside him.

Raven opened the ledger at a random page. Just as Annabel had indicated, it contained dates, dues owed and dues paid. It also contained names. Familiar names.

'"Judges, generals, politicians",' Raven said. 'Magnus wasn't kidding.'

The names of the girls were listed too, along with likes, dislikes and fetishes.

'What's this?' Sarah asked, pointing to a column of larger numbers, some of them substantial.

'Special circumstances,' Annabel replied.

'What does that mean?' asked Raven.

Annabel shrugged. 'Mrs Gilroy didn't specify.'

Some of the larger sums had a V marked beside them.

'Does the V mean what I would assume?'

Annabel's cheeks reddened. 'Yes.'

Raven turned to the back of the ledger, to the most recent entries. The name Leitch appeared several times, the letter V next to his payment. And twice more against a larger sum. What cost more than taking a virginity?

Raven felt something in him curdle as he worked it out. Given what Annabel had described Leitch doing on the night he died, he had little doubt what the larger payments must be for.

Compensation.

He considered it best that Leitch was already six feet under the sod.

'No wonder Magnus wanted this back,' he said.

Raven closed the book, lifted it up. It felt like a weapon.

He looked at Sarah.

'Magnus told us we were in no position to negotiate. But we weren't holding this when he said it.'

SIXTY-THREE

espite the rain, Raven walked the short distance from the Lock Hospital to the Cowgate, having sent Sarah and Annabel on to Queen Street in the carriage. He could not go with them. He had business at the Coffin.

Sanderson was seated at the same table as before. Raven wondered how much money he spent there to be granted such special consideration, or perhaps it was mere coincidence. Sanderson looked up eagerly as soon as he saw Raven approach. There was none of his previous aloofness.

'What news of Miss Fisher?' he asked anxiously. 'She was supposed to meet me after her visit to Pike and Featherstone, but she never arrived.'

Raven noticed that his face was bruised, estimating from the various hues of blue and green how many days it had been since the blows were inflicted.

'They knew who she was,' he said. 'There will be no story.'

'How did they find out?'

Raven stared at his face. 'How did you come by your injuries?'

Sanderson said nothing, picked up his drink.

'Those bruises are not fresh,' Raven observed. 'You were warned off, weren't you? And you didn't tell Sarah.'

Sanderson stared into his glass, unwilling to meet Raven's eye.

'If I find out you betrayed her, that you tipped them off . . .'

Sanderson looked up now, indignant.

'I'm trying to build something here. That story was the best thing to have happened to the *Capital*. Why would I blow my own vessel out of the water?'

'Your face suggests several reasons. Magnus Cunningham has a way of making people act against their own interests.'

'I can't argue with that,' Sanderson said, gingerly touching his damaged face. 'I was warned it would be worse next time if I printed anything else. But I thought if we could bring him down, he would no longer be a danger. I was a fool.'

'What happened to the girl? Mary Anne?'

'Sent from the carriage with some extra money for her trouble. She had no idea what happened after that, where they took Miss Fisher.'

'You should go to the police. They'll have to listen to you. You're a man of some standing.'

Sanderson pointed to his face and scoffed. 'It was the police who did this. Or one of them, anyway.'

'Wilkie?'

'Indeed. How did you know?'

'He's in Cunningham's pocket.'

'So you understand: if I go to McLevy, Wilkie will find out, and I have no wish to invite another visit from him. So, for now, I'll do as I'm told.' He knocked back his whisky, grimacing, and not just at the taste. 'We have to choose our battles,' he continued. 'Fight the fights we can win.'

Raven recognised the resignation in his tone. With the discovery of the ledger, he at least had the chance to get the photographs back, but Magnus and his sordid business would continue with impunity. Raven had all but given up hope of finding justice: if he could merely avert catastrophe, he would be grateful for that much.

SIXTY-FOUR

t was a crisp morning and the skies were clear, the rain finally having ceased. Raven took it for a good omen as he and Sarah entered Queen Street Gardens ahead of their rendezvous with Magnus. Raven had sent a note informing him that they had his ledger. It felt good to be the one summoning him.

Annabel was gone, taken first thing that morning by Forbes in the carriage. They dared not risk the train, even had one of them accompanied her, for fear of her being seen and word getting back to Magnus. By the end of the day, she would be reunited with her mother in Perthshire – home, safe.

Sarah reported that the girl had kept her awake half the night at Queen Street, getting up to look out of the window, convinced that Magnus or Wilkie might arrive at the door any moment. Raven had not slept well either, his mind in turmoil as he took in the previous day's events and tried to anticipate the next. Somewhere amidst it all he had remembered his encounter with Agnes Syme, not sure what to make of that either. His wife had been lying to him about her whereabouts on the night she stayed away from St Andrew Square. Why, he could not fathom. But whatever the reason, he was still sure he could convince her that her future lay with him. Only now he needed to ensure that such a future was not jeopardised by his uncle and the dangerous items he still had in his possession.

Magnus was already in the specified place, alone, taking his ease on one of the benches. He was dressed in a black suit, a top hat upon his head, looking every inch the respectable businessman, the ambitious hotelier. Raven sensed Sarah stiffen at the sight of him. She seemed tremulous. He wanted to reach out a hand in solidarity but knew that was not possible.

Perhaps because it was the first time seeing Magnus outside in better light, or perhaps merely the first time allowing himself to, but Raven saw a resemblance to his father now – what he remembered of him. Beneath the lines etched by the Australian sun, he saw something of himself too. That had always haunted him: the idea of what he might have inherited, and worse, what he might have passed on.

It chilled him that his son carried the same blood, shared something of this man. But Raven had also come to know that, in spite of heredity, he was nothing like his father, and nothing like the man sitting before him now. Neither his fate nor his nature was dictated by his antecedents, any more than his profession had been. Otherwise, he would be a vintner, a smuggler, or indeed whatever this monster called himself.

Magnus watched their approach, regarding it as though it was only of mild interest. He did not get up.

'You could have come to the hotel,' he said. 'You're always welcome, nephew. You too, Miss Fisher.'

Raven gestured to the many people traversing the gardens, taking advantage of the clement weather. 'I consider it wiser, when conducting conversations with men like you, to be in a place where there are witnesses.'

Magnus wrinkled his nose in distaste. 'Where's my ledger?' he demanded.

'Yes. That. I gather you were so keen to retrieve it that you murdered Dr Stokes.'

Magnus sighed, as though bored. 'I don't know what you're talking about.'

'On two previous occasions I have mentioned things you

genuinely didn't know about. One was how Leitch died, and the other was that Todd and Conville were being blackmailed – and not by you. Consequently, you worked out Stokes had the ledger and was making use of the information it contained. So, you burned his house down, with him in it.'

'I don't know who this Dr Stokes is. And nor do I care. Now give me the ledger.'

'You didn't think we would just hand it over, did you? We're offering a trade.'

'For what?'

'The photographs,' said Sarah, her voice steady despite herself. 'The negative plates and the prints.'

Raven could feel the tension in his gut. There was so much resting on this.

Magnus considered their proposition for a moment. He looked past them into the gardens, then took out a cigar and lit it. Taking a puff, a smile appeared on his pockmarked, weather-beaten face.

'A trade is fair,' he said.

Raven felt a surge of relief. He knew that exposing this man and his activities in the press was what Sarah had originally intended, but in their present circumstances this was as much as they could have hoped for.

'But not for both,' Magnus continued. 'For the ledger I will give you *one* of the plates.'

Raven felt everything crumble into dust, like a wall of sand he had built and thought strong, washed away by a single wave. He and Sarah shared a look. They had one card to play, but they had forgotten Magnus had two.

'Which one?' Sarah asked, her voice fading in her throat.

But Raven already knew the answer to that. He would be able to spare Eugenie, for less than it had cost Todd, but it would be a Pyrrhic victory, for Magnus knew that as long as he held Sarah's photograph, he still controlled them both.

'Your wife's,' Magnus said, confirming it. He looked at Sarah like a wolf at a lamb, a man who knew Raven would do whatever it took to protect her.

'There is no need to despair,' Magnus went on, affecting an air of magnanimity. 'This is a lucrative trade, and you will both be compensated for making yourselves useful. In fact, I now have a vacancy for a doctor to examine and certify new girls. But more immediately I have arranged – through a third party – for you to meet with Mr Dalton this morning, with a view to becoming his physician. He has heard you have a marvellous new tonic that you are offering your patients. I will leave the recipe to you, but I want to be negotiating with his widow by tomorrow.'

'Or what?' Sarah asked. 'Or you release the photographs? You can only do that once.'

Magnus took a slow puff on his cigar then blew out a long plume of smoke, his eye fixed upon Sarah the whole time.

'I don't think you understand how this would work, Miss Fisher. See, I wouldn't release all my prints in one go. It would be a little at a time, sending them to select people. No one would talk about it, except to others in the know. You would never be sure who had seen them. Then I would start selling them. In London at first, but they would soon find their way back here. You would just never know the day nor the hour. And all the time you would remain aware that I can always print more.'

Raven could see that Sarah was physically shaking, tears beginning to spill. Magnus looked up at him.

'I wonder, had I made you choose which photograph I returned, which would you have spared? Would you have perhaps revealed something you'd rather keep hidden: that your first loyalty is to Miss Fisher here rather than your wife?'

Magnus took another puff and expelled the cloud into the spring air, carelessly sullying its freshness.

'You've had her, I take it,' he added, looking Sarah up and down with a horrible glint in his eye. 'Of the two, which one is better in the bedroom?'

Raven felt a stirring rage, his appetite for brutality fast returning and straining for an outlet. Magnus sensed it at some animal level but did not flinch. He gestured with his cigar towards the people walking in the gardens.

'I consider it wiser, when conducting conversations with men like you, to be in a place where there are witnesses. You need to calm yourself, Thomas. You have important business to conduct.'

Raven looked at Sarah, thinking her presence might restrain him from what he was about to say. It did not. She deserved the whole truth anyway. And so did Magnus, for different reasons.

'It was me,' he told Magnus. 'I want you to know that.'

'What was you?'

'I killed your brother. My father. He didn't die in an alley. I dragged him there and left him, after I beat him to death with a poker to stop him murdering my mother.'

For a third time he saw that look: something Magnus had not known, had not suspected. He saw surprise, then hurt, then anger.

'It has haunted me every day, though,' Raven told him. Magnus's expression softened just a little on hearing that. 'Haunted me that I had not the courage to do it sooner.'

Raven was shaking as he turned and walked away. He felt Sarah's hand slip into his, the warmth of her touch a greater balm than the ointment she had applied to his cuts that first night they met. It didn't matter that Magnus saw. He had already seen something deeper.

Sarah stopped once they had exited the gardens, turning to face him.

'Why didn't you tell me?' she asked.

'How could I, if I wished you to think me a good man?' Raven took both her hands, looking into her misted eyes. 'It's not a madwoman I have in my attic, Sarah: it's my father's corpse. I would have preferred that you never found out, but given what I now must do, I felt there was nothing to lose.'

Sarah swallowed, tears running down her cheeks. 'You *are* a good man, Will. You always were. And that is why you must not do this thing he is asking. It will destroy you, for ever.'

Raven knew she was right, but he also knew there was no alternative. He might not have thought himself capable of what Magnus was asking, were it not that he would do anything to protect Sarah. And even then, it might not be enough.

SIXTY-FIVE

arah found herself drifting through the streets of the New Town. She could not remember the moment when she had let go Raven's hand and separated from him, but he was gone now. It chilled her to think where he might be headed, the unspeakable deed he believed he must undertake.

They had made their play, and Magnus had defeated it. He held both of their futures in his grasp: hers because she could not live with the shame should the prints be distributed, and Raven's because he would not suffer to allow that. His love for her would be his undoing. And even if Raven did this unconscionable thing, it would merely be the beginning of their torment.

Sarah found herself in Princes Street Gardens, barely aware of conveying herself there. The Scott Monument loomed ahead of her, and she walked towards it as though drawn by its power, its intimidating presence. It had towered over the city as long as she had been here, but it had cast a longer shadow of late. This was where Cameron Todd had taken his own life, but he had done so to save Eugenie, understanding that by removing himself from Magnus's twisted game, he removed the threat to his daughter.

Looking up, it suddenly struck Sarah that she could save Raven the same way.

He was the one his uncle truly wanted to own and control:

she was merely the instrument by which Magnus could do that. But if she was gone, then Magnus's hold over Raven would be broken. As Raven had suggested, she could quit this city, go far enough that the photographs could not follow her, no matter how many Magnus printed in his spite, and neither of them would need to do his disgusting bidding.

The price would be that she could never return. She would be ruined here, but Raven would be free to build his practice, raise his children, live his life.

Sarah headed for the tower. Built in tribute to a great man of literature, the Gothic edifice now represented only the power of an evil man to her.

She climbed the stairs, flight after flight, until her breath was heaving in her chest, her blood pumping in her ears. She thought of what Raven had confessed, the killing of his father, the thing that had tormented him all these years. The felling of a brutal man, terminating an assault on a defenceless woman.

Much as Annabel had done with Leitch.

Raven had carried the weight of it ever since, and she feared Annabel would too. Sarah could not perceive of either incident as a sin nor as a crime. The intention was to save a life, not to take it. It did not compare to the exploits of men like Leitch, men like Magnus Cunningham.

Raven had been afraid that she would be ashamed of him, think less of him. That was not the case. She loved him. This damaged man who already had a wife, with a shameful secret held in the attic of his mind. She loved him despite it all. Perhaps all the more *because* of it.

He had saved her from the fire at the theatre. He had saved her when her pregnancy had threatened to kill her. He was a good man. He would make a great doctor.

She thought of Dr Simpson, and the difference one good man could make to the world. What a tragedy it would have been had something happened to the professor that meant humanity was denied his extraordinary kindness, wisdom, and skill. Raven deserved the chance to make his contribution, but there would be no such chance if he was in thrall to Magnus, bent always to his will. Sarah could not, would not let him do it: not merely to save her.

She reached the viewing platform at the top of the tower. The day was clear, cloudless. So much of Edinburgh was visible from where she stood. The waters of the Forth. Calton Hill. Arthur's Seat. Salisbury Crag. The labyrinth of the Old Town, its decrepit buildings huddled around the castle like limpets on a rock. Everything she had known throughout her adult life, everything she would leave behind. She could live without all of it. Much harder would be to live without Raven, but she would do it because she loved him. He would do anything for her, and she had to save him from that.

Looking directly down from the balustrade, she saw a woman walking with her daughter, hand in hand. She thought of all the other women who populated the city. All with so much to give, so much to contribute, so much light to shine, but surrounded by men intent on extinguishing these fragile flames lest they burn brighter than their own.

She thought of Mina, Mrs Simpson's sister. Smart and vivacious, a keen intelligence left to wither on the vine. Now resigned to a future as an old maid, disappointed with her lot because she had been convinced that the sum of her ambition should be wife and mother, and she had not managed even those.

Sarah thought of Miss Mann, a photography pioneer in her own right but destined to be remembered as merely an assistant to her male counterparts.

She turned her head to the south. She could see the college grounds, the university from which women were barred from entry. The Infirmary, where they were permitted to be nurses and nothing more. The Lock Hospital, tucked away from view so that the city did not have to bear witness to its shamed women. Women whose only role was to fulfil men's needs before being discarded and forgotten, hidden away. Forced to cater to male appetites and then shamed for doing so: proxies for the embarrassment men felt at the baseness of their own desires.

She looked north towards Bonnington Mills, where all those murdered babies had been discovered. More shame. Women shamed by motherhood: the very purpose these men otherwise hailed as a sacred virtue, the panacea of woman's existence.

Shame. Everywhere shame, but always hung about the necks of women. Men using shame as a means of control. Women powerless within a society that could destroy them on a whim, using only a word.

Harlot.

Harridan.

Crone.

Spinster.

Witch.

Whore.

They were shamed over the conduct men demanded of them. Shamed for their own desires. Shamed for their ambition. Shamed for their bodies. Shamed for their weakness. Shamed when they exercised strength.

They were referred to as the opposite sex. But to Sarah's mind, gender ought not to be seen as oppositional. It should be about balance, one complementing the other.

Raven had sought a partnership with her, an alliance to better both of them. Why could more men not see things the same way? Why were some men intent upon making women feel powerless?

From the top of that tower, the answer revealed itself, hiding in plain sight all along.

Fear.

They were afraid that women might come to understand the power they truly had. The many powers they truly had. Afraid they might realise men's only means of holding back that tide was shame.

Sarah felt something kindle within her.

Suddenly she could see a way forward, her path clear. A path that would not end here as Dr Todd's had done, though sacrifice would be required. It was too late to change that much.

She just hoped it was not too late to save Raven's newest patient.

SIXTY-SIX

he death of Reginald Dalton was announced in the intimations section of the newspaper on the day after Raven's fateful visit. He knew that Magnus would have learned of it through other channels, not least the widow. Nevertheless, he had brought a copy of the *Capital* with him, opened at the appropriate page, reasoning that this would obviate the need to speak directly of the deed.

Magnus was sitting in his office at the Clarendon, taking tea. The delicate china cup and saucer in his bear-like paw of a hand made him look faintly ridiculous. Stokes's strongbox sat on the floor next to his desk, the letters HS etched just below the hasp. Raven was certain that its presence was intended as a taunt.

Raven placed the newspaper down on the desk. Magnus glanced at it, then at him. 'You look terrible,' he said.

'Oddly enough, I didn't sleep much last night.'

Magnus noticed Raven's hands. 'Why do you have ink on your fingers?'

Raven ignored the question. 'It is the stain on my soul that concerns me.'

Magnus feigned a look of sympathy. 'Conscience troubling you over killing a man?' He snorted. 'You're long overdue that, aren't you, Thomas?'

'Don't call me that.'

'I'll call you whatever I like. Put a foot wrong and I'll be whispering in McLevy's ear, telling him I suspect foul play in my fellow hotelier's death.'

'After what you've done to me, hanging would be a mercy.'

'Why would you need the hangman?' Magnus asked. 'Perhaps you lack the courage Todd had.'

'Perhaps I do. Like yourself, I seem to have something of a survivor's instinct.'

'You're a Cunningham yet,' Magnus sneered approvingly. 'So, you are not suspected?'

Raven's cheeks flushed, radiating shame. 'Mrs Dalton believes I did all I could to save him.'

'How touching.'

'She has no notion why her husband would not sell to you. But I do. It was because he knew what you are, what you do. That's the truth of it. He did not want his name, or the name of his hotel, tarnished by association with you. But he kept all of that from her. How vulnerable we are when someone we trust has not given us the whole truth.'

Magnus considered this, seemingly oblivious of Raven's insults.

'Women should be told only what we deem it necessary for them to know,' he said. 'I imagine you'll do the same with your wife: keep the existence of the photograph from her.'

Raven hated that Magnus was right about this. He had been wrestling with it since they made their deal. He could let Eugenie know her father's final act was an honourable one, done to protect her, but it would come at the cost of revealing why he had found it necessary.

'She may remain in her state of blissful ignorance,' Magnus added, holding up a letter, 'for you have done well. Mrs Dalton acted swiftly. It seems she still intends to travel abroad, even without her husband. I suspect she was secretly relieved to be rid of him. She will conclude the sale today as long as the first tranche of the sum is paid in cash.'

Raven glanced at the strongbox. 'Then you should act swiftly before she comes to her senses,' he said. 'Or before someone suggests to her that it would best honour her husband to deny you.'

'You wouldn't dare,' Magnus warned. 'Not given what I still have in my possession. With regard to which, have you brought my ledger?'

'To your office? Where you can take it from me in exchange for nothing? I think not. We will make the trade on neutral ground. I will bring it to Dalton's Hotel, your prospective new property, where you can conclude both aspects of this business at the same time.'

SIXTY-SEVEN

arah was sitting in the lobby of Dalton's Hotel alongside Raven and Mrs Dalton when Cunningham arrived, Wilkie at his back bearing the strongbox. Magnus tarried just inside the entrance, surveying his new acquisition with demonstrable relish. It must have been a long journey back from Australia, she reflected, and now he was approaching the promised land.

Sarah found that she much preferred Dalton's to the Clarendon. The decor was more subdued, less opulent, as though its proprietor did not need to try so hard to impress. She wondered what plans Magnus had for it, not that they would be any concern of hers.

She had a bag with her, clutched at her side, inside which was the ledger. The weight of it seemed disproportionately trivial, given all that it contained. Beside her, Mrs Dalton was dressed head to toe in the black of first mourning. She looked unnaturally pale, encased as she was in her bombazine and crepe. Sarah had expected to feel as awful as Mrs Dalton looked, cramped with anxiety, but in practice she felt surprisingly calm. Perhaps it was knowing that matters were out of her hands. She had taken action, and that action could not be revoked. All that remained was for her to convey the terrible news, the truth about Mr Dalton's death.

She watched Magnus stride towards them, Wilkie carrying the money that would form the cash portion of the purchase, in accordance with the agreed terms. The strongbox contained all of Stokes's ill-gotten gains: a sum that could take Mrs Dalton a very long way. Sarah would once have liked the opportunity to sail off into the future herself, explore new places, live a different life, but she accepted now where her path must lead.

Mrs Dalton got to her feet, intercepting Magnus and Wilkie as they strode through the lobby. She gestured insistently to a uniformed porter to take the box from Wilkie, directing her man to convey it to Mr Dalton's office while she fussed over Magnus, thanking him humbly for agreeing to a swift transaction. Mrs Dalton was trembling and her voice shaky, understandably ill at ease despite the fact that she was about to get what she wanted, and what her husband had long promised.

'My lawyer will be here presently,' she said. 'While we wait, I understand Dr Raven has some business to conclude with you. Please, allow me to show you all upstairs.'

Magnus gestured to Sarah to go ahead of him, his first act of faux graciousness as the respectable owner of this prestigious establishment.

Mrs Dalton led the way up to the first floor and into a bright room with a view of the castle. It was warm and welcoming, a fire burning in the grate against the stubbornly unseasonal chill. The strongbox was waiting for them on the floor in front of Mr Dalton's desk, upon which there was a silver tray bearing a decanter of whisky and several crystal glasses. These sat alongside a sheaf of documents: title deeds and a contract of sale.

Magnus took in the view, a look of satisfaction on his face. This was something he had long coveted.

'It's Highland whisky,' Mrs Dalton said, indicating the decanter. 'Dr Raven tells me you have a particular fondness for it. I thought you might like to drink a toast once our deal is concluded. But I will leave you to your business while I locate the whereabouts of my lawyer. He should be here any moment.'

Mrs Dalton had barely closed the door behind her when Magnus turned to address Raven, his expression of politesse swiftly erased.

'Have you the ledger?'

'Have you the photographs?' Raven countered.

'Photograph, singular,' Magnus reminded him, reaching into his jacket for an envelope.

'Plate and prints?'

'All in here,' Magnus told him, holding out the package.

Raven took it from him and slipped the contents into his palm. He held the glass plate up to the light to verify what it showed, then slid it back into its envelope, dropping it to the floor and smashing it beneath his heel. That done, he threw the prints onto the fire.

Magnus observed all of this with quiet amusement.

'Now give me my ledger,' he said.

Sarah began to pull it from the bag. Before she could do so, Wilkie stepped across and grabbed it, wresting it from her grip. He handed it to Magnus.

'Were those all of the prints?' Raven asked.

Magnus made no reply, merely gave Raven a knowing smile.

'How many have you printed of mine?' Sarah asked.

'As long as you know your place and keep your mouth shut, you'll never need to find out.'

Sarah was glad she did not have a decision to make; that it was already done. It made it easier to speak now.

'I've never been very good at either of those things,' she said. 'That's why you should take a look inside your ledger.'

Magnus glanced scornfully at her, but within it she could detect the smallest kernel of doubt. He opened the volume at a random page.

'Do you notice the indentations on all of the entries?' she asked. 'The greasy marks? Those are from the lithograph process. Dr Raven was up all night, working with Mr Sanderson.'

'I told you I hardly slept,' Raven said.

'We made *a lot* of copies,' she added.

Magnus narrowed his eyes. 'You forget the nature of your photograph, Miss Fisher. If you are trying to alter the terms of our exchange, I can make as many prints of that plate as there are leaves on the trees. One for every copy of this ledger and then a thousand more.'

Sarah looked at him, held his gaze. 'This is all about shame, isn't it? That is the sum of your threat. But that will only work should I allow myself to be afraid of it. I can choose not to feel shame. And I do.'

Magnus was staring uncomprehendingly at her. 'What are you talking about? Do not test me, Miss Fisher. You should know I'm not in the habit of making empty threats.'

'Perhaps not, but what if I render your threat empty? Should I choose not to feel shame, what does that leave you with? I'll take my lead from the late Duke of Wellington. Publish and be damned. I have nothing to fear from you, you miserable parasite. Unfortunately for you, the opposite does not apply.'

Magnus scoffed. 'I am most definitely not afraid of you pair.'

Sarah looked him in the eye, relishing his expression of smug impunity.

'It's not us you should be afraid of,' she told him. 'We've already distributed all our copies.'

The enormity of what she had just said began to dawn on Cunningham's face.

'Distributed to who?'

'"Judges, generals, politicians, men of industry and commerce",' Raven quoted. 'Some of the most powerful figures in the city. If I were you, Uncle, I would start running. You might have previously taken these men to paradise, but the moment you become a threat to them, they will destroy you. Such is Edinburgh.'

'You should be running too,' Sarah told Wilkie. 'We have a witness to the murder of Hedley Stokes. His confederate was hiding in the cellar. McLevy took his statement yesterday. He saw both of you, and both of you will swing.'

There was a moment of stillness and silence, Magnus and Wilkie each wearing the look of a man unused to facing a reckoning, but starkly aware it was bearing down upon them.

Then Magnus spoke. 'The box,' he commanded Wilkie.

The policeman seemed so dazed that he appeared grateful to be given an order. He grabbed Stokes's strongbox and Sarah stepped nimbly out of their way as they charged from the office.

Or rather, Wilkie grabbed what he *assumed* to be Stokes's strongbox. The one he lifted was almost identical right down to the initials recently etched on it, but not the contents. This box had already been sitting in Mr Dalton's office even as the porter took the one containing the money, conveying it to another room in the hotel.

Raven looked at Sarah with exaggerated confusion. 'Was it something we said?'

She went to the window and looked down onto Princes Street. McLevy was waiting below, six of his men standing in front of the hotel entrance. It was only as Magnus and Wilkie ran into their waiting clutches that she realised she had been holding her breath.

Then she heard a knock at the door and looked around to see an eager, friendly face peering in.

'I trust all went well?' Mr Dalton asked.

'So far,' Sarah replied.

But it was not yet done.

SIXTY-EIGHT

t was later the same day when McLevy presented himself at Queen Street. Sarah had been hovering at the window in the drawing room for at least an hour before he arrived, anxiously looking out for his approach. For all she had chosen not to let the photograph exercise power over her, she needed it gone from this world.

Having been shown in by Jarvis, McLevy seemed reluctant to sit, keen to get on. He declined Sarah's offer of tea. Cunningham and Wilkie might be in custody, he said, but a policeman's work was never done. No end of reprobates and petty criminals to be dealt with.

He took an envelope from his pocket and handed it to Sarah.

'It was in the safe at the Clarendon. Exactly as you indicated.'

Sarah reached out and took it from him, tried not to snatch it.

'Did you look inside?' she asked. She had told him the envelope contained something Magnus planned to use against her, and had been surprised when McLevy asked no further questions.

He answered without delay. 'No, Miss Fisher. I was as good as my word.'

She stared at him a moment, but found that she believed him. If he had looked at the contents of the envelope, it would have been impossible to hide. She would have known the moment he walked through the door, the way his eyes would have regarded her.

'I understand you found your niece, managed to retrieve her,' he said. 'You must forgive my earlier doubt. I should have known not to bet against you. We could do with someone like yourself working for us.'

'Thank you, Mr McLevy, but my plans preclude future employment with the police.'

'You're not planning on turning to crime, are you?'

Sarah smiled and shook her head, amused at this uncommon display of flattery and good humour from the usually taciturn detective. She wondered if he had been drinking, celebrating the apprehension of a man he had long had his eye on.

'Where are the prisoners now?' she asked.

'Calton Jail. Safely under lock and key. Last I saw Cunningham, he was ranting about us stealing his money.'

'What money?'

'The strongbox he had in his possession when he was arrested. He claimed it contained three thousand pounds, but we found it held only a few banknotes at the top – the rest was newspaper. Bits of Sanderson's newspaper, to be exact.'

'I don't understand,' Sarah said, feigning ignorance.

McLevy shrugged. 'I can only assume he intended to defraud Mrs Dalton in some way. Though I can't for the life of me see how that would work, how he thought he might get away with it.'

He gave Sarah a penetrating look. 'Any ideas, Miss Fisher?'

Sarah stood at the window and watched McLevy leave, then looked down at the envelope she still held in her hand. She opened it and slid out the contents: the glass plate, and a number of prints. As she had seen Raven do, she smashed the plate under the heel of her shoe and then, without looking at them, threw the photographs onto the fire.

As she watched the flames blacken the edges, consuming the image, she felt the tension ease from her shoulders. She flopped down into one of the armchairs by the fire and simply breathed.

It was over.

But now what?

Raven and Eugenie would be reconciled. The return of Dr Todd's money meant that Raven would be able to repay his debts, and with Eugenie inheriting her father's house on St Andrew Square, there would be no need to continue renting the property on Great Stuart Street.

Raven had made it clear that even if he was no longer in need of Sarah's investment, he would still continue to train her. They had discussed it all when she outlined her plan to defy Magnus. Nevertheless, they both knew that Eugenie would prefer Raven to cut all ties with her. Eugenie's wish was for Sarah to be gone; and with good reason, Sarah thought. She and Raven had a closeness that seemed to be missing from his relationship with his wife. And perhaps that would ever be the case with Sarah still around.

She loved Raven. She had no doubts about the strength of her feeling for him, but they could not be together. She had accepted that, and she would not stand in the way of his happiness with Eugenie.

She wondered again whether she should do as Elizabeth Blackwell had and find somewhere far from Edinburgh where she could study and where she might be permitted to practice. She thought about what Emily had said, something that had radically altered her perspective. It was not about merely being allowed to do what men did, and it was not that women needed to enter the practice of medicine. It was that the practice of medicine needed women.

And then there was Callum Somerville. She thought about what he could give her. Unlike Raven, she believed that Somerville would abide by her wishes. In his own way, he was a man of honour, though the codes he lived by differed from those Raven might recognise.

She was fond of him, despite what she knew, and despite Raven's disapproval. There was mutual affection and respect between them, and that was worth something. It was more than existed between many married couples, in fact. He would give her a good life, and if she was married, that would surely go some way to solving the problem of Eugenie's suspicion and worry. Unfortunately, it would do nothing to solve the intractable problem of her love for Raven, nor that she did not love Somerville in the same way.

She was tormented by the fact that men got to have it all: got to pursue their professional ambitions whilst having a family life with a spouse and children. If she married Somerville, she could have most of these things. Not all, but life was about compromises. Priorities.

She sighed and rubbed her tired eyes, felt as though she might sleep for a week.

The door opened and Lizzie came in bearing a tea tray.

'Is Mr McLevy gone already?' she asked.

'He didn't have time for tea,' Sarah explained. She refrained from pointing out that the tea had been asked for some time ago.

'Why don't you have some with me?' Sarah suggested.

Lizzie looked at her as though she had lost her mind. 'Me? Mrs Lyndsay would tan my backside if I so much as sat on that sofa. I ate a wee bit of shortbread that was left on a tray one time, and she was all for putting me out onto the street.'

Lizzie put the tray down and left the room before Sarah had the chance to propose any further outrageous ideas. Sarah watched her go, thinking about how far she had come: further than she would have ever thought possible when she first started working at Queen Street as a housemaid herself.

So why, she thought, did it not feel like enough?

SIXTY-NINE

aven went directly from Dalton's Hotel to the bank, carrying Stokes's strongbox the short distance on foot. It was heavy but the weight of it was reassuring. He was carrying the foundations of his future.

James Quinton had yesterday furnished them with a spare key. He had also told them where Stokes purchased the box so that they were able to buy an identical model. He had been most cooperative, as befitted someone facing accusations of complicity not only in Stokes's blackmail activities but in his work for Magnus Cunningham.

Sarah's epiphany had changed everything. Magnus had bound them with what appeared to be a Gordian knot, but Sarah realised that it did not need to be untied. All she had to do was cut through it. She had seen that what Magnus held over her was as thin and fragile as the glass it was etched upon, only as powerful as she believed it to be.

Sandy, Dr Simpson's brother, was walking through the banking hall as Raven arrived. He rushed across to greet Raven and asked after his business there.

'I am here to repay Dr Todd's loan.'

'You traced his investment, then?'

'After a fashion. I found his blackmailer.'

Sandy gaped. He had many questions, which Raven answered as briefly and honestly as he could.

'And my brother's blackmailer?'

'One and the same. The matter is closed.'

Sandy gripped him by the shoulders and grinned with satisfaction and relief.

Raven felt a vast relief of his own in handing over the box. After redeeming Todd's loan, he deposited the remainder for safekeeping, not comfortable walking around Edinburgh with that amount of cash. Quinton had also informed them how much money Professor Conville had paid, and for what. Stokes had threatened to write to the dean of the university, as well as to the families of all his students, about his activities (and his tastes) at the Elysian Fields. Sarah had suggested they give all of Conville's money to women at the Lock Hospital in order to assist them in finding new lives after their recovery. She felt Conville had brought this upon himself, but Raven persuaded her that the money should be returned to his family. 'The sins of the father should not be visited upon the son,' Raven had said, he of all people understanding that.

Sarah had not argued, the rarity of which indicated that he must be right.

He felt closer to her now than he ever had. They worked well together in so many ways. He felt different when he was around her, always striving to be a better man. And though his wife would rather Sarah pursued opportunities elsewhere, he would remind Eugenie that she was the one he had chosen. She was the one he had married.

Sarah was nonetheless his closest friend, he realised, and always would be. The thought of that was a comfort. Or was it a consolation: for what she could not be to him, and what he could not be to her?

Walking into St Andrew Square, he had to put such thoughts from his mind. He had saved the home that meant so much to Eugenie, and there could be no firmer basis for a new beginning. The recent tragedy had not been the cause of their problems, but perhaps it could herald the end of them. He was looking forward to seeing the joy on her face when he told her. He had missed the sight of her happiness. The sound of her laughter.

As Raven approached the house, the front door swung open and he watched Dorothy Butler step out. He hailed her warmly and thought she might stop to ask after Sarah, but she gave him the most cursory acknowledgement, hurrying past as though his presence was somehow awkward to her.

Maxwell held open the door for him and Raven stepped inside, where he observed that the downstairs hall was cluttered with boxes and trunks. He felt a surge of something that was not quite elation but greater than relief. Eugenie had decided to give this place up and commit fully to their new life at Great Stuart Street. But now she would not have to.

'Where are the children?' he asked Maxwell.

'Louisa has taken them out so that they did not get under Eugenie's feet while she was busy packing. I believe she is finished, though. She is in the drawing room.'

Raven could smell Eugenie's perfume again as he approached the door. He found her on her favourite seat, exactly where he had encountered her on the day they first met.

She was dressed as though ready to travel, ready to leave this place. A part of him wondered, had her father not died, whether in her heart she would have ever truly done so. But now he could tell her it was not necessary.

'I have recovered your father's money,' he said. 'The loan is redeemed.'

She looked up at him, astonished. Clearly this was something she had given up hope of. She bit her lip and her eyes filled. Raven thought she might have embraced him, but she remained seated.

'You found his blackmailer?' she asked.

He thought about what Magnus had said: *Women should be told only what we deem it necessary for them to know.* He also remembered what Sarah had suggested: that he should give Eugenie an explanation, but it did not have to be the whole truth. The knowledge that the photograph had ever existed was something he did not want to burden her with, and once he told her, it could not be undone.

'Your father did not kill himself over money,' he informed her. 'You recall I told you about Mr Dalton's reluctance to sell his hotel to Magnus Cunningham?'

'Yes?'

'Cunningham had threatened your father, demanding that he poison Mr Dalton, knowing his wife would approve the sale once he was dead.'

Eugenie sat up straighter in her chair, giving him her full attention now. 'In what way did he threaten him?'

'The most effective way he could,' Raven told her. 'Cunningham was threatening to harm you.'

Eugenie contemplated this for a moment, then a look of horror appeared on her face. 'Mr Leitch,' she said, 'the patient whose death upset him so much . . .'

'No,' Raven reassured her, shaking his head. 'Your father had nothing to do with his death. Leitch died in a brothel and your father was merely asked to help confect the fiction that he had died at home in his own bed.'

Raven paused a moment, aware she was still taking it all in.

'The problem was that your father having complied once, Cunningham knew he could ask for more. Hence the demand to poison Mr Dalton. Your father decided that the only way to protect you was to take his own life.'

Eugenie swallowed, looking up at him. Raven sat down beside her. He reached for her hand, but she withdrew it.

'And the money?' she asked.

Raven had decided that Stokes's involvement was another of the details he would withhold.

'He made an investment in Cunningham's hotel business before he knew the nature of the man. It was a fraudulent scheme. The return he was promised did not materialise.'

'Then how did you get the money back?'

'Cunningham was just apprehended by McLevy and is being charged with the murder of an accomplice. The money he had in his possession at the time has been disbursed amongst the victims of his crimes.'

'I don't understand. Could my father not have found some other way to protect me? Could he not have gone to the police?'

'Too risky. Certain of them were in Cunningham's employ.'

Eugenie sat in silence for a long time. Eventually she spoke.

'Thank you,' she said. There was relief in it, if no great warmth. There was time, though. Everything had changed.

Raven glanced towards the door. 'I see you have been packing.'

'Yes,' she replied after a moment. There was something determined in her tone.

'There was no need,' he told her, smiling. 'The house is secured, and we can stay here if you would prefer. Were I to run my practice from here, I'm sure more patients would— '

'It is my intention to sell,' Eugenie said, interrupting.

Raven straightened. This was unexpected.

'I had already made my peace with leaving here,' she continued. 'Having had the time to consider, I have come to realise it would be the best thing for me. It is most important the children be with their father. They love you and you them.'

She fixed him with a look: sincere, and yet still not warm. Raven knew her words ought to be music to his ears, but something seemed discordant.

'Of course,' he said. 'If you are sure. Our money will go further at Great Stuart Street, and we will be able to afford the staff if we are in a smaller— '

'I am not going to Great Stuart Street,' Eugenie said.

Raven was confused now. Then he thought of all the times she had been out during the day, leaving the children. Had she been searching for somewhere else they might live?

'I don't understand.'

She turned to face him. Her eyes filled again but there was resolve in her expression.

'I am leaving, Will,' she said. 'Leaving Edinburgh. Leaving all of this. Leaving you.'

Raven felt the world shift on its axis. Implications assailed him as though from all sides, but one cut to the heart, one his deepest instinct was to defend against.

'You're not going to take my children from me,' he said, though even as he spoke, he could not say whether this was a vow or a plea.

Eugenie looked at him. 'I don't intend to.'

He was again confused for a moment, before her words resounded in his head: *It is most important the children be with their father. They love you and you them.*

She was utterly resolute. He could see that. The distance between them that he believed he could bridge, the time he thought would mend her wounds . . . He had been wrong about it all. And though he was dumbfounded by it, he could see now that it had not been sudden. Her seeming indifference towards her daughter, her manner with Jamie, her refusal to *call* him Jamie. She had been leaving them by degrees, ever since Clara's troubled birth.

'A wife can't simply walk out on her husband, on her children,' Raven protested. But his words sounded feeble to his ears, and as he spoke them he thought of what Sarah had just done, cutting a Gordian knot. Now Eugenie was cutting another, and he could not stop her.

They sat in silence for a moment, then she gave him a sad smile.

'You are a good man, Will Raven, and I will always think well of you. But I do not love you. And you do not love me.'

'But I do,' Raven insisted weakly.

Eugenie shook her head. 'You might have married me, Will, but you have always been in love with someone else.'

She held up a hand to forestall any protest, although Raven was not sure he would have made one.

'I know this to be true,' she went on, 'for that has been my lot, too.'

With these words, several more pieces slotted themselves together. The unexplained absences, her coldness towards Raven, rebuffing his every affection. She had been keeping him at a distance while she prepared herself to leave. All the while secretly spending time with someone else.

'Is that who you are leaving with? The man you truly love?'

Eugenie nodded and the tears spilled.

Raven was about to ask who he was, then he pictured Dorothy Butler's face as she passed him earlier.

'Nathaniel Butler,' he said.

She nodded again, wiping her eyes.

'The father of your child? The child you were forced to give up?'

Another nod.

Raven sighed, rubbed his tired eyes. 'Where do you intend to go?' he asked.

'London.'

From her tone he could tell it was not an idle notion. Her passage was already booked.

SEVENTY

arah entered the drawing room unbidden, Maxwell at her back. Eugenie was adjusting her hat, looking into the ornate mirror that hung above the fireplace. Maxwell began to apologise for the unheralded intrusion but Eugenie cut him off.

'It's all right, Maxwell. I'll deal with this.'

Maxwell left, closing the door behind him.

The two women stood staring at each other for a long few moments, as though mutually aware that they were waiting for Maxwell to be fully out of earshot. Looking at Eugenie and feeling the tension build in the silence, Sarah realised how seldom the two of them had been alone together, despite the extent to which their lives overlapped.

'Why are you doing this?' Sarah asked.

'I thought that you'd be happy.'

'Happy? Of course I'm not happy.'

'I'm not blind, Sarah. Anyone can see how it is between you and Will. How it has always been.'

'But he chose you. He married you.'

Eugenie nodded. 'Yes, he did. But that is not the life either of us wants, is it?'

'Do you know what he wants? Have you asked him?'

Sarah heard the sound of a carriage pulling up on St Andrew Square. Eugenie walked across to the window, looked out, then turned to face Sarah again. She was completely calm, a softness to her expression that Sarah could not recall seeing before.

'Sarah, I'm about to leave so I will have to be brief, but I will try to explain this to you as best I can. Put simply, I do not want this life. I do not want to spend my time wishing it were different, regretting not taking the chance to be with the man I truly love. If my father's sudden death has taught me anything, it is that our life here is short, and I want to make the most of the time I have left.'

'But what about your children?' Sarah asked.

Eugenie's expression changed, sorrow clouding her features.

'I do not love them as a mother should,' she said. 'I do not feel towards them the way I ought. They will be better off with their father.'

'But Dr Simpson says— '

'I'm well aware of what Dr Simpson says; I've heard it often enough – that I need time. That things will improve. But they haven't and I don't think that they will.'

Sarah opened her mouth to speak but found she had no notion what to say. Who was she to tell Eugenie she was wrong about how she felt? And did she really want to change her mind? In truth Eugenie was right: part of her was happy at this turn of events, no matter how messy it was likely to be.

'We women are brought up to believe that the greatest contribution we can make is to be a wife and mother,' Eugenie told her. 'No one thinks to ask us if that is what we want.'

She looked down at her hands. Sarah noticed that she was no longer wearing her wedding ring.

Eugenie's voice became softer, less strident, more vulnerable. 'I did want to be a mother once,' she said. 'When my first child was born. But then she was taken away from me, and I think that part of me, the part that was supposed to be *her* mother, has never recovered.'

'But you can't just leave your children,' Sarah said again, though even as she said it, she was aware that there was little conviction in her words.

Eugenie shook her head. 'Men do it all the time. Leave women and children behind and move on.'

'But Will has worked so hard for you these past months.'

'I know he has, and I'm grateful for it. Will is as caring a husband and father as he is a doctor. But he cannot fix what is broken in me. Fortunately, fate has reunited me with someone who might. Nathaniel can make me whole again, and I him.'

Sarah felt a sudden desperation, a fear of what the repercussions could be, and how far they might reach.

'But what will people say?' she asked.

Eugenie looked unrepentant. 'I'm surprised to hear that sentiment from your lips, Sarah Fisher. You of all people. Fear of what people will say is what keeps us in line, renders us compliant. We need to think less of what society wants of us and more about what we want for ourselves.'

ONE MONTH LATER

SEVENTY-ONE

aven looked at Sarah as she sat across from him in his consulting room, the early evening sunlight that streamed through the window casting a glow around her hair.

It was the end of a gratifyingly busy afternoon clinic. Raven had been worried that once word got round that Eugenie had left him, the few patients he had managed to attract would leave him too. That did not appear to be the case. There were more of them every day and he seemed to have their sympathy; their opprobrium reserved for the mother who had scandalously left her children behind.

Sarah was unsurprised. 'If we have learned anything over these past weeks,' she had said, 'it's that the woman is always to blame.'

Raven leaned back in his chair and sighed. 'Tell me again, Sarah. Remind me. What am I going to do?'

Sarah smiled. He asked the same question of her most days.

'The only thing you can do. Keep going. Continue to work, build your practice, look after your children.'

He nodded a weary head. 'She's not coming back, is she?'

Sarah paused before answering. 'I suppose there is always the chance.'

Raven snorted. 'If she does, it'll be for the children. She's not coming back for me.'

'She wasn't happy, Will. And it had nothing to do with you.'

'It had something to do with me, in that she didn't love me.'

He had these moments of self-recrimination, as though there was something more he could have done to stop her. He felt guilty about the children, growing up without their mother.

'She was always in love with Nathaniel,' Sarah said.

'She maintains that I was always in love with someone else too.'

Sarah looked at him directly. 'And were you?'

He looked at her, held her gaze. 'Yes.'

Sarah smiled. She lifted a bottle of claret from a ridiculously large hamper that had been delivered earlier in the day. A present from Dr Simpson: a token of his gratitude and appreciation for Raven's role in unmasking his blackmailer.

Raven did not know how Quinton and Stokes had found each other's confidence, sufficient to conspire together, but he did know that Quinton had been inspired to attempt a little blackmail of his own, having nursed a grudge against Simpson since his banishment. It turned out to be nothing to do with the child Raven had seen Simpson with years ago. Rather, Quinton had been suggesting that Simpson was the real father of the child he and his wife had adopted, and was threatening to make this information public. Utter nonsense, Simpson insisted, and Raven found that he believed him.

Sarah was rooting around, trying to find something amongst Raven's instruments with which to open the bottle. He watched her move a pile of newspapers aside, several copies of the *Capital*. Once Magnus was safely behind bars, Sanderson had run his story, under the headline 'The Fall of Babylon'. The initial report quoted freely from the Book of Revelation, claiming Edinburgh had become 'a dwelling for demons and a haunt for every impure spirit'.

All of Edinburgh had been outraged . . . for a few days, at least. It was long enough for Pike and Featherstone to close their doors, their business in Edinburgh at an end, but that had been the extent of the justice they faced. The two women left the city and would no doubt set up shop doing the same thing somewhere else.

Sanderson had not printed any of the specific details found in the ledger – he was too canny to run the risk of doing that – though he did keep a copy for himself. And canny he was right to be.

Magnus Cunningham did not hang. He was found dead in his cell, presumably poisoned. Nobody found out by whom, probably for the same reason that the investigation into the death of Barrington Leitch was quietly closed. Influential people did not wish there to be any greater scrutiny of the goings-on at the Elysian Fields. But what was without question was that it was dangerous to know too much of the sordid secrets of powerful men.

Wilkie would likely take the brunt himself, though McLevy suggested that there might be insufficient evidence to convict him. Quinton hiding in a cellar did not make for the best eyewitness, and there was no corroboration. There was, however, sufficient evidence for McLevy to sack him from the police force.

Sarah found a small trephine amongst Raven's things and pulled the cork out with that, finding that it served quite well. She poured them both a glass and broke off a piece of cheese from a wheel that also graced the hamper. The wine smelled of warm fruit and sunshine, while the cheese smelled of feet. Both tasted delicious.

'You're going to need some help with the children,' she said.

Raven nodded. They had discussed this before. Eugenie had already agreed to the sale of her father's house, the staff happy to stay on with the new owners. Eugenie had also arranged for a share of the proceeds to go to Raven and the children, so for the first time in a while, money was not an issue.

'Unless Mrs Balfour wants to expand her hours now that you have the money,' Sarah added. 'She's always been so kind and patient with them.'

Raven gave a wry laugh, but he suspected Sarah had an agenda. 'Do you have a recommendation?' he asked.

Sarah swallowed another piece of cheese. 'I do, as a matter of fact.'

'Who?'

'A young girl, most capable, with a good head for numbers.'

'Annabel?'

Sarah nodded. 'What do you think?'

'I'm surprised she would contemplate returning to Edinburgh.'

'She is grateful and wants to help. Edinburgh is a good place for a young woman of talent and ambition.'

'And if Annabel comes to work here,' Raven said, 'will you stay?'

Sarah smiled. 'Where else would I go?'

'Edinburgh is not the only place for a woman of talent and ambition. There are other destinations where she might realise her potential. And I have never wanted to stand in the way.'

Sarah put her glass down and walked over to where Raven sat. She leaned in and kissed him.

'You *are* the way, Will Raven,' she said. 'You are my way, and I am yours.'

HISTORICAL NOTE

he *Death of Shame* draws upon an infamous series of Victorian newspaper articles by campaigning journalist W. T. Stead in the *Pall Mall Gazette*, entitled 'The Maiden Tribute of Modern Babylon'. In lurid and deliberately shocking detail, the articles unflinchingly depicted the trafficking of young girls into what became known as 'the white slave trade', primarily in London but also in Edinburgh and other British cities. Among Stead's sources were several 'procuresses', who proudly described the ways in which they would divert housemaids, nannies and other young women into 'houses of assignation', where they would be 'seduced' (their self-serving and cynical euphemism for rape).

Stead is regarded as a forefather of tabloid-style journalism, and in particular as the inventor of the 'pseudo-event': manufacturing a situation in order to report upon it. The sting dreamt up by Sanderson is based on an instance whereby Stead claimed to have found a mother who was prepared to sell her daughter into the trade, arranging for the girl to meet with a procuress and a gentleman who would verify her virginity. This reckless act led to Stead being imprisoned for three months for endangering the girl, and was described as 'the death knell of responsible journalism'. Nonetheless, the articles scandalised the country and Stead's work is credited with driving the government to pass the

Criminal Law Amendment Act 1885, which raised the age of consent to fifteen. Stead died in the sinking of the *Titanic*, reportedly having given his life jacket to someone else.

The morally upstanding Victorian era was a boom time for blackmail. As Angus McLaren puts it in his book *Sexual Blackmail*, 'Nineteenth-century middle-class society made a fetish of the cult of sexual respectability . . . As legal and social disapproval of certain forms of sexual behaviour rose, so did the profitability and frequency of blackmail.' In 1822, Robert Stewart, Viscount Castlereagh and Britain's Foreign Secretary, died by cutting his own throat, reportedly driven to it by blackmail. McLaren's book points out that as sexual behaviour gradually became destigmatised – less clouded in shame – certain forms of blackmail became less prevalent.

The character of Dorothy Butler is (loosely) based on the English feminist and social reformer Josephine Butler, who in her *Personal Reminiscences of a Great Crusade* describes how one meeting was disrupted by opponents liberally coating the floorboards with cayenne pepper, and another by arson and the intimidation of a violent mob. In the case of the latter, Butler recounts her initial relief at seeing three policemen apparently come to their rescue, then adds: 'We are safe, we thought. But no! These were Metropolitans who had come from London . . . They simply looked at the scene with a cynical smile and left the place without an attempt to defend it.'

Henry Littlejohn became Edinburgh's police surgeon in 1854, serving as medical adviser to the Crown for the next fifty years. However, it was in his role as Medical Officer for Health that he had the greatest impact. His observations on the relationship between living conditions and the health of Edinburgh's citizens led to the demolition of some of the city's worst slums and a programme of urban renewal. Consequently, much of the modern Old Town is Victorian in construction, post-dating the Georgian New Town.

Emily Blackwell came to Queen Street under Simpson's tutelage in 1854, and as Sarah suggests, Lady Byron was instrumental in her being offered this position. However, she was not as charmed by the charismatic Simpson as his patients tended to be. She acknowledged in her letters that he had made many remarkable cures but also suggested that he 'had killed a good many that he said little about' and had persuaded many of his patients that they were much improved when to her mind 'there was really not much difference'. The newspaper article about Emily being refused permission to walk the wards of the Edinburgh Royal Infirmary was published in the *Caledonian Mercury* on 25 September 1854.

Despite being pioneers as women in medicine, Emily and her sister Elizabeth were not exactly manning the barricades on behalf of the gender. Elizabeth lamented her fellow women's 'intellectual inferiority' and consequently was not in favour of universal suffrage. 'What good is a vote if one doesn't know how to think independently?' she wrote.

James Young Simpson's disgraced amanuensis, James Quinton, was involved in a plot to blackmail his former employer several years after being dismissed by him for fraud. He and his wife attempted to extort money by claiming the child they had adopted through him had been fathered by Simpson himself. Simpson threatened legal proceedings and no further accusations were made against him.

Allowing multiple prints to be made from a single image, new technologies such as the calotype and wet collodion processes facilitated a burgeoning trade in pornographic photographs during the 1850s. The ensuing moral backlash led to the passing of the Obscene Publications Act in 1857, which obviously killed the problem stone dead.

ACKNOWLEDGEMENTS

s ever, our thanks go to all at Canongate, but especially to Francis Bickmore and Melissa Tombere for their unfailing enthusiasm for all things Ambrose. Also to Joanna Dingley for bringing her editorial expertise, along with a fresh pair of eyes – the book is much improved because of it.

Our ongoing gratitude also goes to: Sophie Scard, Caroline Dawnay and Charles Walker at United Agents for their unstinting support and wise counsel; the real Eugenie Todd for her eagle-eyed copy-editing; and the indefatigable Fiona Brownlee, the best publicist in the business.